Again, Only More Like You

CATALINA MARGULIS

Text copyright © 2024 by Catalina Margulis

Cover Illustration © Nat Mack
Distributed by Simon & Schuster

ISBN: 978-1-998076-53-6
Ebook: 978-1-998076-54-3

FIC071000   FICTION / Friendship
FIC044000   FICTION / Women
FIC056110   FICTION / Hispanic & Latino / Women

#AgainOnlyMoreLikeYou

Follow Rising Action on our socials!
Twitter: @RAPubCollective
Instagram: @risingactionpublishingco
Tiktok: @risingactionpublishingco

For Gord, and for my sister

To Zach, Zephyr, Zane and Scout:
I dare you

Sometimes when things are falling apart, they may actually be falling into place.
—Unknown

"Midway in our life's journey, I went astray
From the straight road and woke up to find myself
Alone in a dark wood."
—Dante, *The Divine Comedy*

Again, Only More Like You

Chapter 1

S tanding beside the fire, Carmen takes a sip from a glass of water. Beads of sweat trickle down between her breasts as she watches smoke billow from her minivan. From the open windows of the church behind her, notes played on a piano punctuate the air in a slow and steady rhythm. The recital audience inside—doting mothers, fathers, and grandparents, and children both excited and nervous for their turn—clap along while her own heart races at double time and her stomach curdles at the thought of what tomorrow might bring. She feels like weeping, screaming, stamping her foot. Throwing her hands up to the heavens and asking for mercy and forgiveness—a full-on toddler tantrum if she could. Instead, she holds it all in and keeps very still, her whole body clenching against the pressure. She had tried so hard to make today special, only to have it turn to shit anyway.

Forty Minutes Earlier

Carmen swivels into the driveway and slams on the brakes, crushing sidewalk chalk and a Captain America action figure beneath her tires.

Racing home from the train station, past manicured lawns and white-picket-fence houses, she had pictured her own kids lolling about

1

the front porch like The Three Amigos, kicking at her flower bed mulch and stabbing at ants, the front door left wide open, while they waited for her to pull up. But no, when she turns off the blue Odyssey littered with half-empty water bottles, broken toys, and the sticky residue of melted candy, she sees the front door is closed and the porch is empty.

Shit.

Carmen's phone rings, and her best friend's name flashes across the dashboard. Single, childless, Ally has all the time in the world. She is probably on some patio at this very moment, enjoying her endless free time with her equally untethered friends, while Carmen tries to keep her limbs from coming off in an existential tug of war.

"I'm sorry, Carmen can't come to the phone right now. She's busy trying to *not* drive her van into a wall," Carmen says to herself out loud, declining the call and sending her best friend to voicemail.

Ally's timing is always terrible. Or is Carmen's life the problem? There is never any white space for herself, never mind her lifelong friend. Regardless, she doesn't know when they will finally catch up or get around to planning that trip to celebrate their fortieth birthdays—they have been playing phone tag for weeks—but this definitely isn't the right time now.

Carmen holds her breath as she unlocks the front door. Opening it, she sees that even the foyer is desolate. She pokes her head around the corner and peers up the stairs. Tobias is shirtless, racing cars off the contours of his bookshelf. Teo is sitting back on his bed, flipping through a comic book in nothing but his Batman underwear. Only Tyler is dressed, in the same clothes as the day before, and is lying on his rug, playing with his toy soldiers. None of them are wearing the matching khaki trousers and white button-down shirts she had picked out and placed on their beds that morning for the occasion.

"Ugh," Carmen groans. "Come on, you guys! We were supposed to be at the church by now. Why isn't everybody dressed?"

The kids startle and begin to scurry.

"You're late ... again," Dan says, rolling his eyes and shaking his head as he saunters down the hall from their bedroom.

"Which is why it would have been nice if you had gotten the kids ready." Carmen sighs.

"We *were* ready, but the kids got tired of waiting. You were supposed to be here an hour ago."

Carmen sucks in a breath. She wants to throttle him, wants to tell him about all the hoops she had to jump through *just to be an hour late*, but there isn't time. There isn't time, despite racing through the day, through the week, taking lunches at her desk and not breaking for the washroom half as much as she needed to. There isn't time, despite the hours, months, *years* leading up to this moment. There isn't time, because she is a working mother, and time isn't hers anymore.

"This, coming from the guy wearing board shorts and a 'Hang Ten' T-shirt."

"What? It's summer!"

Carmen glares.

"You want me to wear something else?"

Carmen lifts an eyebrow. Dan throws up his hands and turns back around to get changed.

Instead of slipping out of her work clothes into something fresh and summery the way she had planned as she got ready for work that morning, Carmen makes a protesting Tyler change into the outfit she had picked out for him as she helps the twins get dressed and out the door.

By the time they finally reach Ridgewood Congregational Church, Carmen's chest is damp from sweat and her flat-ironed curls have begun to kink up again. She smooths her hair and blows cool air down her shirt as they pause at the open doors, waiting for the program director to go through her welcome speech.

"And finally, I want to thank you, parents, for being here today and supporting your children on their musical journey," she says, her high-pitched voice and ex-Vegas showgirl appearance cutting through a reverent silence. "Our teachers have loved working with your children this year, and we look forward to seeing you again in September. And now, we hope you enjoy the show."

Applause offers cover as Carmen scoots the kids up the carpeted aisle, scanning for a pew that can fit them all while trying to ignore the faces staring back at her. There is no mistaking the side-eye that one mother gives her, though.

"Take a picture, it'll last longer," Carmen says under her breath, turning away. No one that calm, cool, and collected was balancing a high-pressure job *and* raising a family. *Give me a break.*

Tyler's teacher waves him over to where he and the other students are sitting. Dan grabs his hand and pulls him close, whistling into his ear the first notes of "The Autumn Wind," the theme song for the 1974 Oakland Raiders season coverage that Dan would play on his phone before letting Tyler score a mock touch down on him when they played together.

"Hey," Carmen says, taking Tyler's hand and crouching down in her high heels to be at his eye level. "You know I think you're awesome, right? You're gonna be great!"

Tyler nods back as he and Carmen do their secret handshake fist bump/hand explosion.

"Boom," they say in unison, before Carmen gives him a quick kiss on the cheek goodbye, sending him off to his group.

Seeing a stretch of empty bench on the other side of a pair of grandparents, Carmen urges Dan and the kids over to it with a flick of her index finger. Squeezing past the couple, Carmen ignores the annoyed looks on their faces.

As she catches her breath to the tune of "Lean On Me," the wooden bench digs into her sit bones like a judgement from above. Why did life, *her life*, always have to be this frantic? Why did everything have to be such a fucking emergency?

If only Carrie, *Muse* magazine's art director, hadn't called Carmen in to her office over last-minute changes to the issue just as she was leaving to catch the train out of Manhattan for her son's first music recital. ("A doctor's appointment," she had lied. "I'll be home in time to go over any corrections." Another lie.)

If only Meredith, *Muse*'s editor-in-chief, hadn't changed her mind about the cover a million times, Carrie wouldn't have been working on it the same day they were sending it off to the printer—on a Friday after a long week of late nights, no less.

If only her boss didn't always recoil at the words "My kid ..." Carmen could have simply asked for the day off months ago, making Thursday a hard stop for any changes, so they could have avoided all the manic rushing to get the issue to the printer in the first place.

If only she didn't need her job—had courted it as the crowning achievement of her magazine career, finally shedding her outsider status and belonging to the ultimate "In crowd" at the top fashion magazine in the country—she could have told them all to go to hell. She is practically forty. She is too old for this shit.

Taking deep breaths to calm her racing heart, Carmen picks up the program and looks for Tyler's name. There are seven kids to go before his turn. *We're good,* Carmen thinks. *We made it,* she mouths as she and Dan shake their heads in disbelief, smiling at each other.

Two college-age music teachers approach the stage to make adjustments to the microphone stand and swap out instruments. Carmen takes advantage of the pause in the show to check her phone. There is an email from Carrie, with a revised cover attached.

Please approve by 5pm today.

Carmen checks the time. It is 5:17.

The audience claps, and Carmen looks up to see a boy carefully approach the stage. Hands go up and cameras click as he places his music book on the piano ledge and turns the page.

Shit! They forgot to bring Tyler's piano book.

Carmen glances at the cover and taps out "Approved," feeling guilty as she slides her phone back into her pocket. She doesn't have the previous proofs with her to reference, but really, what could go wrong? The words, last time she looked, were good to go, and the image, well, that was on Carrie anyway.

Carmen leans forward and urges Dan to hand over the car keys, miming as the boy on the stage performs a tentative "Twinkle, Twinkle, Little Star."

"Sorry," she says to the grandparents sitting next to her as she carefully nudges past them.

She is already halfway down the church aisle when it hits her: the house keys. They are in the diaper bag, which is tucked under Dan's seat.

"I'm sorry," Carmen says, wincing at the older couple who shoot her confused looks as she pushes her way past them, again.

What the fuck? Dan mouths, giving her a bewildered look as she kneels down in front of him and pulls out the diaper bag, but Carmen only shakes her head and takes the keys.

"So sorry," she says to the grandparents as she crouches past them again, bracing herself against their frowning stares.

The stutter of the van's engine starting up bursts through the church parking lot, and Carmen prays that the recital audience can't hear her leaving. She might not win any mother-of-the-year awards, she thinks, but this, this she could fix. If she made it back on time.

Dodging too-fast corners in a sweaty panic, Carmen pictures a terrified Tyler stepping up to the stage without his music book. She spots a stop sign ahead, but only gently presses on the brakes, rolling through the intersection instead.

"Asshole!" a driver yells, shaking his fist at her.

Shit, Carmen thinks, shrinking in her seat and grateful for the faded, peeling numbers that make her New Jersey licence plate hard to read. Leaning on the gas again, Carmen glances at the clock, calculating the minutes, seconds, really, she has to recover Tyler's music book and place it in his hands as inconspicuously as possible before he steps up to the stage himself. She is a bad mother. She isn't doing enough. She could do better. She must, next time. 'Next time' being a future perfect that dangles like the proverbial carrot, promising absolution.

At home, Carmen leaves the car running, although she detects a faint smell. Something burning. The engine? She doesn't have time to solve that mystery. Instead, she unlocks the front door and lunges up the stairs into Tyler's room, tossing books and stuffies and dirty clothes aside until she spots the rainbow-striped, piano class zippy bag on the floor next to his blue hamper. She checks inside, holds up the music book triumphantly, then leaps down the stairs, and catapults herself into the minivan, which is now engulfed in a cloud of smoke. *Carajo.*

Carmen races back to the church, gas-braking all the way. She swerves into the parking lot in a spray of gravel dust and shoves the gear into Park. Hurrying up the church steps, she glances at the car as she pulls the door open.

Inside the church, Carmen crawls up the aisle and reaches over Tyler's shoulder to hand him his music book. Out of the corner of her eye, she sees the grandparents hesitate, mid-air, ready to make room for her to pass, but Carmen crawls back out of the room instead.

In the foyer, long tables display rows of triangle sandwiches, cupcakes on cake stands, and cookies splayed out on doily-covered platters. Carmen remembers the fruit tray she forgot to bring, but that isn't the thing that is tugging at her, trying to claw its way out of her tangled subconscious. A feeling that something has been left behind, something is missing, at work.

A woman in a long, floral-print dress gently sets out pitchers of fruit punch. She smiles hello, and Carmen's mouth twitches back as she helps herself to a glass of water before walking back outside.

Standing in the church parking lot next to the Odyssey, Carmen takes another sip of water as she watches smoke billow out from her van. God, she is exhausted. Maxed out. Done. If one more thing goes wrong, she will surely break. At least then, maybe, she could finally stop.

A faint echo rises, as the church audience begins to clap. A downtempo rendition of Queen's "We Will Rock You." The same song she has listened to three times a week for the last six months.

Shhhit, Carmen breathes out, closing her eyes. And the sound is like the sizzle fire makes as she tosses water onto her melting tires.

Chapter 2

Ally moves toward the sun shimmering in the distance. As she surfaces, she looks around, anxious for his touch, his gaze. In just a few hours, she will be alone with him. In just a few hours she will be complete. Unless he has changed his mind. Unless she has changed it for him.

Swimming toward the boat, Ally wonders if the ocean has it right. Seahorse males gave birth and cared for their young. Oysters changed genders, depending on which was best for mating. A shrimp carried its heart in its head—Ally wishes she were so lucky.

"How'd it go?" Malcolm calls out, leaning over the edge of the boat. The sound of his voice—a deep, motoring purr—makes her skin tingle. Her whole body vibrates at the sound of him. Though they've been together for over a year now, still she feels an urgency around him. Their time together is always brief, and her need for him is infinite.

"It was a good dive. Just cold ..." Pete, the other diver, answers from behind her as he wades past and passes up his suction sampler to Malcolm. Ally bobs up and down in the water, waiting for her turn. When Malcolm reaches for her note-filled slate, Ally tries to catch his eye, but he avoids her gaze and steps back, giving the divers room to climb on deck.

A chill comes over her as Ally peels off her dry suit, watching Malcolm examine the sample bag of baby lobsters, crab, and seaweed. He is totally ignoring her, but could she blame him? If Pete found out, and word got out at the office, they would both be in trouble. Still, Mac didn't need to be such a jerk about it. You couldn't choose who you loved, could you?

Ally shivers as she pulls on cargo pants and a tank top. She finds the sunniest corner of the boat to sit down in and tries to warm her body in the waning light of the sun.

"Man, I'm thirsty," Pete says, pulling his shirt over his head. Ally looks away. His skin is taut and tanned, a body she would have lingered on if she didn't already have someone else on her mind.

She takes a sip from her water bottle as she watches Mac climb down into the cabin, looking for the moment when she can slip away after him. She knows that she should be cool, patient, but she can't help it. She needs to solidify things with Mac. Needs to make sure he won't head home after they dock. That they still have tonight. All she needs is a moment alone with him, and in the whole day, she hasn't been able to get it.

"Hey Parker, catch," Pete says, tossing Ally a sandwich from the cooler.

"Thanks." She catches it and puts it down. She's hungry but that's not the thing to satisfy her. It's their last night offsite, and it could be weeks before another dive, when she might have another chance to be alone with Malcolm. She needs to make this happen.

Ally gets up and walks over to the bow, away from Pete. The gentle rock of the boat, the rippled repetition of the sea, soothe and quiet her racing mind. Here, she has history. Here, she belongs. Malcolm belonged with her.

"Missing it already?"

"Yeah," Ally answers, walking back to Pete. She peers into the sample bag and pulls out a baby lobster.

"Growing pains, huh," Ally says as it squirms in the palm of her hand. Its flesh is soft to the touch as she strokes it, having shed its shell. "Don't worry. You'll be as good as new before you know it."

Ally measures the baby and takes notes on the dive slate. Instead of placing it back in the bag, though, she lets it go, leaning over the boat and letting it flutter out of her hand.

"You guys sure you don't want to come out for a few? It'll be a good time."

"Thanks, but you know how Malcolm likes to process everything right away. Plus, I'm wiped," Ally says, hoping Pete doesn't volunteer to stay with them to help. "We got it, though. Enjoy your time with your cousin. We'll see you back home."

"Suit yourself." Pete shrugs, and Ally's chest unclenches a little. Now she needs to convince Malcolm to stay the night.

"Ready!" Malcolm shouts from below, and Pete walks over to take the wheel.

"Back in a minute," Ally says, getting up to follow Mac down into the cabin.

"What's that?" Pete yells over the roar of the engine.

"I'll be right back." Ally sweeps her long, blond hair over one shoulder and makes her way across the deck, her skin electric with anticipation.

Climbing down into the damp, briny cabin, Ally sees Malcolm bent over his laptop, tapping numbers into a spreadsheet. His shirt sleeves are rolled up and his tanned forearms strain at the keyboard as he stares at the screen. Ally comes up and hugs him from behind, relishing the heat of his body and breathing him in.

"Ally." Malcolm shrugs her off and glances up the stairs to the deck.

"I just—"

"Just ..." Malcolm says, putting up his hand, and Ally steps back. His cold eyes are more than she can bear.

"Let me do it," Ally says, reaching for the laptop.

"I've got it."

"Please."

"Go," Malcolm insists, urging her out with a nod. "I've got it."

Ally climbs out of the cabin, hot tears burning behind her eyes, a growing ache threatening to break her. Turning her back to avoid Pete, she feels empty, see-through. Looking out toward the harbour, Ally rubs her goose-bumped arms and holds herself in.

Please, she thinks. *Just one more night.* One more night to win back the only good thing in her life.

Ally pulls her phone out of her pocket as she crunches up the gravel path leading to the cottage. She needs to hear someone else's voice, other than the mean girl in her head. She searches for a name in her Favorites and presses Call.

"Hey!" Carmen's voice rings out.

"Wow, you actually picked up! I never get you on the first try."

"Toby's on my phone. We're still potty training, it seems. Say hi to Tia Ally, boys."

"Hi, Tia!" the twins yell back, their giggles like the tinkle of wind-chimes.

Ally feels a slight pang at the thought of Carmen's bustling household as she stands in front of an empty cottage that's not hers.

"So, how's it going?" Carmen asks. "Everything okay?"

It's just like Carmen to cut to the chase. No time for small talk. It always makes Ally feel like she is interrupting something or being a pain in the ass. Why couldn't they just talk like normal people? Like they used to. When hours on the phone or spent together would fly by, with neither one of them wanting it to end.

"Yeah. Just coming in from a dive," Ally says, unlocking the front door and pushing it open with her shoulder. She wishes she hadn't bothered calling Carmen, but who else was there to talk to? So many friendships had dwindled and fizzled out over the years, as friends got busy with work, partners and growing families of their own. Would she lose Carmen too? She wonders if she never called her again, would Carmen even notice. Would she even care.

"How's everything with you?" Ally asks, as she drops her bags on the kitchen floor.

"Oh, you know, just another day in paradise. Hold on a sec—sit back on the potty, Toby! Sit back or the pee will fall on the floor! God, I'm so tired of cleaning up pee everywhere. Not sure what's worse, this or diapers."

"Come on, you know you love it." Ally moves the curtain aside so she can look out the kitchen window. Carmen was always complaining about the kids, and at the same time, it was like nothing—or no one—else mattered.

"I love little faces and toes, not random smudges of poo everywhere. I swear my house is covered in feces. Enough about me, though. How's work? Your boss coming around?"

"You were right, I should have left when I got that offer. I'm still waiting for the promotion he promised me," Ally says, wincing as she watches Malcom and Pete talking by the truck, knowing she's about to get a lecture from Carmen.

"That job was incredible! I still can't believe you turned it down. I would die for summer hours and four weeks' vacation."

"I know, it's just so hard to give up the field work, you know?" Ally says, rubbing her lip and hoping Pete doesn't convince Malcolm to go out with him.

"That's my Ally. You always loved being on the water so much. Though I still think it's hilarious that you became a Marine Biologist after failing Grade 11 Science."

"I blame that entirely on you. For the record, you are the worst science project partner."

"I don't deny it. You know me, I always preferred books to real life. Anyway, you really should start your own company, where you can call your own shots. You're so brilliant, you'd be amazing at it."

"Thanks. Maybe one day ..." Ally says, thinking for a moment if she really could do it all on her own. "What about you?"

"Me? I wish. It's like a jail sentence going to my office every day—with none of the perks."

"Trouble at work?" Ally asks, watching a car pull up and Pete get in. Malcolm waves goodbye. *Phew.*

"How'd you guess?"

"It's the only thing you ever really complain about, feces not included. Your life is otherwise perfect."

"*Your* life is otherwise perfect. Anyway, it's nothing. The usual. I hate my job, and my boss hates me. I'm just so over it. Working at a fashion magazine was fun when I was in my twenties and cared about getting into fashion week. Now I just miss my kids ... hey, what about that date you went on? Anything there?"

Ally recalls the lie she told Carmen to throw her off the trail of her love life as Malcolm walks into the room.

"Nothing to write home about," Ally lies again, following Malcolm with her eyes as he goes into one of the bedrooms and drops down on the edge of the bed. "Besides, I'm having too much fun sampling the local species."

"Ugh! When are you going to get out of there? If you loved yourself, you'd set yourself free. You're so much better than that job, that town, all of it ... oh, Toby, honestly! You peed all over the seat! Ugh, boys are the worst!"

"Did you ever think you would be surrounded by so many penises?"

"Not in my wildest dreams. Listen, I gotta go. Just promise me you'll get a job in a real city, so I can visit you and we can have fun like we used to. And yes, I know, we still have to book our trip."

"Ready when you are," Ally says, thinking it was rich that Carmen was reminding her that they still needed to plan their girls' getaway when she seemed to be avoiding committing to anything Ally put forth as a suggestion.

"I know, I know. Soon. Things are just so crazy right now, but I'll text you with dates. We have to do something good. It's been too long since we had some real time together."

"No kidding."

"I know. Time flies. I just can't keep up. Fuck. Forty. I can't believe we're turning forty."

"Me neither," Ally pauses, painfully aware of what little she had to show for it. "Give your monsters a kiss for me."

"Will do. Love you."

"Love you."

Ally hangs up and checks the fridge. Only a couple of cans of Guinness left. She would save those for Malcolm. He'd turned her on to it and now it was her drink too. She would finish off Pete's Cabernet instead.

It would go well with the steaks and potatoes that she had purchased for their last night, just in case.

Ally glances back at Mac, and her heart soars. She wonders if Carmen still feels this way. If she and Dan even do it anymore, or whether they simply fall asleep to the drone of the TV each night, hardly acknowledging each other's bodies.

Opening a living room window, Ally breathes in the salty gust of air coming in off the water. Boothbay Harbor's Our Lady Queen of Peace sparkles in the setting sun, and Ally can make out Jack Johnson echoing across the water from a neighboring dock. The smell of barbecue reminds her that she hasn't eaten since before the dive, and she wishes now that she and Malcolm could just go out for a night on the town. But she knows he won't be seen alone with her in public, not even in this town of strangers.

Ally turns to Malcolm and notices that he is frowning at his phone. She knows his screen saver well: a photo of Nicki laughing on the beach as she hugs Henry and Sydney to her. God, she is pathetic. In love with a married man. Carmen would kill her if she ever found out. She should walk away. Go to another room and shut the door.

Instead, she walks toward Malcolm. He deserves to be happy. She deserves to be happy too.

"Hey," Ally whispers, kneeling before him.

"Hey," he whispers back, his mouth spreading into a smile as he slides his phone out of the way. "I'm sorry about earlier." Malcolm shakes his head. "It's just ... I just ..." He looks up at Ally, a pained look in his eyes.

"I know," she says, wrapping her arms around him, and nuzzling into his neck. "I wish we could just disappear and start over. Just you and me."

"Me too," Malcolm says, cupping her face in his hands. He pulls her close and kisses her softly on the lips.

Ally breathes a quiet sigh of relief, and a shudder rolls through her. He is still hers, then—at least for the night.

Chapter 3

Up all night. Again. Sleepless nights, not just in the first weeks or months, but in perpetuity, is something the nurses could have warned her about during her prenatal classes. Carmen lies in bed after her phone alarm has gone off, feeling not a bit rested. She recalls with a smirk those early, naïve days, when everything seemed possible. The birth plan and shopping for the perfect baby stroller, as if they made any difference. As if she could control the future.

The illusion of power over her own destiny was shattered early in her motherhood journey. Tyler was late, requiring her to be induced, which made her whole natural birth plan a complete waste of time.

After he was born, he failed to latch, which meant that in the ensuing weeks Carmen was subjected to a host of humiliating strategies used to support Mom and baby with nursing—something she had assumed would come naturally. Instead, she had to experiment with breast pumps and myriad other devices and contraptions that reduced her formally empowered self to the sum of her anatomical parts. It all made her wonder if she, as a mother, was broken. Maybe something was wrong with *her*.

During that first night home from the hospital, Carmen lay on the floor next to Tyler's crib, listening for his breath to make sure he stayed alive. She wonders if she's had a good night's sleep ever since.

"What a great sleep." Dan yawns, grabbing Carmen's hand and reaching down.

"Toby's sick. He was throwing up last night," Carmen says, pulling her hand away and rolling over.

"Really? I didn't hear a thing."

Carmen snorts. It doesn't surprise her. Becoming a mother had gifted her with a sixth sense attuned to the slightest changes in her kids. A cough or nightmare-induced whimper in the middle of the night could wake her from her deepest dreams, so she could soothe a child back to sleep or administer a dose of honey for a cough.

Dan gets up and goes in the shower, while Carmen opens the blinds in the kids' rooms and turns on their lamps.

"Time to get up," she says, patting their sleeping bodies.

As the kids throw off their covers, yawning and stretching, Carmen goes downstairs and places chipped bowls and stained spoons on the table and makes lunch for Tyler. *Shit.* She'd forgotten to make banana muffins over the weekend, again. Looks like it's another week of boxed brownies. She really needed to stop buying that crap—"Basura," her dad would say. *Garbage.* But it was so convenient to have on hand.

"Remember, soccer game tonight. Tyler and I have to leave at 5:45," Dan says as he walks into the kitchen to prepare his own lunch for the day.

"Ugh, I'm gonna be late and I'll have to leave early too—it won't look good," Carmen sighs. "Can't someone else coach so you can watch the twins?"

"Carmen, you know this is what we signed up for. Besides I love being Tyler's coach, and he loves having me there. Those kids need me. We're gonna win this year! Team red is going down!"

Carmen can't help but laugh. While Dan's role as head coach for Tyler's soccer team made their weekdays even more frenzied, she thought it was sweet that he cared so much, sweating over game-day playbooks and spending hours designing practices like the kids were some kind of professional team.

"I get it. I love that you love it. I really do. It's just, when do we get a break?"

"I know, we live in the same house, and I feel like I don't even get to talk to you anymore."

"I wish I could say we'll find a time later, but ... we won't," Carmen says, giving Dan a kiss goodbye. "Have a good day."

"You too."

As Dan and the kids eat, Carmen showers, thinking about how to reorganize her day. She won't be able to take Toby to the doctor; she absolutely couldn't miss work today. Carrie would be in the office early now that she was back from her photo shoot in St. Barths, and Meredith would be waiting, eager to go over cover selects and photos for the inside spreads. Plus, the September issue was due to arrive in the office today and Carmen always liked to be the first to see it. Another trophy for her office wall at home. Evidence of a life well-lived. *Her* life.

Getting dressed, Carmen can hear the door close, announcing Dan has left for the day, off to saw, sand, and paint sleek kitchen and bath cabinets for Ridgewood's wealthiest families. While Carmen is grateful for his early start, which means he can pick up the kids at the end of his workday and start dinner, it doesn't exactly help her when it comes to getting them out the door in the morning and getting to her own job on time.

Carmen carries her heels tucked under her arms as she threads a belt through her pants. Coming down the stairs, she sees Teo and Tyler wandering around in circles in their rooms, in their PJs, as if they'd forgotten what comes next.

"Guys, get dressed! What are you doing? We gotta go!"

"Toby's not getting ready," Teo says, pouting.

"Toby's sick," Carmen says, picking Toby up and giving him a kiss on the forehead. "Don't worry, baby. Mommy's taking you to Grandma's today. She'll take good care of you."

"But I want to stay home with you," Toby pleads, his face crumpling up as he begins to cry.

Carmen sighs as she feels a squeeze around her heart.

"I wish I could, baby."

"Can I go to Grandma's?" Teo asks.

"Not today. Now come on, let's get ready," Carmen says, turning to carry Toby down the stairs. "Tyler, I hope you're getting dressed!"

By skipping the kitchen cleanup and leaving dirty dishes stacked in the sink, Carmen manages to drop Teo off at daycare and Tyler at camp just a few minutes past the usual time. The extra drop-off, though, leaving Toby with her mother-in-law, has her missing her 7:48 train. The next train arrives at Penn Station after nine. *Shit.* If the traffic is good, she could still make it to work before then.

"Thanks again," Carmen says, still holding her son's tiny hand, even after she passes him to Dan's mother. She feels guilty for leaving him. Guilty for running late for work. Guilty for not doing either of her jobs at all well enough.

"Of course, dear. Just drive safe."

They hug and kiss goodbye, and Carmen finally lets go of Toby's hand. Turning toward the elevator, she sneaks a peek at her watch. 8:10. *Shit.* She'll be catching the rush-hour traffic on the Garden State Parkway. She is going to be late for sure.

Carmen slows down to a walk at the front doors of Apex Media, catching her breath and saying a silent prayer of thanks that she didn't break a heel running from the parking lot. She twists her hair up off her neck and blows a breath of air down her shirt, trying to cool herself, hoping too that it will soothe some of the panic rising in her chest.

While Carmen does her best to summon her inner calm and look like those smiling ladies in the shampoo commercials, a flutter of nerves makes her stomach turn, as it's done ever since her first day as Managing Editor of *Muse*. Every day was like the first day of school—the desire to be liked, the fear of not fitting in. Though she preferred Dostoyevsky to fashion magazines, she still got a thrill from working at one of the top glossies in the country.

On the escalator to the main floor elevators—a corporate catwalk serving up the hottest looks of the moment—Carmen does the math: she'll be fine. The rest of the team is probably still trickling in. The art department would have stayed late the night before, prepping layouts for Carrie's return. The fashion editors would be drifting in, groggy from launch parties and distracted by the post-event swell of gossip on who wore what to where. The beauty editors, jet-lagged from product previews in London, Milan, and Paris, would be lining up for their non-fat lattes. Carmen could still look like she was in charge if she arrived before the crowd.

In the elevator, she checks her reflection in the mirror and smooths down her shoulder-length, brown hair, which was already frizzing up again. She and her hair had been at war ever since she could remember, and she had tried every process and product under the sun to tame her impossibly thick and unpredictable waves, so she could look more like the pretty, successful women on TV and in magazines.

Carmen adjusts her black blazer and brushes some lint off her pants. If only she had had time to iron out the wrinkles in her white, button-down shirt. Still, not terrible for almost forty, she thinks, despite the hollowness beneath her eyes. She looks boring but reliable—*non-threatening*—and that's what Meredith wanted, that's what the world expected of her now, isn't it?

A bell goes off, calling Carmen's attention to the twentieth-floor signal above the elevator doors. Another flutter of nerves shudders through her as she checks her profile in the mirror one last time. A white stain on her shoulder catches her eye—a trace of Toby's sleepy drool. *Great.* Carmen tries to look casual as she licks her finger and rubs the spot on her black blazer.

The elevator doors open, and Carmen steps out, blinking at the retail-store brightness of the white-on-white decor, light reflecting from the floor-to-ceiling windows and the Hudson River beyond. The effect is that of a glistening beauty counter, hypnotic with possibility. The American Dream her parents had raised her to go after. She could have it all, it promised her. She just needed to work for it.

Carmen walks past the maze of low-rise cubicles with the practiced poise of someone who belongs here—an affectation. Like the teenagers pumping down the catwalks in power suits and evening gowns, she feels like a child in dress-up clothes. Fake it till you make it? She had made it and still feels like a fake.

Despite the mussy desks and quiet buzz of powered up computers, the floor is empty. Could she be the first to arrive? It is after nine a.m.—where is everyone? Carmen's stomach rumbles and she realizes she's hungry—she couldn't even manage a slice of toast this morning. Perhaps she is coming down with Toby's flu. It would just have to wait now. If she could settle in at her desk and start working, no one would know she was late.

Carmen reaches her office, one of only four on the entire floor. It is supposed to make her feel prized, but instead it feels stifling. A glass enclosure that offers nowhere to hide—her every move trackable, on display. The show is exhausting.

Reaching into her purse for the key to the sliding door, Carmen catches a smudge of movement from the corner of her eye. She turns her head and notices the boardroom. It takes a moment to register all the departments present and accounted for: Meredith, Carrie, Fashion, Art, Beauty, even Online, gathered around the football field-length table in the meeting room.

Everyone but Carmen, it seems.

She has a split second to decide: cut and run, or face the music. Heart thumping, Carmen chooses music and makes her way to the boardroom as if everything were going exactly according to plan, even though her hands are trembling. Walking over, Carmen's brain scrolls back through recent emails, trying to recall something about a morning meeting. Nothing, which is especially surprising given the fact that calling meetings in the first place is her job. It is just like her recurring nightmare of showing up to school naked—only worse.

Carmen gently tries to open the boardroom door without drawing attention to herself, but the glass door is locked and bangs against its frame as she pulls on it. Meredith's icy-blue eyes dart her way, and the rest of the team follows her gaze, all except Carrie, who mercifully looks away.

Meredith points a dagger-shaped red nail at the neighboring door, and Carmen tries it instead. Success. Only Carmen can feel Meredith's glare as she slides into the empty seat next to Sasha, the beauty editor, with her head down. Carmen sits still and holds her breath as a wave of nausea comes and goes.

"As I was saying," Meredith says, drawing out the vowels as if even this simple phrase were beyond Carmen's level of comprehension. "We need to make this holiday issue a hit. We need to send the message that *Muse* is hotter, cooler, younger than ever, especially with the eighteen-to twenty-five-year-old set."

Her voice is high, soft, and feminine, with a movie-star quality that has an eerie effect juxtaposed with her dominatrix-style, slicked-back, black hair, and pursed red lips. Carmen wonders if she uses that voice to make herself seem younger, welcoming, though the effect is more chilling than reassuring.

"Our digital strategy is going to be key for this campaign," Meredith continues, turning to David, the online editor, and Carmen can feel the irresistible fog of sleep coming on. "We need to think beyond print, to the kinds of partnerships and execution that will establish us as an online innovator as well."

A phone rings, *her* phone, and Meredith's eyes dart Carmen's way again, her nose flaring.

Fuck. Carmen hopes it's not one of the kids—the daycare saying that Teo is sick now too, or her mother-in-law calling to let her know that Toby has gotten worse and should probably go to the hospital. Working in the city means that she won't be able to get home any time soon, regardless of the circumstance. Should she pick up her phone and check? Meredith's stare dares her to act.

"We could—" Carmen begins, but Meredith's frown cuts her off and she blanks, forgetting what she was about to say.

"Yes?" Meredith prompts her, holding out her hand and rolling her eyes.

"We could invite someone like Mizz B to guest edit the issue," Carmen blurts out, breaking into a sweat and swallowing down another wave of nausea. The rapper's latest song is still ringing in her head from the drive over, and proposing a guest editor to reboot the magazine, and newsstand sales, had been on her mind since the latest round of budget cuts and layoffs. If she could create a hit idea, maybe she could save her job. If she created a hit idea, maybe she could get scouted to helm a different title, where she could finally be in charge of her time.

"*Guh*," Nadine sighs, grasping her cup of tea as if hanging on for dear life. Despite the July sun baking the room, *Muse*'s pouty fashion editor is hunched over her drink and swathed in nubby knits, as if bracing herself against a winter storm. "I'm so tired of these celebrity *collabs* already. *We* should be the ones headlining the issue. *Muse*'s editors."

Sasha gives Carmen a commiserating smile from beneath her glossy, brown locks. Unlike the beauty editors, who preferred to linger in the background, nerding out on ingredients and label histories, Nadine and her cohorts craved the spotlight, jostling for a spot on the society pages. Carmen marvels at the juxtaposition of the mousy beauty editors, who always seem too busy discovering the next beauty elixir to use the products they so vaunted, and the peacocking fashion editors, who regularly display every color of the rainbow on their eyes, mouths, and fingernails.

"Mizz B will give the issue viral appeal. Plus, it will give us great visual and video assets," David chimes in with an authority Carmen finds grating. The twenty-something bespectacled online editor had been a devoted, loyal intern until recently, but now acts like he is next in line to inherit the place. Just six months on the job and already Meredith was asking for his opinion on everything, as if he held the key to youth, street, and everything current. Carmen would be grateful for his vote of confidence if he didn't sound as if he had come up with the idea himself.

"Excellent point, David," Meredith says. "Carmen, David, draft up a proposal and you, Carrie, and I can meet on it tomorrow morning."

Carmen freezes for a moment, balking at the short turn-around. They had just come out of production and a run of late nights, and now she'll have to pull another late night just to put a solid proposal together. Not to mention Toby is sick, and Tyler has soccer.

"Um, I-I-I might need more time," Carmen stutters to admit.

"I've got the bandwidth. I can have it to you today," David jumps in. "Consider it done."

Meredith cocks her head and looks from Carmen to David as her blood-red lips spread out into a benevolent smile. Carmen's face burns with shame and embarrassment.

"Thank you, David. That is all."

There's no talking as everyone gets up from their chairs and leaves the boardroom. Carmen doesn't dare look the others in the eye as they all make their way to their desks.

As she reaches her office, humiliation turns to anger. After all, it wasn't the first time Meredith had given someone else credit for her ideas. What does Carmen know, anyway? She is just a mom. Just a tired, harried, past-her-prime caretaker.

Thinking of her kids, Carmen checks her phone. There's a missed call and a text from Ally, following up on their trip.

Costa Rica? Hawaii? the text reads, and Carmen's stomach begins to knot.

As much as she misses her friend and could use the time off, the chance of getting away is looking more and more impossible. Things are already strained at work; she doubts she can get the days off. Plus, money is tight, especially since the emergency reno in the powder room due to a leaking toilet. Not to mention having to replace the brakes on her car after the recital debacle—it turns out it was the brakes, not the tires, that were scorching. And now all the back-and-forth planning is turning their long-awaited getaway into another nagging item on her never-ending to-do list.

And yet, while Carmen is losing her appetite for adventure, too worn out from her life to muster the energy to travel anywhere, she misses her friend. Time together always made her feel so free, like she could be, do, have anything. For Ally, that is still the case—she was always off somewhere. The last time they travelled together, though, was a spa weekend over a decade ago, before Carmen had Tyler. It was a far cry from the decade before that, when they had backpacked around Barcelona, sampling tapas, dancing in flamenco bars, and riding around the city on scooters with strangers until the sun came up.

Maybe she could get away just for a weekend. She could really use some time to decompress.

Something closer? Miami? New Orleans? Carmen texts back, sitting down at her desk.

After logging onto her computer, Carmen scans the prompts of articles waiting for her approval: another "revolutionary" eye cream, another trip down fashion's memory lane triggered by the latest trending retro look. The same rotating treatises she has been reading and re-reading for months and years now. The only respite from the banality of it all was the occasional confessional relationships story, which Carmen lapped up like spring water in a desert. *Something real.*

"September is here," Sasha says, waving the latest issue of the magazine as she gently knocks on Carmen's office door. A sheepish smile scrunches up her pretty face as she places a couple of issues on Carmen's desk, and Carmen can feel the heat return to her cheeks from the boardroom blunder.

"Thanks," Carmen says, taking the magazine and mindlessly flipping through. "So, what did I miss?" she asks with forced casualness. "Toby was up all night, sick. I didn't have a chance to check my inbox this morning."

"Oh, save the magazine. Save the magazine. Save the magazine," Sasha says, hesitating in the doorway. "Yup, that's pretty much the gist of it," Sasha adds, pulling away, though Carmen feels there's more she wants to say and can't. A warning.

Sasha's head tilts and Carmen recognizes it for the sixth sense the team shares when it comes to Meredith. Giving Carmen a brief, pitying half-smile, Sasha turns on her heel, and hurries back to her desk. Behind her, Meredith appears, marching toward Carmen with looks to kill.

"I'm totally going to get fired," Carmen declares, struggling to push the double stroller with one hand while the other grips her cellphone.

"Come on," Ally says over speakerphone. "You're being paranoid."

"Well, it certainly doesn't look good." Carmen tries to keep an eye on Tyler as he zigzags on and off the park path, hiding behind trees and pretending to shoot targets like one of his toy soldiers. "Meredith is furious. Not only is there a typo on the cover, but it's a typo in an advertiser's name. I'm totally fucked!" Carmen instantly regrets the slip in front of the twins. She checks, but they're following Tyler with their eyes and seem not to have noticed.

"But it wasn't your mistake. You said someone else made the change."

"It doesn't matter. It doesn't matter that Carrie made the mistake when she was cropping the photo and messed up the cover line. Meredith won't let go of the fact that I approved it. She can't stand me anyway, so now she has the perfect excuse to get rid of me."

"Why would she want to get rid of you?"

"I don't know!"

"I'm sure it's not that bad."

"Maybe ... it's just that, if only Meredith was a parent herself, she would understand. If only the company were run by women rather than men, we might have companies that were kinder to mothers. I really need to go and work for myself ... I'm sorry. It's been all about me today, hasn't it?"

"It's okay, you need to vent," Ally says, sounding bored or peeved, Carmen isn't sure which. She wonders if Ally's mood has anything to do with their trip plans—or lack thereof. God, she can't do anything right, can she? She isn't even a good friend. But the need to release is stronger. Organizing girl trips and fixing Ally's love life would have to wait—Carmen has real problems to solve here.

"It's just that everyone's so terrified of Meredith and she does these things to trip us up, like emergency emails *at night*. Almost there, boys!" Carmen shouts at the twins, who are whining and straining against the stroller straps, eager to chase after their big brother. "Why do women have to be such bitches?" Carmen says, lowering her voice at the sight of two young moms walking along, coffees in hand, with their newborn babies sleeping peacefully in their strollers. She, on the other hand, feels like an eight-legged momster, rising from the depths of the ocean waving screaming children from its long, ugly tentacles.

"Aw, listen. Men can be assholes too," Ally says softly. Carmen notices something is up but doesn't pry. Ally would come out with it sooner or later. "What does Dan think?"

"Same as you: That it's not that bad. He doesn't get it, though. This place, it's a whole other world ... hang on—" Carmen leans over to unbuckle the twins. Teo is wielding a branch like a sword and stabs her in the eye with it by mistake. Carmen bottles a scream and counts to five as the twins stare in horror and wait.

"Sorry, Mommy," Teo whispers finally.

Go, Carmen motions, face squished up in silent rage and index finger pointing at the playground. The twins scramble off the stroller and run after Tyler, who is climbing up a slide. Another boy watches him from the top, at once curious and suspicious-looking, like something out of *The Omen*.

"Who am I kidding, anyway?" Carmen says, slumping down on an empty park bench. "They're talking eighteen- to twenty-five-year-olds. I'm pushing forty. Next, they'll have toddlers Tweeting for them. I don't even know what half of these hashtags mean!"

Ally guffaws across the distance.

"Who sends a nine a.m. meeting request the night before, anyway? Isn't nine-to-five enough?" Carmen asks, instantly regretting polling her workaholic friend on the matter.

"Look, you need to relax. Start having some fun! Put yourself out there more," Ally says. "Events, parties. You need to look interested. *Dedicated*."

"I'm doing my best. I work hard. Isn't that enough?" Carmen insists, though she knows she's talking to the wrong person. Ally lives for her job. It is nothing for her to work around the clock. Carmen is surrounded by women like Ally, had been one herself.

"It's not, though. You need to bring the old Carmen back. Not this Karen that you've turned into—"

Carmen gasps. "I'm not a Karen." Unless she had become her?

"Yes, you are. And no one wants to play with her. You've got to play the system. You need to get *political*."

"Thanks, Mom," Carmen says, her voice hard, although she knows that Ally is right. If she wants to survive, she has to play the game. Recent cuts have everyone inside the building on edge, and thanks to the mobile updates that have replaced the elegant narratives of print, hundreds of laid-off editors and writers across the country are eyeing her job, ready to pounce the moment she is ousted.

Then there are the usual tensions at work that survive regardless of the names on the masthead—as ancient, Carmen is sure, as the legacy of the *Muse* brand itself: The beauty editors jealous of the free samples the fashion team get, and the fashion team jealous of the free trips the beauty editors get. The art and copy departments jealous of them both, and the interns and freelance assistants jealous of their full-time jobs. It all contributes to a Cold War-esque atmosphere that has Carmen scanning job postings and thinking about next steps. Problem is, there aren't any. Magazine titles are folding every day. And online magazines operate on a fraction of the staff and budget. Still, she has to do *something*. If the company doesn't "re-structure" her out of a job, Meredith certainly will.

Teo lets out a scream and starts to cry, his hand reaching out for a stick that the other boy has run off with.

"It's so unfair," Carmen says, motioning to Teo to continue playing and smiling guiltily at the moms eyeing her with disdain. They probably think she is the nanny, with her children's fair hair and skin not quite adding up with her own dark features. "I mean, it's okay to take a day off because you need 'personal time,' but God forbid you miss a day because one of your kids is sick. I work through lunch and take work home with me. But because I leave at five p.m., I'm seen as less than. It's such a double standard."

"So, leave."

"It's the same thing everywhere," Carmen says, shaking her head, and hoisting a still crying Teo on to her lap. "I've hit the glass ceiling. There's nothing more I can do until the kids are grown up. I just can't give it any more time. And my time is all they want."

"The world's smallest violins are playing for you now, Carmen. Don't cry for me, Argentina," Ally teases, making Carmen smirk.

She was right. While the rest of South America danced to a sexy salsa, samba, cumbia beat, her family's country of origin had the whine of the accordion and melancholy of the tango to boast of. Was all this angst and anxiety just ... *genetic*?

"That's right. Give me some of that stiff upper lip, blondie," Carmen teases back. Whereas Carmen's family oozed passion and drama with their loud, love-hate dynamics, Ally and her family were great at sailing through rough waters and transitions—Mom has a weird new boyfriend? Whatever. Dad moving to Australia? No big deal—if you could call ignoring the giant elephant in the room "great."

"Well, it's true. You can walk out the door at any time. So, *leave*."

"Easy for you to say, Miss Free As A Bird. I have a mortgage, a marriage, kids. I can't just do whatever *I* want. Besides, I've spent my whole life getting here. Where would I go?"

"Fine, then, stay. Stop complaining and enjoy your happily ever after."

Happily ever after. Is that what this is? Carmen wonders, stroking Teo's hair. Maybe that's the problem. Maybe she is still trying to steer when she should be on cruise control, riding out whatever life she has created until death do us part. Maybe she is just ungrateful. Her kids, Dan and their parents, are healthy and happy, and that's what really matters, isn't it?

Teo pulls away and skitters over to the playground, where Toby and Tyler are digging in the sand. Her heart aches. The kids will be grown before she knows it, and she'll miss this very moment. And then what? Retirement. Except that she needs a job in order to retire from it. Could she spend another twenty years doing the same thing, bowing to the altar of Meredith and pretending to care about the next big thing? Carmen shudders at the idea.

"My career is at a dead end, I have a house full of kids, and I'm turning forty. How is this me? I don't even recognize myself. I had a five-year plan."

"It's ten years later." Ally snorts. "So? What are you going to do? Stay and play, or take your chances and leave?"

Carmen hesitates, wondering.

"Do I really have a choice?"

Chapter 4

"Meet anybody interesting?" Amanda asks, peeking around the corner of the cubicle and giving Ally a wink.

"Sure. Because Boothbay is crawling with eligible bachelors," Ally says, though she's sure that if Amanda were there, she would be able to sniff out the one single hottie in town, just as much as Ally had a knack for falling in love with emotionally unavailable men.

"In fact, I think it would be perfect for you. If you were, like, seventy," Ally adds, glancing around to see if Malcolm had made it in yet. He'd been avoiding her since they got back from their last trip together, ignoring her texts and emails and sending the new technician, Karim, out on their latest dive in his place.

Amanda laughs, giving her black bob and ample bosom a sexy shake, and Ally can't help but wonder whether Malcolm ever looked at Amanda *that* way. Guys were like putty in her hands.

"We did see a porbeagle shark and humpback whale, though," Ally says, taking a sip from her third cup of tea that morning, the other half-empty cups cluttered around her desk. After tossing and turning for what seemed like hours, she finally got up around five a.m. and ended up pacing for the next couple of hours, anxious to speak with Malcolm.

"So jealous!" Amanda says. "Did he have a big dick?"

Ally chokes on her tea.

"Well, while you've been frolicking in the ocean, I've been nerding out over data in this stupid shirt," Amanda says, gesturing at her uniformed top which is unbuttoned just enough to reveal her cleavage.

"Yeah, I was going to ask why you're dressed like a jerk," Ally says, wrinkling her nose.

"New company policy, didn't you hear? To make us look more legit."

Ally snorts, looking around at the shabby, gray office—a far cry from the sleek labs where she got her start. "If Malcolm and Dave think logoed shirts will make a difference, we're in more trouble than I thought."

"Well, the government announced more cutbacks, which means fewer contracts, so I guess they're getting desperate. It's a good time to sell out. Go big home or go home, and all that. Have you heard from TEC lately?"

"Shh, I haven't told Malcolm yet," Ally says. It sure was time for her to jump ship, except that leaving the company also means leaving Malcolm.

"You should. You do all the work and he gets all the credit. Without you, this place would fall apart. Honestly, I don't know why you stick around, when you could be living it up in Seattle."

"Portland."

"Close enough."

"It's just, I've put so much into the Hatch project, I need to see it through," Ally says, thinking the same could be said for her relationship with Malcolm. There had already been something stirring between them when he decided to leave the company they were at and start his own consulting business. He had encouraged her to come and join him with the possibility of eventually making partner, and in the meantime, offered her more autonomy and field work. He knew her love for the water. But really, it was the unspoken promise of growing closer to him that persuaded her.

"Don't wait too long. You might miss your chance. Besides, bring me on as your assistant and I'll love you forever—I've been trying to get out of Augusta for years ... you coming out for happy hour tonight?"

"I don't know," Ally says, her eyes drifting over her cubicle just in time to notice Malcolm arrive as he walks toward his office. What if he stayed late? What if she did, too? "I have this report to finish ..."

"Well, you know where to find us. It might not be a porbeagle shark, but it can still be a good time," Amanda says with a wink, before disappearing back into her cubicle.

"It's good to see you," Malcolm says, when Ally knocks on his door. His quick, half smile is weak, uncertain, *fake.*

"You too," Ally says, taking a seat in front of him.

Malcolm taps his hand on his desk, and the glint of a gold wedding ring catches Ally's eye.

"How have you been?" he asks, his eyes shifting from side to side. "We haven't had a chance to talk lately."

"I'm good, things are good," Ally says, nodding and trying to keep her mind from chasing theories about why he has called her into his office. Her eyes spot a framed photo of Nicki and the kids, and her heart sinks. Could he be letting her go? "How about you?"

"I'm sorry I didn't make it out to the dive. Things at home ... well, you understand," Malcolm says, biting his lip. She imagines kissing it.

"So, listen ... I'm not sure how to say this, but ..." he says, and his frown sets off alarm bells in her head. Is he breaking up with her. Here? Now? "I know about the job offer from TEC."

Ally freezes, not sure what to say. Malcolm puts up his hands.

"It's okay. I get it. I totally understand if you want to go. I understand ..." He pauses, rubbing his neck and glancing over at the cubicles grid-locked behind her. "If circumstances seem favourable for a move."

"Malcolm ..." she says and what she wants to explain is that she applied for the job out of spite, not because she really wanted to go. That she did it just to hurt him. It was all a big mistake, and she is so, so sorry. She was just sad and mad. She never meant to leave.

"Let me finish," Malcolm says, patting the air with his hand. "It's a great opportunity. You deserve it. And certainly, we can't compete remuneration-wise. But, well, I hope you know how much we appreciate you. How important you are to the team ... to me."

Malcolm holds her gaze for a moment and Ally's heart leaps.

"We can offer you a ten percent raise if you'll stay."

It's something, but it's still short of TEC's offer.

"What about the promotion?" Ally asks, a little piece of hope lighting up within her. If he wouldn't make her his partner in life, she would make him her partner in business.

"I'm still working on Dave."

"The Hatch project has to count for something." Indeed, they would never have gotten their latest contract if not for her proposal.

"You know that I think you deserve it. But I need to get Dave on board, and he's got a lot going on. Right now, all I can do is senior biologist."

"Senior biologist? That's basically what I have now!"

"Okay, then. Group Manager," Malcolm says, rubbing his neck and glancing off again.

"Group Manager. For now," Ally says, thinking that at least it will look good on her resume, if she ever decides to leave—though Department Director would look better. She catches herself tugging on her bottom lip and stops, forcing her hands flat on her lap. "Maybe celebratory drinks after?"

"I can't," Malcolm says, shaking his head and looking back down at the papers on his desk. "It's not a good time."

"It's never a good time," Ally shoots back before getting up and walking away. Her whole life is one big wait.

"Ally ..." Malcolm calls out, but it's too late. She's already out the door. Back at her desk. Facing her computer while her mind is miles away.

Ally closes her eyes and takes a deep breath. She doesn't have time for these games. She doesn't have time, period. If she wanted it all—the guy, the house, the baby—it had to happen soon. And she did want it, didn't she?

Loser, Ally thinks, looking at the empty room around her. *Hiding out in your office because you don't want to go home to your empty apartment. You're so pathetic.*

"Not true," Ally says. She glances around to make sure that nobody heard her. Fortunately, the entire office floor is quiet except for the cleaners, a mother and son. The only sounds come from the vacuum and the occasional tumble of a foreign-tongued exchange between them.

Ally picks up the blue invitation lying atop scattered reports and sticky notes on her desk. She has been holding off on RSVPing to Casey and Erin's wedding, the dates possibly conflicting with her trip with Carmen. But she can tell Carmen is stalling. She will probably cancel, like she always does. It isn't the first promise Carmen would be breaking. How many times has Ally invited her out on a trip? How many times has

Carmen bailed on her, always putting her family, her career, ahead of Ally? Here they are, coming up to their fortieth birthdays, after, what, almost thirty years of friendship, and Carmen can't even spare a few days to spend with her so-called best friend. Sure, Carmen was always inviting Ally to stay with her, but it wasn't the same. Between Dan and the kids, there isn't really any space for her there. She had been squeezed out of Carmen's life.

As for Malcolm, maybe if she went away on this trip, he'd realize how much he needed—and wanted—her.

Ally reads the wedding invite again. The Intercontinental. Koh Samui. Friday November 25. The thought of escaping her life, a new adventure, perks her up, and she checks out flights, simultaneously scrolling airfare deals in one window and Google images of the island in another. *Paradise.* If only she had someone to share it with.

Malcolm. The idea of a romantic vacation with him makes her ache—somewhere they can be themselves, without the fear of being found out. She wishes he would walk through the office doors and take her away. Fill the empty space that haunts her.

Deep down, in a place she does not like to admit to herself, she knows it's not going to happen. That she is just cheating herself. That theirs is just borrowed time. She is tired of waiting.

On her computer screen, Koh Samui glows blue and green, whisking her off to a hot, sandy fantasy. Malcolm isn't the only one who has a life. She can have it both ways, too.

"Fuck it."

She has yet to ask for the time off but clicks "purchase" anyway.

Chapter 5

—————————

"One more story," Teo says as Carmen snaps the book shut. Exhausted, Carmen had skimmed through the latest Pokémon adventure, only reading the tops of each paragraph.

There's always one more story, Carmen thinks, trying to shake off the different tracks of her mind so that she can be in the moment. There is the present, which she is always trying to catch up to. The future, which is constantly being re-written based on the endless to-do lists and unrealistic timelines she can never achieve. And there is the master of them all: the past, which is always reminding her of every misstep and lost opportunity that took place that day, the day before, and the day before that.

Carmen sends Toby to his bed, shuts off Teo's pirate ship lamp, and lowers herself along his body, settling into an old familiar story, the first that comes to mind, given her day.

"Well, there was this old woman, who lived in a shoe," she whispers into his ear. It's a cruel refrain, now that she thinks of it, as her mind travels back to her trip to the pharmacy this morning.

She had so many kids, she didn't know what to do.

It had started off as a nagging thought, the missed period. Carmen was chronically late for everything, but her period was always on time. Perhaps it was early menopause, she hoped. But as days passed, a sick certainty came over her. *What were we thinking?* As much as Carmen had sat on the fence about Dan having a vasectomy after the twins—*maybe just one more,* she would think, as if contemplating a chocolate chip cookie—now, there is clarity. She doesn't want this baby. *It will ruin us.*

Why had they been so reckless? It is so clear to her now—why didn't she see it before? She had spent her whole life trying to be in control—going to college, having a career—so that she could have all the choice and all the power, unlike her single, divorced mother. And now if Dan ever left her, what would she do, with three, four, kids tugging at her skirt?

Carmen switches beds, wraps herself around Toby, and strokes his springy, curly hair. Before she knows it, he will be locking her out of his room with a big sign on the door that reas, *Keep out.* She holds him a little tighter. One more song.

"Goodnight, sweetheart, well it's time to go ..."

Sure, over the years, while choosing whether to store clothes the kids had outgrown, or give them away, she had thought: *Maybe we're done having kids.* But then Carmen would glance at the baby pictures on the wall, and her heart would break. *Maybe just a little bit longer,* she would think, stowing the bags and bins in the attic.

Sometimes, it was the thought of moving on in life that stayed her: if they didn't have any more babies, that would mean they would be the parents of big kids, who turned into teenagers, who turned into adults, which meant that she and Dan were that much closer to *dying.* Sometimes she simply wanted her kids to stay babies forever, and having another one seemed like the only way to do that, each a clone of an earlier iteration.

Carmen gives Toby a final kiss on the cheek, and gently closes the twins' bedroom door behind her, pausing outside. What should she say to Dan? *Should* she tell him? From the top of the stairs, she can see him putting a record on, his night-time ritual after wrestling the kids to bed—play fight, followed by a story, then Carmen's turn to finish them off. But instead of approaching him she goes to their room, panic rising and spreading like wildfire to the sounds of Alice In Chains' "Rooster" floating up from Dan's record player below. It is a wonder their kids have learned to sleep through any of it at all.

Another baby. They could barely pull off day-to-day now. Even though they split the housework and tag-teamed on dinner and getting the kids to bed, they were still outnumbered. Between the cars, mortgage, grocery bills, childcare, karate, swim classes, music lessons, hockey, soccer, glasses, dentist, and orthodontist, plus emergency renos, they were maxed out on their line of credit, and each Visa statement lately was a thousand dollars more than they could afford.

"De Guatemala a Guatepeor," her mother would say. *From bad to worse*. Indeed, as far as stereotypes go, which her father had worked double-time to overcome, she is playing the part perfectly: another poor, oversexed Latina with too many kids. She should win an Oscar. Except this isn't a movie.

Could they fit another kid at the dinner table? Would they need a bigger house? Not to mention her dad would be so disappointed. Each kid was like another nail in the coffin of what was once her bright and shining career.

Could she do it all, again? She would be forty when the baby was born, putting them both in the high-risk category. She can't handle any more drama in her life. What if something went wrong? And even if the baby is perfect, she is middle age, for God's sake. Her career, and belly, had already taken a hit with the twins. Then there are the years of daycare, colds and flus, another picky eater to cater to, not to mention the interruption to career, travel, and retirement plans. Never mind her trip with Ally. The way things are going, Carmen would turn half a century old before she could score a day off on her own. It all weighed heavily in favour of *not another baby*.

Carmen's heart thumps as she takes the pee test she has been avoiding all day. She reminds herself to breathe as she waits for the little pink lines to decide her fate. Before the pastel-colored strips even appear, she already knows her answer.

"I'm pregnant," Carmen announces a few days later, dropping an overflowing basket of laundry on the bed by Dan's feet. She has been waiting for the ideal moment to discuss their latest catastrophe, but she can't wait any longer. No matter the time, no matter the day, there is always another basket of laundry to fold.

"Fuck off!" Dan says, slapping down his iPhone and looking over his reading glasses to get a good look at her. He is wearing nothing but crew socks and red boxers. Despite the odd gray flecks creeping around his dark temples, he still looks as young as she remembers him.

"What are we going to do?" Carmen asks, watching Dan sit up against a pile of throw pillows pressed up against the headboard—it always drove her crazy how he actually used them, wearing them in and distorting their shapes, when, to her, they are just for show.

"Whatever you want to do," Dan says, rubbing his face. "I support you one hundred percent."

"I have a bad feeling," she says, looking away and placing another shirt on an already-towering stack of tops and bottoms.

"I know, I know. It's a lot," Dan says, pulling off his socks, one by one. It makes her want to giggle. What kind of fucked up was she that she wants to laugh when things are at their worst? She wants to change the subject, run away. Anything to not face her too-real reality.

"We can't. We just ... can't," she says again, as if to convince herself.

"But can we? We have everything ..."

"It's too much. We can't afford it. It's not a good time at work. I already feel like I don't have enough time for the kids as it is," Carmen says, shaking her head.

Dan covers his face with his hands. "I know. It's crazy. But—"

"What?" Carmen asks, realizing he has already made a decision, and it's not synching up with hers. She feels another giggle rise inside of her. *Madness.*

"It could be ..." Dan drifts off, and the look in his eyes tells her what they're both thinking: the best thing that never happened to them.

"I know."

"Look, I get it," Dan says, taking her hand in his, rough and stained with flecks of paint. "It's your body. If you don't want this baby, I'll go with whatever you decide."

Carmen feels the love growing under his influence and swallows it back down. Someone has to hold the reality check. Someone has to be in charge. So she doesn't tell him about the piece of paper. A folded-up receipt from last week's grocery run. On the back, she has scrawled her appointment details, date and time. *Not now.* Perhaps not ever.

"It's over," David declares triumphantly. "Print's dead."

Carmen looks over her shoulders to assess who's within ear shot but sees only mannequins and coat racks in the bright glare of the department store's track lights. It's a bold thing to admit, even for David. Even if the ship is sinking, their very lives depend on pretending it isn't. If they don't let on, maybe no one with the power to end things would notice.

Carmen grabs a flute of champagne from one of the servers circulating drinks and appetizers among the seemingly un-hungry editors in attendance. She's so tired she wishes she could crawl into bed right now, instead of pretending to enjoy the department store party with the see-and-be-seen-obsessed glitterati in an attempt to win over Meredith and show that she is indeed *interested. Dedicated.*

Just one sip won't hurt the baby. A little bubbly to make the medicine go down. Carmen swallows.

"I hear they're eventually going to close all the consumer titles," Laura, the recently hired editorial assistant, says. She strokes her stringy, blond hair as her eyes dart around, reminding Carmen of herself early in career, so eager to please. So afraid of not belonging.

Confident no one's listening in on their conversation, Carmen nods along. How could she not? Three titles had been cut in recent weeks, another stripped down to a skeleton crew. *Hello Home*—a monthly newsstand best-seller—had gone quarterly, and *What's For Dinner* is now just an app. The sharks were circling, and it was just a matter of time before they took a bite out of *Muse* too. Carmen would be more worried if it weren't for the fact that she had her work-life struggle to sort through. If only *she* were her own boss. If only she had finally climbed so high up the ladder that she was in charge. She could decide her own call times. She could hire a cook, a cleaning lady, a nanny. She could enjoy only the best parts of both worlds. There might even be a little space left over for herself.

"But they can't close *Muse*! It's too important," Dani says, aghast. Carmen chokes down a laugh. As much as she needs her job, really, there are more important things than another issue of *Muse*. If it weren't for the paycheck, Carmen couldn't care less if the whole gossip-and-glam universe came crashing down. The thrill was gone, the what-to-wear fantasy paling in comparison to her own adrenaline and oxytocin fueled life at home.

"It's a technology company," David says. "The magazines just don't make enough money to justify to the shareholders—anymore, anyway."

A server passes, and Carmen turns down a sashimi-topped toast, wishing she could swallow the whole platter of them down. It reminds her that she still has to tell Ally the trip is off. Whether or not she keeps the baby, with everything going on at work and at home, she doesn't have time to plan an escape—even though she desperately needs one.

Thinking about Ally, Carmen feels a twinge of remorse. Ally was the one who had always wanted a family, mooning over crushes and dreaming of their future life together, while Carmen studied magazine mastheads and schemed of ways to break in and move up. If Ally really wanted a family, she needed to get on with it, with or without a man in her life. But how could Carmen tell her that?

"Do you think Mizz B will be here?" Carmen asks, though what she's really thinking is, *When is this thing going to end?*

The 'Mizz B Havin x *Muse*' invite had teased an announcement, but no one had even approached the stage set up for the night. And although *Muse* is co-hosting the event, there had been no discussion among the editorial team, just an invite. Carmen figured that the guest issue idea had simply fizzled out, like so many of *Muse*'s campaigns. If there had been any meetings on it, they had been closed-door, and Carmen had been shut out of them. She assumed that the event was just another empty ploy cooked up by the marketing team, like the gift bag, to get people to attend. A Mizz B x *Muse* T-shirt perhaps, or canvas shopping bag, like the world needed another one.

"I doubt it. They already had a private launch for her new perfume with the beauty editors this morning," Dani says, shaking her head. "She's probably on her way back to L.A. by now."

"Hey, did you get invited to the MAC launch?" David asks, changing the subject. "The invitations are all over Instagram. I think they invited every influencer in the city."

"I can't believe they invited *bloggers*," Dani says, shaking her head. "Editors should have their own event."

"Style by Sisi has 100,000 Instagram followers. How many do you have?" David says, elbowing her. "Well, I just hope they're giving away more than a discount with purchase gift card. I hear the beauty editors got diamond earrings today."

"Ugh, so not fair." Dani pouts. "Beauty editors have all the fun."

"Tell that to your free Coach bag," David says, tugging on Dani's new purse.

Carmen feigns a smile to show that she's listening, to appear simpatico, but her mind keeps wandering off to her very own Peter Pan and the Lost Boys. She hopes Dan remembers to check that the boys have brushed their teeth properly, though the wet toothbrush trick they pulled on the regular would probably fool him.

Scanning the crowd for Meredith, she notes that she must be the only mom in the mix. Where is everyone? What had the world done with all the thirty-something women?

Carmen remembers how she used to think her life wouldn't change after having a baby—that *she* wouldn't change. It was the only way she could give Dan what he wanted, a family of his own. It was that or break up. But she didn't want to be with anyone else. So, she decided she would continue with her plans. She would have the brilliant career. Her kid would just come along for the ride. She could do it all. The world had promised her she could.

"Hey," Sasha says, joining the group. Her dark hair is tucked around her ears, and Carmen notices diamond earrings, probably the ones gifted to her this morning. Carmen stiffens with jealousy and then remembers baby Ty tugging on her ears the last time she wore a pair.

"Hey," the group answers back.

A pair of male models approaches the group, wearing nothing but briefs, their six-packs glistening. One offers Dani a spritz of Mizz B's new candy-sweet fruity-floral, while the other fans Sasha with a plastic palm leaf. The group stifle giggles, and Carmen forces a smile, feeling ancient next to the light-hearted up-and-comers.

Carmen peeks at her phone to check the time—another twenty minutes until she has to leave if she's going to get the 7:37 train and catch the kids before they fall asleep. Her heart tightens at the thought of missing them again—she'd already come home late the past few nights because they were on deadline. She worries that their frenzied morning routine is casting her as the bad mother without her gentle cuddles to reassure them at night.

"Here she is," David says, placing his flute on a glass countertop. Carmen follows his gaze, spotting Meredith in a gold shift coming down the escalator like Cleopatra herself, flanked by Nadine in an ostrich-plumed bolero and a kimono-wearing Carrie, and surrounded by her latest crop of assistants, interns, and publicists. With her pale skin and signature red lips, she reminds Carmen of a vampire, feeding off her young entourage as if they were the very fountain of youth.

"Ladies and gentlemen, Cruella de Vil has arrived," Carmen whispers under her breath, making Sasha giggle.

"Pity, they would make an enchanting fur coat," Sasha whispers back in her best Cruella drawl, and they both chuckle.

"Game on, bitches," David announces with a wink, leaving the group and taking his place behind Meredith, ready to dish out a quick barb at any attendee's unfortunate fashion mishap.

Meredith approaches the stage, and the crowd shushes as they assemble at her feet.

"Thank you everyone for coming; it's so nice to see all the familiar faces," Meredith says, her voice wavering as if on the brink of laughter, as if someone had just told her the funniest joke—another act. "Tonight, we have a big announcement that we are very excited to share."

A murmur rises from the crowd and Sasha and Carmen look at each other, eyebrows raised.

"Mizz B unfortunately couldn't be here, but she wanted me to thank you all for coming tonight. And she wants me to let you know that she'll be back soon. Only next time, it won't be for the launch of a new fragrance. It will be for the launch of *Muse*'s holiday issue, guest-edited by Mizz B herself."

Meredith pauses, looking pleased with herself, as an excited murmur rises from the crowd. A smug smile stretches across her perfectly made-up face as she stares deep into the crowd, avoiding Carmen's direction. As if it wasn't her idea in the first place.

"That's right, Mizz B is guest editing the December issue of *Muse*. And now I would like to invite our online editor David Chang up to the stage. David is co-editing the issue."

A gut punch sucks the air out of Carmen as David hustles up to the stage, beaming. It was one thing for him to draft up a proposal;

it was another for him to take over managing editor duties—that was Carmen's department. A wave of nausea surges, and Carmen hurries to the washroom, ducking her head to avoid catching Meredith's attention.

Locked in a stall, Carmen tries to swallow down the sick. Not only did Meredith steal her idea and hand it over to someone else, but she had effectively replaced her with a recently promoted intern. *It's official: I'm obsolete.* Carmen gags. She hears the door to the washroom open and holds herself in.

"Carmen?"

Carmen sighs with relief. It's only Priya, probably the only person she can really trust on her entire office floor. Carmen and Priya had worked together at *Muse*'s competitor, *Poise*, bonding over their shared disdain for their mean girl editor-in-chief and art director bosses. *What is it about fashion and beauty that turned people into their ugliest selves?*

Carmen pauses to compose herself before opening the stall door.

"You okay?" Priya asks, her dark curls bobbing as she looks Carmen up and down.

"Not sure. I think I'm going to get fired," Carmen says, walking over to the sink on shaky legs.

"I heard." Priya nods, and Carmen's heart sinks.

"I should never have taken this job. It's so toxic," Carmen says, letting the cold water run over her wrists and patting her neck.

"I warned you," Priya says, watching her. "You should have stayed with me, kid. Recipe testing, toy drives, potty talk. That's life at *Today's Family*."

"I know, I know. I should have listened to you. I am *such* an idiot. I just couldn't help myself. The chance to head a fashion magazine? *Muse*? Me?"

It was true. Though she now looked forward to another day at the office the way she did a Brazilian wax, she had *chosen* to be here. Arriving at *Muse* had been no accident. She wanted to be the best, and *Muse* was it.

"It was just a silly dream ... anyway, what about you? What are *you* doing here?" Carmen asks, trying to change the subject.

"What, can't moms have fun too?"

Carmen shrugs. "You call this fun?"

"It is when your ass isn't on the line." Priya winks. "Besides, it got me out of kitchen duty at home. It's nice to have something to dress up for, for a change. I'm guessing you didn't know about David?"

Carmen shakes her head.

"That should have been you."

"Just par for the course," Carmen says, leaning back against the sink. "What am I going to do?"

"Looks like it's time to leave the dark side," Priya offers.

If only I weren't pregnant, I might actually have options, Carmen thinks. Could she wait until her maternity leave, and then take the time off to figure things out? Would she even make it that far, or would Meredith cut her loose before then? *Maybe I should just be a stay-at-home mom.* The cost of childcare ate up most of her income anyway. Perhaps she could supplement with a part-time job. But where? Doing copy writing work for some no-name marketing firm? It would be a far cry from the glamorous, jet-set life she had envisioned for herself in her twenties. And all that her dad had hoped for her too. Could she give up these years to her children and resurrect her career when they are grown? Would there even be a career to come back to?

If only she weren't pregnant, she might actually be able to think herself through this mess. Instead, the hormones and fear and shame cloud her mind.

If only Ally had never moved away, she could confide in her now. Tell her everything the way she used to when they were kids, either from her heart-shaped phone or side-by-side in their sleeping bags on a weekend sleepover. Instead, their few-and-far-between chats and once-a-decade reunions left them skimming the surface of their friendship. This is too painful, too deep, to get into on a five-minute coffee break call or text. It isn't the first time Ally had let her down.

Carmen wishes someone would just tell her what to do. She feels wholly unqualified for this crisis in her life. The responsibility is more than she can bear. She is just Carmen, the quiet, shy girl at the back of the class who didn't want to make any trouble. Instead, trouble had found her.

Chapter 6

"**B** aby!" Ally's mother squeals, and the sound of her voice is like a splash of cold water.

"Mom!" Ally says, forcing a smile as her mother beams out from her cellphone screen. Though she's in her sixties, there is something ever youthful about her, girlish even. Maybe it's her bright blue eyes, her still-blond hair, or petite, trim body. Maybe it's her lack of responsibility.

Ally holds the phone close as she turns down Mumford & Sons wafting out of her portable speaker so her mom can't see the table set with candles and a bottle of red wine. Not only is Malcolm speaking to her again, but he has been coming out for dives too. Whether things had cooled off at home with Nicki, or he just missed Ally, she wasn't sure, and frankly, didn't care.

"Is everything okay?" Ally asks, doing a quick calculation: her six p.m. translates to three p.m. on the West Coast—rush hour at the coffee shop where her mother works in Santa Cruz. Usually, Ally's mother sandwiched calls to Ally between her morning yoga class and afternoon work shift. The unlikely afternoon call makes Ally suspicious.

"What? Can't a mother check in and see how her daughter is doing?"

"Mom ..." Ally says, placing the phone on the kitchen counter and running water for the pasta. She hopes it isn't another call about money. She'd already loaned her mother thousands to help with everything from paying rent to buying business cards for a dog walking business that didn't even last the week.

"It's nothing. It's just ... well, I broke up with Carlo—"

"Oh, Mom!" Ally says, placing the pot on the stove and turning on the gas. As much as she wasn't a fan of her mom's latest, overbearing boyfriend, at least he had a job, unlike some of the others. And at least her mom wasn't alone.

"It's okay! I'm okay. Really. I just didn't have a chance to call earlier, with everything going on ..."

"What happened?" Ally asks, lining tomatoes up on a cutting board and checking the drawer for a sharp enough knife. Splitting up with her music teacher boyfriend would put the squeeze on her mom for rent. She barely managed with her barista job as it was.

"I found out he was having an affair with one of the other teachers."

"Oh!" Ally says, nicking her finger with a knife.

"That's not all. Turns out he wasn't paying the utility bills either. That was the last straw."

"Ugh, gross, Mom. I'm sorry. Do you want me to come out?" Ally says, sucking on her finger, and hoping this doesn't call for a trip to California to nurse her mother's broken heart. It had been years since she visited her mom—the last time was for her mom's knee surgery, when Ally had taken two weeks off to look after her, and Ally's ex, Craig, had balked at even that.

"No, you're busy, honey. Really, I'm okay. I don't even feel sad, I'm just angry. So fucking angry. Oh! Sorry, honey," her mom says, with a giggle.

"It's okay. You should be angry," Ally says, wincing at the thought of Nicki. It wasn't the same. What she and Malcolm had was different. And anyway, if Malcolm still loved Nicki, what was he doing here with her?

"Thank God for therapy or I would have killed him."

"Therapy?"

"I thought I mentioned it ..."

"No," Ally says, dropping the cutting board and knife into the sink.

"It's called tapping. You tap the pain away, like this—tap, tap, tap." Her mom shows her, tapping her forehead and temples.

Ally turns away from the phone camera and rolls her eyes. No, Ally would not be flying to visit her mother. This was as close to crazy as she liked to be.

"It works. It really works. You should try it! I'll ask my therapist if she knows anyone near you. How are you, anyway? Have you talked to your dad lately?"

Ally feels a tinge of regret and looks out the window at the boats bobbing in the harbour.

"No. He called a few weeks ago, but I still have to call him back. I've been busy," Ally says, and though it's partly true, maybe a little piece of her is still punishing him. He'd kept her waiting for most of her life; now it is his turn to wait.

"I'm sure the time change doesn't help. What day is it even there?"

"Australia? I can't remember. Besides, I think he might be in New Zealand right now. I can't keep track." Or rather, does she even want to?

"Oh well, that's your father for you. Always off somewhere. I guess if it makes him happy."

"I guess," Ally says as she scrutinizes the faded labels on the spice jars in the pantry.

"Well, I hope you're not too busy to fall in love. What's it been? A year?"

"Since Craig? Two. It's been two years since Craig left me, Mom." Ally lowers her voice and glances back at the washroom. As if Ally needed the reminder. She faced it every single morning, when she swallowed down the little pink pill.

"Worse. You need to start dating again."

"It's not that easy," Ally says. *For some,* she thinks. For others, like Carmen, love was a stroke of luck, love-at-first-sight-and-together-for-twenty-years good fortune.

"Of course, but you have to try."

"I am. I am trying, Mom," Ally says, shaking what she thinks is oregano into a pan and giving it a stir. If she just hung on a little longer, maybe Malcolm would eventually leave Nicki, and they could finally be together. After all, he's here with her now.

Ally's ears perk up at the sound of the shower shutting off.

"Mom, the guys are here. I gotta go."

"Fun! Anybody cute? Anybody available?"

"Mom—"

"I know, I know. Okay, call me back later. I love you."

"Love you." Ally waves into the phone and hangs up.

Dropping noodles into the pot and stirring, she watches the bathroom door out of the corner of her eye.

"Not much longer now," she calls out when the washroom door swings open, and Malcolm comes out with a towel wrapped around his waist.

"Hmmm, smells delicious," he says, coming close. "*You* smell amazing."

Malcolm presses his body up against hers and traces her bra strap with his fingers, kissing her neck and sending shivers down her body.

She wasn't totally lying to her mother. She *was* trying. She *had* met someone. Problem was, he was married to someone else.

Ally can't remember her dream, but she can still feel it: a soft, pleasant, undulating happiness. Was she riding a wave? Floating above clouds? The peaceful feeling dissipates as the sound of a door shutting calls her to consciousness. It takes a moment before she gets her bearings, still foggy from a dream she tries to recover. Malcolm. Morning. What?

Ally stretches across the empty bed, opening one eye and then another. She can make out drops of rain hitting the chimney as she checks the time on the clock radio. *6:45.*

"Ugh, what are you doing?" Ally groans, before letting her head drop back on to the pillow.

"I told you, I have to leave early," Malcolm says through the crack in the door. Ally can see him hunched over the tiny bathroom sink, shaving. "Henry's final game is today. I have to leave soon if I'm going to get there on time."

Ally sits up and wraps a sheet around her. She walks over and leans on the bathroom door frame.

"Can't we stay a while longer?" she says, hoping she doesn't sound whiny. "I can make you breakfast. We can watch a movie. You can be home in time to tuck him in tonight."

"You don't get it," Malcolm says, shaking his head in the mirror. "I need to go."

Ally bites her lip. Of course, she doesn't get it. Her own father had been absent for much of her life and she herself doesn't have kids. *That's what you really think, isn't it?*

"Missing a game isn't going to kill him," Ally says, regretting the words as soon as they come out. Her voice sounds shrill and cruel, when what she really feels is hurt and vulnerable. *Henry doesn't need you. I do.*

"You don't get to talk about my son," Malcolm says, pushing past her. "You don't get to talk about my family."

"Then what are you doing here with me?" Ally demands, burning with jealousy and shame.

"Forget it," Malcolm says, rummaging around in his overnight bag. Ally's throat tightens. "This was a mistake. This is over."

"Malcolm—"

"It's over!"

"Please," Ally says, sitting down on the bed next to Malcolm as he buttons up his shirt. She wants to reach for him but she's afraid to, so her hand lands half-way between them. "I'm sorry. Look, I get it. You're a great dad. It's just ... I need you too."

She needs him to stay. Needs to be someone worth staying for.

"I can't give you what you want, Ally," Malcolm says, shaking his head. He gets up. "You stay. I'll catch a ride into town."

"Let me drive you." Ally looks around the room, searching for her clothes. She picks up a pile at the side of the bed, the night before a memory that flickers at the periphery of her mind.

Malcolm slings his bag over his shoulder, and when he looks at her, she almost doesn't recognize him.

"No. I don't want you to."

"Malcolm," Ally says, her voice cracking as she searches his face for a trace of love, a spectre of the passion she felt the night before.

"Goodbye, Ally." Malcolm turns and closes the door behind him.

A sob escapes, and Ally crumples to the ground, the white sheet gathering round her like an abandoned wedding dress.

She does get it. She simply doesn't matter at all.

Chapter 7

A nightmare startles Carmen awake. In her dream, she remembers holding a gun as Meredith stands before her. A single, deafening shot echoes as a thick, bloody spot appears on Meredith's forehead. Then everything goes black. Nothing but darkness.

The nightmare follows Carmen to work. Standing in the *Muse* galley kitchen, Carmen shakes her head, refusing to give in to the bad dream. She drops a few cubes of sugar into her new mug and stirs.

"Life begins at forty," it says, a birthday gift from Dan that she found on her nightstand this morning. It's corny, but it makes her smile anyway.

Though it's a cloudy fall day, she is determined to make it a happy one. Forty would be a glorious year, when all good things would come her way, she had decided on the train to work this morning. It would be a whole new era for her—one in which she would feel less defensive, more assertive. She would own it. And forty would love her back.

Despite her looming appointment, she drinks decaf coffee at the office, just in case she changes her mind about the baby. She can't help it; as much as her inner control freak is against it, her heart is already starting to warm to the idea of another little one. It is like falling in love all over again.

She takes a sip of her coffee, relishing the warmth of the mug against her cool skin, the air conditioning still set for summer even though

September had added a crispness to the air. Even the gray, gloomy skies casting a blue tint over the office can't bring her down. Any hint of stress or worry quickly disperses, like an early headache that can't grab hold.

Back at her desk, Carmen puts her cup down on her desk and pulls out a stack of Thank You cards from her purse. She had spotted them at the grocery store and thought it would be a nice way to acknowledge the team and build rapport. Two years had passed since she first walked through these halls, but it isn't too late to start over. She can still make friends, turn the messy past into another bad dream.

Carmen walks through the empty office, placing the cards on each desk. The room is eerily quiet, the calm after the storm. Another issue put to bed, another round of late nights followed by late-to-work arrivals. Weeks had passed since the announcement, and they had just wrapped production on the holiday issue with Mizz B on the cover. The timing couldn't be more perfect. Three of the singer's hits were now sitting at the top of the Billboard Hot 100 chart. And there were talks about her getting her own Netflix series. Her cover is a stunning rags to riches homage, celebrating her Cinderella rise to fame and fortune with a spectacular Elie Saab champagne-and-caviar number.

For once, the whole team agrees that this issue is a cut above. Meredith had given a warm speech, thanking her "incredible team" for always giving their best, over cake the night before to celebrate the close of the issue. Even Carmen and David had fallen back into a comfortable camaraderie, collaborating on the issue's digital strategy. As usual, Meredith had micro-managed every aspect of the Mizz B issue, proving that David's promotion had been more of a public gesture than a heartfelt intention to loosen her reins on the magazine. Still, Carmen refuses to give in to her resentments. She has made peace with the world. All is forgiven. Even the kids were cooperative this morning. Everything would work out. Today is going to be the best.

Carmen turns to head back to her desk and hesitates, glancing at Meredith's office. No, she will give Meredith her Thank You card in person. Carmen will stop hiding. She will put aside the slights and betrayals. She will smile and she will compliment her boss, making everything warm and easy between them. She and Meredith both need this. With the industry in turmoil, the last thing they need is another enemy. They can be partners. Allies.

Carmen places Meredith's Thank You card on her desk so she doesn't forget it and settles back into her chair. In one more day, Meredith would be flying out for the European fashion weeks, and Carmen would have the whole office to herself. She would make the team, and herself, feel at home. Like family. She just needs to get through the next twenty-four hours.

Carmen takes another sip of her coffee, scrolling through nursery bedding options on her phone, still toying with the idea. She knows she shouldn't get attached but can't help wondering, what if she kept the baby? Maybe everything will turn out in her favour. The baby announcement might even help her keep her job, long enough to figure out her next step anyway.

She hasn't told Ally yet either. Just the thought of admitting she might not go through with it makes Carmen cringe with guilt. Another baby, when Ally is still waiting for the perfect partner to start her own family with. It's a conversation they will have to have, but first Carmen needs to get Meredith in her corner and secure her position for her family and the foreseeable future.

Carmen puts away her phone and scans the headlines on Women's Wear Daily on her computer, clicking through to a story on the latest magazine closure. Despite a three-million circulation, *Simple Living* is being shuttered, though publisher Star Media insists it will be creating jobs for its digital platforms. Carmen wonders for a moment if there might be an opportunity for her there, but the rat-a-tat sound of nails tapping on a keyboard cuts her thought short.

Already? She winces, knowing the answer to that question. Of course Meredith is here already. *Does she ever leave?*

Stop, Carmen tells herself. She will not get annoyed. She will not get passively hostile. She will go over and say hi. Make small talk. God, she is terrible at small talk. Maybe she should finish her coffee first, or would it look more casual if she just brought it with her?

An email notification pops up on Carmen's screen: *Meet me in my office, now. M*

Carmen's stomach drops. Why would Meredith send an email instead of popping her head around the door or simply calling over the partition? The formality of her message sets off alarm bells. Carmen takes a deep breath, trying to suppress her stomach flips. *Everything is fine, everything is cool*, she tries to soothe herself as she gets up from her chair and walks over. Meredith was about to fly out on a fashion weeks tour of Europe; she would be gone almost a whole month—no way she would do anything drastic right now. She needs Carmen on her side more than ever. And Carmen can use those weeks to prove herself and win Meredith over, or else come up with a Plan B. In either case, those weeks are hers, guaranteed. Carmen leaves her coffee behind.

"Good morning," she sings out, trying to sound as cheery as possible, even though Meredith's back is turned to her. A red talon in the air signals her to wait a moment. Carmen takes that as a cue to sit down and works on her smile.

When Meredith swivels round, her face is closed tight, unreadable. She would be beautiful, really, if she weren't so terrifying. Meredith lets out a breath and looks Carmen in the eyes.

"I want to thank you for all your contributions to the magazine, but we will no longer be needing your services," she says in a voice Carmen does not recognize. Gone is the Marilyn Monroe vibrato, replaced with a let's-cut-the-shit tenor she has never heard before.

"Excuse me?" Carmen asks, trembling.

"We've prepared a nice package for you; I think you'll be happy with it. It's very generous," Meredith says, holding out an envelope.

Carmen doesn't move. Her heart is pounding. Should she fight or run away? Is Carrie getting fired too? Or Meredith, for that matter? Carmen had worked so hard, staying late, missing bedtime stories and cuddles, time she would never get back, to get the latest issue done in time. Meredith was always pushing it; Carmen was always making the impossible happen to make it to the printer on time.

Meredith purses her lips, letting the package drop on her desk.

"There's been a restructuring. Your role is no longer necessary," Meredith says impatiently, and Carmen wonders if that's true or if David has been promoted in another back-stabbing move. Whether Meredith and Carrie and David and the whole damn office were just waiting for her to fail.

"But—"

"It's just not working out," Meredith cuts in.

How can she get away with this? Carmen wonders, but all that comes out is, "Why?" The question refers to more than this moment. She hates the sound of her own voice, needy and beseeching. She wishes she had prepared a speech. She just wants the truth. *Just tell me the fucking truth.*

"I think we both know that you don't really want to be here," Meredith says with a sigh. "It's just ... not the right fit."

Not the right fit. Not smart enough, not cool enough, not rich enough, not connected enough, not pretty enough, not thin enough, not white enough. Not dedicated enough. She should just go back home. Back to where she belongs.

Carmen's insides boil with anger. She wants to remind Meredith that the cover was Carrie's mistake. To remind her that the Mizz B issue was her idea. That Meredith had never given her a chance. That Carmen had tried. That Meredith hadn't. That she doesn't deserve this. But the words just won't come out. Carmen can see from Meredith's cold, impatient glare that it's too late. There will be no answers today. Perhaps ever.

Carmen takes the package from Meredith's desk and hurries back to her office, grabbing her blazer and purse. Shaking, she takes one last glance around her office. There's nothing but a cup of cold coffee and Meredith's Thank You card to show that someone was here. In two years, she has left no indelible mark on this space. There's not one photo of her kids, not a single badly drawn picture by one of them. Easily erased, easily forgotten. Perhaps she had always been preparing for this day. Carmen picks up the card and tosses it into the recycling bin beside her desk.

Walking over to the elevator, Carmen spots the top of Laura's head. Did she know Carmen was getting fired today? Did everyone?

Thankfully, Laura keeps her head down. Still, Carmen can imagine the gossip machine in action later that morning.

She punches the elevator's down button with her finger, holding her breath and praying that no one else sees her leave. Hoping that she will be forgotten as quickly as yesterday's news. Too ashamed to go home, she wanders through the city streets, trying to get lost in the white noise of traffic and sparkling storefronts, until her usual train takes her home for the last time.

I'll never believe you again, Carmen says to herself. *Today is the worst.*

Forty. Pregnant. Fired. When did her life become a worst-case scenario?

Carmen stands outside her front door and takes a deep breath, forcing her hand to turn the key. She wishes Ally lived closer so she could call her over, get drunk, and make fun of the whole nightmare together. Around her best friend, life always felt like a game. Only the stakes had gotten higher.

Opening the door, Carmen steps inside and hears a commotion in the kitchen. Voices inside. God, is that her mother?

"There's the birthday girl!" She hears her stepdad, Richard, say from the living room, as she steps into the foyer.

"Feliz cumpleaños!" her mother calls out, making her way over with arms outstretched, makeup and hair freshly done and wearing a smart-looking suit, as if ready to take one of her real estate clients on a showing.

Accepting the hug, Carmen spots the balloons and banners strung over the fireplace mantel in the living room. "Happy birthday!" "40 and Fabulous!" they declare in a show of sparkly optimism.

"Querida, when did you get to be so old?" Carmen's dad says, pulling her toward him for a heavily scented hug. Next to her freshly groomed parents, Carmen feels sweaty and lacklustre, layered in a film of city streets and despair. She wonders if he can smell the failure on her. His only child. His only hope.

"Isn't this great?!" Carmen's stepmom, Debbie, waves a bottle of champagne from the doorway of the kitchen, looking ready to party in a leopard-print top and faux-leather pants.

"Great," Carmen says, grabbing at the empty flute offered to her.

"Let the birthday celebration begin!" Richard cheers as Carmen's dad steers her to a seat beside him on the living room sofa. "This one's not getting any younger," he adds with a wink and a smile, raising his glass to toast Carmen's dad.

What next? Bruno Mars serenading me from the banister? Not exactly the fuss-free birthday she was looking forward to.

"Where's Dan?" Carmen asks, looking around for him.

"Oh." Her mom winces sheepishly. "The twins shot him with a slime gun that your dad bought for them so he went to change his shirt."

"And the kids?" Carmen asks, pocketing a stray Pokémon card and toy car left on the coffee table. She wonders if Dan had bothered to make the beds since this morning and hopes that at least the bathrooms are in decent condition. Despite the walking disaster she has become, Carmen still wishes she could freeze time and quickly tidy up the place for her guests.

"In the basement, plugged in to their iPads. Honestly, Carmela, I don't know why you let them play with that garbage," her dad says, scotch on ice clinking in his glass. He's the only one who still calls her that, even though she had been signing her name as Carmen ever since she and Ally had agreed it was cooler, the summer before the start of Grade 7.

"*You* bought them the iPads," Carmen shoots back under her breath. Her dad takes a sip and studies her.

"So, how's the birthday girl?"

Under her father's gaze, Carmen feels exposed, as if at any moment he will guess at what a failure she has become. She had let him down again, tainting his over-achieving, coming-to-America legacy with mediocrity. Reeling and exhausted from her firing this morning, Carmen can't think of anything to say. All she wants is time alone to think about her life and find the best way to spin things. She needs to come up with the silver linings before she can convince anyone else.

"Basta, Oscar. Give the girl a break," Carmen's mom says, poking a party horn in her mouth. Carmen blows it.

"That bad, huh?" her stepdad asks, wrinkling his nose. Her dad looks at her with suspicious, furrowed brows.

"I'll be back, just need to use the washroom." Carmen hurries up the stairs to her bedroom, away from his scrutinizing stare. Though Carmen was grateful her divorced parents had come together over the years, she couldn't help but think sometimes that her life would be easier if they were still unfriendly with each other. Certainly, it would have been convenient if they had all refused to be at the same place at the same time instead of convening for her disastrous fortieth birthday.

"Babe!" Dan says, coming out of the bathroom. "Surprise?" he adds weakly, registering Carmen's look of horror. "I swear it was all your mother's idea. That woman is relentless."

"I was fired today," Carmen blurts out, unable to contain the words any longer.

"Congratulations!" Dan says with a smile, arms outstretched. He hugs her to him, and she gives in, sinking into his shoulder.

"It happened this morning ..." Carmen says, her voice muffled against his shirt. By now the anger has subsided, replaced by waves of hurt and humiliation.

"It's great news, really!" Dan grabs her by the shoulders and looks her in the eyes. "Honestly, it's the best thing that could have happened."

"Really?" Carmen says, wanting to believe him.

"Really." Dan takes her face in his hands and kisses her. "For us … and the baby."

"Baby? My baby is having another baby?" Carmen's mom says, coming into the room.

Carmen rolls her eyes at Dan as her mom cuts in for a hug. *Cat's out of the bag now,* she silently accuses him, looking over her mom's shoulder.

"Mom—"

"We're having another baby!" her mom calls out, pulling back to admire Carmen's miracle belly.

"Mom!"

"What?"

"Who's having a baby?" Richard hollers from below.

"Nothing," Carmen says, head hanging in resignation. The secret is out. There is no going back now. She braces herself as her mother tows her down the stairs and back into the living room, showing her off like a prized pig.

"Baby? Who's having a baby?" Carmen's dad asks, his brows scrunched together now in concern.

"Carmen's having another baby!" her mom happily announces while Carmen stands by.

"Another baby? But you're forty!"

Carmen sinks into the sofa chair. He always knew how to pile it on.

"Oh, people are doing it all the time now," Debbie says. "Forty is the new thirty!"

"What about your career," Carmen's father demands, looking at Dan accusingly. "How are you going to manage?"

"Actually ..." Carmen begins but stops. She takes a deep breath, gathering courage, and pictures a Band-Aid being ripped off. "I was fired today. So, I don't really have a career anymore to worry about."

The sudden silence is like a slap in the face, and Carmen wonders if she went too far.

"Carmela Maria Mercedes Garcia!" Carmen's father's face is contorted in a look of anger and disappointment she remembers all too well from her rebellious teen years. Though he loved Ally like family, he had always blamed her whenever Carmen skipped school or received a bad grade. His daughter wasn't a *loser*. It was all Ally's influence, her lack of structure at home. Only, he couldn't blame her now. "What happened?"

"Restructuring," Carmen says, parroting Meredith's words. "I just helped the company slash their budget. Who's ready for another drink?" Carmen reaches for the champagne.

"It's okay, dear, you'll find something else," Dan's mom, June, says, pulling the bottle away from her and nodding at Carmen's not-yet-bulging belly.

"Carmen, querida," her mom says, wrapping her arm around her. "I really think it's time you met my Reiki woman. All this stress is not good for the baby."

"At $200 a session? Thanks, but no thanks, Mom."

"Another baby! I can't believe it!" Debbie chimes in.

Carmen's dad shakes his platinum-covered head and looks down at his glass, disconsolately.

"If that's what you want ..." he says.

"*Nothing* is the way I want," Carmen fires back. "It's just the way it is."

Chapter 8

Ally sits in a sticky, dimly lit pub table with Amanda and her friend Jeff, trying not to think about Malcolm as the band plays horny rockabilly music, singing about broken hearts and lustful longings. The bar is stylish and old-timey—wrought iron chairs, brick walls and exposed-beam ceilings—a nod to Maine's quarrying past. The room, raucous with the occasional outburst of laughter, is filled with Augusta college students, Water Street tourists, and locals looking for live music and a good time, with a side of oysters, grass-fed beef burgers and playful microbrews.

"That's your problem," Jeff says, raising a fist to his wiry beard and letting out a beer-and-burger-soaked burp. Ally wonders how much more she can take before she's willing to face her empty apartment, alone. Jeff would be cute if he weren't so annoying—a woodcutter-styled wannabe who couldn't wield an axe if his life depended on it. *Malcolm-lite.*

"That's the problem with women today. You're obsessed with everything being just *so*." Jeff flicks his fingers in the air as if conjuring magic and signalling *fuck you* at the same time. "The just-so career. The just-so house. The just-so fucking life. And then we come along, and you don't know what to do with us. We don't fit into your little paradigm. We're *just so* unpredictable."

Amanda had invited Ally out with her friend Jeff, ostensibly on a blind date. And now here she is, sitting on her hands to stop herself from ripping the beard off his face. It had started when Amanda and Jeff began talking about a friend's obnoxious wedding planning. That had led to a debate about relationships, which led to an argument on the differences between men and women. Which led to sex.

"You made up this whole story, and all we ever wanted was to get laid." Jeff points at Ally with his pint glass. "You're just an itch to scratch," he says, chuckling to himself before taking another swig.

"You're such an asshole." Amanda shakes her head, although she's smiling.

Ally notices Amanda keeps glancing over at a guy at the bar and the whole thing feels like a show for him. Ally, however, feels like punching Jeff in his woolly face. Had she made up the whole story with Malcolm? Was it all her imagination?

She had thought battered wings and a Guinness with Amanda and her friend would tamp down heartbreak. Instead, the roar of laughter and clinking glasses seems to underscore the years between Ally and everyone around her. Their twenty-something sarcasm betraying the boundless optimism of youth. All their years and promise make her want to hit back.

"I don't think so," Ally says, tugging for a fight, though, really, it's her life she wants to strike out at. "I think you're just a bunch of spoiled brats who've been doted on by their mommies too long and now you don't know how to man up."

Jeff's eyes roll as he stretches into a yawn, pissing Ally off even more. *That's just fucking it.*

"You want us to do the cooking and the cleaning, and count on us to bring home the bacon too, and you can't even fix anything anymore," Ally says.

Amanda's eyes open wide, and her full lips form a perfect O of amusement. Ally knows it's wrong, that the blame is misplaced, but the bite of anger feels so good that she wants to dig in.

"We have to behave like men, and then you want us to lie back and worship you. You're entitled and delusional."

"Bravo! Bravo!" Amanda says, standing up and clapping, checking to see if the guy at the bar is looking. He is.

Jeff chuckles and smooths his shaggy, shoulder-length hair behind his ears as Ally takes a thirsty gulp from her pint glass. She's definitely catching a buzz. Perhaps she should slow down with some water. Only, she is just beginning to feel like she is having fun again. The thought crosses her mind that she could still win Jeff over. Take him home for the night. Be the one on top for a change. If only to get back at Malcolm.

"Look, you don't need to get upset or anything. I'm just giving you *feedback*," Jeff says, putting his hands up—man's universal gesture for *I'm guilty; don't shoot.*

"And I'm just giving you *mine*," Ally volleys back, wishing it were Malcolm she was facing off with. Knowing that if it were, she would lose all resolve, and beg him to take her back, the space he left impossible to fill.

Ally pauses and waits for Jeff to serve another comeback. Instead, he glances to the left and right as if looking for an exit from what is fast becoming the blind date from hell. To top it all off, there's that couple across from her torturing her with their PDA. Although it seems that they can't keep their hands off each other, Ally knows it's not love, just the tender edges of a beginning with no end.

"Look, I'm sorry. It's been a rough day. Let's just forget it and move on. Cheers," Ally says, reaching her glass out to toast Jeff. Instead of clinking glasses, though, her hand slips, knocking over his drink and spilling beer on to Jeff's jeans.

"What the fuck!" he shrieks, standing up and wiping it away with his hands.

"Sorry, sorry! I didn't mean to." Ally searches around for a clean napkin and doesn't find any. "Oh fuck. I'm sorry. I—I just ... I gotta go." She rummages around in her purse for money, drops $50 on the table and gets up to leave.

"Ally!" Amanda shouts after her, but Ally is already elbowing her way to the door. The cool, wet air outside soothes her as she takes deep breaths. Three weeks. Three weeks of averted eyes, of unanswered messages. Like she didn't even exist. Like *they* didn't. Malcolm had even bailed on another dive, leaving Ally to spend a week in the cabin with Pete and Karim, pretending nothing had happened there. *Like it didn't even matter.*

"Ally, come back," Amanda says, holding open the door.

"I'm beat. I have to go home," Ally says, waving at an idling taxi.

"I'm going with you." Amanda's tone is firm, non-negotiable.

Ally waits as Amanda goes back in to leave money for the bill, and likely her number for the stranger at the bar, and they both get in the cab. Ally wishes she could confide in Amanda, but how would that conversation go, anyway?

"You and Malcolm? You slut!"

"I know, right? He's married, with kids. Who am I to make demands?"

"Maybe there's nothing wrong with his marriage after all. Maybe he's not just staying for the kids. Maybe he's just an asshole."

"Maybe, but I'm guilty too. What was I thinking?"

"You were thinking with your dick, and so was he. That's the problem."

Ally is already tired of the conversation, which she has played out so many times in her head. The one person she had shared most of her life with being off limits. Carmen would never forgive her.

Ally is tired of herself. Tired of love. Now that her—what should she call it anyway? Relationship? Affair?—with Malcolm is over, she is back to square one in the dating game. Except that she isn't the online-dating type. Which leaves her where, exactly? Oh yeah, with a blind date from hell.

"I'm so tired," Ally blurts. "I'm so tired of being alone."

The alcohol makes her voice feel foreign, brash, overly loud. She wonders if Amanda ever feels the same. It seems she loved the game—locking eyes and sweeping up her lover in an intoxicating flurry of devotion, only to dump him when the next hottie crossed her path. How did Amanda's heart take it? Is she really as hard as she thinks she is? Yet with guys like Jeff making up the still-single contingent, does she really have a choice?

"But you have me!" Amanda insists, grabbing Ally's arm. "You've got friends all over the place."

"Eventually, though, the night ends, and everyone goes home. Then what?" Ally asks, tears stinging her eyes. She feels bad for being a downer, but the days and nights of bottling it in make her desperate. She needs to tell someone. Needs to let it out. Needs someone to really see her.

"Who's going to look after me when I'm old? Who's going to find me when I die? Say something nice?" Ally blinks back tears.

"Stop!" Amanda says, chuckling. "That's what friends are for."

Ally smiles despite herself and dabs at her runny nose with the back of her hand. Only her smile falls when it occurs to her that she doesn't want to grow old with Amanda. If she couldn't grow old with the love of her life, she would want to grow old with Carmen—Carmen who was smart and funny, real and grounded, and most of all loyal and consistent. The slow and steady she could always count on, while everyone else in her life seemed to come and go. But Carmen was taken. And every day, she slipped further and further away from her life. Maybe this trip together would finally bring her back.

Ally catches the taxi driver's eye in the rearview mirror. Embarrassed, she lowers her voice. "Seriously, though. I'll go home now and there will be no one waiting for me. No one who cares whether I come home at all. No one to tell how the night went, or warm up the bed. Someone I can look back with and say, 'Remember that time? That was awesome.'"

Amanda frowns, and Ally winces at the thought of her heading to an empty apartment herself.

"You're still in your twenties. At least you have time on your side. Mine is running out. I'm facing the fact that it might not happen for me—marriage, kids."

"Fuck it, who needs kids?" Amanda says. "The planet is dying anyway. You get to live every day the way *you* want to. With whoever you want. There's no one getting in your way."

"That's right." Ally forces a smile as the taxi pulls up to her apartment, the windows dark and cavernous above. Always empty. Always alone. "No one at all," she says, wishing Malcolm would just pick up the phone.

Chapter 9

On a sunny September morning, Teo slides onto the kitchen table bench and rubs his eyes. "What are you doing?" he asks.

"I'm making breakfast—pancakes!" Carmen says. That's what mothers in her position do, she had decided, lying in bed that morning, her six a.m. internal alarm clock waking her up despite having nowhere to go. Until she figured out what she would do next, until she came up with a game plan for her career, her income, *money*, she would be the best freaking mom in the whole freaking world. A stay-at-home domestic goddess.

"Yay," Teo says sleepily, blinking under the kitchen light.

"Mommy, are you going to work today?" Toby asks as he comes down the stairs.

"Nope. Mommy's staying home today."

"Can I stay home?"

"I wish, honey. But it's the law. You have to go to school." Carmen scoops warmed blueberries onto each plate.

"Awww, I want to stay home with you. I want to watch movies today."

"Is that what you think I do?"

"Mommy lost her job, dumb-dumb. She's not on vacation," Tyler says, pulling out his chair and flopping down.

"Tyler!" Carmen yells, then turns to the twins and uses her sweetest, most-reassuring mom voice. "Mommy's just on hiatus right now, just like your favourite shows when you're waiting for a new season to start."

The kids' blank stares remind her they have no idea what she's talking about. In their lifetime, the next season has always been just a click away.

"I'm just taking a break. I'll be back soon and better than ever!"

Carmen pushes a happy face pancake in front of each of the kids, with blackberries for eyes, raspberries strung in a row for the mouth, and strawberries for ears.

"Does that mean we're poor?" Tyler asks.

"We're not poor."

"Can I have a new hockey net then?"

Carmen bites her lip. "C'mon, eat up, we have to go."

With time to spare, Carmen takes her time driving the kids to school. The trees are red, yellow, and gold, and it reminds her of the cozy, quiet weeks leading up to Tyler's birth, before the chaos of parenthood and being a working mom set in.

"Isn't it beautiful?" Carmen calls out to the kids in the back. They don't answer, and instead look out their windows as if she never said a word.

"You don't have to walk me to school," Tyler says when Carmen parks the car.

"It's okay, honey, we have time."

"Why are you being so nice today?"

"I'm not being nice. I'm being normal."

"You're being weird." Tyler slams the door. Carmen rolls down the windows.

"I love you!" she yells out as he walks away, ignoring her.

Outside the twins' classroom, their teacher welcomes Carmen with a confused smile. It's as if she doesn't recognize her without her high heels and lipstick.

The stores don't open for another hour, so Carmen heads back home. The kitchen is already spotless, so she attacks the walls with gusto, erasing chocolate fingerprints and traces of marker and crayon. On the way up to her bathroom for a shower, Carmen stops at each bedroom, admiring the picture-perfect Pottery Barn vignette she has created. Baby blue and beige for the twins. A gray and navy theme for Tyler. Carefully made-up beds are puffed up with throw pillows and stuffies. The walls are decorated with artfully arranged groupings of framed family photos, showing off smiling family vacation memories. She'd worked so hard to give Dan and the kids everything they could ever want. She is not about to let it all go to shit. *Not without a fight.*

I'll just get a part-time job, any job. All I need is a paycheck, Carmen reminds herself, scrolling through the job postings on her computer after her shower. She would look for something undemanding, something that would allow her to focus on the kids. She would forget about her "career." That's over, for now. Carmen submits resumes to a few lacklustre websites, then goes back to her housework.

She goes after the dressers first, swapping summer clothes for winter, and discarding anything that the kids have outgrown into a pile to give away. When she reaches her walk-in closet, she sifts through the outfits waiting to be dry-cleaned. She pulls out her favourite black knit tank and leather pants and holds them up in the full-length mirror. *Will I ever wear these again?* she wonders, and it's not just the bloated belly she's thinking about.

A gray hair poking out of her head catches her eye, and she grabs hold of it, walking over to her bathroom vanity and sitting down on the stool to get a closer look in her makeup mirror. She scans her hairline, eyes growing wide at the salt and pepper sprinkling through her dark hair. *How did I miss these*, she wonders, dialling the number for the salon.

"Belle Boutique!"

"Hi, I'd like to book an appointment with Jessica?" Carmen asks, noting that her appointments are growing closer together.

"She can see you two Saturdays from now?"

"I can't wait that long. Can she fit me in sooner? I can come in during the week now," Carmen says sheepishly.

"How's Thursday?"

"Perfect," Carmen says, hanging up, and noticing that her frown lines haven't disappeared. *Wait, are those wrinkles?* Carmen wonders as she flips the mirror over to the magnifying side to get a closer look. *Oh, God.* The optometrist at her last appointment had mentioned this might happen, that she might require bifocals soon. *So fast?* Forty is cruel.

Growing up, she'd never obsessed over her looks. And at first, when Dan would tell her she was beautiful, she would deflect. Laugh it off. She was too dark, too frizzy, too thick to be considered anything as such. Still, getting older had evened the plane, and in her thirties, she had aged pretty well, she thought. Until now.

Disgusted, Carmen turns away from the mirror, her eyes landing on the rows upon rows of high heels in her closet. The red espadrilles she ran in through the tunnels of the Metro, chasing the last train of the night with her friends as a foreign exchange student in Paris for her third year of college. The studded black heels she wore clubbing in London's Soho, where a fellow partier offered to give her throbbing arches her first and last foot rub—back when she was a travel editor invited on press trips for hotel openings around the world. Then there's her favourite: the yellow Manolo Blahniks she bought for a steal at a fashion editors' VIP sale, which she wore on her babymoon with Dan in Bora Bora. They all seem worlds away from her everyday life as a suburban hockey mom, whisking Tyler and his teammates off to practice once a week now that she's home. *Is this all she is now?*

The thought of travel brings Ally to mind. All the trips and adventures they had taken over the years slowly waned as Carmen's work and family commitments grew over time. There's a sharp pang of guilt as Carmen remembers the secret she's been keeping from her best friend and for avoiding her calls, so she doesn't have to tell her the truth. Can their friendship survive another trip that didn't happen? Are the memories they shared enough to hold them together when they weren't creating any new ones?

Getting up to finish her wardrobe swap, Carmen pulls down her roomier maternity clothes off the top shelf. The look on her dad's face still stings. He was probably wondering what the point was in paying for college when she was only going to end up here anyway, barefoot and pregnant.

If only she had told Meredith she was having a baby, she might still have a job. Only just the thought of going back to the office makes her shudder. She knew other parents, moms, who were still excited about their jobs and careers. Meredith was right, Carmen thinks, carrying bags of discarded clothes to the front door. She didn't fit in. Only, if that isn't her anymore, who is she now? Even if she and Dan could find a way to make *this* work, the kids would grow up and leave home one day, and then what?

Carmen drops the bags in the trunk of her car and drives to the plaza, where she parks in the half-empty parking lot and stuffs the bags into the donations bin. As she approaches one of the stores, the doors open wide, greeting her with bright lights and sparkling tableware. The smell of perfume and promise lures her in. Carmen decides to go inside and look for a table runner to replace the one Dan shrunk in the dryer, along with matching napkins, for Christmas dinner. It's months away, but the stores are already in holiday mode and, well, she doesn't have anything else to do. *Retail therapy.* She needs therapy all right.

As Carmen scans the aisles, she finds herself studying flameless candles, dazed by the endless displays. Muzak plays over the speakers and Carmen catches herself humming along. *I do not need another candle! I do not need another candle!* she repeats like a mantra, forcing herself to leave the racks.

Moving through the store, Carmen notices the other aimless shoppers cruising around the aisles in slow motion. Surely, there is more to her than this? Surely, she hasn't peaked. She is not ready to be put out to pasture, grazing the stores with the other done-with-it-alls. She hasn't chosen *this*.

Carmen grabs her purse and hurries out the door, embarrassed and ashamed of herself. By the time afternoon rolls around, she is curled up in blankets on the living room couch, surrounded by used tissues, as a boy kisses a girl on the screen.

When she considers her mounting bills and dwindling career prospects, her heart races and her breath grows short. The van is on its last legs and is worth nothing at trade-in. She was hoping to start the twins in skating—another $400 a month. The Christmas season is coming, and with it the flurry of requisite holiday shopping. Her severance package will be over before she knows it, and then what? Unemployment barely covers the groceries, never mind another mouth to feed. And that will eventually run out too, at the worst time possible—with a newborn baby. Between daycare and before/after school programs, the cost of childcare for four kids would outweigh what she made at any job, even if she worked 24/7. Even with Dan pulling twelve-hour days and picking up extra shifts on the weekends, it still wouldn't be enough.

Carmen looks up as if to keep herself from falling. Her eyes land on a framed family photo of their last trip to the Bahamas, and she sighs at the sight of the white sand beach, pink sky, and neon-blue ocean. She wonders if they'll ever go on another family holiday. If anything will ever be so perfect, again. If she could be happy with anything less.

Chapter 10

Where did everyone go? Ally wonders, sitting on the faded beige seat of her rusted-out green Civic. She bought it for $10,000—a steal—when she and Craig had broken up. When *he* had broken up with her. Unsure whether she would stay in Maine, or see how far her Marine Biology degree could take her—could she get a job in New Guinea, perhaps?—she had purchased the car to get herself from point A to point B in the meantime. She is still, it seems, biding her time, between past and future.

Rain and tears distort the view out of her windshield. For her young friends, love is still a game and commitment something to trifle with. Having reached the mid-life mark, Ally knows how quickly time flies and how thin the options get when you reach middle age. Being single in your forties is like being at a party and suddenly noticing that everyone else has coupled off. *Where did everyone go?*

It reminds her of when Carmen met Dan. It was late. A party at his parents' house. Ally had just gotten in a fight with her boyfriend and wanted to leave. She looked all over the house for Carmen, pushing past other high schoolers making out in bedrooms, smoking in the garage, throwing up in the bushes outside. Eventually, she found Carmen with Dan, listening to records in his room, huddled together like they'd known each other forever. A small piece of her wanted to get in the way, but she could tell right away there was no stopping it, that it was inevitable. She would be abandoned, just like she had been before.

Sitting in the car, *always waiting*, Ally is haunted by memories of Malcolm. Building his business together, she had really felt a part of something. He made her feel alive. Important. Like she counted. Sure, the long days had taken a toll on his marriage, and then Dave had come in to help them scale even more, and the cracks began to show. Still, while Craig had always been the centre of attention, the joker holding court, Malcolm ... at least before the fights with Nicki began, and Dave started scrutinizing every project ... Malcolm made her feel like *she* was the only person in the room. Or had it all been a dream?

After Craig, when the betrayal had burned off and all that was left was a dull, aching loneliness, she would wonder if she had ever actually been *in love* with him. She hadn't felt passion, but she had felt the validation of belonging. Without it, she simply floated through the world. Until that night at the cabin, when Malcolm had really looked at her. Seen her. Smiled. And she felt that she belonged again. But could she miss something she never really had?

Malcolm.

Ally flinches at a memory, an echo of an even older hurt. Something that had broken once and never healed. She was sure that he would call. That their fight was just a blip on their timeline and that he'd return to her. And yet, as days and weeks passed, it cast doubts on everything that came before. Had he even cared about her at all?

She wasn't supposed to need him. She had crossed the line. But hadn't he too? Would he again? The thought makes her wince, that she could be so irrelevant. She was just a distraction. A fluffy rom-com flick and pack of M&Ms at the end of the night. *Joy ride.* Real life, real love, was waiting for him at home.

Tugging at her lip, she cannot put Malcolm out of her head, cannot stop replaying their last morning together. She wants another chance. A chance to explain herself and convince him to forgive her. Forgive himself. Win him back. He had suddenly been snipped out of her life, with no chance to explain herself or reconcile, and this, perhaps more than anything, she is having trouble coping with.

Which is why, on a Sunday night, Ally finds herself sitting in her car in the pouring rain. She had been driving back from a game of Catan at Amanda's when she spotted Malcolm's car parked on the street and pulled over, unable to break her stare as she watched him run up to his car-commercial family waiting for him at the entrance to a restaurant. She watched them through the window, ordering their dinner and chatting cheerfully, grieving for the family she never had, her absent father present more than ever before. What kind of damage did he do to make men hate her so? As if being left behind once, she was doomed to be left behind forever.

Is she waiting for a moment that she can slip in and talk to Malcolm? Or is she looking to confirm he is better off without her? She knows it doesn't look good, but she seems frozen to her spot. Finally, Ally sits up to attention as Malcolm gathers his family in his arms under his umbrella. She watches him tuck them into his white Palisade and drive away. Is this the closure she was seeking? Is she trying to hurt herself on purpose? Can she continue to put her life on hold, waiting for him? Will he ever come back to her? And if he does, for how long?

Ally starts up her car and pulls away.

Only a new life might take this pain away. A fresh start.

She needs to get as far away from Malcolm as possible. Away from here. No looking back. Now.

Chapter 11

Carmen is exiting Michaels with a shopping cart full of craft supplies when a wheel gets stuck in the cracks of the sidewalk. She pushes the handlebar with all her might to move the cart forward, and the sudden jolt sends boxes flying out onto the street.

"Fuck!" Carmen shoves the cart over the curb and on to the middle of the intersection.

"What's going on? What's with all the racket?" Ally asks, her voice crackling through Carmen's speakerphone.

"Oh, these shopping carts are so obnoxious. They don't even go in the direction you want them to," Carmen says, huffing as she picks up the stray items on the road while the other cars stand by. "Sorry, I'm at Michael's picking up material to make Teo a robot costume for Halloween." Carmen steers the cart back to her van, wishing just one thing in her life would go right.

"Can't you just buy those at Walmart?"

"Yeah, but he really wants *me* to make it for him." Truth is, without a job, she doesn't have an excuse *not* to do it.

"If I have a kid, they'll be happy with Walmart."

"*When* you have a kid, they'll be perfect," Carmen says, searching around in her purse for the key and unlocking the car doors. "What's going on with you? *Where* are you?"

"I'm home. There hasn't been that much field work lately. Just walking to my yoga class now," Ally says.

There's a hint of sadness in her voice but all Carmen can think about is how delicious it would be to attend one herself.

"Ugh, I need that so bad. I haven't gone since Tyler was born and he pooped all over the blanket during a mom and baby yoga class."

"Maybe we can take a class or two on our trip," Ally says.

"Oh, Ally, I'm so sorry." Carmen's stomach sinks with guilt as she drops the boxes and bags into the trunk. "I can't go. I really want to, but I was fired, and—"

"Oh no! Are you okay?"

"Yah. It's just been so crazy. I'm still trying to figure out what to do."

"Isn't it obvious? You get another job."

"I don't know ..." Carmen says, sliding on to the driver seat and slamming the door shut. Getting another job would be the obvious solution if she weren't pregnant. But how could she tell Ally about the baby now?

"It's slim pickings out there. Every day, another magazine shuts down. I don't even know if I want to do that anymore."

"It's just as well. You hated that job anyway."

Carmen detects impatience in her friend's pat response. She must be upset over another cancelled trip. How many times had they talked about getting away together? Missed concert festivals. Trips for work that they could never quite coordinate. Vacation time that Carmen had ended up spending with Dan and the kids instead. Carmen had let her down, again.

"I know, but a job's a job. It's just not fair."

"Come on, you've always gotten everything you've ever wanted..."

"I've worked hard for everything I have," Carmen insists. Is it because of another cancelled trip, or is something else bugging Ally? Lord knows, she had consoled her friend through enough breakups. Been there for her, when her own family wasn't, while her mom was out on dates and her dad was jetting off to some distant land. Carmen would keep her company after school, inviting her over for weeknight dinners and weekend sleepovers. Even her parents had adopted Ally as their own, bringing her along on theme-park excursions and family vacations. And where was her pity party now?

"I know, I know. It's just that life is going to throw you some curve balls. No one's life is perfect," Ally says.

No one's life is perfect, Carmen thinks, wondering if there isn't a bit of jealousy in her friend's voice. Carmen's own parents' divorce had only multiplied the moms and dads in her life. There were always double the amount of holidays and presents, the flip side of which was double the amount of people always telling her what to do and how she should feel. Once she had moved in with Dan, it didn't take long before her own home filled up with kids. Meanwhile, Ally is still living the single life. Does she want the same things? Is she still having fun? Funny, Carmen can't remember the last time she asked.

"God, when we were twenty, everything was so *easy*," Carmen groans, watching two twenty-somethings leave Starbucks with their Instagram-ready outfits and ten dollar cups of coffee. She and Ally had been them once, but now her ten-year-old son had more in common with these girls than she did. "I knew what I wanted, and I got it. Now I don't even know who I am anymore. Or if it even matters. I mean, money, fame, success—if you haven't made it by now, it's not likely to happen. Am I wrong?"

"C'mon, it's not that bad," Ally says.

"Easy for you to say. You still have a shot at something. Your life isn't written in stone," Carmen says, starting up the car as she remembers that there are still groceries to shop for, lunches to make, homework to fight over and the rest of the day to survive and atone for. She wishes she could run away from it all, if only for a night. Sneak out from her life and skip out on an adventure with her best friend, careless and carefree. "Remember that time we skipped school in Grade 9 and snuck booze and cigarettes from your mom, and she came home early and caught us?"

"I remember the part where even after she found everyone else, you were still hiding in the furnace room."

Carmen cackles at the memory.

"I couldn't show my face at your house for weeks after ... of course, that wasn't as bad as when you stole your mom's car to drive us to that rave."

"Ugh, don't remind me. It's amazing I survived my teenage years."

"You were wild."

"*We* both were."

"Yeah, I guess ..." Carmen gazes out the window. All she can see is the past. "Anyway, until everything gets figured out, I have to be careful with money. I'm sorry about the trip. I was so looking forward to it."

"I know, me too. There's always next time."

"That's true," Carmen says, not believing it a bit.

Chapter 12

Walking through Harvest Natural Foods, Ally keeps her eyes down, avoiding contact with the other shoppers and ashamed of the single woman basket she is carrying: one box of granola cereal, one carton of lactose-free milk, one single-serving meal kit. Worse: she is now a *middle-aged* single woman carrying around the paltry basket, surrounded by young mothers pushing carts of baby cereal and formula, with newborns clinging to their chests in organic-cotton baby slings. It wouldn't be so bad if she could suffer her fate privately, but the cashier checkouts and table-for-one status are really beginning to grate on her.

Stop. It's just your period talking. Of course, she still has to deal with that mess: the mood swings and the headaches, one fruitless month after another.

Reaching up to re-consider the alternatives—menstrual cup or sea sponge?—Ally's basket knocks over a stack of pink and purple boxes of organic cotton pads. *Can I get a fucking break here?* Sighing, Ally kneels down and gathers the boxes in her now overflowing arms. As she stands back up, trying to juggle it all, she thinks she sees her ex out of the corner of her eye. Ally does a doubletake and confirms it: tall, tan, and strong from days logging at the company where he worked and weekends paddling along Kennebec River, with a cocky, I-own-this-town smirk splashed across his face. That is definitely Craig talking to his beautiful wife, who is holding their perfect baby, at the end of the personal-care aisle.

Ally quickly turns to walk the other way, but Craig spots her and calls out, "Ally!"

Ally keeps walking, pretending she doesn't hear.

"Ally!" Craig calls out again, loud enough so that she has no choice but to turn around.

"Craig. Hey," Ally says weakly, forcing a smile as he makes his way toward her with his obnoxiously overflowing grocery cart. "So funny seeing you here." Even though they've been broken up for two years and continue to live in the same town, so far Ally had managed to avoid bumping into him by giving up their old haunts and finding new ones.

"Fuck, right?" Craig laughs. "You know me. I could eat fried chicken and French fries for dinner every night, but Rachel insists on all natural for Maggie. She usually does the shopping; I'm just along for the ride today."

"Of course," Ally says, nodding her head but wanting to run out of the store as Rachel and Maggie join them.

"Ally, you remember Rachel," Craig says, petting Rachel's arm as if stroking a trophy.

"Of course," Ally repeats, trying to force a smile. Seven years. Seven years she had wasted with Craig, the one she thought was *the one*. It's been two years since he left, and still Ally feels the burn of jealousy and resentment. Not only did he dump her for another woman—the "from away," artsy, college radio type he and his friends used to make fun of—but he also married her, and they had a baby, despite having insisted to Ally that he wasn't ready for marriage. And that he wasn't sure he would ever want kids. *Why not me?*

"Hi," Rachel says, her smile tight. An agonizing silence follows, and Ally has the same feeling she has when she is the only single woman at a dinner party. *Persona non grata.*

"She's beautiful!" Ally exclaims, nodding at Maggie.

"She's a real heartbreaker," Craig says. *Just like her dad,* Ally thinks, noting that he's a little thicker now around the middle, and his hairline has receded some.

"How are you?" Craig asks, shaking his head, unbelieving. "How are ... things?"

"Good, good." Ally nods back, adjusting her arms to conceal the pink and purple boxes Craig is staring at. She wishes Malcolm were standing beside her, to give Craig something else to look at. "You?"

"Aw, it's a shit show. Literally. Kids. You gotta love them. You look great, though!" Craig looks her up and down.

"Thanks."

The blatant ogling should feel good—revenge on the girl who got everything Ally wanted—but instead she feels embarrassed, guilty, and glances at Rachel, who is fussing with the baby. She notices shadows beneath her green eyes, and that the angles of her face are more pronounced. Maggie starts to cry.

"Well, we better go. You know how it is," Craig says, stepping forward.

"Yeah, I gotta go, too," Ally says, accepting the hug and cheek-kiss that feels a little too intimate for two people who are practically strangers now. Ally waves at Rachel and Maggie as they walk away. *Have a nice life.*

"Ally," Craig says, dropping down to pick something up.

"Yeah?"

"You forgot your Supers," he says, tossing her a box with a knowing wink. "Nice to see some things never change."

Out of sight, Ally rolls her eyes and slaps her head. *Asshole.* Some things never change, indeed. He is still a jerk. Still has the ability to make her soar and crash. She was always just a plaything to him. Ally recoils in embarrassment. She must have looked desperate and sad with her single-person basket, smiling stupidly as if for approval. Why did she let that go on? Why did she let him humiliate her that way—again? And why oh why did she always let other people call the shots on beginnings and endings?

"I bumped into Craig today," Ally says, sliding her frozen pad Thai into the microwave.

"I hope you kicked him in the nuts," Carmen says, making Ally laugh so that she almost drops the phone cradled between her shoulder and her ear.

"He was at the grocery store with Rachel and their baby. What is it with guys? Why do they always seem better off after they break up with you?"

It occurs to Ally that she might be asking the wrong person: Dan was Carmen's first and only boyfriend.

"Because guys don't care! They just want somebody to feed them. Besides, I'm sure Craig and Rachel aren't even that happy. Behind closed doors, she probably nags him to death, and he drinks too much."

"Oh my god, I'm that girl. The sad friend who doesn't have a date on Friday night," Ally says as she pours herself a beer and takes a sip.

"You don't want to date. You want to be *married*. And, as a married person, I can tell you: on Friday night, I'm probably doing the same thing. Eating chocolate alone in my room, watching *The Girlfriend's Guide to Divorce*—if I'm lucky."

"So, what's the point?"

"There is no point. And then you die."

"Thanks. I feel so much better now," Ally says, and they both cackle. "Actually, I do have some other news ..." Ally pulls the bowl out of the microwave and dips a finger to test the temperature, savoring having something positive and hopeful to share.

"Yummy! Do tell."

"I might be moving to Portland, Oregon."

"Really? You're taking the job?"

"Kind of. They already filled that position, but they offered me something else."

"Of course they did. You're brilliant. They're lucky to have you."

"Thanks." Ally tries to drum up enthusiasm in between bites. She still hasn't accepted the offer. The idea of leaving Malcolm—for good—is still hard to accept. Is she being impulsive? Childish, even?

"No, really. This is going to be the best thing ever. Hold on a sec," Carmen says, and Ally can hear screaming and yelling in the background. When all the baby cuteness was said and done, she had to wonder if she really wanted her own child. What about the sailboat she'd had her eye on? Could she still go surfing in Costa Rica?

"Ugh, the kids are killing each other again. I gotta go. I'm so happy for you, though! Tell me all about it later, okay?"

"Okay. Call you soon," Ally says, trying to keep the noodles from spilling out of her mouth.

"Indian?"

"Thai."

"Bitch. I never get to eat anything but pizza for takeout. Everyone here is such a picky eater. Anyway, we'll talk later. Love you."

"Love you."

The call disconnects, and the silence of Ally's empty apartment is deafening. Even the walls are bare. After the breakup with Craig, she just couldn't be bothered—her new, one-bedroom apartment became just a place to lay her head. And with all the field work and time spent away, it was just as well.

Ally glances around the room and feels the emptiness threaten to swallow her up. Memories of her dad driving away. A piece of the puzzle missing. Home would never be the same. Now Malcolm was gone too. Why did every man she ever loved end up leaving her?

Ally looks at her bowl. All of a sudden, she's lost her appetite. She pushes the bowl away, slides her laptop over and adds an electronic signature to the employment contract sitting in her email inbox.

Home, she thinks, looking around her and rubbing her fingers across her lips. This was never home anyway. It isn't even her town. She's just a tourist. A dumb college student who followed her heart out here and stayed too long.

Home is out there now—waiting.

Chapter 13

*M*om. Was there another word so venerated, and yet so hated? Mom jeans. Mom hair. On Mother's Day, everyone praised the ground mothers walked on, and for the other 364 days of the year, they walked all over them.

Will this be my kids, too, one day? Carmen asks herself, wincing at the missed calls from her mother and wondering if she should finally answer.

"Pero dónde estás? I've been trying to reach you," her mother says over speakerphone as Carmen brushes her teeth.

"Um-huh."

"I'm worried about you."

Worried about me? Carmen had spent her whole life worrying about *her*. Her mom had trusted Carmen's dad and look where that left her: a young, single mom with only a high school education, in a country that wasn't even hers. Thank God, Richard had swooped in, or who knows where she and her mom might have ended up. Carmen promised herself that would never be her.

"Don't be," Carmen says, spitting into the sink. "I'm fine, Mom, really. I've even got a job interview lined up and everything."

Just the thought of her upcoming interview, though, makes her cringe. She wanted something local to be closer to the kids, but anything in the neighborhood is leagues beneath the glamour of Manhattan she is accustomed to.

"Oh, really?"

"Yeah. I mean it's a part-time job writing copy for a local travel agency, but it'll help tide us over."

Her father would be disappointed if she got it. He'd come to America with nothing but a few words of broken English and over time had built himself a nice, shiny career as a real estate developer, appearing in luxury home magazines and trading in Carmen's mom for a younger, flashier model. So far, Carmen, too, had lived up to his belief in the American Dream. Now, though, she is at risk. At risk of being merely mediocre.

"Richard and I want to help you out."

"No way, Mom. I've got this. You don't have to worry," Carmen says, swooping her hair into a top knot.

"Of course I'm worried! You are my daughter, and these are my grand-kids."

"Listen, I appreciate it, Mom. I really do. But we'll be fine."

"But you've been complaining about how hard it is to do both—working and looking after the kids. And now with another ... we think, maybe it's time for a change."

"Trust me, Mom, starting my own magazine won't help," Carmen says, rolling her eyes at the mirror. Her parents had already suggested it, as if it were so easy. Even if she could compete for advertisers, as the kids got older, there would only be more karate tournaments, hockey practices, and music lessons to attend, homework to help with, and general chauffeuring and school volunteering to do. She never planned to be a full-time mom, but was there any other way?

"I wasn't talking about that."

"What then? Start my own business?" Carmen asks, scanning her brows and tweezing a few strays. What would she be able to accomplish with a baby on her hip? It isn't exactly the best time to start a new venture. Nope, she is officially stuck. *Trapped.* Just like her dad had warned her about.

"What if you got a nanny? We'd even help you out, until you got back on your feet."

Carmen cocks her head. Maybe her mom is right. Only, her heart isn't in it.

"I can't. I just can't." Carmen shakes her head, thinking of the other career moms who saved quality time with the family for vacations in the Hamptons in the summer, and the Cayman Islands in the winter. Even if Dan gave up his work to become a stay-at-home dad so she could pursue her dreams, even if she could ever make enough money for the both of them, would she regret it after the kids were grown? "Looking after them is my job. It's a job I *want* to do."

"Well, you have your work cut out for you then," her mom says, and Carmen feels bad for not letting her help. Why couldn't she give her this?

"Mom, I gotta go. Tyler's supposed to be at his playdate in ten minutes. Hang on a sec—Tyler, get dressed! Brush your teeth! We're leaving!" Carmen yells, closing the door.

"Okay. Give him a hug and a kiss from me."

"Will do." Carmen strips down and dumps her PJs into the laundry basket.

"Love you," her mom says, and it sounds like a warning.

"Love you," Carmen says, hovering over the end-call button. There are so many things she wants to say, but there's too much history getting in the way.

"And Mom?"

"Yeah?"

"Thanks."

Carmen hangs up as Toby stumbles into the bathroom.

"Hey, privacy!" she shouts, clutching herself.

"But I have to go poo!" Toby's eyes are wide at the sight of her naked body.

"Why can't you use the other bathroom?"

"Because I need *you* to wipe my bum."

"Where's your dad?"

"In the kitchen."

"Why don't you ask him?!"

"Lunch, boys!" Dan calls out from below, and Toby runs away, leaving the bathroom door wide open as feet thunder through the house in all directions.

Carmen slams the door shut and steps into the shower, keeping an eye on the time through the fogged glass as she quickly soaps up, scrubs her face, and shaves her legs in quick, broad strokes. Towelling off, Carmen hears a knock on the door.

"Mom, we have to go! We told them 12:30!"

Carmen opens the door a crack, crouching naked behind it.

"Tyler, c'mon! You have so many nice pants. Do you have to wear those sweatpants to Dylan's house? It's not gym day."

"Every day is gym day."

Carmen sighs. "Okay, meet you downstairs."

She closes the door and dresses quickly, rubbing foundation over her face and filling in her brows. Walking out the door, she smooths her hair and applies lipstick, layered with lip gloss overtop.

"Remember to say please and thank you." Carmen turns down the music on the radio as she reverses out of the driveway. "And if you have a snack, don't bury your nose in your plate. Manners please. And use your napkin."

Tyler nods along, only to the song, Carmen realizes, not to her. He turns the volume back up.

When they arrive at Dylan's house, one of the newer, nicer builds on the street, Carmen walks Tyler up to the front door.

"You don't have to come with me," he sulks.

"It's polite to say hi. Besides, Anita and I are friends," Carmen scolds, hoping Dylan's mom doesn't bring up work. Thanks to social media, Carmen had discovered she worked in public relations, and ever since then they would update each other on who was doing what every few play dates.

"Hey, so good to see you!" Anita says, makeup free and still in her pyjamas as she opens the door. Carmen feels like she won something but also silly for trying. Why does it matter what she looks like? Who is she trying to impress anyway?

Dylan and his brother hover in the foyer, in matching silk pyjamas, and Carmen admires the new marble floors and sparkling gold chandeliers as Tyler runs in. Her own furniture dates back to her wedding day and is in need of an update. Carmen dissolves.

"You too! It's been a while. How was your trip to Argentina?"

"Amazing, really amazing. The kids had such a good time. The food, the music, the nightlife—oh! Well, you would know. You're from there, right?"

For a second, Carmen pauses. How to explain that she's brown on the outside and white on the inside? That she speaks Spanish with an American accent, and that she's never been back to the country of her birth. That the only time she feels Latina is when others remind her she is. "Yeah, but my parents moved here when I was one so I'm basically a gringa. It looks amazing, though. I loved seeing your updates on Instagram."

"And I hear you're going to Bahamas this Christmas?"

"Oh?" Carmen quickly does the math. She and Dan had talked about doing a trip this winter to make up for last year's missed holiday—Meredith had turned down her vacation request so *Muse*'s copy editor could go backpacking through Thailand, despite Carmen's seniority.

"Yeah, Dylan told me that Tyler said you were going."

"Right, yeah. Bahamas, Turks and Caicos—we're not sure where yet," Carmen lies, a vacation being absolutely out of the question now, even though, finally, she had all the time in the world to take a holiday.

"Oh, the kids would love Turks. We went there a few years ago—they have the best snorkelling."

"I'll definitely look into it," Carmen says, nodding as she turns to go.

"Work keeping you busy?" Anita asks, stopping Carmen in her tracks. Does she tell the truth and face the embarrassment now, or save it for later?

"Actually, I'm taking some time off of work so I can be with the kids. They're growing up so fast," Carmen says, turning back with a sheepish smile. Vague enough to be somewhat true.

"Ugh, I know, right? Lucky you! I'm off to Hong Kong next week for a launch. I wish I could stay home with them."

"Thanks for having Tyler. Let me know when you're ready for a pickup," Carmen says, that old familiar twinge of jealousy rising up at the idea of hotels, dressing up, doing something important, and being somewhere new.

"For sure. You're amazing, I don't know how you do it. All those kids. And your hair is perfect. You look so happy!"

"Thanks," Carmen says, turning back to the car, wondering who is fooling who.

Carmen scans the brass-framed photos hanging on the wall of the travel agency. A man she assumes is Mark Walsh, the owner of Walsh Luxury Travel, is riding elephants in one picture and shaking hands with heads of state in another. Carmen wonders what kinds of compromises he has had to make to get there.

"Well, you certainly have an impressive resume," Janice, the interviewer, says, pursing her lips as she scans Carmen's resume in her hands. Carmen glances around at the vintage teal-blue walls and wood trim. It's a far cry from the hallowed halls of Apex Media.

"*Muse, Poise*—the country's top publications. What brings you here?"

Carmen considers Janice for a moment, wondering which answer to give her. Certainly, she must have been curious to find Carmen's resume in her inbox. The position was far beneath Carmen's experience and pay scale.

"To be honest, I'm looking for something closer to home, so I can spend more time with my family," Carmen says, remembering her father's advice. *Never, ever, mention your family! It's career suicide.* He had coached her to success, only for her to break the rules.

"And how many kids do you have?" Janice asks, cocking her head.

"Three." *Four,* Carmen thinks, trying the number on for size.

"Wow, you must be busy."

"I have a lot of support." Carmen forces a smile and adjusts her cardigan over her belly. She's grateful for the cooler fall weather and wardrobe that are doing a good job of hiding her budding baby bump, though she feels a little guilty interviewing for jobs while she's pregnant. *Just need to nip out for a moment, be back in a jiffy,* she imagines herself saying when contractions begin. She wouldn't need to miss more than a couple of weeks, tops. That's practically vacation time, she considers matter-of-factly.

"So, you've got great experience, but this role requires some late nights and attending events on evenings and weekends. Are you okay with that?" Janice looks at her intently.

"Sure," Carmen answers, thinking that the fall from high fashion grace wouldn't be so bad if she could convince the company to let her work from home part-time. If it would mean being able to balance it all—the bills *and* the kids. She must try anyway. She knows they can't get by on Dan's salary alone. But something about Janice irks her, as if it were her own future mocking her.

"Except Wednesdays," Carmen blurts out, something desperate clawing out of her. "On Wednesdays we have hockey practice. Oh, and on Fridays we have karate. Then Saturday mornings we usually have a game. *Kids.*"

Janice doesn't say anything, and Carmen searches her face, trying to read her thoughts. She knows she has said too much, but the last thing she needs is another boss who thinks they own her. Who promises to understand and doesn't. She wonders how far she can go.

"Thursdays are a little crazy too. Dan will work late sometimes, so he doesn't have to work on the weekend."

Damn the torpedoes, Carmen thinks. *This is me. Take it or leave it.* Except she still hasn't mentioned the baby. That would be too much to give away, at least on the first date. Carmen inwardly smirks, touching her belly. She hasn't given herself the chance to give in to the idea yet, but the secret between them begins to warm her heart a little.

A plaque on the wall catches her eye, a kids hockey team sponsorship, and Carmen remembers Tyler's tournament she still needs to book a room for.

"You need to look interested. Dedicated," Ally had said, as if it were so easy. *"You've got to play the system. You need to get political."*

"I'm sure I can find a way, though. I just need a little notice to line up babysitting," Carmen backpedals, thinking now about all the Christmas shopping she needs to do. *You want this,* her conscience reminds her. *Please try. You're fucked if you don't.*

Janice looks back down at Carmen's resume, and Carmen breathes in, not sure whether to be worried or relieved. For a moment, she is free, in limbo, and she wonders if this is what it feels like to be Ally, if this is what it feels like to be young again. Before the worry and crushing responsibility set in again.

Janice's lips press tight.

Carmen can tell she's no longer a contender.

It's done, then, Carmen thinks, driving back home from the meeting. She couldn't fake her way through another interview. The universe had kicked her out of her career, and there was no going back.

She would stop working, for now at least, and they would go into debt. They would just have to be okay with it. She would use the time to recalibrate. Explore her options. Maybe study toward a new career entirely.

In the meantime, she would enjoy the time with her family. She would volunteer at the school. Bake everything from scratch. Create the best memories possible, so her kids could remember her when she disappeared back into the workforce. Because what other choice does she really have?

"You need to bring the old Carmen back," Ally had said. What did that even mean? And did she even exist, anymore? How would Ally know anyway? Since she'd moved away, she never visited long enough to really know who Carmen is anymore. She has no clue what it's like to be a mother and a wife and manage a career as well. The delicate balancing act that is being a working parent. Their friendship is based on the ghosts of their past. Is it time to cut the cord?

Carmen gently pulls into her driveway, maneuvering around abandoned scooters, baseball gloves, and basketballs. She slides the gear into Park and pulls out her phone, deleting her job-search applications and notifications. She is done with trying to hang on to someone she used to be. Instead, for now, and perhaps forever, Carmen would commit be being what she seemed destined to be: just a mom.

Chapter 14

Outside, Portland's downtown glows like embers after the fire, like the end of all things. Inside, Ally stands at the darkened kitchen counter, a miniature vanilla cupcake before her, which she dips a single candle into.

Ally lights the candle, and the flame dances off the glossy white countertop. Another blank slate. She's still a stranger in her trendy Pearl District apartment, and just beyond its walls, the city lies unfamiliar too. Maybe she was just like her dad: a drifter. She had left home to go to school in Maine, following her passion for the ocean, copy of *The Sea Around Us* in hand. She had stayed on—too long—for a boy who refused to become a man. And now she had run away from the life she created there, just like her dad.

Ally peels back the cupcake wrapper and sucks the icing off her finger. She had made a wish before blowing out the candle, but what did it matter? None of her wishes ever came true anyway. Perhaps the trick is in *not* wishing.

Ally takes a bite. It tastes like regret.

Giving notice had been bittersweet revenge, even if it had meant going back to TEC and asking for a job she had already turned down. It would be a scramble to replace her, especially on such short notice.

Ally pushes the thought away. She didn't leave Augusta because of Malcolm. She wasn't running away. She was running *to* something, something new and exciting. Hopefully that something led to *someone*.

Only, Ally still isn't totally convinced that she has made the right choice. For one thing, she's more alone than ever. For another, she's already feeling restless in her new job, anxious for the great wide open. She misses the ocean. Misses the certainty that there will be another field work assignment soon to look forward to.

There isn't. She has swapped time on the water for a corner office view of it.

Ally holds her breath at the thought of an endless stream of monotonous days at the office. Sitting, trapped, in her ivory tower, when all she wants is to be on the other side.

She wonders if this move is yet another giant mistake. And if so? Ally shakes her head as if to shake off the doubts and takes another unhungry bite. Leaving her job is a risk, she assures herself, that is worth taking. It has to be.

Ally forces herself to chew. She figures she hasn't uttered more than ten words the whole weekend—hellos and thank yous spoken to the various cashiers she has encountered throughout the day, and that was with making an effort to get out and see the city. Yesterday, she explored her new home by bike, checking out the Portland State University farmer's market, and crossing Hawthorne and Tilikum Bridge—that had actually been fun, and momentarily made her forget her loneliness.

This morning, she had treated herself to brunch at one of the city's more popular spots, making her way through a sausage-and-cherry omelet and scrawling notes in her Koh Samui travel guide. She spent the afternoon hiking Mount Tabor—that had killed a few hours. After washing up, she made another outing, this time for some celebratory takeout Indian. She needed milk for her morning tea, so she picked some up at the corner store, which is where she spotted the cupcakes and decided to drown her sadness in sugar and *Man vs. Wild* episodes.

Of course, Ally's Facebook timeline is a steady stream of congratulations. Her mother and Carmen had called while she was on her bike. Her dad had sent her an email, reminding her she was always welcome to visit. Amanda had sent her a text. But here? Now? Nothing. Fucking forty.

Ally puts the half-eaten cupcake down and stares at her phone. Wills it to come alive. This is the part where she should drive home in the middle of the night, falling into her parents' arms and crawling into her childhood bed. Except that home isn't home anymore. It hasn't been for a long time. Her mom is already dating again. A new boyfriend to go with her new part-time job at a clothing boutique. As for her dad, she hasn't seen him since Uncle Jack's funeral, five years ago. And that had been tense and fraught with things unsaid. She'd happily book a trip anywhere in the world, but to fly twenty-plus hours to Melbourne just to have an awkward visit with her dad and stepmom, whom she'd only met at the funeral? No thanks. There is simply too much time and distance between them now.

Ally presses Carmen's name on her phone.

"Hey! Happy birthday!" Carmen sings out. "I tried you earlier, but I guess you were out, and then I got busy. Did you get the flowers?"

Ally looks over at a bouquet of yellow blooms sitting on her countertop.

"I did. You're the sweetest."

"Not quite, but at least once in a while, I come through."

Ally laughs.

"So ... how's Portland? Do you love your new job?"

"It's great. Job's great. The people are great—"

"Sounds like everything is great," Carmen cuts in, and Ally can hear her opening and closing doors. "What's up? You sound terrible."

"I don't know ..." Ally says, and a sob catches in her throat. She wishes Carmen weren't thousands of miles away. She misses her friends. She misses Malcolm. She wishes someone would hold her and tell her everything will be okay.

"Oh, shitty, I wish I was there to celebrate with you. I should have ... we were supposed to ..."

"I know. It's okay. It's not that. It's just ... it's..." *Everything*.

"I know. I mean, I can imagine. You just moved to a new city. A new job. It'll take time, but it'll be amazing. You'll see."

"I just ... I don't know if I did the right thing. I don't know what I'm doing anymore."

"Look, insanity is doing the same thing and expecting different results. You weren't happy. You moved on. Besides, if it makes you feel any better, my life isn't exactly how I imagined either."

Ally can't help but smile at the thought. Indeed, Carmen now is the last person she thought Carmen would turn out to be.

"How's the job search going anyway?" Ally asks, inspecting the cupcake and taking another bite.

"Oh, there are lots of jobs. Hundreds of so-called entry-level posts asking for decades of experience: 'Do you live and breathe social media? Want to work 24/7? Obsess over your client's copy, in lieu of having a life of your own? Would you die for your team? Do anything your manager asks? Are you an expert writer, photographer, videographer, accountant, project manager, brand strategist, open to long hours, fast-paced deadlines, weekends and travel, on contract, no security or benefits, for just $20,000 a year? We've got the job for you!'"

"Seriously?" Ally says, feeling the slightest bit satisfied with her friend's misfortune. Why should Carmen have it all? Why can't Ally? At least, when it comes to her career anyway, Ally is in demand. She swipes at the remaining cupcake icing with her finger and gives it a lick.

"Seriously. It's a sad state of affairs. Anyway, it's just as well ... I'm going to have to put the job search on hold now that I'm showing—I'm pregnant," Carmen says, lowering her voice.

"Wow! You're kidding!" Ally blurts out, feeling a jealous pang. She does a quick calculation in her head. Something doesn't add up. How long has Carmen been keeping it a secret from her? Can they still call each other best friends, when they aren't even being honest with each other? "My, my, were you trying for a girl?"

"It was an accident. I don't know what we were thinking—we should have had the snip years ago. At the rate things are going, I might have to sell the house, pack everyone up, and come live with *you*."

"Aww, everything will work out. You always pull it off." Ally gets up and walks over to the black leather sofa. It's not as cozy as she would have liked it, the smooth finish cool and hard against her skin. But the apartment came furnished, and for a decent price considering the location, so she couldn't complain.

"Because I don't have a choice. It's just ... sometimes, it's just too much, you know?"

"But I don't. That's the problem," Ally says wrapping a throw blanket around her shoulders. Out of the corner of her eye, she spots her Koh Samui travel guide lying on the coffee table and picks it up, flipping through.

"Is it, though? I mean, I know you always dreamed of having a family of your own, but have you seen my life? Look, all I'm saying is that maybe we've been programmed to believe that we need a husband and kids to be complete. Maybe you are complete ... anyway, if you really want a kid, you can have one of mine. Lord knows I have plenty to spare."

"Let me get back to you. I've got a date with paradise first," Ally says, putting the beach-covered book back on the table.

"Take me with you. I need a vacation from my life," Carmen gushes.

"So, come! It's not like you have a job or anything. Besides, better now, before the baby comes."

"It's impossible. My life is impossible. Maybe you could come visit and stay with us instead? Mi casa es su casa. That is, if you don't mind staying with the Goonies. It could be just like old times, only with four little monsters running around."

Ally tries to picture herself crowded into a corner of Carmen's busy home.

"Maybe next summer," she says, not meaning it at all. Visiting Carmen would mean being closer to her family home, only now there is no family to come back to. Maybe some of that hurt had rubbed off on Carmen, and deep down inside she is avoiding her too. Perhaps they are better apart. Maybe if they reunited, they would see how little is holding them together.

"You always say that. Listen, I have to go. Gotta get these kids to sleep, or I don't know how I'll get them to school in the morning. Have a great trip, though! Have sex with a random stranger for me, will you?"

"I'll try," Ally says, thinking that perhaps she just might.

Chapter 15

July 6th,

Today we moved into Richard's house. This place is so different from our home in the city. The houses are far apart and surrounded by so much green. Already Mom has Richard clearing some of the shrubs that cover the front of the house. At night, it feels like we're being swallowed up by a deep, dark forest.

I miss my friends, I miss my teachers. I wonder if I'll fit in and at the same time, I already feel like I don't belong. Mom said she would talk to Shanice's mom about a sleepover, but I don't think she would like it here. We're different and this place is all the same. During the day, I watch Saved by the Bell *and read* Sweet Valley High, *wishing that some of it would rub off on me.*

PS: I put my Janet Jackson and Salt-N-Pepa posters up on my wall. It still doesn't feel like home.

July 10th,

There's a girl who lives across the street. I think she's the same age as me. She spends a lot of time outside her house, swinging on the tire hanging from the tree in her front yard. Sometimes she has a friend over, but most of the time she's alone. I don't think she has any brothers or sisters. I think she's just like me.

July 13th,

Today when dad and Debbie picked me up for their weekend, the girl across the street was watching and waved to me as we drove away.

July 18th,

I found out the girl's name is Ally, short for Allison. She laughed when I told her my name is Carmela. Now she keeps putting on a fake accent and calling out "Carrrmellla!" just to tease me. I don't mind, as long as nobody else hears it.

Ally looks like a real-life Barbie doll, with her long, blond hair, skinny legs and tan. She smells like shampoo, and an hour after she's washed her hair it looks like she stepped out of a commercial and she didn't even have to do anything to it.

Ally says that her dad has a sailboat and I could go sailing with them sometime. He's not around much, though. I think he travels for work.

July 26th,

Today I spent the whole day with Ally. Her parents weren't home so we could do whatever we wanted. We rode our bikes around, swam at the pool and watched Young & The Restless.

I love being at Ally's house. It's messy, and there are always dishes in the sink, but I feel like I can finally relax there. Like I don't need to walk around on tip-toes and worry about how everyone is feeling.

Ally doesn't care what anyone thinks. She's smart and funny and loves to ride her bike with no hands. She sticks her tongue out at strangers and sings from the top of her lungs as we ride through the streets. She's not afraid of anything.

August 3rd,

Today I met some of Ally's friends. They all have names that sound like bubble gum flavours: Kristy and Ashley and Stephanie and Vanessa.

Kristy says no one wears jeans like me, but the ones they wear don't look the same on me. I feel like a chorizo stuffed into a casing that's three times too small. Bubbling over in all the wrong places.

I don't think her friends like me that much, but for some reason Ally does, and she's always in charge. I think it's because I live across the street from her and she doesn't like to be alone.

August 9th,

Today I went with Ally and her friends to the store and they all stole candy. I didn't find out until we left. My dad would kill me if he found out. He cares so much about what other people think. I wish he cared that much about me.

September 5th,

First day at my new school. Thank God Ally is in my class. We sit together and pass notes and Mrs. Mitchell slams her ruler on our desks to get our attention, which only makes us giggle, which only makes it worse.

There's a cute boy with brown hair and blue eyes that I like but I think he likes Ally. All the boys do. She laughs a lot during class and always looks like she's having the most fun. Sometimes it's just annoying. Sometimes I wish she would stop pretending to be someone she's not, just to get people to like her. To make people stay.

November 14th,

Last night I slept over at Ally's house. Usually I go to Dad's for the weekend, but since it was Ally's birthday he agreed to let me have the weekend off.

We had pizza and cake and told ghost stories, and after Vanessa and Ashley went home, and Ally's mom fell asleep, Ally and I snuck out on to her roof from her bedroom window. We sat there under the moon and

wished upon the stars. Ally says she wants to get married as soon as possible.
She wants four kids. Two girls, two boys.

As for me, I can't wait to move far away and be on my own. I've decided
I want to be a writer in Paris. Or live in a hotel in Manhattan, like Eloise.

December 20th,

Dad's angry with me. Last weekend, he had plans for us, but I wanted
to stay home and have a sleepover with Ally before she goes to her grand-
parents' place in Florida for the holidays, so I didn't go. He hates that I'm
spending so many weekends at home with my friends, or that I bring Ally
with me when I do visit. He forgets that he's the one that made things this
way, and I'm the one who pays for it.

Sometimes I'm tired of having two separate homes, two different lives.
Sometimes I just want to be whole.

Chapter 16

Dan is working late, picking up extra shifts to help make ends meet, so Carmen ushers the twins into the van to pick up Tyler from his Friday evening karate class. She's already late and in a hurry, but she can't help piling up the dirty dishes from dinner into the sink and wiping the breakfast table clean before she locks the door.

When they arrive at karate, Carmen's heart sinks: Tyler's class is already over, and the next class, a group of middle-aged students, has already started gathering around the floor.

"You're late! Why are you always late?" Tyler pouts, pulling on his jacket.

Carmen reaches out a hand to console him, but he pulls away and stomps off to the door.

"Mrs. Garcia," the owner shouts, startling Carmen and stopping her in her tracks. *Shit*, she thinks, as the owner walks over. Another belt, another tournament, another upsell Carmen can't afford.

"I'm sorry we're late," Carmen pleads, leaning toward the door. The twins sense a break and scuttle over to the bench where some kids are playing with toy dinosaurs, waiting for their parents' class to end. "Dan has to work and—"

"I need your commitment to hold Tyler's spot for the winter session. We need to know how many families are participating," the owner says, planting herself squarely in front of Carmen.

"I know, I know, it's just, there's hockey too. And piano. I just need some time to figure it all out," Carmen says, looking apologetically to Tyler, who rolls his eyes.

"I know, I know, you're so busy. So busy!" the owner says with a fake smile and a wave. "Super Mom! I don't know how you do it."

Super, Carmen snorts to herself. She couldn't think of anything she was super at lately.

"I know someone who's really busy, though," the owner says, grabbing Carmen by the arm and steering her over to the bulletin board, which is covered in portraits of smiling families. "Now that's a Super Mom. Seven kids!" she says, pointing to a family photo in which the mom, dad, and kids are all wearing matching white T-shirts and blue jeans. Carmen bristles at the comparison. In the photo, she recognizes the lady who sneered at her during Tyler's recital.

"They all go here, even the mom and dad. In fact, mom is right over there, taking a class right now."

Stunned, Carmen turns to look over to where the owner is pointing. In the centre of the group, a woman wearing headgear, with biceps like tennis balls, is fending off fellow student attackers. Carmen marvels at her rail-thin body and wonders how it can actually look concave after pushing out seven kids. Not to mention, how does she find the time?

"So, listen, spots are filling up for winter registration. Can I have your commitment? I'll need a $500 deposit to cover—"

"I'll let you know," Carmen says. She can hardly decide what to do tomorrow, never mind months from now. Carmen looks around, searching for the boys and finding them now hunched over a boy's iPad.

"Boys!"

"Sure, but I'll need your commitment—"

"I'll let you know," Carmen says, walking away and grabbing the twins' hands. As she walks out the door and loads the kids into the van, the image of Super Mom leaves a smear in her mind she cannot wipe clean.

"Hey, you new to the school?" a woman wearing sweatpants and a sweatshirt that reads *I hope you get the day you deserve* asks Carmen as they watch their kids chase each other around the school playground.

"New? Oh no, we just never come here," Carmen says, confused, until she realizes that she's never home early enough to take Tyler to the playground after school. "The playground, I mean. After school. Hi, I'm Carmen."

"Tanya," the other mom says, tapping her chest. "Yeah, I thought you looked familiar, but I wasn't sure."

"Yeah, I'm usually working so ..."

"What do you do?"

"Magazine editor. I mean, I used to be. Until now. What about you?" Carmen asks, wanting to take the attention off herself.

"Me? I'm a teacher. At least I was, before I had kids. Mark travels a lot for work, so it's just easier this way. I might go back. Or do something else. We'll see."

A gust of wind whips a lock of hair across Carmen's face and she tucks it behind her ear. Tanya's shoulder-length hair, however, is flying all around her, without her noticing or caring, it seems. Instead, she keeps watching Carmen, whose face begins to burn under her stare.

"Sorry, bad habit," Tanya says, finally. "I'm just trying to figure out what kind of mom you are. You see, over there to my left—" Tanya says, cocking her head toward a group of women standing behind her on the far side of the playground wearing matching jeans and cardigans, including the woman Carmen now recognizes as Mom of Seven. "We have the Mean Girls of mommyhood, the Preppies, the parent committee. It's like the woman in human resources. You think she's on your side, until you realize—too late—that she's really not. Stay. Away. From her."

"Ah, good to know, thanks," Carmen says with a chuckle.

"You think it's funny, but I'm being serious. They may seem nice but they're only trying to coerce you into doing things around the school. Everything from lunch-room supervisor to pizza-day volunteer, bake-sale fundraisers, book fair and the holiday store, not to mention the Grade 5 graduation."

"Isn't there someone to do all this?" Carmen asks.

"Yeah, us moms."

"Yikes," Carmen says, the words "Grade 5 graduation" ringing in her ears. Maybe that was something she could help out with. Finally make up for all those years of working late, all those missed field trips and track and field competitions, with Tyler.

"Then you have the Mombies. There's one over there," Tanya says, nodding to a mom dressed in sweatpants and a hoodie, who is leaning over a stroller as she fusses with a toddler. "They're not actually even human anymore. Just a walking appendage. Whatever you do, don't get sucked into a conversation with one of them. Your brains will actually eat themselves so you don't have to hear how little Jimmy will break out in a rash if his chicken is not cut up into the shape of unicorns."

"Got it," Carmen says, nodding her head and smiling as a young boy comes up to Tanya and begins tugging at her jacket.

"Hungry? I've got some popcorn," Tanya says, pulling a bag of microwave popcorn out of her knapsack and passing it to him. "Take it and get your sister. It's time to go ... thank you, Mommy," she adds, as he walks away.

"Thank you, Mommy," the boy repeats after her.

"As you can see, I've given up. They just end up eating popcorn anyway, so why bother with anything else?"

"I get it," Carmen says, waving back to Toby who is waving at her from the top of a slide.

"That one yours?" Tanya asks.

"Yup. And that one. And that one."

"Yikes, you've got your hands full," Tanya says, eyeing Carmen's bulging belly that's only partially hidden by her oversized cardigan. "What grade's the big guy in? He looks about the same age as my daughter."

"Tyler? He's in Grade 5. Mrs. Black's class."

"Oh! Just like Mia! God, middle school here we come. I feel like they were toddlers just a minute ago," Tanya says, rolling her eyes.

"I know," Carmen says, her heart breaking a little as she watches him play.

"Is Tyler going to Oakwood Middle School next year?"

Carmen nods.

"You should join me on the grad committee. I never volunteer, but it's Mia's last year at Kennedy, so ..."

"I don't know ..."

"C'mon! It'll be fun. Besides, that way we can make sure the other moms don't ruin it for the kids."

"Okay, I'll think about it, I guess."

"Cool. Listen, I gotta go." Tanya stoops to pick up a couple of frayed backpacks. "Swim practice. It's a fucking nightmare; don't ever try it, but we're committed to win it now. A bunch of us moms get together once a month to drink our sorrows and talk about smutty books. You're welcome to join us at the next meetup, if you like."

"Sounds fun, thanks," Carmen says, thinking she could use a night off from Dan and the kids. She'd never been part of a moms group before. Instead, she had poured all her post-partum feelings into a blog, preferring an online community to spending time in person with a bunch of random moms. Plus it helped raise her profile and personal brand. Maybe it was time to succumb. Maybe she had finally found her people.

"Here's my number," Tanya says, writing it down on an oily piece of paper from one of her kids' backpacks. "Text me and I'll send you the details."

"I will, thanks. Nice to meet you, Tanya."

"You too, Carmen. And remember—" Tanya says, sweeping her arm in the direction of the other moms. "Stay. Away."

Chapter 17

"Not bad," Ally says to herself, checking her reflection in the full-length mirror of her Koh Samui hotel room as she smooths down the long, black bias-cut dress she had picked out for tonight's dinner. She turns side to side, admiring the way the dress clings to her, making curves where she was previously only aware of straight lines. It's something she'd never pick out on her own but had to buy as a bridesmaid's dress for a friend's wedding a few years ago. She had a closet full of such dresses. Indeed, it seemed as if the only dresses she owned were purchased for one friend or another, though lately the number of weddings she was invited to had dropped off as most of her friends were married already.

Ally slides on the stilettos she purchased to go with the dress, which she had swapped out for flip-flops as soon as the ceremony was over and hadn't worn since. She remembers how Craig had looked at her when she stepped out of their room, ready to go to Lisa's wedding—for once, he didn't take his eyes off her all night. Maybe she should have worn them more often.

Ally teeters over to the elevator, keeping her eyes on the plush, red carpet, one toe in front of the other, trying to ease out of her awkward gait. Waiting for the elevator, she looks at her reflection in the doors, and smiles at herself. *If you could see me now,* she thinks, smiling bitterly at the thought of Craig and trying to stop her mind from wandering over to Malcolm.

The elevator doors open, and Ally takes a step forward, but a wobbly ankle makes her trip and she stumbles, reaching out for something steady. Her hand lands on a stranger's arm. Looking up, she sees a man with movie-star looks in a black-on-black suit.

"Sorry!"

"Anytime," he says in a smoky drawl. His warm smile and blue eyes crinkling up at the edges make it hard for her to breathe.

Ally lets go and quickly turns her back to him. She presses the button for the rooftop terrace, her hands shaking. She can feel his eyes on her as the doors close, and a hot flush rises up her neck. The seconds and storeys seem to go on forever, and she wants it to stop and continue all at the same time.

Finally, the elevator doors open to the hotel bar and restaurant, and Ally feels the stranger brush past her. She bites her lip, willing him to turn around. He doesn't, and she watches him join some other suited men in the lounge, before the doors close and her heart sinks. No fairy tale love story. Not for her, tonight, anyway.

When the elevator doors open again, Ally utters an "Oh!" at the beauty of the view from the rooftop terrace. It's decorated with strung lights, potted plants and trees, and sweet allées, with couples and friends gathered close on divans and daybeds, the moonlit water stretching out beyond them. Ally spots Casey and Erin laughing with their parents, and Erin waves her over.

"Hey! You look amazing!"

"Oh gosh, thanks," Ally says, feeling the heat of a blush rise. "Now you! You look amazing."

Erin smiles and takes Ally's arm, introducing her to Casey's parents and friends. Ally tries to concentrate on everyone's names but all she can see are the stranger's soft blue eyes staring into her. Her breath quickens as she recalls the feel of his arm under all that black. Her lip stings as she realizes she's biting down on it.

A server passes, and Ally accepts a glass of champagne, savoring the taste, already a little buzzed off the thought of him.

Hors d'oeuvres are passed around and pictures are taken. For dinner, the group is directed to a private room in the hotel restaurant. She wishes they were seated out in the open so she could have a better view of the crowd, in case he showed up.

Throughout the five-course dinner, Ally does her best to try and look interested. Every person she encounters pales to the wonder of him.

By the time the dessert dishes are cleared away, Ally is dying to escape into the main room. To the possibility of encountering him again.

Finally, Ally excuses herself to get a cocktail at the bar, lying to her seat mates that she needs to stretch her legs.

"Gin and tonic, please," she says to the bartender, secretly hoping she might spot the stranger in the elevator as she glances around while waiting for her drink.

Ally rubs her neck as she sways to the music of a slide guitar strutting and gliding across scales in the background. The bartender places a glass in front of her, and Ally takes a sip. Out of the corner of her eye, she catches a glimpse of black, and someone takes the seat beside her.

"Excuse me," a husky voice says.

Ally's breath catches at the familiar crackle of it. She tries to stay calm as she turns to get a better look.

"Oh, sorry," she says, making more room for him at the bar. She can't believe her luck. Could he read her mind? Had he been looking for?

"Sam," he says, flashing his dazzling smile and holding out his hand.

"Allison," she says, her breath raspy. She reaches out to shake his hand, but instead he gently turns her hand over and kisses it, sending a flutter through her.

"I'll take a Woodford Reserve, neat," he says to the bartender, not taking his eyes off her.

Ally lowers her gaze and takes a nervous sip of her drink. The bartender places the glass in front of Sam, and he picks it up, pointing at her.

"Let me guess. Destination wedding."

Ally laughs, relieved. "Let me guess," she teases back, "client meet and greet."

"Argh, you got me!" Sam laughs, grabbing at his heart. "I guess we'll just have to sleep together then. It's in the cards."

"Speak for yourself," she shoots back playfully. "I'm not that kind of girl."

"No, you're not," he says, considering her seriously now.

"Okay," Sam says pensively, looking for the right words. "Guy walks into a bar and orders a fruit punch. Bartender says, 'If you want punch, you'll have to stand in line.' Guy looks around and says, 'But there's no punchline!'"

Ally winces. "That's terrible."

Sam laughs. "I know, it's awful! Want to hear one more, or should I quit while I'm ahead?"

Ally rubs her chin. "One more."

"Guy walks into a bar—ouch."

Ally groans.

"I warned you it was bad!"

"Okay, my turn," All says, shifting in her seat. "Why do lobsters always fall for each other during mating season? Because they know how to claw their way into each other's hearts!"

Sam chuckles as he shakes his head. "And I thought no one could beat me in the worst joke department."

Sam cocks an eyebrow. "Okay last one. A guy and a girl meet for the first time, and he says ..." Sam pauses for effect, looking right into her eyes. 'Are you a magician? Because whenever I look at you, everyone else disappears.'"

Ally breathes in.

"Listen, I have to go. Don't want to give them the wrong idea." Sam stands up and nods toward a group of businessmen who are stealing glances at them. "I'm here for a few more days before I have to head back to Seattle. Sam Hutchins, room 604. See you around?"

Ally nods. *I hope so.*

Unable to relax—partly due to the encounter with Sam, partly due to the time change, 10:15 p.m. on her nightstand clock translating to roughly 8:15 a.m. back home—Ally decides to take a dip in the pool.

She pads along the wooden deck and drops her robe on a lounge chair. The warm ocean breeze feels delicious on her skin, and she lets it caress her for a moment before diving into the deep end.

Floating on her back, she watches palm trees sway and stars freckle the sky. No, she can't complain about this moment. It is almost perfect.

Ally flips over and does a few distracted laps before taking a break. Hugging the edge of the pool, she hums along to the sound of Muzak while laughter floats down from the partiers celebrating on the terrace above.

"Hey," a voice behind her says.

Startled, Ally looks over her shoulder to see Sam swimming up to her.

"I was just headed back to my room and then I saw you. Mind if I join you?"

"Sure," Ally says, wondering if she is dreaming.

"I was going to pull your leg, but then I thought it might be too soon for that," Sam says with a grin.

"Too soon for that," Ally repeats, hypnotized by his full mouth and smiling eyes. His warm drawl makes her want to curl up next to him and surrender, but she proudly pulls away instead. "I used to take kickboxing, and I know how to throw a punch."

"I would happily take any hits you have to give me," Sam says, his grin widening. "As long as it doesn't come with another terrible joke."

Ally laughs, her heart soaring.

Sam looks up at the stars and starts to hum a familiar melody. Ally turns her head to catch her breath.

"Stars shining up above you," Sam sings softly at her side, his gravelly voice stirring something deep inside her. Ally's eyes close as Sam hums the rest of the melody.

"Dream a little dream of me," Ally sings at the end, opening her eyes and smiling at him.

Sam pulls himself out of the pool and holds out Ally's robe for her. Ally slides her arms in and turns around to face him. *If he asks me to his room, the answer is yes,* she thinks. Instead, Sam pulls her in and kisses her softly. Ally feels her knees buckle, and she grabs hold of his arms to stop herself from falling.

"I have a morning meeting to prepare for. See you tomorrow?" Sam says, pulling back and giving her a tip of his imaginary hat as he walks away. "We could do lunch ... and other things?" he teases playfully.

"Sure, yeah," Ally laughs, waving back as he disappears. Still reeling from the kiss, Ally sighs and flops down on a chaise longue, lying back in her robe. *Is this real?*

"Sam," Ally whispers, as if saying his name confirms the truth of it. Goosebumps travel up and down her arms at the thought of him, and Ally runs her tongue over her lips, which still taste like him. Spicy cigar and the sweet sting of alcohol. *Sam.*

Chapter 18

"What's wrong? Not what you ordered?" Jasmine asks, nodding at Carmen's plate.

Carmen shakes her head, swallowing a wave of sick back down. Though the early pregnancy nausea has passed, Carmen still feels queasy, and the untouched steak and frites lying before her seem insurmountable.

"The kids. They're always bringing something home," Carmen says, tugging at her shirt and shifting in her seat to get more comfortable. Her loose sweater and stretchy, one-size-up jeans are doing a decent job of hiding her bump, but still, she needs to admit she is pregnant before she gets any bigger. They had just talked about her losing her job, though, and she is tired of everyone telling her what she should do.

"Ben is just a dream. He is the *easiest* baby," Tina gushes, pointing to the server for more wine. It's the first time the three of them have gotten together since Tina's baby shower last spring. Friends since high school, they had stayed close through their twenties, hitting the clubs every weekend. As their thirties approached and they hung up their barely-there, club night dresses, they began meeting for Sunday morning brunch instead. But then Carmen moved out to the suburbs and had Tyler, and weeks became months, which became almost years.

"How old is he now?" Carmen asks, glancing around at the other tables filled with the young and the beautiful and the up and coming, and not really wanting to talk about their kids and setting sun status.

"Five months. And all he wants to do is eat!" Tina says, draining the remainder of her glass. "I'm pumping and dumping," she confesses, as if anyone had asked.

"Sure," says Jasmine.

"Sure," Carmen agrees. She remembers marvelling at the women with endless supplies of milk, whereas Carmen would have to pump for what felt like forever to come up with half a bottle of the stuff for Tyler, so she just skipped to formula when the twins came around. Some women were just made to be moms, she guessed, glad for the career that supplemented her lack of self-esteem. Only she didn't even have *that* anymore.

"Look at this," Carmen says, catching Jasmine on her phone, scrolling through Instagram. "Look at all these happy people. Is everyone lying?"

"Of course," Jasmine says, perking up now that the subject of children is past.

"There's this one girl I know who keeps posting about her team at work and all their wins," Tina says, rolling her eyes.

"That's so obnoxious. She's probably just faking it," Jasmine says as Carmen scrolls through her own feed.

"Faking it. Is that really a thing?" Carmen asks.

"Sure. I do it all the time," Jasmine says with a shrug, taking back her phone.

"Like what?" It scares Carmen a little, to realize that maybe she doesn't know her friend as well as she thought she did.

"Okay, L.A.," Jasmine says, putting her phone down and taking a gulp of her pinot grigio. "L.A. sucked. Todd and I had a miserable time."

"Really?" Tina says, turning to the server to mouth thanks and accept another glass. "But what about all those happy pics and posts?"

"Lies. He was a selfish dick, and we fought all the time."

"Why didn't you say something?" Carmen wonders if she is a bad friend for not picking up on the truth. Was she not paying attention? And yet, she has her own secrets she is keeping.

"I knew what you'd say."

It was true. Jasmine had a thing for bad boys, picking up one damaged, narcissistic boyfriend after another like some Florence Nightingale of the dating world.

"Things are good with Lenny now, though, right?" Carmen asks.

"Actually, we just broke up," Jasmine says, stabbing at her gnocchi and popping a creamy dumpling in her mouth.

"Oh, sweetie! I'm so sorry!" Tina reaches across the table to stroke Jasmine's arm. "Dating is the worst."

"What happened?" Carmen asks, pushing the fries around her plate, afraid to pry, afraid not to.

"I made him dinner," Jasmine says, shaking her head. "I took him shopping. Bought him flowers. Nine months, and what did I ever get in return? A fucking coffee. From Dunkin Donuts. I mean, it wasn't even Starbucks."

"Ugh, gross." Carmen groans, wondering how her brilliant publicist friend who helped launch multinational brands into market space could be so stupid when it came to love. The red flags were always there—late night booty calls, not introducing her to his friends or family. Couldn't she see that?

"I mean, all I want is to go for a nice walk. Get a beer on a patio. A simple meal out. Instead, all we do is sit around at his house having tea. And I have to make it! I mean, am I asking too much?"

"No, honey, no. You absolutely deserve *all* of that," Carmen says, thinking it did not sound unlike her own relationship with Meredith, where she did all the work, and Meredith had all the fun. Why had she put up with it so long? Didn't *she* think she deserved better?

"All that and more," Tina says, nodding along. "You guys, it's so nice to be here with you. I miss us. I so needed this. It's my first time out since Ben was born. You can't imagine how sore my nipples are."

"I'm sure Carmen can," Jasmine says.

Carmen scowls back.

"I mean, I love Ben and everything, but it's so good to get away. I just can't do *that* all the time. Know what I mean?" Tina asks.

Carmen nods, slightly ashamed of her new stay-at-home-mom status. She notices Tina's usually perfect blond highlights have grown out, along with the other telltale signs of new motherhood—shadows under the eyes, baggy top, unkempt hair.

"I just don't want to be a boring mom and wife. I'm not fucking boring!" Tina shouts, grabbing Carmen's arm and catching the attention of the tables nearby.

Carmen ducks her head. Are they all trying to avoid becoming their mothers? In her mind's eye, Carmen can still see her mom, so alone, so scared. After her dad left, Carmen had promised herself that would never be her. Instead, she would be the one to do the leaving. She would have all the power. And yet, all these years later, she has never felt so powerless.

"Ooh, your skin is so soft!" Tina says, rubbing Carmen's arm. "My skin is so dry from all the breastfeeding. What do you use?"

"Actually ..." Carmen wonders if she should just come out with it. She is a tsunami of estrogen and progesterone and there is just no point lying about it anymore. "It's probably just the hormones. I'm pregnant."

"Weee! Congratulations!" Tina squeals.

"Jeez!" Jasmine says, grimacing. "You need a TV in your bedroom."

"What if it's a girl!" Tina says, clapping her hands together. "I could totally have a football team. Frank's a hard stop at two, though. He says any more would be disrespectful to the environment."

"God, all those kids. I don't know how you do it," Jasmine says, shaking her head.

"Thanks." Carmen tries to take a bite. The steak feels like rubber in her mouth.

"See, you can have kids and still be cool," Tina says to Jasmine, taking another gulp from her glass. "You can still have a life."

"You can," Carmen cautions, "when you have one kid. Two, maybe."

"And four?" Jasmine asks, her eyes teasing.

"You're just fucked."

"But you love it, right? Right?" Tina demands.

"I do, I do," Carmen says, watching the table beside her break out into raucous, carefree laughter. All around her she can feel hope and possibility. First dates and fresh friendships. Her own life was already mapped out—work nine-to-five until the kids move out, then retire, sell the house, downsize, and wait to die. "It's just that, kids kind of take over. Like, completely."

"You still have your career, though," Tina says, and catches herself. "I mean your boss was a bitch, but that doesn't mean you won't get something even better. Right?"

Carmen wants to tell Tina everything will work out, but more and more, it feels like a lie.

"I used to think so," Carmen says, staring at the uneaten food on her plate. "I mean, it's so unfair. You spend your whole life working up to your career, and then when you finally make it, the kids come, and you have to step off the ladder, and it's near impossible to step back on again.

And then *Forbes* publishes a story wondering where all the female CEOs are. They're at home, making fucking dinner!"

Carmen looks up and catches Tina and Jasmine staring at her in surprised silence.

"Forget it, it's all good. Everything's going to work out," she says, trying to reassure a doubtful-looking Tina.

"Please, anyone, change the subject," Carmen pleads.

"Okay, talk to Ally lately?" Jasmine asks, bringing another forkful to her mouth. The smell of cheese and garlic makes Carmen's stomach turn.

"Yeah, she just got a new job in Portland. *And* she's in Koh Samui right now for a friend's wedding," Carmen brightens up at the thought of beach, hotel, *room service*. She's chuffed to still have the inside scoop on Ally, despite the years and distance between them. Even among their old high school friends, Carmen and Ally were always a team. Inseparable.

"So amazing." Tina looks off wistfully. "Good for her."

"A job. Travel. Just think, that could have been you," Jasmine says, playfully pinching Carmen's arm. It stings more than Carmen will admit. Just because she usually has her shit together, doesn't mean it doesn't hurt when it all falls apart.

Carmen is sitting on the tan-colored couch in Tanya's living room. The arms are threadbare, and there are stains on the cushions. Carmen doesn't feel so bad about her own worn and dated furniture now.

"Red or white?" Tanya asks, holding out two bottles.

"Just a water would be great, thanks," Carmen says, grabbing an empty glass from the coffee table and holding it up for Tanya to pour into.

"Oh, shit," Tanya says, looking over Carmen's head.

"What?" Carmen glances to her left and right.

"Don't look behind you. There's a giant booger on the wall. Scott and I have been daring each other to clean it up, and I forgot all about it. This is so embarrassing. I'm sorry. It's probably calcified by now. Impossible to take off."

Carmen turns around and sees the glob of yellow smeared on the wall and nudges forward on the couch.

"Ugh, you do not want to see our walls," Joanne chips in. "I'm just waiting for the kids to grow up, and then we'll have everything painted."

"I mean, honestly, what's the point?" Sarah agrees. "We've given up too. The kids win."

"And what about bedtimes?" Joanne says. "It's like a sleepover party every night. Lately, our kids are going to sleep after *we* do. I can't even have a smoke in my own garage without being afraid I'm going to get caught."

"Wait till they're Anthony's age," Sarah says. "Then you can't even have a drink on Saturday night because you might have to drive *them* home from a party. What's with fifteen anyway? I honestly can't understand a word Anthony is saying. All he does is grunt."

"What are you guys doing for lunches these days? I just found out popcorn is carcinogenic and that's the only things my kids eat."

"Ugh, don't even get me started."

"Have you seen the lunches Alex makes? She literally makes each kid their very own all-organic bento box. And delivers them fresh at lunch time. Is she *trying* to make us all look bad?"

"She *did* graduate from Harvard ..."

"I heard she used to be a scientist *and* a yoga teacher ..."

"What, is she an astronaut too?" Carmen asks.

"Wouldn't surprise me," Tanya says with a snort. "She did finish the Ironman."

"I heard Alex has a calendar for each kid. With pictures and reminders and stickers for each day of the week. I mean, I wish *I* had a calendar like that! Are we supposed to be our kids' VAs now too?"

"Don't think it'd make much of a difference. Pretty sure none of my kids will end up in college. Unless they come out with a degree in Fortnite."

"We spent thousands of dollars and hours on hockey, and now Bryce wants to play basketball."

"It's like, we do everything for them, invest every penny we have, and then when they're finally old enough to finally help out and mow the lawn, they still charge *us* by the hour!"

"Kids are such assholes."

"They are. But I love them so freaking much."

"So freaking much."

When Carmen leaves Tanya's house to go home, she feels like she's walking on air. Or the perfect, clear fall night sky. She isn't the worst mom ever. And her life isn't as bad as it seems. In fact, for the first time in a long time, she actually feels normal.

Chapter 19

Ally's phone sends her to Sam's voicemail, again. *Where is he?* After a blissful few days together, feeling like *they* were the ones on a honeymoon, Sam had a meeting this morning. Still, he would have been in touch by now. In the meantime, Ally had done a workout on the bike at the gym, followed by a lacklustre Caesar salad at the open-air restaurant under the shade of an almond tree while trying not to check her phone. All her calls had gone unanswered or straight to voicemail. And now here she is, alone and sitting on a stool under the thatched roof of the beach bar, sipping on an Old Fashioned as beach bathers pack up, abandoning the late afternoon sun.

Ally tries not to think about last night. About why he might not be answering. She won't let her mind go there.

Around her, wedding guests congregate between blanketed banquet tables. Ally takes one last scan of her phone and tucks it into the straw cross-body bag she purchased at the market—despite her vacation status, she can't help stealing glances at her work email now and then. And yet, even work has lost its appeal, paling to the technicolor of Sam.

A breeze flirts with the edges of Ally's white dress, another new purchase to supplement the cargo pants and tank tops she packed for her trip. Ally feels she owes it to the black dress to keep pace with their first encounter, so she has already worn the floral sundress she brought to wear to the wedding. She wonders if Sam will have a chance to see her new white dress, if the $500 she spent at the hotel gift shop is worth it.

Ally scans the hotel guests again, pretending to adjust her straps for something to do, and catches a whiff of the sweetly fragrant frangipani blossoms. The turquoise ocean stretches out before her, while heady acid jazz wafts down from the speakers above. She takes another sip of her drink and leaves it at the bar as she follows the other guests to the beach at the urging of the wedding planner.

Drums sound out like rolling thunder, announcing the arrival of the bride. Glancing around for her but secretly wishing to see Sam, Ally spots Erin making her way past the pool to the beach, followed by an entourage of ceremonial drummers. Ally can't help but smile when she looks over at Casey, who is grinning like a kid on Christmas morning as Erin walks up the orchid petal-lined path. As happy as she is for her friends, though, Ally feels a twinge of regret, and if she dares to admit it, worry. *Why won't he answer his phone?*

Is she delusional? Had she made this all up? Days of exploring beaches and villages together, visiting temples, gushing over Thai delicacies—sweet salsas, sour soups, crispy rolls and savoury noodles. Despite her conscience warning her otherwise, Ally could feel herself falling for Sam. He was smart, savvy, well-travelled. He knew what to order and where to go. The conversation was hurried and filled with laughter. They had so much to share and so little time together.

They talked about places they'd been and places they wanted to go. Sam was friendly and warm and sweet, but with a darkly unpredictable edge—a quirky sense of humor and the occasional playful outburst—that pulled her in, daring her to discover more. He was different than the other guys she had dated. Less outdoorsy, more worldly and sophisticated. But where had her type got her? Maybe it was time for a change.

How is it possible he's still single? Ally would sometimes wonder, though she didn't dare to ask. Ally, for her part, did not want to go over her own history of failed relationships. She wanted a clean start, no past, and here, they had it.

From that first lunch together, when Sam waved her over to his dining table after their late-night encounter at the pool, the two would plan their days together. It didn't matter where they were—in a songthaew careening past fruit stands, on crowded Fisherman Village streets at night, the air thick and smelling of grilled meat, in bars loud with the laughter of drunk backpackers and businessmen—Sam would pull her to him for a kiss, without shame. No, she hadn't made it all up. Yes, she is getting attached. How could she not? They were enjoying paradise together, one perfect day after another.

Exploring the grounds of the Wat Phra Yai Temple, Sam steering her this way and that with just a gentle pressure on the small of her back, warm breeze caressing her skin, Ally had felt inspired by the peaceful expression on Buddha's gold, painted face. Hopeful.

Ally and Sam had headed back to their hotel as a torrential rain started up. Still their clothes were soaked by the time they arrived, and they had laughed running from the taxi to the resort entrance, thrilled by the force of the wind that whipped their hair and promising to meet each other in the dining room after getting changed.

After dinner, Sam had walked Ally to her room. So far, both had seemed reluctant to take things further, as if more might spoil the fun.

Still, reaching the door to her room, Sam had lingered as Ally stepped inside, watching her quietly, and it was she who pulled him in, hungry for more.

That was yesterday.

She hasn't heard from him since.

Casey and Erin receive their water blessings, and the wedding party follows them to dinner. Throughout the evening, as the sky takes on the candy-colored palette of sunset, Ally tries to tamp down disappointment with forced smiles and more glasses of wine than she's accustomed to. She can't blame him, really. That morning, as they woke up to each other, shy and embarrassed and uncertain, she had given him the evening off since she would be spending it with Casey and Erin and their friends, trying to act nonchalantly about it all. To her disappointment, he didn't try to fight it, and instead, promised to try and catch her before she checked out the next day for her flight home to Portland. She feels hurt that he hasn't stopped by to check in on her already and that he didn't insist on getting together after the party. She could have invited him to the reception, but she had been nervous about introducing him to her friends so early and didn't want to ruin their fresh romance with friendly teasing. She was enjoying the private space they had to get to know one another, without friends or family or colleagues getting in the way. That didn't stop him from answering her calls, though. Had she sent the wrong message? Could he be doubting his feelings for her the way she now did?

As the wedding dinner comes and goes and the dancing begins, Ally wishes she had invited Sam after all. That he were here with her now to dance with, or even just to sit together, holding hands. Watching the other couples embrace, she feels a lonely ache.

Ally walks over to the pool, kicks off her sandals, gathers up her dress, and sits down, letting her legs hang over the edge. Rolling her ankles in the water, she tries to push away thoughts of tomorrow and what lies beyond, keeping an eye on the glass doors and willing Sam to walk through. Looking up at the stars, she imagines the entrance he will make, with his dapper swagger, the other party goers drawn to him. But the doors only release a stream of insignificant hotel guests, none of whom she recognizes.

Finally, when she has had enough and feels it is not too early to leave the party, Ally says goodnight to Casey and Erin and heads back to her room, swaying a little. She knows she is drunk when she fumbles to open the door, but still, she couldn't have the wrong room, could she? Ally follows a trail of rose petals tracing the way to the bedroom, where they make a heart shape on the king-size bed. She wonders if it's a gift from Sam maybe, but then it occurs to her that room service must have decorated the wrong room, mistaking Ally's suite for one of the newly married couples celebrating at the resort.

Ally lets out a groan and feels her head begin to spin. Turning away from the bed in disgust, she collapses on the couch instead, falling into a deep sleep.

Chapter 20

At the kitchen table, the boys giggle and shove each other, almost knocking over yet another glass of milk as Carmen awkwardly folds over her baby bump to sop up the spill.

"Hey, watch what you're doing!" Carmen huffs, holding out her hand to stop another glass from falling.

Carmen leans over the sink, wrings out the dish towel, and wipes her forehead with her forearm, wondering if *Muse* and Meredith weren't so bad after all, compared to the little shits who had hijacked her days. It's only 3:45. *Four more hours to go until bedtime.*

Snack time over, Carmen sends the boys off to the TV room, thinking she might lie down on her bed *for just a minute*, but as she reaches the stairs, she spots dark shadows on the carpet. *Footprints?* Carmen follows the trail like a sleuth, finding more footprints in the boys' bathroom. There, she discovers dark smears on the floor and on the toilet bowl. The hand towel is lying on the floor, and Carmen picks it up to place it back on the towel bar but notices a brown smudge just in time.

"Who did this?! Who did this?!" Carmen yells.

The boys come running, pointing fingers at each other and yelling, "Not me! Not me!"

"Don't come in here! Animals!" Carmen shouts.

The boys slink off, shoving each other.

Seething, Carmen gets to work, getting down on all fours and using baby wipes that she still stocks the bathroom with to clean up the mess. She wipes the toilet down and the floor all around, including the footsteps leading out of the bathroom. Turning around, Carmen spots a small turd by the vanity and picks it up, only it slips out of the wipe and falls into the grate. Carmen pulls out the grate and searches around with her hand. She finds the turd, pulls it out with another wipe, and drops it in the toilet. A splash of water hits her in the eye. *Shit!* She wipes her forehead. Carmen gets up and flushes the toilet. Washing her hands, and wiping at her eyes, she looks up at the mirror and spots a smear on her forehead. She hears a flash go off and sees Tyler giggling in the doorway.

"Get out of here!" she yells as he runs off with her phone.

This is not what I signed up for, Carmen thinks as she starts to tackle the stairs, rubbing out poo stains from the carpet. She doesn't care if they are just being kids. She doesn't care if this is normal. She is still a human, and she deserves their respect. She is cool, goddammit! She had seen The Strokes in Paris. Attended fashion weeks in New York. Been wined and dined in the best hotels around the world. Don't these little shits know who she is?!

When the stairs are as clean as they're going to get, Carmen seeks out the solace of her walk-in closet. All she wants is peace and quiet, and instead her life is literally covered in shit. The baby. The mounting debt. The lack of options. She fears for their future. The future of her kids. What kind of world are they leaving them anyway? The opioid crisis. Climate change. Terror attacks. All Carmen sees are cries for help, and she doesn't know where to start. Not even with herself. It all makes it hard to breathe. And to top it all off, her back is killing her. And if it's not that, it's her ankle. And fuck, getting older sucks. Her life is half over and what had she done with it so far? What did she want to accomplish before she died, and can she even make those dreams come true anymore? It is all too much. She wants to give up. Just go to sleep. Curl up in the fetal position and cry for mommy. But she can't because SHE *IS* MOMMY.

Carmen hears a door creak open and slam shut. Dan is home.

"Hey, where is everyone?" he calls out, as he wanders room to room.

"Where's Mom?" Carmen hears him ask the kids. She can picture them staring at the TV like kid-size zombies, but she doesn't hear an answer.

"Carmen? Carmen?" Dan prompts, his voice getting closer. She knows she should answer, but she just doesn't know what to say.

"Carmen, you in there?" Dan asks, knocking on their closet door. He opens it a crack and she suddenly feels silly, seated on the floor, holding a half-eaten bar of chocolate and wishing it were a cigarette.

"What happened?" Dan asks, chuckling and holding out a hand to help Carmen up. Already she can feel the weight of her thoughts lifting.

"We gave birth to monsters," she whimpers, rising up with difficulty. "Yelling, fighting. Milk on the floor. Poo all over the carpet." The fragments tumble out of Carmen in a high-pitched vibrato. *Definitely hysterical.*

"I'm done. Exhausted. And now we're going to have another. What are we doing? I can't do this. We have to stop it!" Carmen urges, grabbing Dan by the shirt.

"I know," Dan says, and for a moment Carmen thinks he's going to agree with her. *You're right, we shouldn't have this baby.* Even if it is too late to do anything about it.

"It's time to kick some ass. Get old school on those punks. Daddy's home," he says, taking her in his arms and giving her a big bear hug.

"Don't worry, everything's going to be okay," he says, kissing her on the head.

"Aren't you scared?" Carmen whispers into his shirt.

"Of what?"

"That we can't afford it. That we don't have the time to look after another kid. That we're too old to start again. That something might go wrong."

"Wow, no, not until now." Dan pulls back from her, frowning. "Listen, I know you're freaking out. I know you're tired, and you should be—you're carrying around another human for God's sake."

Carmen chuckles despite herself.

"But we're gonna be fine. We always pull through. Together."

Carmen nods her head.

"I'm just so happy and excited! We're going to have another baby!" Dans pumps his arms in the air triumphantly.

"You're crazy." Carmen laughs, feeling a little guilty. She knows she should be grateful. It might not be how Carmen imagined, but it could still be good, beautiful, and right.

"Seriously. What else are we gonna do? Go clubbing?" Dan grabs Carmen and starts to dance, making deep techno base sounds. "Guh juh guh jug guh juh."

"Sto-op." Carmen giggles. "I'm being serious."

Dan dances up to her. "Me too. C'mon. Don't you want to do some E? Stay up all night? Have crazy sex?" he teases, pawing at her.

"Don't! Gross. You're making me feel hungover." She laughs. "It's hard to believe that was ever us."

Dan is serious now, waving at the room, gesturing at the whole house over. "This is us now. This is what we do. We're *pa-rents*. This is it," he says, giving her a big, consoling hug.

It's not the answer she's expecting, not even an answer she's sure she can live with, but Carmen can't help but feel buoyed by his cheeriness. Her life might be in freefall, but at least she had him to cling to.

"I know this is crazy, I know," Dan whispers into her ear. "But I love it. I love them. I love you."

Carmen blinks back tears, noticing Dan's hazel eyes are wet also.

"Me too," she says. "I love us, too."

Chapter 21

P lacing her backpack in the plane's overhead luggage compartment, Ally drops into her seat, trying to hold back the tears. *Did you really think it would last?*

All along the taxi ride to the airport, she berated herself for getting attached. And while she had tried to keep up a stoic front, she noticed Casey and Erin, the hotel checkout girl, and the taxi driver all being a little kinder, a little gentler, with her. Clearly disappointment was written all over her face.

Sam still hasn't called, even though he knew she was checking out at 9:30 a.m. She hasn't called him again either, although waiting in the checkout line, she had glanced around, hoping he might come running to her with some apology for being absent the last twenty-four hours.

"You wouldn't happen to have any messages for me?" Ally asked the young woman at the hotel front desk. The clerk searched her computer and shook her head, leaving Ally feeling like a rejected groupie, a one-night stand who didn't get the memo.

Sure, it was an unexpected romance—a fling in a far-off land. Still, she thought they had something, a connection, real feelings for each other. In any case, they seemed to enjoy each other's company—wasn't that worth something? Or was she all wrong about Sam? Had this been just a game for him, that ended when he finally got what he was after? Did she really know him at all?

On the plane, Ally picks up her book and opens it up, trying to see the words through the tears blurring her vision. She can feel someone standing over her, but she refuses to look up or make space. She is done with making room for others.

"Is this seat taken?" a husky voice she's come to love says. Ally almost chokes on her tears when she looks up and sees Sam smiling down on her.

"Wha ...? Of course. I mean, of course not." Ally stumbles, shaking her head, not sure what to think or say.

"Sorry I missed you," Sam says, leaning over and giving her a kiss on the cheek. "I've been in meetings and on the phone non-stop in between, trying to arrange things back at the office."

He presses in to make way in the aisle for another passenger. Ally is still blocking the way to the empty seat beside her, but she's frozen to her place. He isn't on the same flight as her, is he? Or is she on the wrong plane?

Sam leans over again to whisper something into her ear, a grin spreading across his tanned face, sending a warm shiver through her. "I'm coming home with you."

Ally startles and jumps up to hug him, but her seat belt is already strapped in, and she's yanked back down. She laughs and unclips the seat belt. They hug awkwardly, crammed between the aisle and the overhead compartments. Ally catches the other passengers staring at them from the corner of her eye and pulls Sam down into the empty seat beside her.

"I can't believe it. I can't believe you're here," she says, shaking her head and trying to push the voice of reason from her head. Is this really happening? Is this crazy? Are they?

"Yeah, well, my boss isn't thrilled, but work will be fine. I've got my laptop," Sam says, running a hand through his sandy hair. "So, you don't mind? I thought I'd surprise you ..."

"No! It's the best surprise ever." Ally gives him a kiss.

They pause and look at each other, smiling, as if for the first time. It occurs to Ally that real life, this life, of home and work and distances negotiated, feels surreal in contrast to the fantasy glow of their holiday together.

"I can't believe it. I can't believe it," Ally repeats, still in shock.

"Believe it. I'm all yours," Sam says, steering her chin toward him and giving her a long, deep kiss. "Besides ... I couldn't pass up the chance to join the mile-high club with you," he adds with a wink.

Ally blushes her whole body through and looks down at her lap, suddenly feeling shy. Sitting there beside him, she's keenly aware of how strange and different they are to each other. For a moment, Ally wonders what she's getting into. Truth be told, she hardly knows him. Sure, they had shared days together, but she still doesn't know that much about him. Is everything a game to him? Could he be trusted?

And, most importantly, would he leave her too?

Sam gives Ally's hand a reassuring squeeze and her fears melt away. He is worth betting on.

Chapter 22

Carmen taps her feet on the suspiciously sticky floor as she tries to avoid making eye contact with passersby, dreading the next laundromat customer who might walk in, another witness to her fall from grace. Thanksgiving has come and gone, but Carmen is feeling anything but grateful, except for the fact that the place is currently empty besides her. The metal bench she's sitting on does her no favors as she waits for the bed sheets to dry in the industrial-size dryer before her.

Fuck my life, Carmen thinks with a sigh. *You couldn't write this shit.*

Just a few days before, she had been setting up for a deliciously cozy afternoon. The kind of day she used to dream of as she chased after trains and side-stepped office politics. Just her in her PJs, a cup of hot cocoa, and *The Holiday* cued up on Netflix.

Then the school called. Tyler had lice, and they wanted her to pick up all three boys right away, so Carmen swapped out her PJs for a sweater and tights, put on her coat, and drove to the school. She found the boys waiting for her in the office, heads down, like criminals. Worse yet, that mom from karate was there, chatting with the receptionist and principal like she ran the place, her rail-thin body stiff and straight in a starched button-down shirt, pressed trousers, and thin-lipped frown. Did she have her own office here? Did she never leave?

Carmen ducked her head to avoid making eye contact and steered the boys out of the school, shuttling them all off to the pharmacy for some lice-killing shampoo. She then spent the rest of the day on a seek-and-destroy mission, applying treatment to one squirming child after another, as she meticulously combed through each head, extracting the microscopic enemy that had ruined her perfectly relaxing day.

"I think the water heater is leaking," Dan says later that day. "I put a load in the wash, and now the floor is wet."

"Well, that's really great news, Dan, because I have to wash all the kids' bedding, in case there's lice crawling around." Carmen shut off the kitchen sink tap so they don't have to yell.

"Hey, I didn't break the thing. I'm just telling you. I'm going to have to shut the water off until we can get someone in."

"Can I finish washing the dishes at least?"

"With cold water maybe? I need to get back down there and see if I can do something before the basement floods."

Great, God. Keep it coming, Carmen thinks as she turns the tap back on. *I hope you're enjoying the show.*

"Damn it!" Dan shouts from the furnace room the next day, and Carmen can hear him all the way upstairs in her bathroom, where she is sitting on the edge of her bathtub, hunting for stubborn survivors in Round 2 of Mom versus ectoparasite.

"What now?" Carmen asks, looking up from Tyler's scalp, when Dan walks in moments later.

"They can't fix the water heater today. *Maybe* tomorrow. And it'll cost us extra. A thousand dollars for a new venting system," Dan says, looking like he is about to cry.

Watching his crestfallen face, Carmen feels like she might too.

"Toby is sick now, also." Carmen sighs. "He's in bed with a fever."

Dan throws his hands up in the air and turns and walks away.

While they wait for the next technician to come and save them, Dan devises a plan to help them get by, wedging a bucket under the water heater to catch the water leaking from it.

After waking up the next morning, Carmen creeps down the stairs in her PJs to see if Dan's plan has worked. The towels spread out on the floor are dry, though the bucket is now full. Quietly, she does a football touchdown dance, shaking her fists in the air, triumphant. She empties the bucket and puts it back as Dan had left it, turns out the lights, and goes upstairs.

Thinking she could just keep replacing the bucket and resume a civilized life, Carmen showers and readies the kids for school as usual, feeling almost normal again. In control. When she returns home from dropping off the kids, though, she opens the furnace room door and finds the floor flooded.

"Dan, I'm so sorry," she pleads to him over the phone. "I messed up. You were right, though. You were brilliant."

"At least the floor will be clean now," Dan says, non-plussed. "Oh, and the company called. They can't come today."

In the middle of the night, Carmen sits up with a start. She thought she heard choking noises from the twins' room. She runs down the stairs and turns on the light, blinking as she makes out Toby with vomit all over his bed. Teo is sitting up too, crying.

"Oh no, my babies!" she cries out.

Toby looks worse, so Carmen grabs him first and hugs him to her. A shudder and then more spit up as she scoops him up and carries him to her bathroom, where she climbs into the bathtub.

"Dan! Dan!" she whisper-shouts. "Get up!"

Instead of Dan, though, Tyler comes into the washroom, blinking at the light and scratching his head.

"Mama, my head is itchy again."

"Okay baby. Mama will be right with you—Dan! I need some help here. Dan!"

Dan runs into the bathroom, looking startled and ready to fight.

"Wha, what's wrong?"

"Toby. He's sick. I think I have to take him to the hospital."

"Okay, what do you want me to do?" Dan asks, shaking the sleep from his head.

"I'll take Toby to the hospital," Carmen says, passing Toby's tiny body to Dan so she can get dressed. "You look after Teo—he's sick now too—and wait for the tech guy to come."

Carmen pulls on pants and a sweater and dumps her spit up-stained pyjamas in the tub, along with the soaking sheets and blanket from Toby's bed.

"And stay away from Tyler. I think he has lice again."

At the hospital, Carmen waits with Toby's head on her lap. If it wasn't for the consistently bad news, she would just chalk it up to having a bad day. But the past few months are breaking her. Perhaps this was her life now, just one long, very bad day after another.

"It's just a virus," the doctor says when he finally made his way to them. *Just a phase,* Carmen thinks, recalling her mantra of the first few weeks and months after Tyler was born. Just a phase, the newborn colic. Just a phase, the chronic colds of daycare. It isn't just a phase though. It is her life all over again now that there was yet another baby on the way.

"You'll just have to ride it out. Lots of fluids. Rest. Here's something for the nausea," the doctor says, passing a tiny white pill to Carmen for Toby to swallow. By the time they reach home, the nausea has passed and the green tinge has faded from his face. In her bathroom, Carmen surveys the mess in the bathtub and the dishes piled up in the kitchen sink.

"The technician is here," Dan says. "They need to keep the water off for a few hours while they work."

"I need to clean Toby's sheets, and I used up most of the towels to dry up the basement. Tyler's bed is probably infected, too. I'll have to go out to do the laundry," Carmen says, rubbing her eyes.

"Promise you'll come back," Dan says, only half joking. "Promise you won't leave and keep driving."

For the first time in days, Carmen smiles.

"I promise."

He was right, Carmen thinks, watching the sheets tumble in the dryer and feeling that is her, a crumpled up hot mess.

It was just like her dad had said. This life would swallow her up. Take everything she had, leaving nothing for herself. This is all she is now. Rinse and repeat.

Carmen rests her arms on her thighs and lets her belly drop between her knees. Nothing else to do but sit and wait, so she checks her Instagram feed. There's a notification, a post from Ally, and she clicks on it to see a photo of Ally jumping off a cliff into the bluest ocean she has ever seen. Twenty years ago, that would have been her. Fearless, confident that the world would catch her. If Ally is in paradise, Carmen is in hell. What the hell happened to them?

With the water restored, kids feeling better, and last of the bugs wiped out, Carmen and Dan get down to the business of sorting through the storage boxes damaged from the basement flood. Dan puts on a record, and they head downstairs.

"Should I keep these?" Dan asks. He's holding up a few trophies in each hand from his high school days.

Carmen shrugs. "If you want to."

He tosses them into the garbage bin.

Arcade Fire's *Funeral* album floats down, and Carmen has a flashback to Dan's parents' basement. A party there, while his mom and dad were away in Florida. He knew all the right songs to play. She kissed him first.

Looking at the mess surrounding her, Carmen is filled with despair. Even the littlest bit of disorder stressed her out. Ally used to tease her about it back when they were still neighbors.

"You can't control everything," Ally once told her, placing an empty glass of milk on her parents' wood coffee table like a dare, as Carmen picked up her discarded things—a sweater here, keys there—and bundled them up on the bench by the door.

"I can try," Carmen said, wiping up the milk ring, and they both knew they were talking about their parents' divorces too, and how no amount of tidying up would ever make her feel completely safe again.

Carmen pulls a wilted stack of water-stained notebooks out of one box. "Oh, God."

"What?" Dan asks, cracking open a can of beer.

"My journals." Carmen debates whether to read them or throw them out. "I kept one for pretty much every year from the time I could write, until I met you."

Dan chuckles. "Now they're just memories in a box."

Carmen's nose prickles. She isn't sure if it's the pregnancy or turning forty, but lately, she is always close to tears, thinking about the past.

Where has the time gone? And more importantly, how much time does she have left?

Carmen flips through the pages, wrinkling her nose and covering her eyes with her hands. Had that really been her? That girl feels like a stranger now.

"Ugh! I haven't written, I mean *really* written, anything since high school," Carmen says, glimpsing at the entries and cringing at their messy, full-frontal honesty. They conjure up an almost forgotten period of freedom between doing everything her parents told her to, and doing everything the world expected her to.

"I remember you in high school." Dan raises his eyebrows and grins from ear to ear.

"Stop!" Carmen laughs and tosses a scrunched-up piece of paper at him. There have been so many yous, she muses silently. School-age Carmen: Straight A student, introverted, serious, and then when Ally became her friend, a little bit reckless too. There's the careerist. The newlywed. The mother. Which is she now, or is she becoming someone new yet again?

The song stops, and Dan comes over to her, wrapping his arms around her.

"I remember you," Carmen whispers into his shoulder, thinking back to a time before careers and job titles. Before kids and responsibilities. When he was just a boy, and she was just a girl.

Carmen pretends to scratch her eye, but really, she's wiping away a tear. For all the grown-out Carmens. For all the years that have passed. For all the lives she has lived. The memories and moments like so many ghosts in the room.

Dan leans her back onto the rug, and Carmen gives in, his arms steady and strong, amid the ruins of their youth. They rarely kiss anymore, but in his arms, she is always eighteen again.

Chapter 23

Ally shimmies into her new red dress. She'd spotted it on display in the window of a plush boutique she would usually pass with just a fleeting glance on her way home from work—a store filled with pretty bags and sparkly shoes, elegant pant suits and tailored jackets, the sort of thing she had no occasion to wear. Until now.

Sam had made a reservation at Cava, something that set her younger colleagues abuzz when she told them what she was up to for the weekend. Apparently, it was the hot new place to see and be seen, a tapas bar and restaurant, helmed by a celebrity chef Ally had never heard of, that had a waiting list spanning months to get in.

Of course, Sam knew about it. He was a heat-seeking missile for whatever was happening and trendy. Already, he knew more about Portland than Ally did. In particular, where to eat and drink. He loved food, liked reading out the menus, reciting flavours like poetry and making her laugh. He also liked cold, dark bars, where everything was sleek and everyone was sexy. Places to be noticed. Ally sometimes wondered what he was doing with her. All American girl. Sporty Spice, not Posh. He belonged with someone sophisticated. An heiress, maybe. Or an actress. Someone who could speak multiple languages and talk about literature from any era, someone like Carmen. It is something she tries to ignore.

Ally slicks on her new red lipstick and rubs her lips together. The color is shocking at first. It's wearing her instead of the other way around. She lets it sit and soak in. She slowly gets it, the look of it, the way it brightens her face, the way it anchors the eye, brings pink to her cheeks. She learns to like the look of it.

She knows now that being with Sam is living under the spotlight. Out with him, she floated above the crowd. Rooms vibrated with his frequency. People were drawn to him. Other women eyed him like a cool drink on a hot day, like a red dress in a window. It made her feel proud. And a little scared.

Sam was like her dad in that way: the life of the party, captivating Ally and dinner guests with stories from his business trips. Her dad always used to bring something back for her, whetting her appetite for travel and adventure and lightening some of the sadness that seemed to haunt her while he was away. A twinge of guilt makes Ally wince. Her birthday had come and gone and still she hadn't called him, just sent him a curt email back thanking him. Then today she let his call go to voicemail when he called to wish her a merry Christmas. Tomorrow, she'll call him. That will give them something safe to talk about, where neither would have to feel guilty about all those missed celebrations. All those lost yesterdays.

Ally tries to shake off the guilt and resentment in the taxi on the way to meet Sam, who is coming from an office Christmas party. She wants to be happy for him. It's the holiday season, and for the first time in years, she won't be spending it alone.

The taxi pulls up and Ally gets out, smoothing her dress and tucking her hair over one shoulder. Inside, the restaurant glows warm gold, and the cacophony of conversations pushes the last wisps of melancholy away. Everyone is beautiful and well dressed and smiling. Even the pretty hostess looks like she's here to enjoy the evening.

"I'm meeting someone. He might already be here?" Butterflies of excitement take off as Ally cranes her neck to see around the divider into the main dining room.

"What's his name?"

"Sam Hutchins?"

The woman checks her list.

"Yup. Right this way."

An electrical current runs through Ally as they make their way into the room, setting her heart racing as nerves ball up in the pit of her belly. When Ally spots Sam, her heart jumps, and she has to step carefully for fear of swooning.

"Found him," Ally says to the hostess, who looks at Sam and looks back at Ally and smiles. They are a dazzling couple. A Hollywood romance.

The hostess moves out of the way to let Ally pass between the tables. Shy now under Sam's gaze, Ally walks with her eyes down, trying to be as graceful as possible. A wave of pride makes her blush. She is loved. She belongs. *She is someone.*

Looking back up at Sam, Ally breathes out a sigh. Standing with his hands in his pockets, wearing a fitted blue suit, white shirt unbuttoned at the top, he looks as comfortable in his skin as if he were wearing shorts and a T-shirt. Like he owns the world.

Sam tips an imaginary hat and pulls out Ally's chair. Her heart soars.

"You look amazing," Sam says, leaning over and whispering into her ear as she sits down. His warm breath makes the hairs on her neck stand up, and there's a flutter down below. "You look good enough to eat."

Chapter 24

"Whoa, cool, Mom! Can we get some too?" Tyler asks, pointing at a life-sized Santa on someone's lawn on the way to school.

"Sure, after we get the Tesla SUV and the indoor pool," Carmen says, glancing at Dan to see if she made him smile. Instead, he stares ahead, frowning, still sore over their fight about the Christmas lights and Carmen's over-spending.

"You're kidding me," Dan had said when she tentatively placed the box on the living room coffee table before him. "What's wrong with the Christmas lights we have now?"

"Well, they don't really match," Carmen said, sensing a fight and glancing around to make sure the kids couldn't hear. "Remember last year? One of the strings crapped out and you went to the hardware store and bought the last box they had and now our house looks like the Halloween candy bowl nobody wants to touch."

"You're out of control," Dan said, nostrils flaring. "Our line of credit is higher than ever, and have you seen our Visa bill? How are we supposed to pay this one off?"

"Out of control? Do you know what time of the year this is?!" Carmen yelled back. "Do you actually believe in Santa? Do you *really* think Santa is coming to this house? *I'm Santa!*"

"Well Santa needs to remember who pays the bills around here. Especially now," Dan said, tossing on a jacket and shoving his feet into his boots.

That was two days ago, and he still isn't talking to her.

Driving past the stately homes blanketed in snow, their warm and cozy hearth fires glowing within, Carmen wonders how long Dan will punish her. Their fight reminds her of her own Christmases growing up, alternating the holiday between her divorced parents, always feeling like one half of her was missing.

Since having Tyler, Christmas had become a chase toward a bigger, better high. This would be the best Christmas ever. This year, she would make Gingerbread cookies from scratch, the kids would love each one of their presents, and everyone would get along. This year, everything would be perfect. This year, she would feel complete.

Carmen can almost smell the freshly baked cookies as they pass windows lit up by sprawling, fresh-cut Christmas trees. Her own kids had demolished a box of Mr. Christie's as Carmen and Dan dragged their own plastic tree out of the crawl space and assembled it in an awkward corner of their living room, where it dipped under the weight of DIY ornaments crafted by the kids at school, including faux gingerbread cookies she had to remind them not to eat. Carmen had begged Dan for a real tree this year, but he had refused, saying their PVC one was perfectly fine, and it was just a waste of money. And then she had brought the new Christmas lights home.

"Dan," Carmen pleads. "Dan!"

"Mom and Dad are fight-ing," Tyler teases in a sing-song voice from the back. "They're going to get a di-vorce."

"What's a divorce?" Teo asks.

"We are not getting divorced!" Carmen takes a few breaths to calm down.

Dan turns the car radio up, so Carmen looks back at the kids and forces a reassuring smile.

"Excited for the Christmas concert?"

"Do we have to? It's always so boring," Tyler whines.

"I'm with Tyler," Dan says. "What's the point anyway?"

"The point is that Christmas is about more than presents," Carmen says, shaking her head. "It's about the Christmas spirit. Being good to one another. Being generous. Remember the Christmas spirit, Dan?"

"Huh, I thought it was about being right all the time," he fires back, parking the car and shutting off the engine.

The kids tumble out, racing ahead and joining the other families funnelling into the front doors.

"Dan, come on, don't be like this," Carmen says, reaching out for him.

Dan pulls his hand away.

"It's like you're in some kind of race," he says "Where are you going?"

"I don't know."

"Then stop."

Dan walks off in direction of the kids and Carmen tries to catch up to him, but her now sizeable belly and sciatica keep her to a hobble while he drifts further away.

"Carmen! Hey!"

Carmen turns and feels a sense of relief as she sees a familiar, friendly face. Tanya speed walks toward her as Carmen smiles and waits. She's wearing the same sweatpants as usual, her frizzy, curly hair wild and blowing around her. Carmen at once admires her for not caring what the world thinks but also wonders, would this happen to her too one day? The giving up and giving in? And why did Carmen care anyway?

A car cuts in front of Tanya, and she punches the trunk. "I'm walking here, you jerk! Jeesh, you'd think I'm invisible."

"You okay?" Carmen asks.

"Yeah, happens all the time. People and their phones. Where are your boys?"

"They've gone ahead," Carmen says with a shrug.

"Mom, Jack is here. Can I go say hi?" Tanya's son asks.

"Okay." Tanya glances toward the front doors as both her kids run ahead. "I guess Alex won't mind if they tag along. She's only got seven kids, what's two more?"

"What?" Carmen asks, cocking her head.

"Alex. Mom of Seven. That's her up there with your boys."

"I thought that was a group of families."

Tanya shakes her head. "I have a hard enough time with just two. I don't know how she does it."

"Seven! How is that even possible?" Carmen asks, secretly admonishing herself that she could barely manage her three.

"Yeah, I'm surprised you haven't met her yet. She only has a kid in like every class at the school. Except her daughter that she homeschools because she competes in gymnastics."

"Whoa," Carmen says, wondering if Tyler would be better off if he were homeschooled. His marks rarely floated above a C, and his teacher had mentioned he was easily distracted. Removing all the variables from the classroom might help him focus, but Carmen would rather work for another Meredith than spend all day doing homework with her kid.

"You done your Christmas shopping yet?" Tanya asks as they wait to go in, a crowd bottlenecking at the doors where the principal is greeting parents.

"Just a few odds and ends. Stocking stuffers, you know," Carmen lies. Truth is, she had been stockpiling gifts ever since she was laid off and had the time to get a head start on Christmas shopping, instead of her usual last-minute scramble. Now she can't even remember what she has already bought or what's left to get. What she is sure of, however, is that she has gone entirely overboard with presents this year. And it still doesn't feel like enough. Dan will be furious.

"What about you?"

"Almost." Tanya shrugs. "Not like they deserve it. Ben has to travel for work and only gets home on Christmas Day, so Christmas Eve and Santa are all on me."

"I don't know how *you* do it," Carmen says, recalling her own divided family holidays, and how the sadness only seemed to lift when she started hanging out with Ally, and Christmas became a joint adventure in crafting IOU cards from homemade paper and later, shoplifting soap bars and body creams for gift sets, until eventually she started replacing those too with the cozy new memories of Dan and her own growing family. Now Ally would probably be spending the holidays alone and Carmen still hasn't called her to hear about her trip. She is a terrible friend.

"Oh, the joys of the holidays," Tanya says as they wait to go in.

As they pass through the doors, Carmen spots Tyler and the twins. They're shoving each other on the other side of the principal while Dan stands by, waiting for her but still refusing to look her way. He sticks out in his winter work jacket and boots among the suited-up Wall Street dads, and Carmen feels another twinge of guilt. She loves that he never sold out, that he is still the man-child she fell in love with. Has *she* changed though?

"Come, I'll introduce you to Alex. She's in charge of the Grade 5 grad committee," Tanya says after they nod hello to the principal, pulling Carmen away from Dan and the boys.

"What? Oh no, that's okay—" Carmen's face burns with shame, but Tanya has hold of her arm and is already dragging her up to Mom of Seven, whose brood is calmly lined up behind her, patiently waiting while she chats with another mom.

"Alex! Hi!"

"Tanya, nice to see you," Mom of Seven says, turning with her whole body to look at Tanya. Carmen recognizes the stone-faced mom from karate.

"Great job on the holiday store. Spencer had a blast. Have you met Carmen?" Tanya asks.

Mom of Seven considers Carmen for a moment. Her eyes are black, inky pools that reveal nothing, reflecting an anxious Carmen back at herself. Carmen wonders if Alex remembers her from the office the day that Carmen was called to pick up her lice-ridden boys from school.

"No, I don't think we've met."

Carmen breathes a sigh of relief. "I'm Carmen. Tyler's mom. Mrs. Black's class."

"Alexandra. Nice to meet you. Tyler must be with my Carter then," Mom of Seven says stiffly, her eyes shifting to a solemn boy around Tyler's age.

"Carter, right! That name sounds familiar," Carmen lies.

"Carmen was wondering if she could help out with the grad committee," Tanya offers.

Carmen winces at the thought of spending any amount of time with this monolith of a woman.

"That would be great," Alexandra says flatly. "We're actually having a meeting tomorrow to talk about the Grade 5 graduation. It's at nine a.m. at Starbucks if you want to come."

"Sure," Carmen says. She could think of a dozen other things she'd rather do—hunt for the perfect Christmas stockings, wrap gifts, find *some* way to help pay for it all—but without a full-time job to report to, she's out of good excuses.

"I'll see you there." Alexandra's mouth twists up into a smile, and she turns, heading toward the gym where the concert is taking place.

"Thanks a lot," Carmen says, shoving Tanya in the arm.

"You're welcome. Enjoy the show!" Tanya sings out as Spencer yanks her away.

"You too," Carmen says to herself, locking eyes with Dan and nodding. *Let's go.*

Tyler and the twins follow her to his classroom. Inside, the noise is deafening, as kids run around in circles, shouting at one another. Outside, the wall is covered with letters to Santa. Carmen finds Tyler's. His letters are twice the size of his classmates' and his sketch isn't even colored in. How is he going to get through high school?

"Cute, huh? Which one's yours?" a dad standing beside her in the hall asks.

"That one," Carmen says, pointing to Tyler's letter. She wants to tell him she tried. That she quit smoking before she got pregnant, fed Tyler an all-organic diet for the first few years of his life, and didn't even let him watch TV until he was two. She'd done everything she knew to do, controlled every possible variable, and still, it wasn't enough.

"Carmen," Dan calls. "Gym's filling up."

They grab the last seats available, at the back, and wait for the show to begin as a room full of parents jockey for the best view of their shell-shocked child. By the time the lights go out, the twins are bouncing in their seats.

It's Carter who appears first on the stage, standing stoically and staring out into the audience.

"Welcome, friends and neighbors,

And everyone we know.

All the bugs have gathered,

For a merry Christmas show."

Bugs? Whatever happened to Santa Claus or Charlie Brown? Carmen thinks, looking around to see if the other parents are as confused as she is, but they look on, rapt. Why can't she just enjoy the show like everyone else? What is wrong with her?

"Oh, what fun it is to ride, In a one-horse open sleigh!"

Tyler's class appears, and Carmen looks over to catch Dan's eye, but he still refuses to acknowledge her. She tries to get a good view of Tyler with her camera, but he's either hidden by the giant child standing in front of him, looking the other way at his classmates, or pawing at his nose. Finally, she gives up and puts her phone away. The twins are crawling under the chairs now, so Carmen takes them into the hall. There, they run back and forth as she peeks through the gym door window, watching families enjoy the show together, while her own is split in half.

Is this the beginning of the end? Would this baby be the death of them, as a couple, as a family? Could she do this on her own, without Dan? Would he survive, perhaps even thrive, without her?

From the outside, the darkened gym and lit-up stage remind Carmen of the classic holiday films she loved as a child. Movies where everyone hated each other, but they still stayed together as a family and learned to love each other by the end. With wild, rambunctious kids. With the desperate, harried mom. And the curmudgeonly father, usually played by Steve Martin. There was always a lesson there, something about forgiveness.

Those movies are her whole life now. Only *she* is Steve Martin.

On Christmas Eve, Carmen works in the kitchen while Dan serves drinks and tends to the fire and kids. She is willing to forgive and forget, but he is still avoiding whichever room she is in.

"Anything I can do to help?" Carmen's mom asks, poking her head into the kitchen.

"I got it. You go enjoy," Carmen says, wiping her forehead with her arm as she mashes the potatoes. Her mom had never been much of a cook, and neither she nor Carmen had prepared turkey before. Usually, the holidays were split up between all three sets of grandparents—dim sum with her mom and Richard, steak and salad with her dad's signature chimichurri at his place, and turkey and stuffing with Dan's parents, who are seasoned Christmas dinner experts. But this year, with Carmen home and out of work, she thought she could bring everyone together and kill three birds with one stone. *As a full-time mom, isn't it the least she could do?* Only the kids had been up since six o'clock in the morning, thinking it was Christmas Day. Carmen had already made breakfast and lunch and just finished cleaning up from the kids' snack when Dan's parents arrived—early, and while Dan was still vacuuming the house and cleaning the washrooms. Carmen's growing belly made her feel like she was carrying a bowling ball around, and her back and shoulders were cramping from standing in the kitchen all day. She didn't know if she could keep this up much longer.

"Okay, but don't take too long. We came here to be with you."

Carmen knows her mom is only trying to help, but it just feels like more pressure. More pressure to hurry up. More pressure to do more.

Carmen enters the living room to check if they need more apps and picks up the shrimp plate, empty except for leftover tails.

"Need any help, Carmen?" June asks.

"Nope, I've got it all under control," Carmen says, taking the empty platter and dirty napkins away. She wants to prove she can do it. Wants to prove she can do it *all*. Besides, the last time her mother-in-law helped out in the kitchen, it took Carmen months to find the steak knives, which turned out to be stowed in the bottom pantry shelf with the lunch box Tupperware and other containers the kids liked to play with.

"Oh, can you believe we're having another baby?" June exclaims.

"Yes, I can't wait. Hopefully it's a girl!" Carmen's mom coos.

"Tyler, I have something for you. Wanna see?" Carmen's dad asks.

"Yeah!" Tyler says, shoving a handful of chips into his mouth.

"Papi, we agreed—no presents before dinner," Carmen says, already dreading the mess of wrapping paper and sticky tape the kids would be leaving in their wake.

"It's nothing. Just a little thing. Come, Ty, let me show you."

"Not now, Pa. Please. He's got chips all over his hands."

"Basta! I'll bring it to you," Carmen's dad says, breathing heavily as he gets up from his chair.

"What is it, Abuelo? Is it candy?" Tyler asks, shoving another handful of chips into his mouth and coming over to see the package his grandfather is pulling out of a gift bag.

"Do you like it? It's a dinosaur. Dinosaurio. I got it for you. Do you like it?"

Tyler nods his head, banging the dinosaur against his fist.

"Tyler, what do you say?" Carmen reminds him.

Tyler mumbles back.

"Ty! What do you say? Gracias, Abuelo."

Tyler ignores her and keeps playing with the dinosaur.

"Tyler!" Dan shouts, turning his head from stoking the fire.

"Aunk you," Tyler says, opening his mouth to reveal a mouth full of food that falls out as he speaks.

Carmen shakes her head, her eyes settling on the twins who are sitting on the living room couch on either side of Dan's dad, who is flipping through the pages of one of the family albums as the boys point and giggle.

"Daddy is my daddy," Teo says, inspecting a photo.

"That's right, your daddy is your daddy, and he's my son," Dan's dad explains.

"And who's your daddy?" Teo asks.

"Oh, my daddy died a long time ago."

"Who killed him?"

Back in the kitchen, Carmen places warmed buns in a basket. June walks in and opens the fridge, reaching for the white wine.

"Smells wonderful, Carmen. Are you sure there's nothing I can do to help?" she asks as she tops up her glass.

"Nope. It's already done. We're just about ready to go," Carmen says, trying to stir the lumps out of the gravy. The veggies are overboiled and dishes are piled in the sink. Dinner is yet to be served and already it is falling short.

"Oh, I love those Christmas photos you got. So dear!" June says, looking up at the kids' picture with Santa on the fridge.

"Thanks," Carmen says, regretting the $75 she had spent on the "Santa Experience." Tyler did his usual fake smile schtick and Toby had managed to get a goose egg on his forehead the night before, after falling off the bed in a wrestling match with his brothers. Teo, meanwhile, had started crying the moment she placed him on Santa's lap.

"Now run!" the Elf had called out, waving at Carmen to get behind the photographer as a terrified Teo reached out for her to save him from the strange Santa monster.

"The best worst photo you'll ever get," the Elf whispered into her ear, as the photographer snapped away. Indeed, as far as terrible Christmas photos go, these are perfect.

"What's wrong with Toby's face?" Carmen's dad asks, squinting at the photo with an empty tumbler in his hand.

"Okay, everyone, time to sit at the table. Dinner's ready," Carmen calls out as she pulls the turkey from the oven, wishing everyone would just get out of the kitchen.

Instead, Carmen's dad and Dan's mom linger, watching over her shoulder as she pulls the tinfoil off the wings and moves the bird to the carving board for Dan to cut.

"Carmen, it's a little pink," Dan says as she watches him slice into a leg. Beneath the crisp, golden surface, the meat is still pink.

"I've never cooked a turkey before, but this looks raw to me," Carmen's dad says, peering over Dan's shoulder.

"Oh yeah," June says as she squeezes between them to inspect the bird. "This turkey's not cooked yet."

"But I followed the instructions to a T!" Carmen whines.

"Did you use a thermometer?" June asks, and Carmen blanks.

Dan and Carmen's dad look at each other.

"No, but it *looks* done," Carmen pouts, and they all groan.

"You have to take the turkey's temperature to make sure the meat is cooked right through. Especially meat on the bone," June says, poking at the bird.

"It's gotta go back in," Dan says.

"At least another half hour," Carmen's dad agrees.

"Wine, anyone?" Carmen's mom asks, waving a bottle of Chardonnay.

The kids race off to their rooms to play while the adults file back into the living room for another drink and Carmen slides the turkey back in the oven. Ashamed and deflated, she slumps down at the kitchen table, thinking about her latest defeat. She had thought that not having to catch the train to her nine-to-five job every day would mean that she could be a better wife, mother, daughter. Now she could see, she still isn't enough.

"Can I help?" Carmen's mom asks when she enters the room.

Carmen shakes her head.

"Come on, you're missing out on all the fun. Forget the turkey and come join us. Or let us join you."

"Forget it. It's hopeless. Impossible. I just, I just can't seem to do anything right," Carmen whimpers, bringing her hands to her face.

"Carmen, it's your first turkey," her mom says.

"No, it's not just the turkey. I totally suck at this. All of this." Carmen waves her hands around her. "I couldn't keep my job. My kids are out of control. Dan is mad at me. And to top it all off, I'm a terrible cook. Is there anything I am good at?"

"You're putting too much pressure on yourself," Carmen's mom says, giving her a hug. "It's not a competition."

"I dunno ... do you ever wish *you* had done things differently? That you had a chance to live your life without me? Without *him*?" Carmen asks, pointing through the wall.

"Sure, I do," her mom says, resting her chin in her hand and studying her. "You know, Carmen, you can be a mom and still want other things too. It's okay to feel that way. Sometimes we think we're supposed to disappear after we have kids, or like that's the right thing to do. And sometimes when I felt differently, I felt like I was failing you. Maybe you thought I was failing you too ... god, I made so many mistakes. Most of all with you. But make no mistake, you are the *best* thing that ever happened to me."

"Really?" Carmen croaks, her throat closing up, wondering if she could say the same about her life.

"Really," her mom says, pulling her in for a hug. "You're doing fine," she whispers into her ear. "You're doing great."

Tucking the twins into bed that night, Carmen is so tired that she worries she'll pass out before the kids do and miss Christmas altogether. Although she and Dan have finally finished cleaning the kitchen, they still have to wait until the kids are asleep before they can bring the presents out and place them under the tree. She wishes he would finally forgive her and turn back into the jolly old elf she married.

"What happens when you die?" Toby asks as Carmen curls up beside him.

"You go to heaven," Carmen says, wondering what he might have overheard from the grandparents that made him worry.

"But you and daddy are older than Teo and me, so you're going to die before us," Toby says.

"We'll always be near, even if we're not right here," Carmen says, borrowing a line from their favourite bedtime book. She can't stop the tears from falling.

"I don't want you to die," Toby whimpers. "I don't want to live without a mommy and daddy."

"We're going to be here for a very long time," Carmen says, her voice cracking. She didn't want to imagine a life without Dan, without their kids, without their moms or dads, either.

"Is there a ghost in your body?" Teo asks.

"It's called a soul, Teo! A soul!" Tyler yells from the doorway.

"No, there's no ghost in your body," Carmen says softly.

"Is a soul a ghost?"

"No, it's a soul," Tyler shouts.

"Tyler, please!" Carmen says, turning back to Teo. "There's no ghost, only a soul."

"There's a soul and when you die your soul goes to heaven," Tyler says, silhouetted in the bathroom light streaming into the darkened hallway.

"Will my ghost go to heaven?" Teo asks.

"There's no ghost, Teo!" Tyler shouts.

"When I die, I'm going to turn into a tiger," Toby says.

"That's karma, silly!" Tyler laughs.

"Karma? Is that a ghost?" Teo asks.

"When I die, I want to come back as a crocodile," Tyler says.

"When I die, I want to come back as mommy's mommy," Teo says.

"Shh," Carmen says, her eyes heavy. She wishes she could lie here all night, but there is always something that needs doing.

"If you guys don't fall asleep soon, Santa is going to skip our house. Now sleep."

Tyler leaves to go back to his room, and Carmen strokes Toby's head as she sings. "Good night sweetheart, well, it's time to go. Good night sweetheart, well, it's time to go. I hate to leave you but I really must say, Good night, sweetheart, good night."

Why can't she just tell Dan she's sorry? Why can't she just ask for help? Why is it so hard to tell the people she loves how she really feels? Why is it so hard to say I love you?

Chapter 25

Carmen Garcia <Carmen_m_garcia@hotmail.com>
To: Ally Parker <allswell69@hotmail.com>
Re: I made it!

Ally! How is life in Maine? Full of cute college boys and squishy sea things, I'm sure.

Paris is yummy—just one rotisserie and boulangerie after another. I'm getting fat on baguettes and brie, and eating *waaay* too much chocolate, while my university exchange roommates drink wine and smoke cigarettes until the wee hours of the morning and no one does their fair share of cleaning around here. I feel like the nagging mom and mostly hide out in my room with Zola and Sartre—I think I was born one hundred years late. You, though, would fit right in. I miss home. I miss Dan. I miss you.

Carmen Garcia <Carmen_m_garcia@hotmail.com>
To: Ally Parker <allswell69@hotmail.com>
Re: New guy

That's interesting about Sylvia Reade. I didn't know she came from New Jersey too. It makes sense you've gone vegetarian, but don't expect me to. My dad would disown me if I gave up steak. I think it's my family duty to keep eating it.

Charlie sounds like a great guy and so cool about all the hiking and camping you've been doing. You and your love of nature! You won't find much of that around here—the only plants are potted ones, dripping over balconies. There's the famous Bois de Boulogne but I haven't made it there yet. I've been to Bois de Vincennes, though, and it's surrounded by vans where married men meet with ladies of the night. I love Dan, but I am *never* getting married.

Carmen Garcia <Carmen_m_garcia@hotmail.com>
To: Ally Parker <allswell69@hotmail.com>
Re: Are you coming?

Hey, how was Halloween? I ended up at a party around Gare du Nord, and for Day of the Dead, I went by myself to Père Lachaise. That's the cemetery where Jim Morrison is buried. It was just before closing time. The crows were cawing and the clouds were gray, the trees black against the sky, and it was so delicious. This place makes me want to write, but I don't know what to say.

At school, I'm learning about the Impressionists. I like Monet's Water Lilies.

"All I did was to look at what the universe showed me, to let my brush bear witness to it."

PS: How are you feeling about spring break? Think you'll be able to come visit me?

Carmen Garcia <Carmen_m_garcia@hotmail.com>
To: Ally Parker <allswell69@hotmail.com>
Re: Happy birthday!

Happy happy birthday! I hope you had a great one! I'm sorry I missed you again. I tried calling you but maybe you were on the water.

So what did you do, anyway? I wish I were there to celebrate with you. Or rather, I wish you were here to celebrate with. It took me a little while to get used to things, but I think I'm finally finding my groove here. School's a joke and we barely have any homework, so I mostly walk around the Louvre. My favourite is the sculptures. I'm in love with Rodin. I adore being in a room full of marble, where everything is quiet and the echo goes on forever.

There's something so pure about it. Like Michelangelo said of the David, "I simply carved away everything that was not David."

Carmen Garcia <Carmen_m_garcia@hotmail.com>
To: Ally Parker <allswell69@hotmail.com>
Re: Christmas

Dan was going to come for Christmas but we decided to meet up in Spain in May. Instead I'm going to spend the holidays with some friends in London. It's just as well. I'm beginning to wonder if we're really meant to be, or if I'm from another planet. I'm not sure I can give him what he wants. I think I'm turning into someone else here. Maybe someone more like me.

Carmen Garcia <Carmen_m_garcia@hotmail.com>
To: Ally Parker <allswell69@hotmail.com>
Re: Happy new year!

Happy new year! Hope you had fun however you celebrated. Do they serve champagne under the sea? :)

That's cool you're thinking about doing your Master's Degree in Australia. It would be great for you to be closer to your dad. A part of me is afraid you'll never come back. And a part of me understands if you don't. I guess it doesn't matter anyway. We already live so far apart, it's not like we see each other all the time. What's a few thousand miles more? Plus it would give me another reason to visit the land of Oz.

Carmen Garcia <Carmen_m_garcia@hotmail.com>
To: Ally Parker <allswell69@hotmail.com>
Re: Your future

I can understand why Charlie isn't a fan of you going to Australia—it's a lot farther than France. But I wouldn't give up on the dream just yet. What if he came with you? I'm sure he'd love it too.

Anyway, I just think you should follow your heart and your passion. And if you're excited about the program in Australia, you should go for it. If it's meant to be with Charlie, it's meant to be. That's my two cents.

Carmen Garcia <Carmen_m_garcia@hotmail.com>
To: Ally Parker <allswell69@hotmail.com>
Re: Spring break

I'm bummed you didn't visit but your research trip sounds amazing! I don't know how you do it—I get claustrophobic just at the thought of being stuck under water. Remember the time that girl was having an epileptic fit at the mall and you jumped right in to help her while everyone else froze? You were always the bravest person in the room.

Carmen Garcia <Carmen_m_garcia@hotmail.com>
To: Ally Parker <allswell69@hotmail.com>
Re: Forget him!

Oh gosh, I'm sorry to hear about Charlie! He sounded like a keeper. Oh well, better you found out sooner than later. I know you don't like to hear this, and pardon the pun, but there are many more fish in the sea! You're a great catch! Okay, I'll stop now :)

Anyway, it sounds like you've made your decision to stay on in Maine. That's definitely a great offer they made you. I've been scouting out opportunities post-grad and looks like I'll have to intern—FREE—for a year before I can apply for anything. Maybe I should have studied to be a marine biologist like you. Journalism is dead.

Carmen Garcia <Carmen_m_garcia@hotmail.com>
To: Ally Parker <allswell69@hotmail.com>
Re: Eek!

Ally ...

Dan and I got engaged! I know, it's crazy. But we were in Seville, which is gorgeous and magical by the way. We saw this amazing gypsy flamenco show, ate tapas under the stars and okay, maybe we both got a little carried away in this fairy tale world—that and the sangria, anyway. I know I said I would never get married, but then I realized: I don't have to turn out like my parents. It can be different this time. So I said yes! Anyway, don't worry, you don't have to buy a bridesmaid's dress any time soon—we agreed on a looong engagement.

PS: I am still NEVER having kids.

Carmen Garcia <Carmen_m_garcia@hotmail.com>
To: Ally Parker <allswell69@hotmail.com>
Re: Coming home

So this is my last letter from Paris. Tomorrow I fly home.

This year has unravelled in the strangest of ways. Nothing I thought would happen came true. My French still sucks, and I did more reading than writing. Now that it's over, I wish I had more time. There are still so many corners of Paris to explore that I haven't touched yet. I spent too much time with my nose buried in books, or in bookstores. You know me, I can't help myself.

I know you wouldn't have wasted your time here. I know you would have been fluent in French by now, leaving a dozen heartbroken French lovers in your wake.

Sometimes I wonder if I travelled so far just to lose some part of me. But wherever I go, there I am.

PS: Let's definitely plan a trip together soon. Maybe for our next birthday.

Chapter 26

Ally floats to the surface and gently opens her eyes. The sun streams through her blinds, casting a warm caramel glow across her bedroom. She carefully turns over, nestling her head in the palm of her hand as she looks at Sam. His eyes are closed and his face is relaxed, peaceful. She wonders what he's dreaming about. If he's half awake even. The hills and valleys of his movie-star face catch the light. She wants to stay like this forever.

Ally turns onto her back, not wanting to think about when Sam has to go back to Seattle. She loves the fresh love buzz, even if it's a long-term relationship she really wants—a real partner in life. Someone who is *all in*.

Watching Sam again, she breathes a deep, happy sigh. No, this moment is perfect. This time it will last.

Ally reaches down and feels around for her nightie, a cute little black negligee she bought for Sam and wears instead of her usual oversized tee. She pulls the silky slip over her head and tiptoes out of the room, closing the door behind her. Giddy with happiness to the point of bursting, Ally thinks of Carmen as she readies a pot of coffee. She needs to tell someone, needs to share the news. To make it real. She picks up the phone.

"Happy New Year!" she says softly into the phone when Carmen answers, not wanting to wake Sam.

"Happy New Year! Hung over?"

"Nah," Ally says, feeling more alive than ever.

"We were in bed before midnight. What did you do?"

"I had sex with a random stranger."

"Seriously? Good for you! Tell me all about it ..."

"He's amazing." Ally sighs, flopping down on the sofa and wrapping a throw blanket around herself. "He's funny, smart, sweet. And so fucking hot. We met in Koh Samui, and he came home with me!"

"What? Wow! Must have been some pickup line," Carmen says and they both giggle. For a moment it feels like they're back in high school again, cracking each other up behind their teacher's back. They were so close back then that they could finish each other's sentences. They even got in trouble for cheating once because they had the same answers on their Grade 11 biology test. Maybe they still have things in common. Maybe they are more alike than she thinks.

"I was going to ask you how your trip was. Looks like you've brought home a souvenir."

"True. And it's the gift that keeps on giving."

"Ohmygawwwd," Carmen squeals, and Ally tries to smother her laughter so as not to wake Sam. "Well, I'm glad *someone's* having fun. While you've been frolicking in paradise, I've been in parent committee hell—planning Tyler's Grade 5 graduation party."

"Are you kidding me? Tyler's going into Grade 6? What happened?"

"I know. Time flies too fast. Remember Mrs. Mitchell?"

"How could I not?" Ally says, pulling out a photo album from under the glass coffee table and flipping through old class pictures. "God, she hated us."

"She hated everyone. We drove her nuts! Remember how we used to pass notes in class? I still have some of them! Found them with my journals the other day, while I was cleaning up."

"Oh my God, really? I have to see them!"

"I'll save them for you. And get this—Mrs. Mitchell is still teaching! I saw her at Oakwood's orientation day for incoming students."

"You're kidding!"

"Nope. It's a small world."

"Especially when you never leave home," Ally teases.

"Who would have thought that *I* would be the one to stay. I'm like the opposite of how I thought my life would turn out."

"You and me both, lady. You and me both."

"Anyway, I'm happy for you. Really, it's great."

The downturn of her voice makes Ally think otherwise.

"I know what you're thinking," Ally says, glancing back at her bedroom. Carmen had seen her through enough breakups to distrust her romantic choices.

"What am I thinking? I'm not thinking anything! I'm excited for you."

"You're judging. You're judging him already." *Typical.* Even though Carmen is just a couple of months older than Ally, she was born an old soul and naturally stepped into the big-sister role from the moment they met, the voice of reason and caution. *Maybe we shouldn't. What if we get caught?*

"Am not." Carmen sulks. "Well. Maybe a little. So, when do I get to meet him?"

"Not a chance. I'm keeping him all to myself for as long as I can," Ally says, walking over to her bedroom door.

"Go on. You deserve it. You really do. Enjoy."

"I will," Ally says, peeking into her room as she hangs up the phone. She savours the sight of Sam lying there on her bed, his holiday tan contrasting with her white comforter. It makes it hard to breathe. Desire courses through her, and her whole body hums to the music of him. The coffee maker has stopped hissing, but Ally strips off her nightie instead and slides in naked beside Sam. Underneath it all, she senses an urgency to go to him now, as if she doesn't trust the moment to last.

Chapter 27

*A*sk and it is given.

"Ask and it is given," Carmen repeats, reading from the happy, yellow-covered self-help book that she had picked up while shopping for a birthday present at the bookstore with the kids. She had felt embarrassed picking it up, had slid it underneath the pile she was carrying, but something inside her had insisted, and what did she have to lose anyway?

With the boys busy outside building a snowman, Carmen had decided to crack open the book. She could use some fresh new year's resolutions.

Expect, and enjoy, the unexpected.

"Expect, and enjoy, the unexpected."

Find the humor.

"Find the humor."

It's not working. Nothing is happening. She still feels the same: angsty and distracted. Like a speedboat skimming over the ocean with water splashing all over her face. Ally could always make Carmen laugh, make her feel like it was okay to be silly and carefree, but without her, she has a harder time loosening up.

It doesn't help that the boys are playing in the ditch by the side of the road, so that Carmen has to keep glancing out the living room window to check they're still alive. She always warned the boys that a car might veer off the road at any minute and kill them, but they always eventually ended up there anyway.

Carmen notices her fists are clenched. It feels like she's been hanging on for dear life, for forever. White knuckling her way through the days, months, years, when all she really wants to do is to let go of the wheel.

She remembers when she first spotted the For Sale sign on the front lawn. It was spring and all the trees and flowers were in bloom as she pushed the newborn twins in their double stroller on their morning walk. *We could never afford it*, she had admitted to Dan later that day, still coveting the two-storey house that was massive compared to the three-bedroom bungalow they were all crammed into then. Somehow, though, they had made her wish come true. If only she knew what to wish for now.

The front door slams shut, startling Carmen out of her reverie.

"He hurt me!" Toby cries.

"What happened?" Carmen rushes toward him.

Toby offers up his cheek, red and glistening with snow. Carmen takes a closer look and notices that his neck looks raw and burning too.

"Who did this to you?"

"Tyler!" Toby cries, his face crumpling up. "Tyler threw a snowball at me. And he put snow down my back!"

Furious, Carmen opens the door.

"Tyler!" she yells out the open door. She pulls on her boots and stomps out onto the snow-covered front lawn in just a sweater.

Tyler turns to her, covered up to his knees in fresh-fallen snow.

"You don't do that!" Carmen shouts, shutting out the thought that the neighbors might be watching. "You don't throw snowballs, and you especially don't put snow down people's neck! That's what bullies do. That's not having fun."

Carmen turns to head back inside and tend to Toby, but she hears Tyler mutter under his breath. "You don't know what fun is."

Stunned, she turns back, narrowing her eyes. "What did you say?"

"You don't know what fun is," Tyler says, louder this time as he looks straight at her.

At a loss for what to say, Carmen scowls and storms back into the house.

"Fun!" Carmen huffs, slamming the door behind her. "I used to be fun!"

Her head whips side to side as she searches for something to kick, punch, throw. Some way to prove that she is still Carmen. Cool, smart, sexy, fun. Carmen is still here.

She storms off to her closet. Tries on one dress after another, but, of course, none of them fit over her swollen body. So, she leaves her Diane von Furstenberg wrap dress hanging open over tights and a black tank top, with her engorged winter-pale breasts spilling out over the top. She slides on her Manolos and tucks into her desk and starts tapping away like a deranged Carrie Bradshaw.

If *Muse* doesn't want her, she would publish something anyway. Maybe it would be a blog. Maybe it would be a book. It didn't matter either way. She would write what she wanted to write and say what she wanted to say. There would be no one to report to, no one to get permission from. No editor to dance around or advertiser to dance for.

She wouldn't do it for money. She wouldn't even use her name.

She would do it because she said so.

She would do it just for fun.

"Carmen?"

She looks up and sees Alex staring at her from the head of the school staff room table.

"Yes?" she asks, realizing she had disappeared again. Her baby brain is off the charts, and it seems she can't get through five minutes without wandering off in her head.

Carmen shifts in her seat and loosens the scarf around her neck, the room stuffy and the air stale.

"The Grade 5 yearbook. How's it coming? Do we have all the kids' questionnaires filled out yet?"

"Just a few left to go," Carmen says, resenting the line of questioning. She had run entire magazines. She doesn't need babysitting for the school yearbook.

"What's the holdup?"

"The flu—some of the kids have been sick," Carmen says, clenching her hands under the table.

"Just as long as we get them all in on time."

Carmen gives Alex a quick, tight smile and checks the time on the clock hanging above the door. 10:15 a.m. The bell would go off soon, releasing the classes for recess. Even Tyler's Grade 5 class would be hurrying out the doors to play. One last year before the who-kissed-who middle school drama kicks in. *Good, go be kids,* Carmen thinks. Real life would catch up with them soon enough.

"We have photos, the kids Q&As, teacher bios—anything else we can include?"

"Actually, I was thinking it would be fun to open it up to the kids—let them submit their own stuff," Carmen offers.

"We could give out prizes for best painting or story," says Shari, Alex's equally intense right hand, and Carmen wonders why everything fun must be ruined by turning it into a competition. Why is *she* always measuring herself against others?

"Great idea, Shari. Let's go with that," Alex says.

The more things change, the more things stay the same. Carmen sucks in her breath and wonders if there is a sign over her head that says, "Irrelevant."

Alex and Shari take notes in their tiny, neat script, as serious as if they were deliberating a case before the courts. Carmen looks down at the stack of answers on the table before her.

What do you want to be when you grow up?

It was a ridiculous question to ask a ten-year-old. Carmen was forty and she still didn't know.

"A professional gamer."

"A YouTuber."

"Rich."

Copying the kids' replies into the yearbook layout on her computer had reminded her of the playful, scrapbook feel of the magazines she fell in love with growing up and wanted to be a part of. Those magazines had been real life mixed in with make believe. Full of promise and possibility on the one hand, and truth or dare on the other. Somewhere along the way, though, the excitement of creating something had disappeared. The whole thing was treated with such reverence, it had sucked out all the fun. Grownups had ruined it.

The bell rings and kids flood the halls, racing outside. The rush of energy feels like freedom and joy. Like driving around in Ally's car with the windows down and nowhere to go. It feels like writing.

Carmen, Dan, and the kids take off on a frigid January morning. Dan puts the gear in reverse, and the van groans under the weight of all their belongings: one double stroller, one hockey bag and stick, one duffel bag, three knapsacks packed with toys and candy, and two grocery bags stuffed with snacks. Even the diaper bag is bursting with every kind of emergency item they could possibly need: more granola bars, juice boxes, band-aids, children's Tylenol, changes of clothes, hand sanitizer, and a brand-new pack of baby wipes. Though the twins are out of diapers, Carmen still takes the bag with her wherever they go. *You never know ...*

It's a quiet drive to Westchester for Tyler's hockey tournament as the twins watch movies on their iPads with their headphones on and Tyler plays his Nintendo Switch. Though Dan is talking to her again after their fight over the Christmas lights, and Carmen is finally letting their credit card cool off from all the holiday spending, there is still a formality to their interactions. Each not sure what is safe to say to the other. Their conversation as colorless as the streets outside.

I used to do Milan, Paris, Carmen thinks as they drive past salt-and slush-encrusted sidewalks lined with grimy motels and dilapidated homes with taped-up sofas sagging on their crumbling porches. Instead of resentment, though, the thought makes her smile to herself.

"Boulevard of broken dreams," Dan says, turning to her and smiling back.

The cold gray of winter casts a powdery quality to his pale skin, and she notices more crinkling around his eyes and flecks of gray at his temples. She knows she has more wrinkles and grays too. They are getting older, had grown older together. It isn't the fresh flush of Ally's new love affair, but it is home.

At the community centre, the front hall is packed with exhausted parents clutching take-out coffee as children run back and forth, grabbing at the souvenirs for sale by nervous vendors. As they wait for the tournament to start, the twins badger the vendors, whine for hot chocolate, and fight over the popcorn. Tyler scores a goal, but also gets a penalty for body checking another player who keeps slashing his skates. Carmen's not sure which Dan is more proud of. Not sure which *she* is more proud of. So much of her own childhood had been about not rocking the boat. Not getting it wrong. If her own kids aren't afraid to be kids and stand up for themselves, that must mean she is doing something right, right?

After the game, they head out for dinner, the kids racing up funhouse sidewalks lit with holiday lights. They grab a greasy bite at a diner, and afterwards Carmen and Tyler face off in an arcade, battling zombie pirates and seeing who can get the most basketballs in net. Carmen takes a picture in her mind's eye. She isn't sure what it will turn into yet, but there is something here to explore.

The more she wrote, journaled—she isn't yet sure what to call it—the more she appreciated these kinds of moments. The everyday and seemingly mundane haloed by the words she framed it with. Little bit by little bit she is coming back to herself. The more she does, the more it feels like love.

Driving back home, they spot a park decorated with holiday lights arranged in the form of characters and animals—Mickey Mouse and Big Bird, a unicorn and polar bear. They pull over and stroll through the celestial scene, marvelling at the glowing creations up close, like so many stars and constellations. A world of possibility. No past or future, just now.

Dan squeezes Carmen's hand, and she knows what he's thinking. The moment is so perfect, she wants to freeze time, if it didn't mean giving up tomorrow.

No, it isn't Milan or Paris, but this, this is everything.

"What's wrong?" Dan asks as Carmen dries tears on her coat sleeve.

"I think I found my feelings. I can't stop," she says, wiping her nose.

"Good, 'cause sometimes I feel like I married a rock," Dan says with a smirk, making Carmen laugh.

Toby starts whining, and Dan scoops the twins up, making them break out in giggles.

"Are you having fun?" Carmen asks Tyler, taking his hand in hers as they walk back to the car.

Tyler nods his head and swings their clasped hands while Carmen smiles with her whole body and soul.

"Me too."

Chapter 28

They're late for the party. Ally is never late for anything, but Sam is in a mood tonight. Even as he gets dressed to go out—a birthday party for Davis, a fellow biologist at Ally's work—he lingers, brooding and restless, first on his computer, then the TV. He changes his top, from button-down to sweater to T-shirt. Cracks open a beer.

"We're supposed to be at the party by now," Ally says, waiting at the kitchen counter by the door.

"What's the rush?" Sam says, flopping down on the couch and pointing the converter to turn up the volume. Ally sucks in her breath and pauses for a moment before letting it out. She's still getting to know her colleagues, still getting to know Sam. She doesn't want to make a bad impression by arriving late to the party, but she also doesn't know how far she can push him.

It seems there is no hurrying Sam without a fight, so Ally sits down on the other end of the couch, tapping her foot and glancing at the time on her watch. There had been a time when she was the centre of attention. When all the world was at her command. But time and disappointment had quietly ebbed away at her, eroding the spontaneity and confidence of her youthful self. Now she is afraid to ask for what she wants, needs.

"Let's go," Sam finally says, placing an empty beer bottle on the table.

At the party—*after* he had finished watching the basketball game and had changed back into a white button-down to go with a charcoal-gray blazer—Sam puts on a good show. He dazzles with his smile, pats new friends on the back, laughs louder than everyone else in the room. Ally sees two Sams emerge: one that he leaves back at her apartment and another he has brought out to play. The fans love it.

"What do you do?" Francesca, one of the technicians, asks Sam, and he launches into an explanation of his company, regaling his audience with tales about the seemingly clueless, childlike founders who run the tech start-up where he works. Ally has heard the stories before. She wanders over to another group.

"Ever see a five-year-old dribble?"

"We dropped my son from A level to house league. He just couldn't handle the pressure. *We* couldn't handle it."

Ally feels the absence keenly. If Carmen were here, she would know what to say. Ally could let her do the talking, fit in by association. She just couldn't win. Back in Maine, she was surrounded by post-graduate singles. Here in Portland, everyone is married with kids.

Sam comes up behind Ally and wraps his arms around her, hugging her close. Ally blushes, grateful for the shift in his temperament and attention.

"Actually, the principal was asked to leave, because he was having an affair with one of the mothers. They both left their partners to be together."

"They call it divorce row, where all the dads end up, and the wives get the house and kids."

Sam secretly rolls his eyes at Ally, making her giggle to herself. God, is that what she is in for? Parents living out fantasies through their children, marriages that become battlegrounds. Their world seems so small and desperate. No, that would never be her, Ally insists to herself. She and Sam would be different. Better. If *they* ever happened.

"I don't know, I kind of like my life," Sam says with a shrug, when Melanie, Davis's wife, asks if he wants kids, as if it weren't a private matter, as if his lifestyle were something he had to defend. "I mean I wouldn't mind, I guess, but I don't really care either, you know?"

Wait, did he just say he does or doesn't want kids? Ally double takes. They should have had that conversation already. They should have that conversation soon.

"Besides, I already have everything I need," Sam adds with a wink at Ally, as he takes her hand. She smiles and squeezes his hand back.

"And you, Ally? Do you want kids?" Melanie asks.

"I do," Ally says, looking at Sam. He holds her gaze, and she wonders if that means it's a yes. "I do."

"Coffee ..." Sam groans from the bedroom, and Ally rolls her eyes from the living room, where she is catching up on some work. It would be nice if he made her a cup for a change. If he were ever awake early enough to make her one. Sam slept like a teenager and drank like he was still in college.

"How's your head?" Ally asks, placing a steaming cup on the nightstand beside him.

"I think you're gonna have to go to the museum without me today. I'm out of commission."

Ally sighs. While she'd rather spend the day exploring the city's network of trails and parks, she had planned on taking Sam to the Portland

Art Museum today, thinking he would enjoy it more. She has already bought the tickets.

"You didn't have to do those shots."

"Davis started it. I just finished it." Sam laughs, sitting up and grabbing his head. "Ouch."

"Well, you're paying for it now."

"You know what would make me feel better ..." Sam says with a grin, reaching for her arm and pulling her toward him.

Ally shakes him off, though it takes all her might to deny him anything.

"Bacon's on."

Back in the kitchen, Ally cracks eggs for an omelet.

It's not just the shots. It's not just the tickets. She isn't the jealous type, but hadn't Sam talked to Elena a little long? After all that whining about not wanting to go out, about wanting to stay in and spend time with *her*, then he spends half the night chatting up the recently divorced office manager.

Then there's the evolution of adventure Sam into homebody Sam. When they weren't at her apartment, she was driving up to his place in Seattle, where they'd order in and watch basketball. He always used work as an excuse—too many client dinners and industry meetups—for the reason he wanted to stay in. But how was she ever going to make friends and get settled in her new city—whether they ended up in Seattle or Portland—if they didn't actually get out to explore and experience it? She's tired of being a ghost; she wants to plant roots and belong. Make it her *home*.

The smell of bacon and eggs finally rouse Sam from bed, and he walks over in his black silk pyjama bottoms.

"Another coffee?" Ally asks.

Sam nods his head yes. His mussy hair and sleepy eyes are almost enough to make Ally give in to his every whim—almost.

"Over there," Ally teases, pointing to the coffee machine, the lone accessory, besides the toaster and kettle, on the kitchen counter. Though she keeps the fridge and pantry stocked for Sam, the condo still looks unlived in—tidy and spare. He likes it that way.

"Smells amazing," Sam says as he makes his way over and pours himself a cup. He takes a seat at the island and hugs his mug, while Ally sets a place for him and serves up the eggs, bacon, and toast, along with a fresh-squeezed orange juice—one of her few regular indulgences. She watches Sam dig in.

"A thank you would be nice?" Ally says, once his plate is cleared.

"Thank you," Sam says, wiping his mouth with a napkin and getting up. "Thank you," he says, grabbing her hips and pulling her in for a kiss. His lips taste warm and sweet. "Let me show you how thankful I am," he says, leading her back to the bedroom.

Pulled along by Sam, Ally recalls her college boyfriend, Charlie. All it took was one call—"Come over"—and she would get dressed and walk to his place, whether it was seven at night or two in the morning, winter or summer, desperate for whatever piece of his time he was willing to share. Is she doing it again? Is that what this is? Just another booty call, as Carmen would call it?

"What are we doing?" Ally asks, pausing at the bedroom door, and the voice in her head sounds like Carmen. She is not afraid to ask questions or tell a guy to buzz off. She is not afraid to be alone.

Sam turns, confused, and she almost wishes she could take it back, but something steely and demanding inside emboldens her. She is done wasting time on Mr. Wrong. She will not make that mistake again.

"What do you mean?" Sam asks as he drops her hand.

"Where are we going with this? With us?" Ally asks, unable to stop. She is baiting him, she knows—her desires a growing inconvenience, evidenced by a hardening of his eyes—but the suspense is killing her. Is he the one? Is she the one for him?

Sam falls back on the bed with a groan.

"Oh God! Why do women always want to talk about this? It's so boring!"

So that's it—she is just another woman. Ally turns to leave the room.

"Ally ..."

"Seriously, why are you here? Why are you even with me?"

Sam sits on the edge of the bed and combs a hand through his wavy hair. "Because you're smart. And fun. And you've got an amazing body," he says, looking up, his eyes twinkling mischievously as a grin spreads across his face.

Ally walks away.

"Ally! Come back! I was just kidding!" Sam calls out, laughing. "I love you!"

The words freeze in the air, the first time he has uttered the phrase. Ally turns and cocks her head. Did she hear him right?

"I love you," Sam says, smiling warmly as he gets up and walks toward her. "I love that you know the mating rituals of lobsters. I love that you're not afraid of the deep end or the dark. I love how you cry at commercials and laugh in your sleep. I love the way you tell the *worst* jokes."

Sam takes her in his arms, and she softens as he nuzzles his bristly face into her neck. The warmth of his familiar smell makes her melt. He is hers and she is his.

Sam looks up and traces a heart on Ally's lips.

"I. Love. You," Sam says. He sweeps her hair to the side and kisses her neck, then her mouth, slow and deep. Ally kisses him back.

"I love you too."

Chapter 29

Carmen checks her phone. There are sixteen comments on her latest blog post and almost 5,000 page views in the last month. The blog about no-filter motherhood was taking off in ways she hadn't dared dream of. She had put it all out there, all her messiness and not-enoughness, and the other moms were eating it up. She could monetize it soon, if she wanted to. If she dared.

There is just one thing: The blog is still anonymous. And the bigger it got, the more she risked being found out. What if she wanted to go back to her old career one day? Or work for anyone else? There would be a lot of dirty laundry to apologize for. She was far from perfect and the deeper she went, the more cleaning up there would be to do. And yet, could she speak so freely and unapologetically if everyone knew those words were coming directly from her?

It's something she'll have to address—one day. For now, there is a baby to prepare for, and a yearbook to create. Her blog had brought her so much joy that she now wants to pay it forward and inspire the kids to do the same thing with *their* yearbook. To make it about them. To bring them closer to one another as they shared their own stories and experiences—the real ones, not the filtered versions Alex and Shari were insisting on.

Carmen checks the clock by the door and taps her foot as she scans the walls of Tyler's classroom, savoring the checklists and affirmations. She had loved school. Loved books and homework. Everything packaged up in neat, little cause-and-effects that made sense and which she could count on. It used to be reassuring, the predictability of it all, but now something grates on her. She wants to turn it inside out.

Carmen still remembers the day she met Ally. It was Ally who drew a shy and withdrawn Carmen out, inviting her to go with her friends and giving her the stamp of approval she needed to make others notice, make them care about her. Together they would ride their bikes to the store, pool, beach—all the things Carmen's overprotective parents wouldn't let her do on her own. Carmen smiles, thinking back. It felt like the world was theirs for the taking. For Ally, perhaps, it still is.

There's a knock on the door and Carmen looks over. A girl stands in the doorway, with curly dark hair and glasses. She's wearing baggy jeans and an oversized long-sleeved shirt that says, "I paused my game to be here."

"Hi, come in. I'm Tyler's mom, Carmen," she says, waving her in.

"I know," the girl answers, looking Carmen right in the eyes as she strides into the room and sinks into her seat.

Carmen pauses, reminding herself that this is just a child. She is the adult here.

"You're Olivia Flores, right?"

"Is this going to take long? I have a music recital to practise for."

"We can take as long, or as little, as you want," Carmen says, smiling tightly. Olivia looks on stone-faced as Carmen presses start on her recorder.

"Okay, so let's begin: What will you miss about Kennedy Public School?"

"Nothing. This school sucks. I can't wait to get out of here."

"Okaaay," Carmen draws out, thinking there's a teachable moment in here somewhere. "There must be something you enjoy."

"Fine. The library. Pizza day."

Rote answers. Doesn't she have any friends? Carmen decides to talk to Tyler when he's home, make sure he's being nice to her.

"Next, what's your best memory?"

Olivia pauses and a flicker of doubt passes over her face. "The talent show. I won second place for my speech about climate change."

"That's awesome," Carmen says, inspecting Olivia's face for more. She's too composed, too grown up. Carmen wants to knock the adult out of her. See her break free. The way Ally did with her when they were in school together.

Carmen looks at the next question. It feels like a betrayal.

"What do you want to be when you grow up?"

"Dunno. CEO of something, I guess."

"Why CEO?"

Olivia blanks. "Is that a question on the questionnaire?"

Carmen baulks but quickly recovers. "Just wondering."

"Because that would make me the best. I want to be the best."

The best. Carmen's mouth goes dry. So much pressure and expectation rolled up into those two little words. Her own dad had impressed upon her the need to be the best, constantly reminding her of how he came to this country with nothing, built his company from scratch. "Mírame ahora! Everything I have and everything I gave you is because *I* was the best. No excuses, Carmela!"

Carmen swallows and focuses back on Olivia. "But why?"

Olivia lets out a sigh of impatience. "I want to be special, I guess."

"But you are special. I think you're special."

"Why should I listen to you?"

Carmen's throat feels raw. It's hard to swallow. What can she say? What can she teach? Aren't they all ten years old, reaching for someone's approval? When did it end?

Olivia thrusts her chin forward, waiting. "Are we done here? Can I go?"

Carmen hesitates. She wants to impart some lesson. To save this girl from herself. Carmen blinks and sticks out her tongue. "Blah!"

Oliva startles back in her seat.

"Buhalooaugoughghg gighoesgi ghoeiisttt."

Olivia's eyes widen, and a smile creeps across her face. "Are you okay?" she asks, her voice thick with sarcasm.

"Come on!" Carmen says, standing up. "Do it with me! Let's have fun! Let's act stupid. And not to make other people like us, but to make *us* like us."

Olivia glances side to side as Carmen starts shaking her hips and waving her hands in the air.

"Should I get someone? A doctor maybe?" Olivia asks, smirking.

"What are you afraid of?"

"You? Looking stupid?"

"Come on, nobody's looking. Nobody cares. Truly," Carmen says, letting the words sink in.

Olivia smiles and starts rocking her shoulders. "Lalallal, alllalall lallalalla."

Carmen laughs. "That's it. That's it!"

"Lalal lalalala lallalal," she chimes in, and does a silly dance. Olivia gets up and starts to dance for real.

Carmen stops and watches her as tears well up. If only someone had done that for her ... Ally had. Given her permission to be herself. The confidence and courage that comes with unconditional love.

Olivia pauses, noticing that Carmen is watching.

"I have an idea," Carmen says.

Olivia raises an eyebrow.

"Let's rewrite the questions. Let's make up our own."

Olivia's eyes widen and a smile spreads across her face. "Won't we get in trouble?"

"*I* might. But I'm a big girl. I can handle it. So, what do you think? Want to play with me?" Carmen asks, cocking her head with a wide grin.

Olivia nods back.

"Cool. So, what if ..."

Carmen holds the laundry basket out, her arms barely long enough to make up for her extra girth. Her biceps burn as she carries the load up the stairs, and she rests the basket on the landing for a moment as she catches her breath, doubting again if there's enough of her to go around for yet another child.

Dan and the boys are pillow fighting in the twins' room so she starts with Tyler. Putting away his clothes, she looks around his room, as if seeing it for the first time, through new eyes. The blue-and-white walls Dan painstakingly painted years ago, which took double the time than had he painted the room in just one color, but did so just to make her happy. The printed and framed photos she picked out to cheer Tyler in the morning, and comfort him at night: trips to Disney World, the beach.

Carmen kicks a sweater on the floor closer to the closet, her toe brushing the plush Pottery Barn Kids rug she had searched everywhere for so Ty and his brothers could comfortably roll around on it. She was thrilled when she found it. It was the same sky-blue shade as his accent walls. It cost over $700, and she couldn't remember the last time she spent that much on herself, her husband, or their home, but she slapped her credit card down with zero qualms. Her son. Her firstborn. The one who turned her life upside down. She was never the same afterward.

Carmen moves over to the twins' room and the boys migrate to Tyler's, where he talks the twins through his hockey cards, teaching them about the different teams, players, and statistics. When the twins were born, Carmen worried that she wouldn't have enough love left over to give them. But her love only grew, along with her patience, strength, and endurance. Sleepless nights and non-stop days just became a part of their existence, so she and Dan hardly felt the pain, mostly the joy. That, and sheer exhaustion.

Carmen shuts off the overhead light, and on her way out pauses at the door of the guest bedroom. *The baby's room,* she thinks, smiling as she walks down the stairs. This time, Carmen doesn't worry she might be short of love—she knows it's boundless. It's her time and energy she is worried about. While she is anxious about the baby's health results—*could it be too good to be true? She is forty now, after all*—deep down, when she allows herself this much, she believes that it is meant to be.

"Everything okay?" Dan asks from the living room where he's folding another load of laundry.

"Everything is perfect," she says, and gives him a real kiss.

"Tongue," Dan says, looking surprised.

"Why not? Neither of us is contagious," she teases back.

"Mommy? My tummy hurts," Teo whines from the top of the stairs.

Dan and Carmen frown at each other. *Of course.*

"I'll take care of him, you relax," Dan says, scooping Teo up into his arms and carrying him to bed.

Dan was right. They are parents. And that's enough. She should just be grateful for what she has and enjoy the ride. What else were they going to do? They were already in it. And they loved it. The kids, the house, the work, the craziness. It was exhausting, but she was desperate to enjoy every second of it, aware of how quickly babies become toddlers, and toddlers become school agers. It would be over before they knew it, and she would miss it all terribly.

Perhaps another baby isn't so bad. They could enjoy this moment a little longer—bills be damned. There were plenty of big families out there, and they managed with less, didn't they? The kids wouldn't miss out, would they? Maybe this baby would be a gift to them all.

"Time to brush your teeth, boys," Dan calls out, placing Teo on the potty.

"Teo, are you doing number one or number two?" Toby asks, leaning against the door frame.

"Two," Teo says, matter-of-factly.

"Ewww!" Toby cackles from the doorway.

"Teo, do you know what the biggest poo is?" Toby rebounds.

"No, what?"

"Diarrhea!"

The boys laugh hysterically as Dan inspects Teo's bum.

Carmen sweeps the kitchen while Tyler helps himself to a piece of toast, which he eats standing up, letting more crumbs fall to the floor.

"At recess today, I invented a new game," he confides.

"Oh yeah?" Carmen asks, sweeping up the fresh crumbs into the dustpan.

"It's called reball."

"What's that?"

"It's like baseball, but completely different."

"Tyler! Bo-oyz!" Dan calls from the bathroom. "Time to gather round! I have a tutorial for you."

Curious, Carmen follows Tyler upstairs as Dan corrals the kids into the bathroom.

"Now children," Dan begins, wild-eyed. "I have a little tutorial for you. Today we're going to learn how to brush our teeth. *Properly.*"

The kids are giggling and wiggling around in their pjs as Dan squeezes a big blue blob of toothpaste onto his brush and starts brushing furiously, coming up to each kid for a close-up.

"See! None of this fancy pants stuff! Like a rabid dog!" Dan shows them, frothing at the mouth. The kids laugh and heckle their dad, and Carmen chuckles by their side. Dan spits and rinses and gets each kid to demonstrate.

"Good, Tyler, good. C'mon Toby, get in there, that's it! Teo, you're letting me down, my man."

Wiping tears from laughing, Carmen suddenly stops, as if she remembered something. She had worked so hard to make everything right, perfect, but this, this was what it was all about. The poo jokes and the sagging belly. The terrible Christmas play and the anxious parents. Carmen runs to grab her phone and snap a photo of her twisted Norman Rockwell tableau. The kids are pushing now, so she knows she only has a moment before the crying starts. And when it does, she takes a photo of that too.

Chapter 30

"Another glass?" the captain of the boat asks Ally.

She shakes her head, thinking she would swallow the whole bottle down if she didn't have to drive home from the marina.

"He's not coming," Ally says, trying to sound nonchalant. The only thing more embarrassing than being stood up is being stood up on Valentine's Day, and she is pretty sure by now that Sam isn't going to make it.

"There's been an accident on the I-5, and he doesn't think it'll clear up anytime soon," Ally lies.

"Oh, what a shame. I hope it's not something serious," the captain says.

I hope it is, Ally thinks, finishing the last of her wine.

Until a half hour ago, she was having a nice time. She had booked a charter—a forty-four-foot-long catamaran—for a catered sail along Willamette River. The captain and crew were friendly and attentive, busying themselves in the cockpit and galley while Ally sat at a table in the salon, admiring the sun setting over the city skyline.

It felt good to be back on the water, even if it was cold; her winter parka and the blanket over her lap not quite managing to keep the wet chill from her bones. Being on a boat always brought back memories of sailing the Jersey Cape with her dad, of speed and adventure, the spray of water whipping at the smile across her face. They had picked out his thirty-foot Beneteau Oceanis together, and when he sold the boat a few years after he left, it broke Ally's heart almost as much as the split between her parents did. He would not be coming back.

Now, thinking about the happier times she spent with her dad, she misses him, though they could never go back to the way things were. Even wishing each other a simple happy New Year had been strained with all the things unsaid. There was too much to catch up on, too much resentment on both sides, making them strangers to each other.

"You'll have to come back—it's a real light show at night. Just give us a minute to wrap up your food. I'm sure he'll be starved when he gets home," the captain says.

Ally gathers her purse as he goes back into the galley. She fights the urge to check her phone, again. She had been so sure Sam would still show up, even though there hadn't been a call or text to say he was running late, or forgot, or even Happy Valentine's Day. Is he still on this planet?

The captain returns and holds out his hand, helping Ally off the boat. As she walks back to her car, takeaway in hand, her phone begins to vibrate. She pulls it out and sees a text message from Sam. Not even a call.

<<Rain check? I'll come 2 u.>>

She wants to answer back. Something mean and hurtful, the way he hurt her. Instead, she shoves the phone back into her purse.

Blinking back tears from the sting of shame, Ally wants to call Carmen. Carmen wouldn't put up with any of this. Carmen would know what to say.

It's too late, though. She would already be in bed. Since the kids had come along, it was never a good time to reach out to her. She was never there when Ally needed her. It was just as well Ally was tired of her own story anyway.

Thoughts of Carmen cocooned at home, surrounded by her kids and loving husband, make Ally wince. While her own home had splintered apart after her parents' separation, Carmen's home life had only multiplied—more parents, more money. She never had to work to put herself through school. She didn't know what it was like to only have yourself to rely on to pay the rent.

Now Carmen is on her fourth baby. And Ally can't even get a date with her boyfriend on Valentine's Day.

Not even two weeks had passed since her broken Valentine's Day, and here she is again.

"Ally ..." Sam yawns from the other room.

"Coming," she can't help cooing.

After Valentine's Day, she had given Sam the silent treatment. She'd decided she was done with jerks. She would come first from now on. She would be all she needed.

And then he had swooped in with a flurry of texts and voicemails. "Miss u." "I'm sorry." "Give me one more chance."

He promised he would make it up to her. Would take her cliff diving in Jamaica. Horseback riding in Montana. Would make her breakfast in bed and build her a cabin in the woods. Anything if she would just pick up the phone. Still, she held fast.

Until one day when she turned the key in her door, sagging at the thought of another lonely Friday night. A shock of color had greeted her. A hundred balloons filled the space, so that she couldn't see the living room from where she stood at the door. And then Sam had stepped forward and bowed. And she had breathed in, as if for the first time in days.

She fell into his arms, and they stumbled into the bedroom, kissing and making love as the colors of the rainbow floated around them.

It didn't take long for things to go back to the way they were. A week later and here she is, catering to him again. Sam had come down with a cold and didn't feel up to the three-hour drive to her place, so she offered to come to him. Then they spent the night on the couch, eating chips and watching basketball. He wasn't too sick to put away a six-pack of craft IPA.

Ally pours a coffee and takes it to Sam.

"How are you feeling?" she asks, placing the mug on his nightstand.

"Better now that you're here," he says, stretching out and smiling. "Come back to bed."

"Stove's on." Ally turns and walks away.

In the kitchen, she flips bacon as she tallies up the casualties. Even last weekend, he had been quick to lose his temper when she suggested they meet up with her friends from work for a drink, calling them boring and fake. And last night, after her shower, he had complained about the water in the bathroom and her clothes lying everywhere. (Not everywhere, just on the chair in his bedroom—what else was she supposed to do when there was no room for her in his closet?) He was obsessively neat, and her normal was not quite synching up with his.

All those trifles stack like small resentments. Mere growing pains or signs of a mismatch? Are they growing together, or two people too set in their ways to change?

Sam grabs her from behind and kisses her neck.

"Careful, you might get burned," Ally says, turning an omelet, her body stiff and unforgiving.

"Hmm, can't wait." Sam sits down at the kitchen island.

Ally slides a plate of bacon and eggs toward him.

"You're the best." Sam grins.

Am I being too tough on him? Ally wonders. *All couples have their moments, right?*

Ally sits across from him, eating her omelet and pretending to read her tablet, while her mind tries to consolidate the two Sams. There is the one who seems to want her, and the one who pushes her away. She feels like a plaything, a toy he flips over and over. Happy sad. Happy sad. To see if she might break?

Ally wants to be happy. She wants to be happy *with him.* But there's a voice of doubt—*Carmen's* voice—in her mind. She still hasn't met his friends. Why? It's a question she doesn't like to think about.

Ally pauses, feeling Sam's eyes on her. She looks up, but he looks away. When she turns back to her tablet, she can feel his eyes on her again, but the moment she looks up, he looks away.

"What? What is it?" Ally finally asks. "Do I have something in my teeth?" She runs her tongue over her teeth.

"Let's move in together," Sam says, daring her with his eyes.

"Really?"

"Yeah, why not?"

Ally tries to imagine what their home would look like. Sam's condo is impeccable, everything cool and untouchable—all porcelain tiles, marble countertops, and monochromatic grays. Ally's things, meanwhile, are like an old couch, worn and frayed, including throw blankets collected from her various travels, mismatched picture frames, and random souvenirs from her trips. Sam often teased her about her "old lady" taste and "quirky" collection of sailboat figurines. She wishes she could relax in his space, and he in hers—an inconsistency in the meaning and sentiment of home. And yet, if they made a home *together* ...

"What about work?" Ally asks, though she had already thought about it. There is a Seattle office. She could put in for a transfer and work remotely, coming into town as required, until it came through. It's what she wants, isn't it? To make a home with him together?

Sam shrugs. "We'll figure it out," he says, dismissing the question with a wave of his hand and walking over to her. "All this back and forth. It'd just be so much easier if we lived together. If we didn't have to make 'plans,'" he says, making air quotes, and she knows he's referring to the Valentine's Day fail, as if it were just a harmless calendar conflict. As if it weren't her who was usually doing all the back and forth.

"Are you sure?" Ally asks, suddenly not quite sure herself that she is ready to commit. A voice in her head urges caution.

"Yes, I'm sure," Sam says, grinning as he grabs her arm and pulls her close. "C'mon, make a home with me," he purrs as he kisses her hand and leads her toward the bedroom, as if the matter were settled as easily as deciding what to order from takeout.

"But how would it work?" Ally asks, pulling back and cocking her head, daring him to prove it's not just another one of his whims.

"We'll figure it out," Sam says again, pulling her in close and dipping her down playfully. "Later," he adds with a wink and a kiss, and pulls her back up again.

Sam rocks Ally in a slow dance, turning her round and round, until they reach the bedroom door. Leaning her against the wall, Sam runs his hands up and in between her thighs. Hanging on to her hips, he slides down.

"Now let me tell you about the dream that I had ..."

Chapter 31

Selena's "Como La Flor" blasts from the speakers of her bedroom as Carmen cumbia dances around, embracing her belly in the final days of her pregnancy. Although by the end of the day, her belly, back, and feet are sore from the extra weight she is carrying, she is still sorry that the time is coming to an end. Her last baby belly. Her last pregnancy. She is lucky to have come this far.

The phone rings and Carmen feels a kick in her groin.

"Hey, ow!" she calls out, rubbing her belly. "Be nice."

Carmen picks up the phone to see the call display reveal a number she doesn't recognize. Lately, the only business her phone gets is from Dan, her mom, and the library reminding her of books that are late. Even Ally has gone MIA.

Carmen flops down on her reading chair and answers the call.

"Hello?" she says, still catching her breath.

"Hi, Carmen? It's Emily from Arrow! We saw your profile on LinkedIn. I'd love to chat with you about a position that has opened up. Is now a good time?"

"Absolutely," Carmen says, a tightening around her belly causing her to grip the arms of her chair. She isn't sure if it is excitement or nervousness, or just the Braxton Hicks practice contractions that had started picking up in recent weeks—an uncomfortable reminder that the peace and quiet she had been enjoying at home, alone, these past months would be coming to an end any day now.

"Great!" Emily says. "We just love your whole story. The big family. Super Mom. Plus all your publishing experience. You're just what Arrow is looking for in an editor-in-chief. They want someone who really gets the millennial mom demographic, and your Instagram feed is just what they're looking for. Your kids are so adorable!"

"Awww, you're so sweet! Thank you so much!" Carmen says, quickly scanning her Instagram feed to make sure she hasn't posted anything damning.

Nope. Nothing but wholesome family fun here.

"They'd love to explore you joining the team to help launch a new parenting platform. They're in a hurry to get going, though. Can we set up a phone interview with you and George, our senior manager of content and digital strategy, next week?"

"Of course," Carmen says, wincing. She can take that call. As long as she isn't in the hospital, giving birth to baby number four.

"Great! I'll send you a calendar invite, and we can take it from there. Talk to you soon."

"Looking forward to it. Thank you." Carmen shifts in her seat. The belly ache begins to spread along her sides and lower back.

Carmen looks out the bay window at a sunny March day. Crocuses are sprouting out of the ground, and she can hear the birds chirping as they flit from tree to tree.

Though money is still tight, she has accumulated some small freelance writing assignments to help make ends meet. She certainly didn't miss commuting to the city, the boardroom meetings, and the anxiety. Dare she give this all up? Does she have a choice?

And yet, she can feel her old ambitions spark back to life at the thought of changing out of her tights and tanks and into the power suits and colorful party dresses hanging in her closet. There's a slight thrill at the thought of spearheading a launch, her name back in circulation. She could become an industry player again, making everyone who thought she was washed up take notice. Prove that she was important. Worthy. Special. To Meredith. Carrie. Her dad. All of them. Best of all, they wanted *her*—kids and all. Everything everyone else had shunned her for.

She could pay down their line of credit. Maybe the van too. Perhaps they could even get a new car. They could take a trip somewhere with palm trees and a beach. They could go from merely surviving to thriving.

They could make it work. They could get a nanny this time, to look after the baby, pick up the kids from school, and make dinner. God, if she never had to cook or clean up after dinner again, taking a full-time job would be worth that in itself.

It strikes her that she would be dispensing domestic advice to legions of struggling mothers while she outsourced and delegated her own responsibilities at home. How could she make promises about raising perfect kids, making healthy meals, maintaining a picture-perfect home, and accomplishing work-life balance, when she couldn't make those things happen for herself? Then there are the late nights—she is sure there will be plenty of those. How bad did she want it?

Carmen rubs her belly and the logical, practical thing to do evaporates. She only wants to be here, now. To see her baby's first steps, hear their first word. The excitement is already building to pick up the boys from school, when her heart would pitter-patter at the sight of them like some groupie at a rock concert. Soon, Tyler would be walking home with his friends. She'd be lucky to get a hug from him at bedtime. The deafening chatter at the dinner table would be replaced with just the sound of Dan's jaw clicking. Carmen's throat closes up at the thought of the kids moving on. It is far away but her life as it is now will be over before she knows it.

And then there is her blog, her passion project. She isn't sure what it will amount to yet, but she is having fun watching it grow. If she goes back to work now, she will have to abandon it. Could she wait a lifetime to write her next chapter? For the first time in a long time, it feels like she is doing something for herself. Something just for the pure joy of it.

But to be able to give Tyler the shoes he asks for next time they go shopping? To afford the things they need, want? To rise from ignominy? Isn't it a dream come true? To save her family? Or dare she save herself?

Carmen is at the party store picking up balloons for the twins' birthday party when it hits her—a squeezing in her gut that reminds her of diarrhea. *Not here. Not now. Not like this,* she thinks, holding on to the handlebar of her shopping cart as a cold sweat breaks out across her forehead.

The young girl in front of her is taking an eternity to blow up balloons, and Carmen wonders how many more to go before she gets to the life-size Minions she has purchased for the twins. She still needs to pay for the napkins, paper plates, and Happy Birthday streamers in her cart, and that line is growing, too.

Just a few more hours, baby. Just give me a few more hours, she thinks when the contraction subsides. Enough time to finish her errands, drive home, and host a party, she calculates, as the girl finally hands over the Minions.

"Please, let the twins have their special day. Then I'm all yours," she whispers to the baby, rubbing her belly.

She should have known better than to think she could pull a fast one on Mother Nature.

Her first-born had been perfectly planned, timed to her career goals and deadlines. She gave up smoking, became a vegetarian, and cleansed her body of toxins with an all-organic diet. She practised breathing and the right way to push during prenatal yoga classes, to protect her vagina from being ripped apart by a giant watermelon of a baby making its way through. After interviewing several midwives, she hired one, though she planned to deliver in the hospital so she could have the best of both worlds.

In the end, Tyler had refused to come out on his own, and Carmen had to be induced three times, requiring an epidural and cancelling her plans for natural delivery. The lesson: birth plans are meant to be broken. And with the twins? Well, they made planning *life* impossible.

So, when it came time to prepare for her new baby's birth, Carmen left it up to destiny. The baby's sex went undiscovered. The nursery unpainted. The C-section unscheduled.

Of course, today of all days, Carmen thinks, pushing the cart out to the van. She had opted out of another C-section to avoid the scheduled date, which landed on the twins' birthday, only for her to go into labour on the day of their birthday party anyway.

Carmen drops the supplies in the trunk and stuffs the Minions balloons into the back seat. As the car warms up, she checks her messages.

<<How R U?>> reads a text from Dan.

<<I think today's the day!>> she texts back and waits a beat.

<<It's early!>> Dan writes. <<What do we do?>>

<<Keep going.>>

Dan texts her a thumbs-up emoji.

The show must go on.

At the grocery store, the woman at the bakery counter can't find Teo's cake order, and Toby's Minions cake already has his name scrawled across it.

"But I ordered it last week and confirmed yesterday!" Carmen cries, feeling another contraction coming on.

"Keep calm," the woman says, nervously eyeing Carmen's heaving belly. "I know just the trick. We can do this up for you. It'll take just a few minutes."

Carmen nods and moves aside to let the next customer through. Her phone rings, but she waits until another contraction subsides before she answers it. It's her mom.

"Is everything okay?" her mom asks when she calls her back.

"I'm having contractions, but hopefully it's just Braxton Hicks," Carmen says, trying to sound casual, as much for herself as for her mom.

"Are you still up for the party?"

"I have to be. Everyone will be at our house soon."

"Oka-ay," her mom says, doubtfully. "Call me if you need anything."

The woman behind the bakery counter nods at Carmen, and she comes over to peek inside the box. It's not Toby's artfully illustrated Minions cake, but it does have 'Happy Birthday Teo' spelled out in yellow and blue icing, along with Bob, Kevin, and Stuart figurines sitting atop a white cake.

"Thank you," Carmen says, breathing out.

"No trouble, dear," the woman says. "You take it easy."

Back home, Carmen carries the bags of supplies inside.

"We're not going to make it!" Dan panics, waving packages of hamburger and hot dog buns in the air. "Everyone will be here soon!"

"Hey, can you not be a diva? I'm the one having a baby here," Carmen snaps, dropping the bags and slamming the door shut behind her.

"Sorry, sorry," Dan says, rushing over and rubbing her back. "I'm just freaking out. Are you sure we shouldn't go to the hospital already?"

"It's the twins' birthday. We can't miss it. We've just got to get through the next few hours."

"Okay. What do you want me to do?"

"Get the barbecue going. People will be here any minute. And what happened to this place? Tyler, Toby, Teo, come and tidy up, now!" Carmen yells, carrying bags into the kitchen.

The kids tumble down the stairs, half dressed, scooping up toys and screaming orders at each other.

"Eww, Toby's underwear!"

"Tyler! Your shirt's here!"

"Teo, your Beyblade!"

Dan is setting up the barbecue and Carmen has started decorating for the party when the doorbell rings. Crossing paths in the hallway, Carmen and Dan give each other a nervous look. Surely not the guests?

"How can I help?" Carmen's mom asks when she opens the door.

Tears rise to Carmen's eyes, and she gives her mom a hug before closing the door behind her.

Twenty minutes later, Carmen opens the front door, looking pretty and fresh in a floral-print, long-sleeved dress. She calmly welcomes in the in-laws—her contractions, thankfully, abated. *Maybe it was just Braxton Hicks after all.*

With the party in full swing, Carmen and Dan grab each other's hand in passing. *Good job! We did it.*

As the evening comes to an end, the contractions start up again, more intensely this time, and Carmen decides it's time to go to the hospital. Her mom and the kids wave goodbye as Carmen and Dan pull out of the driveway. The sun is setting and the sky glows in shades of pink. Despite the pain, Carmen feels like crying, it's so beautiful. Just her and Dan together, like the morning before Tyler was born. Before everything changed forever. Carmen squeezes Dan's hand through the contractions.

In the hospital parking lot, Carmen can barely walk, doubling over through the contractions, which are coming on fast now. When they make it to the emergency desk, a roomful of eyes turn to her, but the receptionist turns them away.

"The maternity ward is that way," she says, pointing down a stark, empty hall that seems to wind on forever.

"'Scuse me," Dan says to a young orderly after they turn down a fourth wrong hall to no avail, with Carmen whimpering as she hobbles through the labyrinth, each double door leading them deeper into the abyss. "The maternity ward?"

"Oh, that's on the other side of the hospital," the orderly says, shaking his head. "You have to go all the way back down this hall, then turn right at the gift shop. Look for the sign that says Labour Assessment Unit. It will take you the rest of the way. It's a bit of a walk," he says, watching Carmen clench through another contraction.

"Like how far?" Dan asks, rubbing his chin and looking at Carmen doubtfully.

"Oh, about five minutes or so?"

"Can someone just get me a fucking wheelchair already!" Carmen cries out.

"Oh, right, sure!" the orderly says, and hurries off. When he comes back with the wheelchair, he keeps his hold on the handlebars and escorts them all the way to the maternity ward.

"Let's get you registered," the nurse at the desk says, waving Dan over to a chair beside her as another nurse guides Carmen into a room.

"You can take everything off and put this on," the nurse says, pointing to a folded hospital gown. "Then lie down. I'll be right with you."

When the nurse returns, Carmen is lying down with her knees clenched together. The nurse pushes them apart, flips up the bottom of Carmen's gown and sticks her arm in.

"Eight centimetres dilated," she reports, before popping Carmen's amniotic sac with what looks like a crochet hook. Warm liquid gushes out between Carmen's legs, and she is simultaneously ashamed and terrified before a rush of contractions block out any feeling but pain.

"Can you walk? We need to get you to the birthing suite," the nurse says.

A little late for that now, Carmen thinks as two nurses help her up and guide her to another room. The contractions make it impossible for her to stand up straight and she continues to leak as she hobbles over, her backside completely exposed.

"Can I get something for the pain please?" Carmen whimpers as they lay her down on the hospital bed.

"What's your name, hon?" one of the nurses asks, ignoring her request.

"Carmela Garcia," Carmen says, wondering why they are asking stupid questions when she is practically dying here. "Can I get some medicine now?"

"What's your birthday?"

"September eighteenth," Carmen says, panicking now. "Is the epidural on its way?"

"Smile for the camera!" Dan says, holding up his phone as he comes into the room.

"Shut it!" Carmen shouts back.

"Please," she says, turning back to the nurses. "Can you give me something for the pain?"

The nurses ignore her and look up as the doctor blows in to the room, waving his arms in the air and grinning ear to ear as if it were all one big joke.

"Carmela!" he calls out wryly. "VBAC?"

Carmen nods, doubting her choice for a post-Cesarian natural birth. Doubting the nurses for withholding pain relief. Doubting that anyone is looking after her best interests.

"High risk." He shakes his head, hardly quelling Carmen's fear. "You're lucky you didn't have this baby in the parking lot."

"Please, can I have something for the pain?" Carmen pleads.

"It's part of our protocol that we let you know about all the risks involved with a Vaginal Birth After C-Section. You're at risk of a uterine rupture. Complications include heavy bleeding for the mother, and it can be life-threatening for mother and baby. Sometimes, the uterus might need to be removed by hysterectomy to stop the bleeding. If your uterus is removed, you won't be able to get pregnant again. Do we have your consent to proceed?"

Another contraction takes Carmen's breath away, and it takes her a few moments before she can speak. The doctor waits while she sobs through her breaths.

"Sure, but please, something for the pain," Carmen groans weakly.

"It's too late for epidural," the doctor announces gleefully. "You're having this baby now!"

"No!" Carmen screams.

"Screaming's not gonna help, honey. You just need to push," orders the nurse.

Carmen feels a pressure that threatens to rip her in half. *And this is when I die.*

"Carmela?" the nurse asks as Carmen's eyes roll up to the ceiling. "Don't quit on me now. You're almost there. But you're holding on too tight. You need to let go."

Carmen looks at her hands, which are clenched. She breathes and releases them, feeling her whole body give in as she does so.

"Good, Carmela. Yes. Now push!"

Carmen grunts and bears down, pushing with all her might.

"You're doing great, babe!" Dan cheers. "Oh my god, the baby's coming!"

Carmen pushes a few more times.

"It's a girl!" Dan suddenly shouts, jumping up and down and laughing.

Carmen falls back from exhaustion as the doctor places the baby on her chest.

As the nurses clean her up, Carmen stares at her baby, enthralled. She remembers when the midwife placed Tyler on her chest when he was born, and how she shrank in horror at the tiny, squirming alien-like being before her. Dan was overjoyed and held him close, the bond between them instant. For Carmen it came six weeks later, with her baby's first smile.

The twins, born one month early, spent two weeks in the neonatal intensive care unit and it was days before she got to hold them in her arms—the moment too heartbreakingly brief, before she had to return them to their incubators.

This time, when the doctor places her baby on her chest, Carmen knows just what to do. She hugs her close, their bodies fitting right into place.

"You little witch," Carmen whispers, marvelling at her baby's tiny fingers and the strange magic that brought them here. How close it came to never happening. The spinning atoms, odds and chance that led to now. *A girl.*

"Isabella."

It occurs to Carmen that she has never felt more right, more whole, more complete, than she feels now, stroking Izzy's back as she lies in her infant hospital bed. All her pieces come together. Even her body feels healed.

A knock on the door interrupts the feeling, so that she pauses to savour the last wisps of it before turning to the door.

"Carmela?" her dad asks, ducking his head around the corner.

"Papi!" Carmen calls out, waving him in. She would have many more moments with Izzy. For now, she is happy to share.

Her dad and stepmom tiptoe over to the baby.

"Is she sleeping?" her dad whispers.

Carmen nods.

"Oh, Carmen, she's bea-u-tiful," Debbie coos, peering into the infant cot.

"She has some bruising still. It was pretty intense. It'll fade away," Carmen says, noticing that already she is self-conscious about her daughter's looks in a way that she wasn't with the boys. *What's up with that?*

"She's perfect," her dad assures her, looking down at Izzy.

"Wanna hold her?" Carmen asks.

Her dad nods his head, and Carmen gently picks Izzy up and places her in his arms.

"Isn't she the best?" Carmen asks, her nose tingling as she watches her dad melt before her eyes.

"Second best," he says, smiling down at Izzy's tiny body.

"So, you're not mad anymore?" Carmen asks, only half teasing.

Her dad shakes his head, and she can see that his eyes are wet too. "Why would you think I want anything other than for you to be happy?"

Carmen shrugs her shoulders and shakes her head. Truth is, she can't remember anymore either.

"Carmen, hija, I'm sorry if I ever made you feel like I was angry with you... I push you because I think you *are* amazing, not because I don't believe in you. I just don't want you and the kids to struggle the way your mom and I did. We just want you to be happy."

It doesn't change the past. It doesn't even make all the hurt go away. But it's a start. And she knows, this may be her and her own kids too, one day.

"I *am* happy," Carmen says as tears stream down her face. "I am the happiest girl in the world."

Chapter 32

Lying in bed, Ally tries to force her mind blank but still she can't sleep. Sam's side of the bed is empty, the blanket smooth and pillows undented as she left them this morning.

In her head, two stories battle it out, one a lingering doubt—that perhaps she's always had—and the other, a wisp of hope that this time might be different. That *they* might be. Which is the voice of reason, she isn't sure.

Ally rolls over and checks the time on her phone—12:20 a.m. She's usually asleep by now, resting for her six a.m. alarm and seven a.m. bike ride to work so she can be the first one in and get a head start on the day's work. But Sam hasn't called to wish her goodnight. And he still hasn't returned her call.

Where is he? No texts. No messages. Maybe his cellphone is dead after being at the conference all day. Except, Ally knows he has an early morning flight. She knows what can happen in Las Vegas.

Ally's head drops back onto her pillow. She can picture him now, swaying a little, as if to a song that only he can hear. A sheepish smile and mischief in his eyes. *Sorry, lost track of the time.*

She'd seen more of that Sam since "moving in together," as he called it, though Sam continued to keep his place in Seattle. Staying up waiting for him while he was out late with clients and colleagues from the Portland office. *Part of the job. Don't wait up for me.* Is this who she is now?

Though his expensive suits are taking up space in her closet, she is still absent from his life back in Seattle. He insisted it was just a place to crash when he needed to visit head office, but there is something about the arrangement she doesn't trust. Sometimes Ally wishes he would move the rest of his stuff in. Sometimes she feels like he is squatting on her life. *What's yours is mine and what's mine is mine.* She needs to know if she's being a fool.

Ally sits up and searches for the hotel number on her phone. She dials it and holds her breath while it rings, her heart racing. What if Sam's asleep and she wakes him up? What will she say? *I just called to say I love you?*

"You've reached Planet Hollywood Resort & Casino. How may I help you?"

"Sam Hutchins, please?" Ally says, her hands shaking.

"And who's calling, please?"

"Allison Parker."

"Please hold a moment."

Ally waits and then hears a click as the call connects.

"Hello?" a woman answers.

Ally's phone falls, smashing against the bedroom floor.

When the key turns in the lock, Ally is waiting on the couch, staring at the TV. The TV is off.

"What's going on? Why weren't you at the airport?" Sam asks, dropping his bags and closing the door behind him. His face is flushed, as if in the bloom of health, although Ally knows the truth. Knows it's a late night coupled with too many drinks.

"Ally?" he asks, when Ally doesn't answer. Despite running through what she would say when she saw him over and over in front of the mirror, in the shower, by the kettle, she's tongue-tied now. He looks different, taller, new. A stranger.

"Why didn't you answer the phone? I've been calling you," Sam says, walking to her.

Ally catches a whiff of smoke and honey. His face is unshaven, and his hair looks longer than she remembers it. Could she do this? Now? There is still time to pretend nothing happened. To keep the peace. Buy them time. She wants this so bad. Did she dare give it up? But what if?

"A woman answered the phone," she blurts out, not wanting to give herself the chance to talk herself out of it. She watches him, looking to see how he reacts as the words register. His eyes are soft and lips swollen, and if he lies to her now, she'll believe it. Anything to stop this from happening.

"A woman?"

Ally starts to doubt herself. Sam looks so confused she wonders whether she got the wrong room. The wrong number. Maybe she had imagined the whole thing.

"I called you," Ally says, wincing. The train had started up, and there was no stopping it now. Ally stares out the window, though the morning sun hurts her eyes. Anything to avoid his face and recall the things that made her fall in love with him in the first place.

"A woman answered the phone."

Sam steps back and slaps his forehead. "Oh God, I'm sorry! I should have said something as soon as I found out. Our company made a mistake and booked us a room together. I was so mad, I guess I forgot to tell you," he says, dropping down on the couch next to Ally.

Ally searches his face, trying to uncover the lie. She wants to believe and yet, the thought of his hands on someone else's hips ... somewhere deep inside, she knows. Perhaps she always even suspected.

"I only found out when we checked in," he says, wrapping his arm around her. "The hotel was already full, and we know each other so we figured, no harm, no foul. There was nothing I could do ..."

His eyes burrow into hers, willing her to accept. A struggle inside makes it hard for her to speak.

"Nothing happened," Sam insists, shaking his head. He strokes her arm, but his touch makes her cringe.

Ally pushes his hand away and gets up. She needs time to think, to process what he is saying. Is her fear real or imagined? Is she being paranoid or naive?

"Are you going to talk to me?" Sam pleads.

"Are you going to tell me the truth?"

Sam hesitates for a moment before throwing his head back on the couch and running his hand through his hair.

"Fuck. Okay, maybe some things happened," Sam admits.

Ally squeezes her hands into fists, wanting to scream and cry all at once.

"I had too much to drink. She was all over me," Sam says, patting the air with his hand as if to stop her. "What do you want?"

"It's her fault that you slept with another woman?" Ally whispers-screams, not wanting to alarm the neighbors.

"I didn't sleep with her!"

"Don't lie to me!"

"Okay, okay!" Sam says, covering his eyes. "I slept with her."

"Ugh!" Ally screeches, squishing her eyes shut to stop the picture from coming to her mind.

"I was drunk! It didn't mean anything!"

Ally shoots him a glare and throws a sofa cushion at him. "It means something to me!"

She stomps over to the window. Outside, the city is waking up to just another morning. Riding cars to work. Streetcars, buses, trains. Counting the hours until they return home. To someone they love. Someone who loves them back. Ally rubs her lips, trying to figure out how far she is willing to go. Fight or flight. *Do I stay or do I go?*

"Baby," Sam says, coming up behind her and putting his hands on her shoulders. "I was stupid. It was a huge mistake. I just missed you so much."

Ally turns and drops her head onto his chest. The sweet warmth of his body makes her want to give in. Stop the fight. He does love her, doesn't he? But how long will it last? And what will be left of her when it ends?

Ally plants her hands on his chest and feels a surge of energy move through her.

"Babe!" Sam says, stumbling back.

She pushes him back, back, back, all the way to the door. There was a time she might have fallen for it, denied it all on his behalf, but she is not that woman anymore.

"Get out," she says, opening the door.

"This is crazy!" Sam says, his face distorted in anger now, and Ally has a flicker of doubt. Before she can change her mind, she grabs his bags and tosses them out into the hallway.

"Out!"

Sam walks out and turns to face her. "Don't do this," he says, as if warning her.

Ally slams the door shut.

"Why are you doing this?" Sam calls out as Ally collapses to the floor, back against the door.

"Because I'm too old for this shit," she whispers to herself.

"Ally. Please," Sam says from the other side of the door, breaking her heart. "I love you."

Ally breathes out a sigh. Already the words have lost some of their power.

Chapter 33

C armen's a jumble of nerves as she pulls into the school parking lot. Still sleep deprived from nursing Izzy, she's a little delirious too—excited to introduce her new baby and also a little nervous to hear back from Alex on the yearbook she had emailed to her over the weekend. She's sure it's more than Alex or any of the moms expected, thanks to all her publishing experience. Still, she hadn't discussed her and Olivia's little pet project and she hopes the surprise is welcome.

"Carmen, come in," Alex says when Carmen reaches the door of the parent-teacher conference room. Though the meeting had been scheduled with Alex directly, the rest of the moms are present as well. Tanya gives Carmen a sympathetic smile and quickly looks away. Spread on the table are print-out copies of the yearbook she and Olivia have drafted up.

Carmen's stomach knots as she sets Izzy's car seat down on the glossy, tiled floor and takes a seat herself in the only chair left that's empty. She feels like the only one not in on a joke and wonders how all these mothers can feel so distant and disconnected when they've been through the same thing.

"We just wanted to thank you for all your contributions to the yearbook, but we'll be taking over from here," Alex says, sitting poker-faced across from Carmen. "It's just ... not what we had in mind."

Anger mixed with shame lights a fire in Carmen's belly as she looks away and glances down at Izzy, not sure what to do. The urge to argue feels like a scab she wants to pick, but she's terrified too. Afraid that something might break. Would Izzy let the world walk all over her, though, or fight back? She wants her to be a fighter.

"And what did you have in mind?" Carmen blurts out, daring Alex with her eyes.

Alex balks and turns to the other moms. Carmen starts to panic. She focuses on the yearbook lying in front of her. The sight of the young, hopeful faces makes her feel protective. For fun, Carmen and Olivia had gathered silly face selfies and bad jokes from the kids in the graduating class. They had put out a box to collect anonymous notes. Some kids had even submitted poems and drawings—some signed, some nameless. She wanted it to feel like it belonged to *them*—not to the moms around the table and their notions of what Grade 5 should look like.

"Kennedy is a school of excellence. The yearbook should showcase that," Alex finally says, letting out an impatient sigh.

"Is it so wrong to let kids be kids? To let kids be themselves?" Carmen lets out, though she' struggling to breathe. She wants to run, but she wants to right things at the same time. She wishes Alex would drop her veil of composure. She wishes the other moms would speak up. She wants them to argue out in the open. Anything but this passive aggressive cold shoulder.

"Carmen, this isn't college. It's not even high school. We have a chance here to really set an example," Alex says.

"But shouldn't we teach our kids to like themselves, and each other? Not force them to be something they're not?" Carmen pushes on. She is done with other people telling her what she should and shouldn't do. How big or small she should be. Or her daughter.

"The committee disagrees," Alex says, looking side to side at the other moms, who all look away under her gaze. "Kennedy is one of the top schools in the district. This is an opportunity to showcase that."

"Is this *your* yearbook or *theirs*?" Carmen fires back, feeling like she might pass out. Even if she loses this fight, she can still make a point. Show them there is another way.

"Go home, Carmen. I'm sure you have enough on your plate. Look after your family. Enjoy your baby."

The slight makes Carmen want to hit her, but she has no strength left. Her arms hang numb by her sides.

"What about Olivia? She worked so hard on this."

"We'll look after Olivia. We know she's innocent in all of this. She'll get the credit she deserves."

Carmen searches for words to say but none come to her. She gets up and grabs the car seat. A piece of her knew they wouldn't go for it, but a piece of her still had hoped. Had hoped there might be room for at least a little bit of something true.

Closing the door behind her, Carmen spots Olivia down the hall at her coat hook, putting books into her knapsack. Olivia looks up and smiles, and Carmen gives her a reassuring smile back. It may be just a flicker in her timeline, but Carmen hopes she remembers when this is all over. Hopes she remembers what it feels like to be free.

Thank God no one here knows me, Carmen thinks as she tries to shut out the mayhem the boys are creating. The baby is crying. The twins are screaming and giggling through the grocery store aisles, bumping into people and displays as Tyler chases after them, leaving boxes of cereal and cookies in their wake. She had thought taking them all to the grocery store on a PD day would be a great way to free up the weekend, so they could spend some quality time with Dan, who had been putting in long days at work. But bringing the kids is clearly a mistake.

Instead of herding them into a checkout line, Carmen focuses on the magazine rack, pretending her kids aren't hers, in spite of the other shoppers who are staring at her, waiting for her to do something.

What's your problem? Carmen thinks. *I'm the one who has to live with them.*

Some days she cherished her family's wild, quirky side, watching fondly as her boys climbed trees, chased each other with sticks, and wrestled on the rug. They were loud, unpredictable, and messy. Real, independent, and unique.

Sometimes she wished they would just fall in line and do exactly what she said when she said it, like Tyler's toy soldiers.

"Shh," Carmen says, bouncing Izzy up and down to soothe her as she moves her cart up the checkout line.

Carmen scans the magazine rack, eyes grazing over covers of tanned, toned bodies glowing like Greek gods, with cover lines that shout out "Win at Work!" "Hot and Happy!" "Live Your Best Life!" Carmen sucks in her tummy as she marvels at one celebrity's impossible curves and breathes a sigh of relief to see another star is still youthful-looking and gorgeous in her fifties—there is hope.

Carmen spots the latest issue of *Muse* and hesitates. She hasn't picked up the magazine since she was fired. A familiar feeling of shame washes over her, and her heart starts to race. She doesn't need to feel worse about herself and yet, she can't help reaching out to grab a copy.

Carmen holds her arms out high so as not to disturb a now-dozing Izzy and begins flipping through the pages. For a moment, she debates whether to look at the masthead, but her fingers are already taking her there. David now reigns at the top of the page as editor, and Carmen can't find Meredith's name anywhere. Turning to David's editor letter, her stomach drops.

Meredith. She had given her whole life to the magazine, only to be dumped, most likely because of her age. Perhaps it was fear all along that had made her the way she was. Did she know her head was on the chopping block? Had she been doing everything she could to hold on to her job as well?

Carmen would have done the same. She doesn't even blame her anymore. They were all throwing each other under the bus to gain an inch. She wishes she had known sooner. Wishes she could have made a difference.

And yet, here she is, still sitting on the offer from Arrow. Still toggling between their contract and all it promised, and her latest passion project, wondering which she should place her faith in.

Working on her blog and the school yearbook had given her an idea—to create a parenthood magazine like no other. Absent are the meal-planning guides, toy reviews, and room makeovers. Instead, she would include the kinds of stories she and other magazine editors would have turned down for being too out there, too controversial, too real.

Inspired by the kids' honest, vulnerable yearbook shares and the comments left by other moms on her blog, Carmen had already started drafting up articles, on postpartum depression and parenthood pet peeves, sex after childbirth, and how parents really feel about their kids. How sometimes they're afraid for their kids and sometimes they're afraid *of* them. How sometimes they're just afraid of themselves.

Her magazine wouldn't include just the angry parts, though, but the lovable ones too. And the fears, hopes, and desires. Just like the journals she wrote in growing up. Truth or dare.

Using fake bylines, Carmen feels a little like she's cheating, but figures that the end result—raw, authentic sharing—is what really matters. If it worked, she would get other women to share their stories. If it worked, she would put her name on it.

Unless she took the job at Arrow, that is. Then she would trade in all the cracked and bleeding motherhood stories for a shiny bright future moving up the corporate ladder. A road paved with money and fame, that would only open more and more doors once she walked through them.

Could she trade it all for her no-name, private label magazine? Is the price she will pay at home, with her family, worth it?

She doesn't want to miss the opportunity with Arrow, and yet, she isn't ready to give up Izzy and the boys, either, even if they do drive her crazy ninety-nine percent of the time. She wishes she could have both, in the best ways possible. The money *and* the freedom, without missing time with her family.

Anxious to hear another voice in her head, Carmen pulls her phone out and texts Ally, <<I miss you!>>

Waiting for a response, waiting to be told everything will be okay, Carmen keeps the phone in her hand as the young checkout girl begins scanning her groceries. No answer.

Carmen watches the cashier move through the groceries, her mind pulling herself to multiple places at once.

"Sorry, I won't be taking these," Carmen says, catching the extra boxes of Twinkies the boys had thrown in her cart and passing them over to the checkout girl.

"Do you have any lollipops?" Carmen asks. The girl nods and reaches under the cash register to pull out a tray. Carmen grabs all of them. "I'll be just a second," she says, leaving her cart behind to track down the kids.

"Boys!" Carmen shouts when she spots them in the soup can aisle. They freeze, guilty looks spread across their faces.

"We're going!"

The boys follow her back to the checkout counter and she gives them each a lollipop, which they suck on while hanging off the checkout railing as if it were a monkey bar set at a playground. Again, the looks from other employees and passersby. Again, the guilt and shame and wanting to disappear into the ether, the wishing she were as invincible as her avatar byline.

"Here, play with this. We're almost home," Carmen says, passing Tyler her phone to distract and subdue the kids as she places the last of the groceries on the checkout belt.

The twins gather round him and point, looking through Carmen's pictures on her phone.

"Awwww, so cute! What a cute baby!"

"Look at Teo's fat face. Teo was a fat baby!"

"I remember that beach house. Mommy, can we go back there?"

"Shh!" Carmen says, struggling to get the last packages from under the grocery cart. Even squatting until she is hovering just above the floor, it's still hard to reach the pizza boxes that have slipped to the middle part of the bottom tray, with the baby carrier in the way. If she has any dignity left, this visit to the grocery store is destroying it.

"Can I help?" a white-haired woman offers, lifting a pizza box and placing it on the belt.

"Oh, you're so kind, thank you."

"I remember those days. Still, four. You have your hands full. Can I help you with the rest?"

"I'm okay, but thanks," Carmen says, transferring the last of the items on to the checkout belt.

"Aren't you afraid to leave them with your phone like that?" the woman asks, nodding at the boys, who are giggling over the phone.

"I'm just trying to survive," Carmen confesses with a sigh as she digs around in the diaper bag for her wallet.

"Yes, well, good luck!" the woman says, with a smile and a wave.

"I'm going to need more than that," Carmen whispers under her breath, feeling more exposed than ever.

Carmen is emptying the dishwasher at home when she finally receives a call back from Ally. She debates picking up. She just finished putting away the groceries and doesn't have the energy to talk to her right now. All she really wants to do is go to bed already and sleep. Put decision making and laundry off for the rest of her life. Then again, maybe Ally would know what to do about Arrow.

"What's up? You texted?" Ally asks, and her let's-get-right-to-it tone makes Carmen want to get off the call already. What is her problem?

"Yeah, sorry, I was having a moment. I'm fine now, if you have to go."

"Have to go? I called you."

"Because I texted you."

"Whatever," Ally says with a sigh. "Anyway, I saw your Instagram posts. It's causing quite a stir."

"What do you mean?" Carmen asks, trying to put the dishes away as quietly as possible.

"The posts you published? People are going crazy over them."

"What posts?" Carmen asks, wondering if her blog had somehow gotten linked back to her, even though she'd left her name out of it.

"On Instagram. Didn't you hear me the first time?"

"I haven't been on Instagram lately. I've been a little *busy*," Carmen says, reaching up to slide the coffee cups into place.

"Well, if I were you, I'd leave the kids alone for a minute and see what's happening in the rest of the world."

Carmen cringes as a fork slips from her hand and clatters to the base of the dishwasher.

"What's that noise? Are you putting away the dishes *now*?"

"Oh yeah, sorry. I'm just afraid that if I don't do it now, I'll be too tired to do it later."

"Are you getting enough rest?"

"Probably not. Anyway, you were saying?"

"Are you listening to yourself? You're afraid you'll be too tired to put away the dishes? And can't you give me just five minutes of your time without catering to the kids or cleaning the house? Can you look at yourself right now? Like, really, don't I deserve a little more of your attention?"

Carmen feels whatever energy she has left drain out of her. All this judgement, all this resentment, like being beaten with a stick. She wants to remind Ally of all the times she fucked up. Getting blackout drunk at parties while Carmen fended off high school seniors with ill intentions. Who held Ally's hair away from her face while she puked her guts out over the toilet bowl? Who stayed with her through the night until she could stand on her feet long enough to walk home?

"You know, that's easy to say when you don't have anyone else to look after," Carmen says, knowing she's delivering a hit to Ally directly where it hurts most. "And for your information, I spend like six hours a day in the kitchen, so I basically live here. I can't just shut it all off every time you call."

"Are you saying I don't matter because I don't have kids? Because it sure feels that way right now."

"Oh, Ally, give it a rest. What do you want? To stare into each other's eyes while you tell me all about your latest breakup?"

"How did you know?"

"About what?"

"Sam and I. We broke up."

Fuck, Carmen mouths, throwing her head back. "Oh, Ally, I'm so sorry."

"Whatever. What do you care anyway? It's not like you ever ask."

Carmen checks herself, about to relent. It's true, she recognizes. She is so caught up in her own drama, she hardly pokes her head above the waters she is drowning in long enough to notice other peoples' suffering. But then she remembers Alex, *Muse,* and she wants to keep fighting.

"What about you? When was the last time you visited anyway?"

"Wow."

"Yeah, wow," Carmen says, and the sensation of something breaking feels good.

"So that's how you feel, huh?"

"That's how I feel, Ally."

"Well, I guess that's that."

"I guess that's that," Carmen says, wondering how she let it get this far, but also relieved. One less person to worry about. And really, what do they even have in common anymore, anyway? What are they hanging on to? Is whatever it is even worth it? It's not like she has time to waste.

"You know, I always knew your world revolved around your family. I guess I just never realized that you didn't care about anyone else. Until now."

"Ugh! You're so selfish and self-righteous, you can't even imagine what it is to be me," Carmen says, each word feeling like a punch she wants to throw. At Carrie, David, Meredith, the world. She feels like breaking something. Anything. So she thinks of the worst thing she can say, pulls her elbow back and delivers the blow. "You're just mad because, unlike your loser boyfriends, I'm always there for you. I'm all you've got."

"Yeah, Carmen. Keep telling yourself that," Ally says, hanging up.

Carmen looks down at her phone, trying to remember how they got to this moment. Then she remembers what Ally said.

Clicking on her Instagram profile, Carmen's heart begins to race as she recognizes the photos, one by one. Moments captured and kept, just for fun, just for her and the kids. Pictures the kids had taken too that she didn't even know were there—Dan's plumber crack, puffy eyed and hungover and drinking an Alka seltzer after a late night of record playing. Carmen before her morning coffee, scrunchy-faced and pouchy-bellied in her PJs. Kids making faces instead of smiling politely for the camera, wielding toy guns and swords while wearing Halloween masks like some slaughterhouse horror movie. Carmen pleading, then yelling. All the pictures she scrapped before choosing the best one, cropping, filtering and posting with a clever aside. To top it all off, there's a video of her Christmas fight with Dan. One of the kids must have been spying on them and filmed it.

Adrenaline surges as the realization sets in that the boys must have posted them by mistake when they were playing with her phone at the grocery store. Now those bloopers—her life—are out there for the world to see. Now the world would know what kind of mother, wife, *person*, she really is. There is no more hiding and pretending now. Not anymore.

Chapter 34

A lly wakes up. It's her eyes that open first, before her mind comes to. And when it does, she immediately recognizes a throbbing headache.

"Ow," she groans, gently touching the back of her head.

And then she remembers.

Ally slowly turns her head, making out the body lying beside her. *Oh God, no. Did I?*

The night is a blur. After stomping around her apartment all day, mad at Sam, mad at Carmen, mad at herself, she had decided to go out, instead of being alone in her apartment, and in her head.

As much as she wanted to forget Sam, she wanted to punish him too. So she showered, put on her red dress that he loved and grabbed a taxi to Cava. She would show him. That she could be happy without him. That she mattered.

How many drinks did she have after that? She tries to remember, but the count is blurry. She remembers distinctly ordering three gin and tonics, but then the shots began, and everything is fuzzy after that.

Including exactly how she ended up in bed with Jeff, the jerk her friend Amanda tried to set her up with, back in Maine.

Did he spot her at the bar? Or did she see him first? Who was he with again and what happened to them?

Ally remembers his surprise. Her dress had clearly captivated him, and she felt grateful and warmer toward him and happy to see him. As if she were bumping into an old friend. All was forgiven.

They drank shots, and got sloppy together, perhaps on purpose. Perhaps both knowing where this would lead. A small piece of her wished Sam could see her having so much fun with someone else. Like someone she used to be. Just one of the guys, always up for a good time.

Ally can't remember who suggested going home to whose place—Jeff was in town, visiting a friend. After that—nothing.

And now this.

Ally reaches for her oversized T-shirt that's lying on the floor, slides out of bed, and creeps out of her room.

She boils water for tea, rubbing her face as she tries to figure out an exit strategy for Jeff. Does she wake him up? Or does she leave a key under the door mat and ask him to lock up after he goes? She doesn't want to see him again.

Making her tea, she assesses the damage. Their clothes are strewn throughout her apartment. Instead of feeling smug and satisfied, though, she feels gross and used up. She wonders who she is really hurting—Sam or herself. And what's the point, either way?

Now she's just another notch in Jeff's bedpost. He got exactly what he wanted, Carmen would say. And what did she want, exactly?

She only seems to be getting further and further away from the truth.

"How are you, Dad?" Ally asks, her voice sounding loud and coarse. She is the one who called him, and yet she feels annoyed. It doesn't help that she's sitting on a restaurant patio alone, back to her table-for-one status. Just her, a Caesar salad, and a front row view of the ocean. Talking on the phone with her sunglasses on makes her look less lonely, she hopes.

She'd already tried her mom, but she was off having the time of her life with her new boyfriend. Ally couldn't call Carmen. Which left ...

"Ally! It's great to hear your voice. How are you?"

"I'm good," Ally lies. *I just broke up with the man I was going to spend my life with, or so I thought. Again.*

"You been on the water lately?"

"No, Dad. I don't get to do much field work anymore with my new job."

"That's a shame. I know how much you love it. Remember when I thought I was going to have to sell the boat, and you ran away, and we found you sleeping inside? God, you gave me the scare of my life. You said you were going to live on that boat forever."

"I remember," Ally says softening. There's pain in the memory but love too.

"Listen, the Hamilton Island regatta is happening this summer, and, well, I thought it'd be fun for us to go together."

Ally sucks in her breath. A part of her wants to. A part of her can't seem to let go.

"If money is an issue, I can help you with your ticket if you want," her dad says, and the vulnerability of his voice makes her heart break.

"Money's not the problem, Dad."

"Then what is?"

"Time."

There was a time when all she wanted was his love and attention, she thinks. Unfortunately, that time has passed.

"Huh," her father says, half-chuckling. "Isn't it always, though."

"What's that?"

"Nothing. Well, I hope you can make some time for your ol' dad one of these days. I won't be here forever, you know."

"I know, Dad."

"I know I haven't always been there for you, Ally. Your mom and I, we're just a couple of kids with gray hair and new knees, looking for answers just the same as you. That doesn't change the fact that I care about you. And I miss you. I love you, girl."

And the way he says it, the way he's always said it, makes her choke as if she's trying to hold back a dam of tears.

"I know, Dad. I love you, too."

Something inside her still wants to hurt him. Only when she does, it feels like she's hurting herself too.

Chapter 35

Carmen slaps another magazine on top of the fire, her last issue with *Muse*, with Mizz B on the cover. She recalls Carrie coming back from the photo shoot, setting the team abuzz as she put cover mock-ups up on the wall. Playing a part in Mizz B's transformation from underground sensation to mainstream star had brought the team together. Made them feel like they too were creating magic and reaching the stars. Even a jaded Carmen could feel the excitement, like anything was possible, even a former stripper's wildest dreams. Now she can see it for the lie that it was. The lie that *she* is.

"What are you doing?" Dan asks, peering out into the darkness in his pyjamas.

Carmen turns to him, tears streaming.

"I'm saying goodbye."

White rabbits erupt from the chiminea and drift off, mixing with the stars. The smell of wood burning is earthy and ancient.

Dan walks over and gives her a hug, which she sinks into, gratefully. "Want me to stay with you?"

"Naw, I need some time alone." Carmen pulls away and waves him off. "Go to sleep; I'll be fine." Dan obliges and heads back inside.

Carmen raises her flute in salute to the past. It had been a decent run. Sparks clap at the top of the pyre.

Burn, baby, burn.

Carmen's pics had gone viral. Become memes. A movement. Mothers everywhere posting their best worst motherhood moments in response.

At first, the attention was unsettling. Even after she deleted the photos, the reverberations rippled on. Carmen was fearful to leave the house, talk to the other moms at school. She felt exposed, raw, embarrassed. Of course there was judgement. Cold shoulders and cruel comments. But there were white flags too. Pats on the back and DM acknowledgements. "Same here." "I can sooo relate." "Thank you!" And she didn't die of shame, even though she thought she might. In fact, she got stronger.

Arrow was not impressed, though. She had gone too far. This was not the vision of motherhood they had signed up for. This was not a table of contents of glossy solutions, slickly edited by someone who was never home to make dinner in the first place. This was motherhood, for real, and they did not like it, not one little bit.

So they retracted the offer.

"The client has decided to go in a different direction. I'm sure you understand," Emily explained.

What am I doing? Carmen thought as she listened, watching rain drops land on the van through her bedroom window. Just a gray sky, no relief in sight. The tire sensors needed replacing, spots for camp were filling up, and the line of credit was maxed out, again. Success could not come soon enough.

If only she had accepted the offer straight away. If only she hadn't been distracted by her little projects. She might have started scrubbing her life to live up to the image Arrow was buying into, of a good mother, one who could masterfully balance both a high-powered career *and* a perfect family and look impeccable while pulling it all off.

All Carmen could do was stare at her screensaver after Emily hung up. A photo of her three boys silhouetted against a setting sun as they dipped into the lake for an evening swim. Even if she had taken the job at Arrow, the kids wouldn't wait, would they? They would just keep on growing, and then one day leave her, off to make their own dreams come true. Quality time with her family isn't something she could stage, like some home for sale. Perfectly timed moments tied up in neat little vignettes. It is every day, here and now. Making the kids a snack after school and chauffeuring them from activity to activity while hearing about their day. It is cuddles in her bed in the morning, and their beds at night. It is taking time with bedtime stories and lineups at the mall. And if she had to rush through that, then she missed it all, didn't she? And she would never have that time back.

Still, God had sent her a lifeline, and she had messed it up. Would they lose the house? Would the kids suffer? She has just lost the offer of a lifetime, her last chance to recover her career, perhaps. And yet every fiber of her being resists it. A steely reserve is building inside of her, something immovable, inflexible, non-negotiable. Something she doesn't quite have control over. A secret Id that doesn't bend to the whims of fear or shame. A hungry something. A fighter. A stander upper. A mother.

"I don't want to go back," she had confessed to Dan, after the offer came in from Arrow. A six-figure salary. Benefits. Four weeks vacation. Summer hours. A dream job. More than she could ever have hoped for. All she had to do was sign on the dotted line.

"I don't want you to," Dan had said, pulling her in closer and nuzzling into the crook in her neck.

Maybe God had heard that too. Maybe it was a gift after all. The rejection. Another closed door. There were so many stories that she wanted to tell. The world was full of them. The sadness and the beauty. The spaces in between. It was all life's great work. She was ready to promise herself to them.

Looking up after Emily's call to retract the offer, she noticed, as if for the first time, her framed magazine covers.

Sitting in the heat of the fire, Carmen can feel the anxiety creep up again, the mounting to-do list, the choking doubt. Her old life is dead to her now and yet isn't she too old to start over? She has no right to follow flights of fancy. The time for achieving impossible things is long past.

Purpose has finally found her, though. Cruelly, at a time when she has the most to lose.

Carmen wonders if she is chasing a mirage, deliriously moving further away from the very shores that can save her. But the thought of not seeing the magazine through makes it difficult for her to breathe. Giving up would turn her into a ghost of herself, and what kind of mother would that make her?

So, she gives in. Lets the past go. Let's Meredith, Arrow, *life*, pull the trigger. The way, deep down, Carmen wanted them to.

She is done pretending her life is perfect. Pretending everything is okay. She is done trying to fit into a mold others created for her. Or thinking anything less is anything less.

There would be no more hiding. No more lying and sneaking. She would own it, all of it.

There's no more anger. No more shame. The red fury turned to ash. Stars sparkle like jewels in the dark sky.

No more back door. No looking back. She would embrace the unknowable, uncontrollable future with open arms and open heart and welcome it in.

Whatever it holds, it is hers now, and hers alone.

Chapter 36

S tupid, stupid, stupid! You're gonna die out here. Alone, in the desert, Ally thinks as her legs grow weak. Her tongue is thick and velvet-like in her mouth. She pulls at her sweat-drenched tank top for relief, but the shifting only angers the bruises on her back.

Another mistake, bringing steel water bottles instead of a drip bag. Her worst nightmare is coming true. She had wasted precious drops cooling off her face and head in the late morning sun. Had miscalculated how much water to bring, how long the hike would take her. And now she is going to die in the middle of the desert, and no one will even notice.

"I am not going to die," Ally says out loud, glancing around again to see if she can spot anyone in the distance. Nope, nothing but sagebrush for miles and miles. *Yes, you are.*

Panic continues to build as the midday sun bears down on her. It is hotter than usual for this time of year. What she thought would take three hours to hike instead took six, hopping from lava rock to lava rock and trying not to trip over cobbled paths along the canyon rim. The Owyhee River below, impossible to access, teases her. She had burned through her water supply in half the time, and there is no water source anywhere near her—not that she can reach, anyway.

Ally turns to her mindfulness app mantras for affirmation. *I am one with the universe. The universe loves me. The universe will provide.* She had made so many mistakes. Maybe *she* is the screwup. Maybe she had overreacted with Sam. With Carmen. Maybe she had pushed them all away. And now her worst nightmare is coming true: Dying alone, with no one to save her.

Ally pulls a Ziploc bag out of her pocket and unfolds the sheet of paper, checking her map of the Oregon Desert Trail against the view all around her. None of it reminds her of the features on the map. And although the GPS tracker on her iPhone is working, she forgot to download the base map. Once again, the compass clipped to her watch tells her she's headed in the opposite direction of where she wants to go. How could she get it all wrong?

C'mon. Keep going. You're almost there.

Ally forces her body to carry on through the desert, hot, angry tears streaming down her face. She feels like she's climbing a mountain, against the wind, the air thick as molasses. Her body screams for water and rest, rest, rest.

Just a little break, her body begs, but Ally knows that if she stops now, it will be that much harder to get going again. Yet the relief when she drops her pack is so overwhelming, she almost doesn't care. Looking at the parched earth around her, she thinks about dumping the water filter in the bag, out of spite. *No water in a desert, silly.*

"Help!" she shouts weakly to no one in particular. "Help!"

Get back up, she says to herself after checking the bottles for any last drops. Her body refuses to move.

"Up!"

Reluctantly, knees bend and legs straighten. The backpack feels like the weight of the world. A step forward. Orbs of light blink before her, making it hard to see, and she reaches out her arms, as if they could stop her from falling.

"Sssssssssssssssssssss."

A rattlesnake comes into focus, and Ally screams and jumps back. Her racing heart makes her break out in another wave of sweat, and she panics over her growing thirst.

"Fuck, fuck, fuck!" she screeches at the dessert, the skies, herself. "Can I get a fucking break here! Please!"

Breathe. Breathe. Please don't lose it. You can do this. You have to.

Ally focuses on the horizon to steady herself and notices a dark smudge growing in the distance. *Could it be?* Ally wonders as she strains her eyes to make out the figure, afraid to blink even. *Thank you,* she praises the heavens, when she finally recognizes a woman walking toward her.

"You're the first person I've seen today," the woman says brightly, her gray hair pulled back into a ponytail half-hidden by her hat.

"Please tell me you have some water," Ally begs.

"Here, you can have some of this," the woman says with a pitying smile as she passes a bottle to Ally.

"Thank you ..." Ally takes a few deep gulps from the bottle.

"Beverly."

"Thanks, Beverly. I'm Ally," she says, reaching out to shake her hand. Ally nods to the woman's pack. "I thought I brought enough. How'd you get it all to fit?"

"Oh! My husband Mike is carrying the rest of our stuff," Beverly says, pointing behind her. "Aren't husbands the best?"

"Sure," Ally says, passing the bottle back. "But it's not like you can get one at Walmart."

Beverly smiles. "You keep it, hun. Mike's on his way with more. Follow that canyon, about a couple of miles in, and there's a ranch with a cow tank where you can fill up."

"Thanks, and thanks for this," Ally says, waving the bottle in the air. Beverly waves back and walks away.

As Ally watches Beverly shrink in the distance, she can't help but think, *What am I doing here? What am I doing here—alone?*

"What's the fucking point?" Ally says to herself, looking around her.

Off in the distance, Ally spots another smudge. As the new figure comes into focus, she notices a growth the size of a boulder on its back. *Mike, the water mule?* Ally cackles to herself. Well, at least she isn't carrying anyone else's baggage. Not anymore, anyway.

"Lucky girl!" Ally calls out as Mike approaches, nodding in Beverly's direction.

"I'm the lucky one," Mike says with a smile, and Ally wishes that anyone she ever loved felt the same way about her.

"You good?" Mike asks, hesitating before he walks on.

Ally nods, convincing herself.

"Sure?" Mike says, checking for someone that's not there.

"Sure."

Mike nods and continues on.

Fuck it, Ally thinks, watching Mike disappear in the distance. She didn't need anyone. She'd only ever had herself to count on. So why did she keep looking for someone else's coattails to hang on to? *She's* the one who stepped up and raised herself while her parents were off figuring out life and finding themselves. *She* put herself through school. *She* built her career on her own merit. She even dehydrated and packaged her own food for her eight-mile hike through the Oregon desert. She isn't just a pretty face. She has beauty *and* brains, and the college degrees to prove it.

I am a survivor. I am triumphant, she tells herself, holding her head a little higher as she finds new strength in her stride.

She might not know what she is doing. Or where she is going. But at least, now, *she* is leading the way.

Ally takes a step forward and feels lighter somehow. She would forgive and forget. She would move on. She would stop waiting. She would buy a place on her own. Maybe even a boat. She didn't need anyone. She could do it all herself. And if, when, she met someone new, it would be on *her* terms. It is her party, and she is done crying.

Back at her car, Ally takes a moment to relish the shade of a cottonwood tree, drinking from a fresh bottle of water. She made it. Everything would be fine.

"You have one new message," her phone tells her, as she checks her voicemail. Three missed calls from her mother. *What now?*

"Ally, it's your mother. Call me back as soon as you can, okay?" Mom's voice on the message says.

Getting into her car and waiting for the A/C to take effect, Ally debates whether to call her mom back now or after she's had time to settle and eat at the campground. What if it really is urgent? Ally calls her.

"Where have you been? I've been trying to reach you all day."

"I can see that," Ally says, eyeing the orange canyon walls behind her in her rearview mirror as she reverses out of the trailhead parking spot. "I had my phone on airplane mode, to conserve the battery. I've been hiking. In the desert."

"Alone?"

"Of course. Who else would I be here with?" Ally says, shifting into Drive and making her way out of the lot.

"Oh, Ally, you know that I really wish you wouldn't."

"Mom, can we talk about this later?"

"Oh baby, I'm sorry, it's just ... there's something I have to tell you. I just ... I hate to tell you like this ..."

Ally can hear her mom choking on a sob and her heart starts to race as she slowly merges on to the paved road.

"It's your dad," her mom says. Ally's heart begins to pound. "He had a heart attack."

Ally brakes suddenly and a car behind her honks.

"Ally, he's gone."

Chapter 37

Carmen is shopping online for clothes for Tyler's Grade 5 graduation party and music recital. Scanning shipping options, she glances at the family calendar on her desktop. She had all year to prepare and yet here she is, having to pay extra for shipping express because she had left it to the last minute—again.

Izzy stirs on the bed beside her and Carmen holds her breath, wanting her to wake up, wanting her to stay asleep. Suddenly not caring about anything else at all other than those tiny hands, those perfect feet.

The phone rings, interrupting the peace and quiet like a record scratch. Carmen picks up the phone to see the call display reveal Ally's number.

For a moment, her heart stops. They haven't spoken in weeks, since their fight. Carmen wonders what she might want. She's afraid of another confrontation. Should she just let it go to voicemail? Then she notices the time: it's only 7:15 a.m. on the West Coast. Ally never called this early. Her heart starts beating again, harder this time.

Carmen gently places Izzy in her bassinet without waking her, and tiptoes out of the room, shutting the door behind her. She knows she's developing a bad habit of letting her fall asleep in their room, in their bed. But she loves cuddling her to sleep, and Izzy is her last baby. She wants to treasure every minute of it.

"Hello?" Carmen breathes softly into the phone, peeking at Izzy from behind the curtained doors to her room.

"Ally?"

Silence.

Carmen swallows. "Ally, is everything alright?"

Another pause. Carmen thinks she can hear Ally struggle for breath.

"My dad," Ally says, in a raspy whisper. "He's gone. He had a heart attack."

Ally's voice is shaking. Carmen doesn't know what to say. Everything seems trite. There's too much hurt here. She's not good at this.

They've been here before.

Wandering among the oak trees on the far side of the school yard at lunchtime, kicking at the amber- and rust-colored leaves like so much nostalgia on the ground. The way she said it, quiet, trembling, Carmen knew she must have been holding it in for a while—days, weeks maybe. They had been talking about boys. Carmen had a crush on quiet, freckled Noah. Ally liked the loud and boisterous Jason, even though he smothered Ally's face in the snow that winter, as a joke.

"He's such a jerk," Carmen had declared. "I don't know why you like him."

The bell rang, and when Carmen started off in direction of the doors, Ally held back.

"Hey, I'm sorry. I didn't mean anything against you ..." Carmen backpedaled.

"My parents are getting a divorce," Ally blurted out, her big blue eyes pleading.

Carmen searched for something to say, noticing for the first time the mole beneath Ally's right eye, or was it a freckle? Sun streaming through the trees picked out the strawberry streaks in her blond hair. *How pretty,*

Carmen thought. She hadn't seen it before, or maybe something about Ally had changed, and she had been too busy to recognize it. She felt self-conscious, all of a sudden, of her glasses and see-through braces, which weren't as invisible as they promised to be and frequently sliced the inside of her mouth.

She knew she was supposed to do something, put her arms around Ally and console her. That it was what Ally would have done. But instead, her body tightened, her arms lay heavy by her sides. Carmen could hear laughter in the distance and looked away. She wanted to join the fun. She didn't want to be here. She felt like a tourist, vulgar and intruding on someone else's grief.

She should have known better, having been through it herself. Did she tell someone? She didn't remember. She didn't think so. Instead, she tucked it up somewhere small and cast it out. The fear of losing a parent. The desperation of not knowing what comes next. Opening a door to catch her mother crying on the edge of her bed. Closing the door and pretending not to notice. Pretending it was all okay. Until one day it was.

When Carmen glanced back at Ally, she was wiping her nose with the back of her hand. Her shoulders looked small, vulnerable, in her fall jean jacket.

"C'mon, we're gonna be late," Carmen said, tugging at Ally's sleeve. She offered her an earphone from her yellow Sony Walkman, and they walked together, listening to INXS' "Never Tear Us Apart." The throbbing of the synthesizer, the wail of the sax, seemed to sing just for them. A gust of wind scattered the leaves. It was the first time Carmen witnessed Ally cry, and the last. Until now.

"I'm so sorry," Carmen says into the phone. *Weak*, she thinks. Why isn't she capable of more? First their fight, and now Ally is struggling with this loss on her own. *And that's the best you can do?*

"Thanks," Ally says.

"What can I do?"

"Nothing. I'll be fine. I just ..."

Carmen tries to find the right words to ease Ally's pain. Deep down, she wants to say, "I'm coming over." She wants to say, "Come home." She wants to say, "Everything will be okay." But it's not that easy. There's soccer practice tonight and dinners to cook, and Tyler's recital to prepare for, not to mention his graduation party next week, plus her magazine to keep going and growing too. It all seems so trivial by comparison, and yet they are paramount *to her*. Then there is the terrible truth, that nothing she can say or do will bring him back.

"Are you sure you're going to be okay?" Carmen asks, still searching for a way to fix it all, and coming up empty.

"It's fine. Really. I'm fine."

"Okay," Carmen says softly, somewhat relieved to be let off the hook. "Look after yourself. I'll call you later, okay? Love you."

"Love you."

The call ends, but Carmen rubs her forehead, something still tugging at her, refusing to hang up. She couldn't possibly afford to fly out. Just the thought of the mess she'd be leaving behind makes her mind reel. But even if Ally could come stay with her, Carmen wouldn't be able to drop everything, now, could she? Would she?

Chapter 38

*T*here's a crack at the window. And another. And another. Ally climbs out of bed and opens the window.

"Ally! It's me, Carmen! Open the door."

Ally quietly pads out of her room and down the stairs to the front door, trying not to wake her mom. It reminds her of her high school days, when she would sneak out after curfew and sneak back in before sunrise, not that her mother ever noticed when she was gone or even seemed to care where she went.

"What are you doing? You're supposed to get married in—" Ally looks at her watch, "Sixteen hours?"

"I'm not going through with it. We had a fight. Dan wants me to change my last name like I never even existed. My parents are fighting over the seating arrangements. It's a disaster. None of this is about getting married or being in love or Dan or me. It's too much. I can't," Carmen says, reaching for her throat.

"Hey, hey, it's okay," Ally says, patting Carmen's shoulder and leading her over to the living room sofa. The tufted design and roll arms look out of place among the cheap floorboards and chipped drywall of her mom's two-bedroom apartment above a corner store. Ally hates coming home, but she agreed to stay an extra week because Carmen begged her to be there for the rehearsal dinner, a whole week before Carmen's wedding day, even

273

though that meant postponing the date she was scheduled to defend her PhD thesis. She can't wait to get out of here and back to Augusta, where she is not her history—her broken family and party girl reputation— and instead is known for being smart, capable, and accomplished. "You don't have to do anything you don't want to do."

"I don't want to get married," Carmen says, shaking her head.

Ally takes a moment before she answers. The right thing to do would be to tell Carmen these are just last-minute jitters, but competing for her attention is the thought of how nice it would be to have Carmen all to herself again and how they could Thelma and Louise it, travelling the world, rocking their respective industries and casting off lovers, never having to be afraid of being alone because they would always have each other. They could be the family she never had and always wanted.

"You're right, it's probably a mistake. Marriage isn't for everybody," Ally says, nodding her head. Indeed, the older she got, the more she believed it, her own dreams of everlasting love still eluding her. She had already had her share of college relationships that quickly fizzled into nothing. Now she had something brewing with her supervisor, though at her last visit to his office she spotted a photo of his wife and two girls and that just made him seem sad and desperate. She needed to end it, whatever "it" was. "Listen, why don't you come and stay with me in Maine. Take some time to figure things out. Hell, maybe we could go somewhere else altogether. We could go to Hawaii ..."

"I love Hawaii ..."

"Or Spain. We could look up those two guys, see if they want to take us for a ride again," Ally says with a wink, making Carmen laugh.

Carmen's face falls, and Ally knows it's not going to happen.

"I'm scared. What if it doesn't work out? What if we don't? You and I both know that they don't always stay together. It's not always a happy ending."

Ally takes Carmen's hand. "It is for you," she says, her voice cracking. "Listen. I'm scared too. But remember what you said to me? You and Dan don't have to turn out like our parents. We don't."

"Do you really think so?"

Ally thinks about it, searching for the truth. For a moment she actually believes it. Ally nods.

"Besides ..." she says with a smile. "I dare you."

In the morning, Carmen's three moms swoop in like a SWAT team, whisking Carmen off to her hair and makeup appointment, leaving Ally holding the door, and her secrets.

Hours later, in the limo to the chapel, Carmen sits fanning herself, beads of sweat trickling down her hairline.

"Can you turn up the A/C, please?" Ally asks the limo driver.

"It's broken," he says.

"Oh God, I think I have diarrhea," Carmen says, clutching her stomach. "We have to stop. Pull over."

All three women—Carmen's mom, stepmom, and future mother-in-law—stare at Ally with terrified looks on their faces.

"Look at me," Ally says, grabbing Carmen's chin. "You're just having a panic attack. You are not going to poop yourself. You're going to calm down and marry Dan and live happily ever after. Okay?"

Carmen nods back, keeping her eyes locked on Ally's.

"*Breathe,*" *Ally says, leading by example. She takes a big breath in and lets a big breath out, and Carmen follows suit.*

"*Good,*" *Ally says, and everyone in the limo lets out their breath. "Again.*"

At the chapel, waiting for their cue, Ally smooths out Carmen's Spanish-style white lace wedding dress, admiring how resplendent her best friend looks.

The hall's wedding organizer scuttles toward them. "We're ready for you, Carmen."

Ally takes Carmen's train in her hands and Carmen looks back at her, shaking her head. "I can't."

"*You have to. You love him.*"

"*I do love him, but it's not enough.*"

"*You love him. That is enough. That's all you need.*"

Carmen slowly turns and faces the chapel doors as they open, and the crowd looks toward her. Ally waits for her to start walking, but Carmen is frozen in her spot. Ally checks in with herself. It would be so easy to end it. To take her friend's hand and run away, disappear. But deep down, Ally knows Carmen wants this. Loves Dan. That it's just their shared history jutting itself between them.

A surge of energy rises inside her and before she knows what she's doing, Ally gives Carmen a gentle push forward. Carmen stumbles but Ally catches and steadies her. She takes her hand and gives her a reassuring look as they walk down the aisle together.

Passing Carmen off to her dad, Ally falls in line behind them.

After the ceremony and photos, while everyone is seated in their place, glasses clinking, Ally gulps down the rest of her champagne and gets up to walk to the mic and make her speech, her hands shaking.

"Despite Carmen's momentary lapse of sanity ..." Ally says, and the room erupts into laughter, which makes her feel even more buzzed. "She is the best friend a girl could ever ask for. Carmen, you are beautiful and brilliant, and I look up to you so much. And Dan, if you ever screw this up, I will hunt you down and kill you."

Dan and Carmen chuckle, and the rest of the room laughs along.

"I'm not kidding."

There's an awkward silence, and Ally can hear her heart thumping in her ears.

"Congratulations, my friend. You deserve all the happiness in the world. And just so you never forget it ..." Ally says, stepping close to Carmen. Ally grabs her hand and slides on a plastic pink ring. "I will always be your best friend."

Chapter 39

Seventy-five minutes. It used to be she couldn't run forty minutes without her body giving up. Now Ally could run all day, all night. If it meant she could keep the clock running. If she never had to sit alone in her apartment, again.

Jogging back from the waterfront park trail, she had passed some young boys trading cards on a park bench. It reminded her of summer days that seemed to last forever. Classroom mornings that dragged on. Now time was numbers on a spreadsheet, projects completed. All the while, her internal clock ticking, a countdown to nothing. Month after month of periods, and how much time left? How quickly could she make it happen? The boyfriend, the house, the pregnancy test, the baby shower. Looping calculations calibrated against her daily relationship status. Where is her fairy tale ending?

Waiting at a red light, alongside a young father pushing a stroller, Ally is surprised that she ever thought she had so much time. Time to make the life she hoped for happen. Time to heal. Time to rebuild the life she lost. Time to forgive. Time to get to know her dad again. Ally's throat closes up and she swallows down a sob.

Goddamn time.

The light turns green, and Ally jogs ahead, trying to outrun the past.

If only she'd had one more chance to talk to him ... and yet, what would she have said? Thanks for nothing? Why did you leave? Why didn't you come back for me?

Then it happens again. The closing up of her throat. The heaving of her chest. The reason she left home in the first place. *Breathe.*

Ally concentrates on the sidewalk to escape what's in her head. The bubble gum stains, spit and left-behind dog shit. A garbage truck makes a crashing *sis-bum-ba!* The scent of something spoiled wafts her way.

Crumbling facades. Pockmarked roads. The lonely and forgotten napping in doorways between cardboard sheets. It's just a matter of time before they are kicked out from here, before the buildings on these streets are replaced by something shiny and new.

Ally eases up her pace as dark alleys are replaced by tree-lined avenues. Set piece cafés. People dying to be seen, sitting and drinking their ten dollar coffees on outdoor patios. At least she still fits in here, among the yoga groupies and bearded hipsters. But for how much longer? How long before she too becomes one of the invisible? Another outcast? Forgotten?

Ally shakes her head and glances ahead. A red Toyota Corolla is parked in front of her place that she hasn't seen before, and she notices a figure sitting on her front steps. A head that turns, a hand that waves. The past breaking through.

"Ally!"

Throat closing. Gasping for air. Tears streaming. Ally bends over, leaning on her thighs for support.

"I'm here," Carmen says at her side now and rubbing her back, as Ally lets it all go. The wasted time. The loneliness. The disappointment. The regret. Until there's nothing left but the pounding in her ears, and empty space. A warm touch.

"I'm here now."

"Now what?" Ally asks, coming out of her room, her hair still dripping from her shower. She still can't quite believe her best friend is here. After all this time. Is this what it takes to bring the two of them together? A death in the family?

"Bubbly!" Carmen says, holding up two glasses, her brown eyes twinkling. "What? Isn't two friends reuniting worth a little celebration?"

"Isn't it a little early?" Ally asks, glancing at the clock, which reads barely lunch time.

"Who's being the big sister now, huh?" Carmen says with a wink. "Party pooper. I'll add some OJ."

"What about Izzy?"

Carmen nods at the car seat sitting on the ground next to the couch, with Izzy dozing inside. Ally swallows down another sob.

"Pour me a double," Ally says, her voice hoarse as she sits down on the couch next to Carmen, who is pouring them each a drink.

"All I could find in your fridge," Carmen says, nodding at the meagre cheese and cracker plate.

"Sorry, I haven't been that hungry lately. I used to have Sam to cook for and now, well, what's the point ..." Ally grabs a piece of cheese and a cracker and takes a bite, chewing thoughtfully. Even though they've known each other for so long, it still feels strange to share this space, after so much time apart. An energetic dissonance. As if parallel universes had overlapped, and each of them were out of time and place.

"Don't give me that look," Ally says with her mouth full, after catching Carmen's frown.

"What look?" Carmen picks up her glass and takes a sip.

"That look! The one that says you knew it all along."

"That's not what I was thinking." Carmen puts her glass down.

Ally narrows her eyes. Even after all this time, she could still pick up on her friend's unsaid cues. Knew what was going on inside her head, without her saying it aloud. Could finish off her sentences, if she wanted to.

"Okay, that's what I was thinking. But am I wrong?" Carmen says.

There it is. The upper hand. She always had to have it, as if it were some kind of competition. All of a sudden, Ally feels exhausted. Carmen is too strong to fight. Ally can never win an argument. Carmen's practical, sensible writer brain running laps around her, while Ally can't help but navigate by feeling. She wants to give up.

"No, but why do you have to always be right? Why can't you just let me be happy?"

"Fine, go back to Sam! Be happy!" Carmen says, waving her hands in the air.

Ally's eyes burn with tears. She wishes someone would just hug her.

"Sorry." Carmen touches her arm. "I'm just really tired. Like, existentially."

"I get it," Ally says, noticing now the shadows under Carmen's eyes, and constellations of moles she can't recall marking up her cheeks.

"You couldn't possibly," Carmen says, shaking her head and reaching for her glass.

Ally sucks in a breath. The words hit her like a punch in the gut. "Why do you say that! It really hurts, you know. Every time you remind me of what I don't have. How I'm not like you."

"I didn't mean that!" Carmen slams her glass down.

"You didn't have to! That's how you make me feel!"

There's an awkward pause. It feels like all the times Carmen wasn't there for her. When Ally needed a friend, but Carmen was too far. Too busy. With Dan. The kids.

"Look, I appreciate you coming all the way here. But I didn't ask you to come," Ally says, getting up off the couch.

"Whoa," Carmen says, leaning back with a look of disgust on her face. "I guess I made a big mistake coming here. I can't believe how ungrateful you're being."

Ally knows that look by heart. The time she kissed Dan. Home from college, drunk. She just wanted to see what it felt like. To belong. Dan pushed her away and that's when she noticed Carmen walk into the room. Saw the look on her face. Knowing no amount of apologies would clean this up, they psychically agreed never to mention it again. Would Carmen blame Ally forever?

"Well, it's true. I never asked you to come and take care of me," Ally says, walking to her room, wishing Carmen would just leave.

"Well, if I don't, who will?"

There's silence and another pause. A sting of shame. All the late nights. Breakups. Too drunk to drive home. Ally wheels around and turns to face Carmen.

"So that's what I am to you? A burden? Poor, lonely Ally, who has no one? Well, know this: I'm letting you off the hook. You don't have to save me anymore."

"Ally, I didn't mean that," Carmen says, getting up.

"You are so selfish. You have no idea." Ally shakes her head with disgust. "You think the world revolves around you, and that your life is the only one that matters. You blame everyone for everything. You think you have it so hard, and you can't even see how good *you've* got it. You're such a hypocrite."

"Shut up! Just shut up!" Carmen stomps her foot.

Izzy starts to cry, and they both look to each other.

"Go on," Carmen urges Ally. "You think you're so great? You think you can do better? Take her."

"No."

"Take her!"

"Okay, okay!" Ally says, picking up Izzy, who is flailing and screeching now. Ally's hands are sweaty, and she's so afraid to drop her, but gradually the volume on Izzy's cries die down as Ally soothes her, bouncing up and down with her little body snuggled to her chest. When Izzy's breathing settles and her eyes close again, Ally places her back in the car seat. They both watch her fall asleep.

"She's beautiful," Ally finally says, breaking the silence. All of a sudden, she's overwhelmed with admiration for her friend, for her ability to keep this tiny human alive and safe.

"She looks like Dan," Carmen says, leaning over and stroking Izzy's blond head.

"She'll grow out of it," Ally says with a wink. Carmen's face crumples and she collapses onto the couch.

"Oh Ally, I'm so sorry," Carmen starts to cry, holding her face in her hands. "I don't know what's wrong with me. I don't even feel human anymore. I can't even blame the hormones because, let's face it, I've always been this fucked up. I don't know how to fix any of it."

"Hey, shh," Ally says, dropping down on the couch and wrapping her arm around Carmen. "I already know that about you, remember?" They both laugh through tears.

"Takes one to know one," Carmen teases back, blowing her nose, her eyes red and swollen. Ally grins.

"What happened to us? I used to be the one who always had her shit together," Carmen says, rubbing her face.

"Maybe it's time to let other people take care of you for a change, mama bear."

Carmen nods along.

"I can't believe you're here," Ally says, helping herself to another cracker and cheese. "Doesn't Tyler have a graduation or recital or something?"

"Both. But he's eventually going to dump me for another woman one day anyway, so..."

Carmen and Ally smile at each other, a wave of memories washing over them. So many nights and days together. Good and bad.

"I'm a horrible person." Carmen says, looking like she's about to cry again.

"No, you're not."

"Yes, I am. I'm a horrible person who yells at her best friend after she gets dumped and her dad ... I'm a terrible friend. And I suck at being a wife and mother too."

"Well, you're very good at making it all about you right now." Ally smirks, making Carmen laugh the way they used to. It feels like forgiveness.

"So you don't deny any of it," Carmen says, daring her.

Ally shakes her head, smiling.

"It's all true. And I love you anyway."

"So, what are we watching?" Carmen asks, dropping down on the sofa and passing Ally a tub of chocolate ice cream with two spoons poking out of it. Ally passes her the TV converter.

"Rom-com? Story of my life?" Ally teases.

"Hmmm," Carmen muses, as she flicks through the movie guide. "You know, we don't even belong in the same movie."

"What are you talking about?"

"You and me. It's a wonder we stayed friends all this time. We don't even exist in the same universe. I'm a writer, I know these things."

"You're probably right. You usually are ... you know, I don't really see you that way."

"What do you mean?"

"I mean, you stereotype yourself like you're some TV sitcom mom, but that's not who I remember."

"Maybe I'm not that person anymore. Maybe I never was ... I just, I'm so tired of feeling like I don't tick off the boxes. Like I can't get any of it right. I don't fit in anywhere."

"Maybe that's because you get to break the box."

Carmen thinks it over and nods her head. "What about you?"

"What about me?"

"Who are you?"

Ally tugs on her lip, trying to think of an answer.

"Dunno. Haven't figured it out yet," Ally shrugs.

"How about modern marine superhero, saving the ocean one species at a time."

"I like it but ... it's missing something."

"Like you said, haven't figured out the rest yet."

Ally smiles. She realizes they don't need joint vacations in Costa Rica to feel connected to each other. It is who they are when they show up that matters the most.

Carmen chews on her lip thoughtfully and clears her throat. "Do you think we can start over again?"

Ally nods slowly, unsure at first, and then game. "Yeah," she says, tears suddenly gathering around her eyes, her voice thick with emotion. "I'd like that."

Carmen swings around to face her and extends her hand. "Hi, I'm Carmen."

Ally laughs. "Nice to meet you, Carmen. I'm Ally."

Chapter 40

T he next morning, Carmen's chest tightens as she watches Ally skim the waves at Otter Rock. She can't remember the last time she could do what she wanted without having to think about anyone else. She closes her eyes, trying to imagine it's her on the water.

Izzy stirs on the beach towel beside her, and Carmen freezes and holds her breath for a moment, hoping she'll sleep just a little bit longer. As much as her body aches to pick her up and nurse her, she is enjoying her moment of peace.

When Izzy doesn't wake up, Carmen takes advantage of being hands-free to stretch her legs and back. Even though Ally had let her and Izzy sleep in her bed, Carmen is still stiff, and her joints crack as she bends them. A night on the couch didn't seem to bother Ally, though. Carmen watches her friend effortlessly climb out of the ocean carrying her surfboard.

"What are you girls up to?" Ally asks as she approaches.

"I'm living vicariously through you." *I think I always have.*

"You'll have to come surfing with me next time," Ally says as she strips off her wetsuit in front of Carmen.

"I'd love that," Carmen says, knowing that next time won't happen any time soon. "How is it possible that you got skinnier after high school?" Carmen adjusts her T-shirt over her loose belly, noticing how

Ally's thighs are smooth and free from the varicose veins and stretch marks that cover her own body.

"I don't have four kids." Ally drops down onto the beach blanket beside her.

"Do you realize how good you have it? I mean, I know it's not what you hoped for, but it can still be amazing..."

"I know ..." Ally says, looking off, as if the ocean holds the answers. "It's just, sometimes I feel ..."

Carmen watches her friend. Ocean water collects like tear drops on her shoulders.

"You're not alone," Carmen says, taking her hand. "I should have been there for you when Craig ...when Sam ..."

Ally places her hand on Carmen's. "You're here now."

Carmen smiles at her and squeezes her hand. Izzy's eyes open and they both giggle, watching her become aware of her surroundings. Ally gently picks her up, clutching her to her chest.

"I can't believe Dan let you leave," Ally whispers, breathing Izzy in and kissing the top of her head.

"He didn't have a choice, really," Carmen says, making Ally cackle. It reminds her of summer nights on Ally's roof, howling at the moon.

"You so lucked out. I've never even heard you guys fight."

"Yeah, I prefer to save my fights for the office," Carmen says with a wink.

"Everybody needs an outlet."

"I guess."

"Maybe the universe is trying to tell you something."

"Like what? I'm unemployable?"

"Maybe ... maybe it's time for something different. New." Ally raises an eyebrow.

"I lost the job at Arrow. I guess I just wasn't what they were looking for."

"Well, you are an acquired taste," Ally teases.

Yes, Carmen recalls, this was why they were friends in the first place. A perfect match. A worthy foe. *Someone who gets me, all of me, and loves me anyway.*

"To be honest, I don't think I really wanted it. I think I want to start my own magazine."

"So do that then."

"Can I? I mean, it's crazy, right? Four kids. A mortgage. I'm forty, for God's sake. I can't just go off and have fun. I have *responsibilities*."

"Fuck that! You have a responsibility to *yourself*. Besides, if anyone can pull it off, it's you. Forget about Arrow and go for it with your magazine."

Carmen smiles, her eyes wide with excitement. "Eeek! Do I dare?"

"*I* dare you."

"Thank God for you." Carmen wraps her arm around Ally.

Izzy cries out and Ally passes her to Carmen, who tucks her under her shirt.

"I wonder how Dan's coping without you," Ally says, watching Carmen nurse. It makes Carmen feel embarrassed and proud all at the same time.

"I'm sure no one has brushed their teeth, and their eyes are burned out on screen time. Shit! I forgot to switch the laundry. I better text Dan and let him know," Carmen says, reaching for her purse. "That stuff is going to stink by now. Damn! I have the worst memory ever. Stupid!"

"You're too hard on yourself," Ally says, passing Carmen her purse. "You might be superwoman, but you're still *human*. Humans make mistakes. *You* make mistakes. It's okay to ask for help."

"I know ..."

"Do you though?"

"Maybe," Carmen says, digging around inside her purse for the phone. "Maybe not."

Carmen texts Dan with one hand and then pulls Izzy out to burp her.

"Four kids ..."

"Yeah." Carmen pats Izzy's back, thinking of the cuddles at night, and in the morning. Her heart hurts for her friend. For what she doesn't have. For what she might never experience.

"Sam texted me this morning," Ally says, scanning the horizon. "While you were in the shower."

"You're talking to him again?"

"Just texting. It's ... nice."

"You know how this ends, right?"

"Do I though?" Ally says, turning to Carmen.

Carmen bites her tongue. She doesn't want to ruin this. Two steps forward, one step back. And yet...

"You can't change him."

"But—" Ally says and catches herself.

"You have such a big heart ..." Carmen says. *It's just misplaced*, she doesn't add. She doesn't have to be right about it.

Carmen lays Izzy back on the blanket and they sit quiet for a moment.

"I miss him so much," Ally says, her eyes growing red and wet, and they both know she's not talking about Sam now, but her dad. "It's so weird. All these years, I was so mad at him. And now, I just feel love."

Carmen puts her arm around Ally's shoulder and hugs her close. She checks herself. She can do better. She gathers more of Ally to herself and squeezes harder, longer.

"Do you think I can do it?" Ally asks, wiping her eyes and nodding at Izzy.

"Alone?" Carmen pauses, trying to picture Ally in her shoes. "Yeah. You're amazing. You can do anything. But are you sure you want to? It'll change everything."

"That's kind of the point."

"It's just, I know it's been hard lately. But this is hard too," Carmen says, and all the doubts and fears begin to surface again like so many clouds in the sky. "Sometimes I miss me."

"*I* miss you." Ally wraps her arm around Carmen.

"I miss you too," Carmen says, hugging her back.

Parking the stroller at the airport gate, Carmen wishes she could stay longer. Wishes she could hand Izzy over to a flight attendant to take her back home so that she could go live it up with her best friend. Properly. At the same time, she aches to wrap her arms around her family. She wants to squeeze them and never let go. Though she agrees with the saying, 'You can have it all, just not at the same time,' it doesn't exempt her from wanting all things at once.

"Bring it in," Ally says, opening her arms up for a hug.

"What am I going to do without you? I'm afraid of my life." Carmen squeezes her back.

"Aww, you'll land on top. You always do. Here, this is for you," Ally says, handing Carmen a stack of papers.

"A gift?"

"They're yours. Letters from Paris. I printed them out. I figured since you've got your girl now ... I think Izzy would like to read them one day."

"Wow, thank you." Carmen tucks them into her diaper bag and gives Ally another hug. "What about you? Are you going to be okay?"

"I'm gonna be fine," Ally says, nodding her head, as if she's just deciding this now, knowing that even when she's not, Carmen's got her back, no matter what. "I'm just going to go ahead and do it, all of it, and whatever—whoever—happens, happens. They'll just have to come along."

"What have you done with my friend?" Carmen teases in mock surprise. "You mean you're ready to give up your college dorm lifestyle?"

"I mean, yeah, I guess. It's time. Husband or not."

"Remember what I said. You first." Carmen looks into Ally's eyes to make sure she understands.

"I know, I know. The right one will come along."

"*If you build it, they will come!*" Carmen sings out, with a laugh. "So, I'll see you at Christmas?"

Ally nods.

"Good, because I already bought your ticket."

Ally smiles and tears up, then crouches down, meeting Izzy at eye level. "Be good to your mama," she says, poking Izzy in the tummy before standing back up to face her friend. "Be good to yourself."

"Love you," Carmen says, giving Ally one more squeeze. It's hard to breathe. There's so much more she wants to say, so much unsaid through the years. She makes a silent promise. This time, she wouldn't let life get in the way. This time, she would be a better friend.

"Love you," Ally says, rocking back and forth, as if in agreement.

Ally lets go, but Carmen is reluctant to walk away. She wants to bring her home. Give her something solid to hang on to. She knows, though, that the best thing for her friend lies ahead. That where she must go, she must go alone.

Carmen pulls her back in, one last time.

"You're not alone. You *are* loved," she whispers in Ally's ear, giving her a final squeeze. Carmen grabs Ally's hand and opens it, placing on it a purple plastic ring to match her pink one. "And you will always be my best friend."

On the plane, Izzy sleeps as Carmen pulls out the letters and reads them one by one. Little by little, she remembers where she comes from. Paragraph by paragraph, she remembers who she is. Wine and cigarettes, cemeteries and books, Rodin and Monet. *"I simply carved away everything that was not David."*

Maybe she had it all wrong. Maybe all this time, it wasn't her saving Ally. Maybe, it was Ally who had been saving her, carrying a piece of her she could come back to. She thinks maybe she can carry this piece with her now, and for always.

Chapter 41

"See, baby? Everything happens for a reason. If Jenny hadn't come into the store that day, looking for a dress to wear to her rehearsal dinner, we wouldn't have started talking about my breakup with Carlo, and she would never have introduced me to Mark, who is just wonderful! And I wouldn't be on this cruise right now looking at the Mediterranean Sea. Oh, Ally, you have to see it! It's just heaven!"

"Sure, Mom," Ally says, keeping an eye on the driver behind her as she scrutinizes the doors on the street.

"Ally, are you listening to me? I'm talking about *signs*, honey. You have to watch for the signs."

"Yes, Mom! I'm happy for you! I'm just ..." Ally looks around. "I'm totally lost."

"Lost, where?"

"If I knew, I wouldn't be lost, would I?"

The car behind her starts honking.

"I know! I know! Just give me a second, okay!" Ally yells into the rear-view mirror. "Why do they always make the numbers on buildings so hard to find?" Ally asks, pulling over to let the other car pass.

"Ally, please drive safely. Tell me where you're going, honey. I'll see if I can find it on my phone."

"I'm house hunting. I'm buying my own place," Ally says, and the words sound crazy, even to her.

"Alone?"

"Exactly—"

"Fucking tourist!" the other driver yells at her as he passes. Ally sticks up her middle finger at him.

"Don't you think you should wait until you meet someone? I mean, how's this going to work when you do find someone?"

"I'm done waiting, Mom. It's time for me to move forward," Ally says, pulling back into the lane.

"But—

"Mom, I gotta go. I'll call you later," Ally says, spotting an empty parking spot.

"Ally—"

"Bye, Mom."

Ally hangs up and parks the car. Walking past entrances, she searches the door numbers for the address, until she finds the building. A pierced twenty-something stands in the doorway, smoking. Ally squeezes past him and buzzes the apartment.

"Hello?"

"Hi, it's Allison Parker. I have an appointment?"

"Oh, yes! Come in."

Riding the elevator up, Ally's not sure the building has ever seen better days. The elevator shakes and rattles on the way up, and the wallpaper in the hallway is stained and peeling, but buying a condo instead of a house means she can travel without worrying about break-ins and maintaining the property while she's gone, and at least she is building equity to save up for something bigger, better, down the line. She doesn't plan on being home much anyway. She had promised to visit her mom soon, and that she would spend Christmas with Carmen. Then there's her trip to Costa Rica with Amanda this winter. She also wants to go to Melbourne, to visit with her stepmom and spread her dad's ashes.

"Hi, come in," the real estate agent says, and Ally steps inside. The smell of the past lingers heavy in the air. There are holes in the wall and stains on the laminate floor. Too much history here.

"It could use a little TLC. Nothing a little paint and polish can't fix," the woman says, sizing Ally up with heavily made-up eyes.

"There's a balcony?" Ally asks, hungry for fresh air.

"Oh, yes, just over here."

The woman guides Ally into the bedroom, where a sliding door leads her onto a ledge that looks directly into the apartment across the alley. A white-haired man is sitting in his underwear on a step on the fire escape, reading a book. He looks up and waves at Ally.

"Thanks," Ally says, turning and walking out of the room.

"So let me know ..." the woman says.

"I'll keep you posted," Ally lies. If this is what her single income buys her, she'd rather rent forever, nest egg be damned.

Back on the street, Ally checks her phone. Another missed call from Sam. While he seemed to be leaning in, she was putting on the brakes and ignoring his messages. As much as she still has feelings for him and gets a thrill from the attention, she doesn't want him to influence her plans, one way or another. She wants to do this for herself.

Ally puts her phone away and looks around for her car. The impatient driver and her mom had her so distracted, she forgets where she parked it. She notices now a pretty park down the street. There's a for sale sign at the corner, and Ally follows it, past elegant homes facing the park, up to a handsome brownstone. Her heart swells. If she had conjured up a dream home, this would be it. But she couldn't possibly ... could she?

"I'd like to see the house for sale?" Ally asks, when a pretty thirty-something woman answers the door.

"Did you make an appointment?" the woman asks, looking to see if she is with anyone. Ally shakes her head.

"Oh, it's by appointment only. See?"

Ally checks the sign at the bottom of the steps, and her heart sinks.

"Well, I'm here now, so ..."

"Sorry," the woman says, giving Ally her best get-lost smile. "Here's our card. Call and make an appointment, okay? We'd love to show it to you."

Hurt and annoyed, Ally stomps down the steps. Turning left to head back to her car, Ally feels an ache, like she's already missing something. She stops and pauses, looking back up at the house. Through the front window, she can see a smartly dressed man, showing a young couple around inside. Of course. It is perfect for them.

Ally takes another step toward her car and hesitates again. She shakes her head. This house is too big, too nice, has too great a location. For sure it's outside her budget.

Looking back at the house, Ally rubs her lip. Behind the couple, she can now make out a canvas, in shades of blue. A woman with long dark hair rises out of a swell. As impossible as it is, deep down inside, Ally knows this is for her. Knows she will find a way to pull it off. That she is enough.

Ally dials the number on the for-sale sign. The woman answers.

"I'd like to make an appointment to see the house," Ally says.

"Sure. Have your agent call and schedule a visit."

"I don't have an agent."

"Okay, then. You can call us back on Monday so we can qualify you and make an appointment."

"Oh, I'm qualified, all right," Ally says.

"I'm sure you are," the woman sighs, "but we have protocol to follow."

"Can I talk to Daryl, please?" Ally says, reading out the agent's name on the sign.

"He's with a client right now."

"He's expecting my call."

Ally can hear the woman whisper, and Daryl takes the phone.

"Daryl speaking."

"Hi Daryl, my name is Allison Parker, and I'm interested in your listing on—" Ally checks the street sign. "Park Street." *Like her name?*

"Sure, we can schedule a visit. When would be good for you?"

"Now is good. I'm standing outside. I'm staring right at you."

Ally sees Daryl glance out the window at her. Looking at him confidently in the eyes, she lets him know she is not going anywhere.

"Okay, Lori will see you inside."

"Thank you."

Inside, Lori takes Ally on a tour. The house boasts a sun-filled open-concept living/dining/kitchen, two spacious bedrooms upstairs and a big, standalone clawfoot tub in the bathroom. Ally runs her fingers along the handrail on her way back down the stairs, imagining the memories yet to be made in each room. A peaceful feeling replaces the restlessness she can never shake. She never wants to leave.

"It's perfect for a young family. Room to grow. Playground across the street. And yet shops and restaurants just steps away," Lori says.

"I'll take it," Ally says.

Lori laughs. "I'm glad you like it."

"I'll take it," Ally insists.

Lori shakes her head. "Don't you want to show it to your partner first?"

"It's just me," Ally says, daring her with her eyes.

"You know, I have other, smaller, homes you might be more interested in. Maybe a condo? It would be more manageable, for someone like you."

"This is perfect," Ally says, without a doubt.

Lori sighs.

"Okay then. Let me get my file and we'll get you started."

Ally takes a seat at the dining room table and looks out the window at the park across the street. She knows it's more than she can afford. She also knows she would do anything to keep it. Here, finally, is something she can build on. Something that is hers and hers alone. A stake in her own future. No more one foot in, one foot out, waiting for the right guy to come along to build it with. *She* is in charge.

As Lori begins to fill out the forms, Ally watches the children outside swinging on the playground. Moms and dads pushing strollers, coffees in hand. People going to work. People coming home.

Home.

Chapter 42

It's her kids' voices Carmen hears first as she comes to.

"Is she breathing?"

"Is she dead?"

"Mommy?"

Carmen looks around. Someone has propped her up on a bench and Sensei is holding a crowd of students back to give Carmen some space. Tyler, Teo, and Toby are kneeling before her, wide-eyed. Dan is off to her right with Izzy pressed to his chest, a stern look on his face.

"Back up everyone," Sensei orders, and the crowd shuffles back.

Carmen can hear whispering. Her head throbs. Slowly the fog clears and she remembers the fight.

She didn't mean to break her nose. It just worked out that way. What had been meant as a block—arm up, elbow out—had become a jutted offense. The way when you're skiing down a hill, the thing you're looking at is the thing you're headed toward. She should have looked away, turned her gaze away from the trees, away from danger.

All Carmen had wanted was a little time out. A little space to be herself and not Tyler-Teo-Toby-Izzy's mom. Not wife. Not daughter. No expectations. No story. Just Carmen, right here, right now.

So she signed up for karate, figuring it would be a fun way to shed the baby weight, build confidence, and prepare for the end of the world. If you can't beat 'em, join 'em, she had decided, imagining the smile it would put on Ally's face when she found out. *I dare you.*

Alex's blank, shark-like eyes, however, they drew her in, a puzzle to be solved. They made Carmen want to claw closer, discover the depths, understand the mechanics of her. Carmen wanted to hear her say it. Wanted to hear how she wanted to be free too. Wanted her to admit the flaws of her family, her own failed career. Wanted to know she was not alone.

But that wasn't what she was thinking at the time. *Homework. Dinner. Toilet paper.* That was the ticker tape that was running through Carmen's head as she positioned herself for attack. It was Carmen's first time sparring, but she knew what to do—besides the introductory classes, she had seen it while picking up Tyler from karate.

Homework. Dinner. Toilet paper. Carmen's to-do list repeated in her head as she listened to the instructor punctuate the air with her raspy voice, giving orders to the class to move to one side of the room. As Carmen stood ready, she could see Dan and the kids out of the corner of her eye, sitting off to the side of the room. She gave them a tight little wave.

Homework. Dinner. Toilet paper. Carmen shook her head to clear her mind and bit down on her lip to focus her attention. She knew she looked like an idiot with her head gear on. She felt stupid standing there, waiting. She was not the proud warrior woman she imagined she would feel like when she signed up for the class. She was clumsy. Weak. Broken.

Homework. Dinner. Toilet paper. Sensei barked "Starting in three, two, one!" and Carmen dug her feet into the ground, bent her knees and put her arms up, just the way her flat-bellied, twenty-three-year-old instructor showed her. Fear and excitement surged as her classmates arranged themselves in a line. They were all watching Carmen, so she looked away, uncomfortable with the attention.

Sensei called out "Hands up!" and Carmen turned back, locking eyes with Alex, who was first in line. Terminator mom. Carmen couldn't help but wonder, did she feel bad at all for firing her from the yearbook team? *Homework. Dinner. Toilet paper.* Are she and her family really as perfect as they pretended to be? *Homework. Dinner. Toilet paper.* Did she even fucking *want* for herself anymore?

"Go!" Sensei shouted out.

So, Carmen let go. Like a matador waving his cloak as the bull charges toward him, she closed her eyes and threw up her hands.

First came a knocking sound, as elbow connected with nose.

Then a screech, like tires burning rubber on a dead-end road.

A flinch, the move was more a slip than an intention. After all, Carmen didn't want to hurt anyone. Still, she hadn't felt sorry. Standing there, holding her breath, as Alex reeled, it occurred to Carmen that she might actually be a little angry, and that it felt good. To be angry at Alex. Meredith. Arrow. At the way things are. At the way things could have been. Even angry just for the sake of being angry, because she knows now that even if she breaks something, even if things fall apart, she can put them back together again.

"What the hell?!" Alex shrieked, grabbing at her nose. Blood was running through her fingers, and Carmen was at once horrified and elated. All of a sudden, she could breathe. She smiled.

There it was. Something she could connect to. Super Mom is human.

Carmen let out a whooping noise—a cross between a hiccup and a laugh that surprised her.

And then, *whack*. A thumping noise. Darkness.

"Mommy has a boo-boo," Teo says, and Carmen looks up to see Dan frowning, as if she got what was coming to her.

"Gimme my phone."

"Carmen, let's just get out of here."

"Let me see!"

Dan passes her the phone, and Carmen clicks on the camera app to see herself. Already, blues, golds, and greens are gathering around her eye. The bridge of her nose is swollen. She has never looked more hideous.

Ready for my close-up, she thinks drily, as she takes a photo. Underneath she types a caption. A maxim. A call to arms.

#thisismotherhood

And so she can't bury this post too, or hide behind yet another fake byline, she adds it to her Instagram profile photo and blog cover, inextricably linking the two. It was all her. Take it or leave it.

Chapter 43

"You're still talking to him? Don't do it. Don't let him back in," Carmen warns, after Ally tells her about Sam.

Ally gazes out her office window at the river, not sure how to feel about any of it. Thinking Carmen doesn't know what it is like to wake up to an empty bed, day after day. How badly she misses being touched. The aching in her heart to love and be loved. How no amount of busy can fill the void.

Ally looks down at Sam's text again and bites her lip.

I miss you, he had written. What did that even mean? Does he want to get back together? Can she be with him again? Can she forgive him? And if she did, would it be out of loneliness, or does she really love and miss *him*?

"Of course not," Ally says, although she can feel the excitement building. Sam still thinks about her. Still loves her, maybe. But does that change the way she feels about him?

"You've already moved on. You're doing so well!" Carmen insists, as if she can read Ally's thoughts and see her relenting.

It's true. Ally loves her new home. And her roommate, Jackson, a friend of Jared, the research analyst at her work. Although Jackson is renting her basement apartment, he could usually be found on Ally's couch, watching *Property Brothers* and *Love It or List It*. A real estate

304

agent himself, he is saving up for his own home after a breakup with his boyfriend. Thanks to Jackson's rent, Ally has enough money left over that she herself is saving up for her own sailboat. In the meantime, she spends weekends kayaking Willamette River and meeting up with friends afterwards for drinks.

"Trust me, we are not getting back together."

"Good. Keep it that way. Listen, I gotta get the kids from school. Call you later?"

"Later."

Ally turns back to her computer screen, trying to focus on the words, but the letters don't mean anything. Her eyes keep going back to her phone, staring up at her from her desk. Should she answer him? What should she say? Does he deserve to still be punished? Who is she to judge, anyway? Though Malcolm had grown cold in her heart, the guilt and shame of their time together still lingers. Perhaps it is her who should be asking for forgiveness.

Ally begins to tap. She taps her forehead, taps her temples, taps all the way down her nose, cheeks and across her chin, just like her mother had showed her, as if to tap the memories away.

"Ally?"

Ally turns around and sees Christine standing in the doorway. Her technician is nine months pregnant, and her belly looks ready to pop. Ally will miss her while she is off on maternity leave. She'd proven herself invaluable on their latest crab survey project.

"Sorry to bother you. I knocked but ..."

"Of course! Come in," Ally says, rubbing her forehead as a flush rises up her neck and cheeks.

"I've finished analyzing the data sets. I've sent you the link," Christine says. "Want something to eat? Jared and I are going out for lunch now."

Ally does an internal check-in. The butterflies in her belly from Sam's text have obliterated any feelings of hunger.

"I'm good, thanks."

"Okay, well message me if you change your mind."

Ally nods, picking up her phone as Christine leaves. She turns it over and over in her hand like a Magic 8 Ball. Could she forgive him? Should she? The thought of Sam with another woman still stings, but let's face it, isn't she a little too old to believe in fairy tales? Just because he fooled around with someone else when he was drunk one night doesn't mean he doesn't love her. But would he do it again? Could she bear it if he did?

Looking up, Ally spots a dark movement at the other end of the office floor. A tall, lean shadow wading through the sea of gray cubicles. She recognizes the shape of him, the swagger, and a breath catches in her throat.

As he comes closer, she sees it's Sam, carrying a bouquet of candy-colored daisies like a guitar. Ally's chest tightens. The people in the background disappear, and he feels like the only real thing in the entire made-up world.

"Look, I'm sorry," Sam says, sliding her office door shut. His clean-shaven face gives him a boy-next-door vulnerability, and Ally doesn't remember seeing him this way. Her whole body vibrates at the sight of him. "I want to come home."

Ally wants to say yes, wants to smother his face in kisses, but something holds her back. Say yes to what? Permission to repeat?

"How do I know it won't happen again?" is what comes out, and she hates herself for it.

"Let me show you," Sam says, negotiating the space between them as if she were a wild animal in a cage.

"No," Ally says, and the voice is one she doesn't recognize. Yet the fact that she has let him stay this long reveals a different answer.

"No?" Sam asks, shaking his head but grinning. "Never, ever, ever?"

Ally feels butterflies rise again, and she can see people at their desks looking over at them. There's an expectation. A pressure to perform. Perhaps he planned it this way.

"Listen, I know. I know! I fucked up. I'm a fucking, fucked up, fucking piece of shit," Sam says.

Ally turns her head to hide her laugh.

"I just want to make it up to you," Sam says, coming closer. Close enough to kiss.

"You're not going to leave until I say yes, are you?" Ally asks, hoping it's true. Deep down, she wants to give in. Deep down, she wants him to make her.

Sam slowly shakes his head.

Ally rolls her eyes and grabs the flowers. She can't help but find the attention thrilling, as embarrassed as she feels in front of her colleagues, and toward herself for being so easy.

"If you ever—" she says, but she knows it's an empty threat. It feels so good to be wanted again.

"Never," Sam says, taking her hand. "Never, ever, ever."

With his other hand, Sam reaches around behind his back and holds up two pieces of paper.

"Mademoiselle?" he asks, and Ally looks closer to see that they are concert tickets. One for him and one for her. A new adventure. Together.

"Care to join me in Paris? My favourite band is playing."

"Yes!" Ally squeals, feeling like the whole world is coming together in her favour. Yes, she is building a future of her own. Yes, she could share it with him too.

Ally takes Sam's face in her hands and covers it in kisses.

"Yes. Yes. Yes."

Chapter 44

S itting at her desk, Carmen stares at the debut issue on her laptop computer. Her face is on the cover of the magazine, a poster girl for everything wrong, for all the mad, bad moms out there who still don't know how to cook and are never on time. Who struggle to make ends meet and enjoy time with their kids. Who are never enough, no matter how hard they try.

Inside, there's a single-page photo of a mom with her head in her hands. A kid monster is having a tantrum in the background. Carmen had a hard time sourcing it from stock images. Most of the pictures featured serene, happy moms and sweet, smiling children. No one wanted to imagine a mother could be anything other than infinitely patient and giving. Selfless. With zero wishes of her own. Desires that fell outside the lines of what they were told they should want and expect, by tradition, by society, by Arrow itself.

Carmen is done with moms being used and abused. With impossible definitions for something that didn't, couldn't, exist. She is done with being a door mat for the world. It is time to embrace the "other" in "mother." The dreamers and dream chasers. The working moms. The stay-at-home moms. The single moms. Even the single and stay-at-home dads.

At the bottom of the screen, there are two buttons: One says SAVE, the other SEND.

Carmen weighs her options. One is a private declaration. The other, a movement.

Carmen's finger hovers over the mouse, thinking back to the yearbook meeting. She may have lost that fight, but what she is fighting for is clearer than ever. The not so pretty truth. The chance to rewrite the questions. The freedom to be truly you, *all* of you.

Alex. Meredith. Arrow. Out in the world, they might be able to tell her what to do. But this is *her* house.

Carmen scrolls over to the Letter from the Editor page. At the bottom, she types in her name. Before she has a chance to change her mind, Carmen presses SEND.

It feels like letting go. It feels good.

Chapter 45

They're at a Paris bar with Sam's friends Ollie and Manuela. The walls glow pink and red, with thick curtains framing the doorways that separate rooms while Chinese lanterns hang from the ceiling. A DJ plays deep house as VIPs look down from balconies above on diners below. Everyone is on display.

What is she doing here? What is she doing here *with him*?

While Ally is no stranger to clubbing, and even enjoys her dinners out with Sam, she's decades away from wanting to be part of a scene. She feels like she has stepped into the wrong movie. Sam, however, is right at home, effortlessly fitting in with the local Parisiennes. They all seem so cool and confident, with their elegant scarves and nonchalant faces, picking at hors d'oeuvres and cuddled up on banquettes.

From the dark, heady bistros to the endless boulevards and avenues, he knows the city inside out, thanks to a marketing stint with Disneyland Paris early in his career. His friends—French, Spanish, German, Austrian expats and locals he's acquired over the years on business trips like charms on a bracelet—welcome Ally warmly, though she couldn't feel more alien, even though Sam boasts about her, his scientist, deep-sea-diving girlfriend. He carries her Marine Biologist title like a trophy. An exotic kill.

Comparing herself to them, which she does often, Ally feels clumsy, unsophisticated, as the conversation moves fluidly between languages she can't understand, every once in a while, landing in an English that's impossibly eloquent.

Here, Sam is at ease, patient and charming as ever. Ally wonders how long it will last when they are back home.

As Sam and Ollie catch each other up on their expat friends, Ally stares at the tables of friends laughing and toasting each other "À ta santé," and couples kissing and fighting like there's no one else in the room. Sam taps her arm.

"The French call it joie de vivre," he says, as he grabs a stem of Baby's Breath from the centrepiece and picks the buds off one by one. "Joy. Love. Music. Sex," he says with a smile and a wink. "I like to think they're worth dying for, don't you?"

Sam breaks off a piece of the naked stem and pops it in his mouth like a toothpick, before holding it between his fingers as if he were smoking a cigarette.

"You know, my dad, he did everything right. Married young. Worked hard. Took care of his family and his health. Total teetotaler. And he fucking died. Brain aneurysm. Just like that." Sam snaps his fingers, making Ally jump in her seat. Manuela and Ollie let out sounds of sympathy. Sam shrugs his shoulders. "I'm still pissed at God."

Sam tosses the stem on to the middle of the table. "He never did see me make it. I was just a punk ass kid, playing in a shitty band. Always disappointing him. Turns out all that music taught me everything I needed to know about marketing. So, I got a job at Disney Paris, and the rest, as they say, is history. Anyway, I'm not gonna make the same mistakes. Like Jim Morrison said, I'm gonna get my kicks before the whole shithouse goes up in flames. Wanna join me?" he says, grabbing Ally's hand and nodding at her.

"I dunno, seems kind of empty," Ally says, looking back and forth between Manuela and Ollie. The idea of chasing one thrill after another sounds exhausting when all she really wants now is to anchor.

"Really? You really want to submit yourself to a bunch of thankless brats who will stop answering your calls and definitely won't look after you when you get old? Or do you want to live your best fucking life right up to the end? No regrets? No compromise?" Sam places his hand on Ally's. "Who wants to be normal? Normal is for assholes. Let's be extraordinary together." Sam leans back in his chair and waves the server over. "Come. Allons-y?" Sam says, and Ally loves the way his mouth stretches to form the words. Just like his suits, he wears the accent well.

"Où tu veux, mon ami," Oliver says, pulling out his wallet and placing his credit card on the table.

"Where to, my love?" Sam reaches a hand to help Ally out of her chair. She feels embarrassed by the attention and is sure that whatever suggestion she offers will sound corny and trite.

"Well, we haven't seen the Arc de Triomphe, yet. And it's our last night?"

"Baby, your wish is my command." Sam kisses her hand.

Except that's not exactly true, Ally thinks, steadying herself with a hand on the table, the whiskey tonics now catching up with her.

Before leaving Portland, Ally had done her research, gleefully dog-earing travel guide pages and underlining passages of places to visit: Shakespeare & Company, Montmartre, crêpes and ice cream on Île Saint-Louis. On the plane ride over, Sam had laughed, calling her "cute" and her choices "cliché."

Instead, he had taken her for falafels in Marais, to a porn-plastered bar in Bastille, and to too many friends' smoky apartments, passing precious evenings with touchy-feely girlfriends. Ally couldn't help but wonder if he'd been intimate with them. If he is still. Would their whole life together be like this? The wondering, waiting, suspicion?

Despite their picture-perfect American in Paris days, at night Ally lies awake in the king-sized bed of their plush hotel suite. She feels out of time, out of synch. Sam himself seems more caught up in his history here than in his present with her. Perhaps they are both grasping to a facsimile of each other. Each playing roles past the curtain call. Maybe it's just a one-night stand gone on too long.

As they leave their table, the house music playing overhead makes Ally's head spin. She can't see the floor, so she holds on to Sam's hand and lets him guide her out of the bar. She's ready to go home.

Outside, Sam adjusts his scarf and waves a taxi over. Standing on the cobblestone street, surrounded by strangers, Ally has to doubletake to remember where she is. *Who* she is. There's a hint of fall in the crisp air. Time is passing.

"Arc de Triomphe, s'il vous plaît," Sam says with a flourish to a cab driver, making Ally blush.

As the Patchouli-scented car drives forward and the lights of Paris blur past, the chatter of Sam and his friends fades out into a low buzz. Ally notices something new emerging within. Who she is becoming clearer than ever, in contrast to him.

"Merci bien," Sam says when they arrive, helping Ally out of the car.

Stepping out onto the street, Ally feels excitement bubble like champagne. The Champs Elysées rolls out before her like a red carpet, cars whizzing past like shooting stars. Standing under the spot lit arches, Ally understands the thrill of the city, the sparkling life splayed all around her. Its beauty is intoxicating.

Sam wraps his arms around her and rocks her side to side, humming their song, "Dream A Little Dream." She knows he feels it too. All the possibilities of the world laid out before them.

When the song ends, Sam turns Ally around and looks at her, his blue eyes soft and seeking.

"Marry me," he says, giving her hands a gentle squeeze.

Ally's body suddenly freezes, and her mind goes blank. She doesn't know what to say. There's an awkward pause, and Sam cocks his head, as if he's about to ask the question a second time. Before he has a chance to say anything, Ollie and Manuela rush them with congratulatory hugs and kisses.

Ally lets them carry her away.

It turns out the proposal isn't Sam's only surprise. He had rented a boat, a sleek, retro-style Vedette, for a private river cruise along the Seine—just the two of them. As they glide past Notre Dame, their guide points out little-known facts about the area's history.

"The Seine is the second-longest river in France, after the Loire," she says in her exquisite French accent. "It takes its name from the Gallo-Roman goddess of the river, Sēquana."

The boat passes under a bridge, and a shiver runs over Ally. She still hasn't given Sam her answer, but he doesn't seem to notice. She wonders how long she can stall. Sam smiles at her and rubs her arms until the golden streetlamps light their way again.

The guide notices their empty flutes and gets up. "I'll get you more champagne."

There's a guitar leaning against the bench, and Sam picks it up now, strumming the first notes of Taylor Swift's "Invisible String" before he breaks out into a velvety serenade, with an ironic wink and grin at first, and then serious and sincere.

Sam lays down the guitar and watches her for a moment.

"I really love you, you know that?" Sam says, brushing a stray lock of hair from her face and looking deep into her eyes. "I never felt this way about anyone. You're special, Ally. Don't ever forget that. No regrets. No compromise."

Ally nods and curls up into his lap, feeling like she could cry.

Back at their hotel room, Ally lies stiff against Sam's kisses, her body revolting against his will. This is not supposed to be how it goes. She's supposed to fling herself into his arms, squealing with delight as if her life's wish were being granted by her very own Prince Charming. Isn't this what she wants? Isn't this what she hoped for? So what if he isn't perfect—is she? Just one simple word and she could have it all. *Yes.*

"I love you so much," Sam says between kisses, and Ally wants to believe him. Wants to say the words back. She wants to give him what he wants, but something inside her resists, something secret and determined making itself known inside her. Never has she felt power like this to choose the direction her life goes in. Never has she felt so powerless.

"What do you say?" Sam says, pulling back, his smile twisting into a question. "I don't think I heard an answer back there ..."

Ally bites her lip. For the first time, she really sees him. The flecks of yellow in his blue eyes. The boyish, clean-shaven face, with only the lines at the edges of his eyes hinting at the passage of time. His uncertainty makes her wince. She feels like a vengeful god.

Just say yes, and you can save him. You can save yourself too, a voice inside her says. But she can't. Won't. Maybe this is how her dad felt. Maybe he really did love them with all his heart but just couldn't give up who he was. Maybe the problem wasn't him, maybe it was marriage. A box he just couldn't fit into. Maybe she is just like him.

"Ally?" Sam asks, his voice shaky now, eyes pleading. "Is it a yes?"

Ally wishes she could freeze time and call Carmen. Call her mom. Turn back time and call her dad too. This is too much responsibility. Too much choice. Endless outcomes. Which one is the happy ending? For her or for Sam? Who does she love more?

"No," Ally says, her stomach plummeting with a deep inner knowing. Her heart mourning the life she can't have. The truth is she doesn't need him. Not anymore. "No."

Chapter 46

Carmen hears a baby cry, and it makes her breasts tingle, but it's not Izzy, who is gnawing on a rubber giraffe at her feet, her tufts of auburn hair making the corners of Carmen's mouth turn up.

Downstairs, dishes clink and cupboard doors slap shut as Alex serves a snack to the little ones, getting them ready for a pre-nap stroller walk. Soon, the house will be full of school-age kids, tweens, and teens taking over the dining-room table to tackle their homework, playing games in the rec room. The detritus of family life lies everywhere, on tabletops, under chairs and strewn across sofas—broken crayons, loose, scribbled-on slips of paper, Pokémon trading cards and tablets. In the backyard, skateboards, bikes, and tricycles wait their turn under a muddy layer of spring thaw.

A year ago, Carmen would have been itching to clear everyone away so she could tidy it all up, wipe it all down. Now, it just feels like home. Carmen carries Izzy downstairs for her afternoon snack.

"Can I help?" Carmen asks, sliding Izzy into a high chair.

Alex shakes her head. "We've got it," she says, sliding a bowl of Cheerios closer to her. "One year. Can you believe it? I still remember when you were pregnant."

"I know." Carmen pouts. "It goes too fast."

Carmen gives Izzy a quick peck on the head and climbs back upstairs, stopping by Maya and Eddy's office.

"How's it looking?" Carmen asks, passing Maya a hat that has fallen on the floor as she works Willow's chubby little arm through the sleeve of her jacket.

"First proof's almost ready for you. Just waiting for a few more photos to come in," Maya says, nodding at the wall, where rows of thumbnail pages are pasted up.

"Wheee!" Carmen squeals, scanning the mock-ups. "Looks awesome, great job," she says, giving Maya and Eddy a high five each.

Carmen returns to her office and reviews a story idea for the next issue. The blog had turned into a popular magazine where moms everywhere shared everything wrong, everything real, the perfectly imperfect.

"Like *Mad Magazine*, but for moms," is how one critic described it.

"The anti-magazine," wrote another.

Thisismotherhood was now the title of an Arrow-sponsored podcast and YouTube channel—50,000 subscribers being enough to change corporate minds. Even Laura Prepon's manager had called, requesting for her to come on the show.

There's a knock and Carmen turns to the door.

"Ready?" Tanya asks, carrying her laptop.

"Freddy," Carmen says, getting up and following Tanya to the podcasting studio. Not only did Tanya make for a hilarious co-host, but she was also brilliant with the tech side of the podcast too. And now that she was working again, she looked amazing in her own Manolo heels—even when they were just working "from home."

While Tanya checks the sound levels, Carmen sits at an armchair by the window and quickly responds to an email on her phone. She flags a couple of messages from her clients but sees nothing urgent. When she isn't working on the podcast or next issue of her magazine, she is creating content for companies that want a slice of something real.

Like she'd told Ally, *If you build it, they will come.*

To pull it all off, she had brought together a team of moms and dads in job-sharing roles and had rented a house in the neighborhood where sick kids could rest in bed while their parents worked within reach. Alex is in charge of the daycare program—Carmen had figured who better to run it than a seven-time, homeschooling Super Mom whose kids were now all in school. To support her, they had hired Gloria, an ECE-trained caregiver to help look after the little ones. The parents took turns picking the older kids up from school, and in the afternoon, everyone congregated in the kitchen for a snack and coffee break.

No more working-parent guilt. No more feeling alone in the struggle. No more "room for only one of us at the table." The saying "It takes a village" had followed them into the twenty-first century, but the ethos hadn't. She saw they could change that, uniting families the way they had been before industry had separated them by demographic.

Carmen knows now what had happened to the thirty- and forty-something women missing from the boardroom. They had gone home, sacrificing everything they had worked for to have more time with their kids. They had gone freelance, changed careers, taken part-time jobs or jobs they were overqualified for, become entrepreneurs, to offset the costs of childcare and to have more ownership over their life.

They had been lied to. Her generation and the generations after her had been told, *you can be anything*. But she knows now that it isn't true, at least not the way they designed it. She understands how only a few women rise to the top, and how they have to give up everything to reach it. And that when they finally get there, they only have a brief, fretful moment to shine before ageism took it away. And how hard it is to be a mother and wife, omnipresent and selfless, without denying yourself and becoming the thing you regret, the thing you hate even.

Carmen gives her dark curls a shake, settles into her chair and leans into the microphone. Time to tell the truth.

What a year, Carmen thinks as the server clears their plates. The boys are kicking at each other under the restaurant table, and Dan moves the newspaper over on to the banquette lest one of the boys knock over a glass of water. On the books page, there is a blurb. It's not very big and there is no photo, but there it is, nonetheless. A review of Carmen's self-published collection of essays about second chances and U turns—Again, Only More Like You.

The server returns with a birthday cake, and they all sing along.

"Happy birthday to you ..."

Izzy claps her hands, and Carmen helps her blow out the single candle.

At home, there's one more present to open, only it's not for Izzy.

On the outside, the package is addressed to one Meredith St. Clair. Inside, there's an advance review copy of Carmen's book, with a dedication scrawled across the title page.

"Thank you."

The book. The magazine. The blog. Like Izzy, they almost never happened. They were roads she might not have taken. Though in the moment they seemed like wrong turns, looking back now, she can see how fortunate she is. How everything had happened *for* her.

Life had taught her so many reasons to say no, but when she finally dared to say yes, it made miracles happen.

Chapter 47

"**A**re you kidding me? You forgot *the wine*?" Ally says, as she readies a cheese plate for their guests.

"I know, I know!" Jackson insists, waving his oven mitt-sheathed hands. "I was just so caught up with the menu, I totally forgot about it, and then I thought I would still have time to go but..."

"Why didn't you tell me? I would have gone out earlier to get some. They'll be here any minute now," Ally pouts, as she places the platter on her coffee table.

"Please, Ally. I'm sure Jared and Cassandra will bring more. Just get one red and one white so we have something on hand. I would go, but I really need to get the carrot mash ready."

"Jackson, if I didn't love you ..."

"But you do."

Ally grabs her jacket in a huff, but she can't help smiling. Jackson's roast smells of pure comfort, and an evening with close friends is the perfect way to celebrate the new business she has just launched.

"Just one white, one red, right? You didn't invite the whole world, did you?"

"Ally, you just signed your first client. It's a big deal! But no, since you're wondering, I didn't invite everyone we know. Just Jared and Cassandra, and Christine and Andrew. And baby Abby, if you're counting. Oh, and my brother's friend James! Remember the one I told you about?"

"The one who did the Arctic expedition?"

"Yeah. He just moved to the city."

"Okay ..." Ally says, taking once last glance to make sure everything else is ready for their guests. Looking around, her eyes linger on the cozy beach house-style throws and cushions Jackson helped her pick out that make her want to flop back down on the sofa and help herself to some of the cheese and crackers she just put out. The framed photos on the wall of her various trips and adventures, including her last visit with Carmen and her family, send her into happy reveries. She couldn't ask for more. She is no longer the woman she saw on the canvas, alone and caught in a swell. She is surrounded by people who love and care for her. She is home.

"Back in a minute," Ally calls out, shutting the door behind her.

A cool spring breeze welcomes her as she walks down the front steps, buoyed by the warmth inside. Carmen was right. Build it and they will come, indeed. It might not be the stuff of romance novels, but life is good. With Jackson, she had skipped all the messy love stuff and jumped into an easy domestic rhythm. Even work is looking up. The fact that her client, a major national player, had awarded her the contract to do their marine survey is sure to open other doors for her company. She had shattered the glass ceiling, and on top of it all, she's back on the water. Free.

Sam, too, has lost all power over her. He is a picture with the pain pulled out. Even her hunger for a baby of her own had dissipated. She got plenty of baby time now that Christine was working for her, the flexible schedule more amenable to Christine's new life as a mom.

While Ally loved holding Abby when she was over, she was just as relieved when she and Christine left for the day. She is perfectly happy playing the aunt.

Walking to the store a few blocks away, Ally takes in the buds blooming on the trees, the colorful arrangements of potted plants on front stoops. At the store, Ally grabs a white and red and, what the hell, a bottle of champagne that catches her eye.

Dusk settles on her walk back. The sky is electric with streaks of blue and yellow. Ally can spot her porch light from the corner and catches herself practically skipping home. As she reaches her house, she notices that the blinds are closed but the music is loud. Climbing the front steps, she can hear voices inside. She tries the door, but it's locked. She realizes that she left her keys behind.

"Fuck!" Ally says, shaking her head. After a few knocks, Ally hears the lock slide, and Jackson opens the door, smiling.

"*Surprise!*" her friends shout as they raise their glasses to toast her.

"Jackson! Guys! You're terrible," she says, giving Jackson a hug, and scanning the room full of friends.

"Anything for family," he says, taking her hand.

Ally blinks back tears of joy. It wasn't the family she'd imagined, but yes, it is.

"A drink, darling?" Jackson asks, steering her into the kitchen.

"I brought champagne."

"Me too," Jackson winks. "Wouldn't have it any other way."

Many glasses later, only crumbs remain from the platters of hors d'oeuvres Ally and Jackson had put out, but they are holding off on serving his pièce de resistance—his roast—until his brother's friend arrives.

"Are you sure you didn't give James the wrong day?" Ally asks. She is still hungry, but more than that, she is eager for tips for item 7 on her bucket list.

"Five more minutes and then we're serving, full stop," Jackson says, topping up everyone's glasses.

When the doorbell finally rings, Jackson is already plating the roast and veggies, and Cass is helping to hand out the dishes.

"Not on your big day," she insists when Ally tries to help.

"Must be James," Jackson calls out from the kitchen.

As Ally goes to answer the door, she has the feeling of moving in slow motion. Maybe it's the champagne, but it feels as though she is wading through water as she approaches the front door, her friends swimming behind her.

"Coming," Ally sings. She feels so happy she could burst. She has everything she could ever ask for. Home. Family. Love. Life is good. Perfect.

Reaching for the door handle, Ally pauses and closes her eyes, relishing the moment. Her wishes *had* come true. It just took her this long to discover them.

Ally takes a deep breath and mouths a silent thank you. Pulling the door wide, she opens her eyes, and when she does her gaze is met by the kindest eyes she has ever seen.

Chapter 48

"Car-men! Carmen! We gotta go!" Dan calls out from the front door.

"I know, I know, okay? I'm coming! Just get everyone in the car," Carmen shouts back, waiting for the turning wheel on her computer to acknowledge that her final changes to the magazine have been uploaded to the printer, who is waiting on the other end.

Could you not be late just one fucking time in your life! Carmen silently berates herself, as she nervously shakes her leg. *Could you just, for once, have your shit together!*

Finally, the circle turns green and Carmen closes her laptop, races out to the front step and locks the door.

"Owwwww!" Toby cries after she buckles him in and slams the van door shut. "You pinched my finger!" he whines, nursing his hand in her rear-view mirror.

"My baby!" Carmen coos, closing her own door without missing a beat. "I'm so sorry!" Carmen looks over her shoulder and cringes at the sight of a pouting Toby. "Mommy's so sorry, Toby! It's just ... ugh, we're so late." Carmen glances side to side as she rolls down the windows of the idling van.

"Dan! Dan!" she calls. *Where is he?* Why isn't everyone cooperating? Wasn't her magazine, her podcast, supposed to fix all this? Give her time for the kids, her husband, *herself*? That reminds her, she needs a pedicure. And a facial. *Fuck, where is he?*

"Quiet!" Dan whisper-shouts as he closes the backyard gate behind him. "The whole neighborhood can hear you!"

"We gotta go! The recital's started!"

"I know! *We've* been waiting for *you.*"

"WAAAAAAAAH!!!!"

"Oh, Izzy, baby, shhhh, we'll be there soon. Just a minute, okay? Give mommy one more minute and I'm all yours," Carmen lies, looking back to see that all the kids are buckled up.

"We're late," Dan says, when he gets in the van.

"I know, I know, okay! I'm doing my best! Mommy's doing her best!" Carmen says, checking the mirror and slicking on lipstick.

"Mommy—"

"Tyler, seriously! Give us a minute here."

"WAAAAAHHHHHHHH!"

"Mom!"

"Hold on Ty!"

"Everyone, shut up! Just shut up!" Dan yells, pulling out of the driveway with a screech.

"Mom! My sticks!"

Dan slams on the brakes and everyone falls forward.

"Ty! Why didn't you say so earlier? You have to be more responsible!" Carmen shouts as Dan backs up into the driveway.

Carmen jumps out and lets Tyler into the house to get his drumsticks. Back on the road, Dan maneuvers the quiet, tree-lined roads like a race car driver on a track, swerving past carefully tended gardens and serene porch vignettes, while inside the van, everyone waits on pause, electric with anticipation. At a stop sign, the van screeches to a halt, sending birds aflutter like darts in the sky. When the van pulls into the church parking lot, Tyler runs ahead, notebook and drumsticks in hand.

"Tyler!" Carmen shouts, and Tyler stops and turns. "*Te quiero!*"

"Love you more," he says, smiling and turning back.

Dan unbuckles the twins while Carmen pulls Izzy out of the car seat, wiping away tears with her fingers.

"It's okay, my baby. Everything's okay," she coos, as she lifts and cradles her to her chest.

They hurry up the church steps and shuffle in as quickly as they can down the aisles, looking for Carmen and Dan's parents. Carmen spots Alex and her family and gives them a little wave, then slides into the row behind their parents, giving them quick pecks on the cheek over their seat backs.

As the first performer takes the stage, Carmen catches her breath. She's as nervous as if it were her own recital.

Tyler looks over his shoulder and gives a shy wave. Carmen, Dan, and their parents smile and wave back. She is grateful to have them all together.

When it's Tyler's turn, he calmly steps up and takes his place behind the drum kit. He hits the first beats, cueing his college-age teacher to start the music. Carmen's heart breaks for him when the music doesn't quite synch up with his beat. She wants to go up and fix it, apologize to everyone in the audience and to Tyler. Instead, she stays in her seat, trying to enjoy the moment, as Tyler stoically carries on.

My brave, beautiful boy, Carmen thinks, blinking back tears as it occurs to her how cool it is to be here with her husband, parents and kids. Dan looks over and gives her a knowing wink and squeezes her hand.

When Tyler's performance is over, the audience gives him a standing ovation.

"You did great!"

"We're so proud of you!" Carmen and Dan say, joint-hugging him as he returns to his seat.

As the next performer steps up, the twins spring into action. Scurrying after each other between the church pews. Hiding behind dusty curtain panels and trying to climb out open windows.

Carmen chases the twins, hissing and reaching for them as they giggle and run away while Dan soothes Izzy in his arms. Carmen grabs hold of the end of Toby's shirt and pulls him in, collapsing on a nearby bench and squeezing him tight. She kisses his neck, the top of his head, then lets him go, sighing and smiling as the chase begins again.

Carmen follows the twins to the front yard of the church, laughing as they roll on the grass in a fit of giggles. In her back pocket, her phone vibrates, and Carmen pulls it out and sees a text notification from Ally. In the message, a photo: two pink lines. Carmen's heart jumps.

<<It's a girl!>> the next message says, and Carmen breaks out into a grin.

Another message follows. This time a photo of Ally with her arms around a mutt of a dog with a snout the color of a five o'clock shadow. James is in the background, laughing.

<<My baby.>>

Carmen smiles and texts a kiss-face selfie back.

<<Perfect.>>

The twins take off again, just as a new song starts. The melody rings familiar, tickling at Carmen's memory. *What's that song again?* she thinks, trying to place it as she jogs after the twins. The stripped-down version on an acoustic guitar makes it hard to recall. Single notes singing out a beautiful, unadorned truth.

Never mind. No time to think, feel. *Go.*

Acknowledgments

First and foremost, thank you to God, my wonderful and magnificent co-author, both in my book and in my life. Thank you for being the most loving, supportive, encouraging, funny, playful, inspiring, wonder-ful and majestic co-creator anyone could ask for.

Thank you to my other co-author, my husband, for asking me to marry him and writing the story of our lives, together. You were right all along, and I'm so grateful for every minute with you.

Thank you to my kids, my muses, for making me the happiest girl in the world, and for being the greatest adventure I could ever ask for. Our life together isn't perfect, but boy, does it ever make for great material ;)

This book also wouldn't have been possible without my lifelong friend Victoria Burdett-Coutts. Thank you for being a true friend, and loving me anyway.

Thank you to Alexandria Brown, Tina Beier and the team at Rising Action for making this book available to readers everywhere and making my little girl dream of being a published author whose book is on book-store shelves come true. Thank you to Alex, Tina, Marthese and Katrina for your thoughtful (if challenging!) edits, and to my fellow RA authors for your always great tips, advice and encouragement. I'm so grateful to be a part of this team and family.

Thank you to my parents—Mom, Dad, Gina, Hans, Elizabeth and Gordon—for your love, encouragement and support. Your belief in me has always carried me through.

To my sister, Paula—I couldn't ask for a more powerful, dynamic, beautiful, generous soul to share my life with.

Thank you to my girlfriends, and all the playground, hockey rink and soccer moms I've gotten to know over the years, whose lives and stories helped inspire this book. I may not have always been the best friend, but you make me want to be better.

Thank you to all my book coaching clients, members, authors, writers and now friends who made books and creative writing my full-time job, and who helped create space for me to dedicate myself to my own books. Working with you has brought me some of the greatest joys of my life.

Thank you to my leadership families, teams and communities for inspiring me, challenging me, growing me, loving me and showing me how to love others better.

Thanks to Sage Clegg for walking me through the Oregon Desert Trail, and Alexandra Babayan for helping me to render Portland. As well as Sarah Ferguson, Pete Vargas, Robert Lyons, Captain Shane, Captain Zach, Terry Barkman and Jay at Sadle Real Estate for helping me fact-check different aspects of this book.

Thank you to my mentor Michelle Winters for your encouragement, and for holding me high and daring me to swing all the way. To David Bezmozgis for facilitating such a wonderful workshop at the Humber School for Writers, where I was fortunate to make lifelong writer friends. Thank you to Lisa Hepner, Chris Carlone and Laura Keil for your early feedback and encouragement. Thank you, too, to my beta readers Paula Margulis, Taneet Grewal and Rachel Schnaiter, for the same. And a special thanks to Monica Mann for your beta read/proofread that gave this manuscript its final polish, and to Karlene Kerr for all your support with my book launch and the many laughs we shared along the way.

Last but far from least, thank you to all my friends, family, communities, and fellow readers, writers and authors, for inspiring me, cheering me on, giving me hope, and being on this writing journey with me. I wouldn't have gotten this far without you, and hope that I'm able to pay it forward exponentially.

About the Author

Catalina Margulis is an author, speaker and mother of four who has written for many of Canada's top publications over the past 20 years. Cat was an editor at ELLE Canada, Flare and Today's Parent, she was a regular contributor to SavvyMom, Mabel's Labels and Walmart Canada, and has written for more than 40 publications, including The Globe and Mail, Reader's Digest, and Yummy Mummy Club. She is also the host of Passion Project (passionprojectpod.com), a podcast about making your dreams happen. Born in Buenos Aires, Argentina, she lives with her family in the suburbs of Toronto, Canada.

www.catmargulis.com/books
Instagram: @catmargulis

For Book Clubs

Hey, if we haven't met before, I'm Cat. Thank you for picking up my book.

I wrote this story when I was in a deep funk—so deep, the only thing I could do was write my way out of it. The funny thing is, as I started to lay down the tracks of this story, things in my life started to happen. A friend would call and tell me about her day, and it would look a lot like a scene from my book. So much so, that I even began to wonder, Am I writing this book, or is it writing me?

Maybe you're reading this before you've even started the book—so I'll try to avoid any spoiler alerts. Maybe you're reading it after you're done. Regardless, I hope this book about reinvention, second changes and U-turns (again, only more like you) makes you feel less alone in your struggles, more seen, and gives you even a smidge of hope that maybe, just maybe, even your wildest dreams can still come true. Most of all, I hope it inspires you to trust, surrender and have faith, the way it did for me. Believe in your power to create something new and different, moment to moment. It doesn't mean things will be perfect, but it could still be good, beautiful, and right.

Over the years, I've had so many fascinating conversations with early readers, editors, publishers and friends that were sparked by this book. Those dialogues helped me to see new things in my characters, and frankly in myself too. I'm excited for what this story will bring to your own groups and circles, and hope you'll write me to let me know how it goes.

Cat xo

Conversation starters:

1. Throughout the book we see Carmen struggle with work-life balance. Do you think work-life balance should be a goal? Is it an impossible or attainable one? What would need to happen for people to achieve it?

2. Ally goes from desperate for love, to learning to love herself. How do you feel about the ending? Should she hook up with the stranger at the door at the end, or continue on her own? Why?

3. At times, Carmen and Ally wonder whether their friendship is worth saving. Do you believe in best friends forever, or do you feel that people can come and go in our lives and that's okay? How do you deal with friendship transitions?

4. For Carmen and Ally, turning 40 is a reckoning with the life they have built for themselves, and whether that's even what they want any more. It's also the beginning of a discovery of who they really are, and what they really need to be happy. Where did their ideas and values come from? Has there been a moment in your life when you realized you were on a wrong path? What did you discover about yourself along the way?

5. By the end of the book, Carmen and Ally have re-written their stories so they can truly be themselves and feel fulfilled. They also re-introduce themselves to each other, inviting their best friend to get to know them as the woman they are today. Do you think it's possible for people

to change? What areas do you feel you are your most fully actualized self in? What areas are you holding back in?

6. One way to look at the novel is as a story about friends. Another is to see a story about paths not taken, lives not lived, and thinking the grass is greener on the other side. What paths do you wish you'd taken? And is it really too late to pursue them?

7. Both women struggle with identity and feelings of unworthiness. Where does your sense of self-worth come from? And is it time to rewrite that story?

8. At different times, Carmen and Ally blame fate or destiny for the turn their lives are taking. Do you believe in fate? What about destiny? How much is in our control?

9. If you could write the perfect happy ending to your own story, where would it take you? Where would you live? What would you be doing? Who would you be sharing it with? And what first step could you take toward it?

10. If you could do anything again, what would it be? And how would you do it differently? How could you apply that to your life today?